P9-APQ-852

PRAISE FOR RANDY SINGER

"At the center of the heart-pounding action are the moral dilemmas that have become Singer's stock-in-trade. . . . an exciting thriller."

BOOKLIST
ON *BY REASON OF INSANITY*

"Readers will be left on the edge of their seats by Singer's latest suspense-filled thriller."

CHRISTIAN RETAILING
ON *BY REASON OF INSANITY*

"Writers of courtroom dramas and thrillers can often fool a non-lawyer but rarely a lawyer. Randy has painted an accurate picture of what an insanity defense entails."

DON GUTTERIDGE,
ATTORNEY, ON *BY REASON OF INSANITY*

"In this gripping, obsessively readable legal thriller, Singer proves himself to be the Christian John Grisham."

PUBLISHERS WEEKLY
ON *FALSE WITNESS*

"*False Witness* is an engrossing and challenging read. . . . Part detective story, part legal thriller—I couldn't put it down!"

SHAUNTI FELDHAHN,
BEST-SELLING AUTHOR, SPEAKER, AND NATIONALLY SYNDICATED COLUMNIST

"[Singer] is every bit as enjoyable as John Grisham."

PUBLISHERS WEEKLY
ON *SELF INCRIMINATION*

"Singer . . . hits pay dirt again with this taut, intelligent thriller. . . . [*Dying Declaration*] is a groundbreaking book for the Christian market. . . . Singer is clearly an up-and-coming novelist to watch."

PUBLISHERS WEEKLY

"[Singer] delivers a fresh approach to the legal thriller, with subtle characterizations and nuanced presentations of ethical issues."

BOOKLIST, STARRED REVIEW,
ON *DYING DECLARATION*

"Singer delivers Grisham-like plotting buttressed by a worldview that clarifies the dilemmas that bombard us daily. Don't miss this book."

HUGH HEWITT,
AUTHOR, COLUMNIST, AND RADIO HOST OF THE NATIONALLY
SYNDICATED *HUGH HEWITT SHOW* ON *DYING DECLARATION*

"[A] legal thriller that matches up easily with the best of Grisham."

CHRISTIAN FICTION REVIEW
ON *IRREPARABLE HARM*

"Realistic and riveting, *Directed Verdict* is a compelling story about the persecuted church and those who fight for global religious freedom."

JAY SEKULOW,
CHIEF COUNSEL, AMERICAN CENTER FOR LAW AND JUSTICE

"Randy Singer's novel of international intrigue, courtroom drama, and gripping suspense challenges readers to examine anew issues of faith and ethics. *Directed Verdict* is an apt story for times such as these."

JERRY W. KILGORE,
FORMER ATTORNEY GENERAL OF VIRGINIA

I will visit the iniquities of th

BY REASON OF INSANITY

fathers unto the third and fourth generations

Avenger of Blood

TYNDALE HOUSE PUBLISHERS, INC., CAROL STREAM, ILLINOIS

RANDY SINGER

Visit Tyndale's exciting Web site at www.tyndale.com

Visit Randy Singer's Web site at www.randysinger.net

TYNDALE and Tyndale's quill logo are registered trademarks of Tyndale House Publishers, Inc.

By Reason of Insanity

Copyright © 2008 by Randy Singer. All rights reserved.

Cover photo copyright © by Veer. All rights reserved.

Interior inkblot © by Cheryl Graham/iStockphoto. All rights reserved.

Author photo copyright © 2008 by Don Monteaux. All rights reserved.

Designed by Dean H. Renninger

Published in association with the literary agency of Alive Communications, Inc., 7680 Goddard St., Suite 200, Colorado Springs, CO 80920, www.alivecommunications.com.

Some Scripture quotations are taken from the New American Standard Bible®, copyright © 1960, 1962, 1963, 1968, 1971, 1972, 1973, 1975, 1977, 1995 by The Lockman Foundation. Used by permission.

Some Scripture taken from the HOLY BIBLE, NEW INTERNATIONAL VERSION®. NIV®. Copyright © 1973, 1978, 1984 by International Bible Society. Used by permission of Zondervan. All rights reserved.

Some Scripture quotations are taken from *The Holy Bible*, King James Version.

This novel is a work of fiction. Names, characters, places, and incidents either are the product of the author's imagination or are used fictitiously. Any resemblance to actual events, locales, organizations, or persons living or dead is entirely coincidental and beyond the intent of either the author or the publisher.

Library of Congress Cataloging-in-Publication Data

Singer, Randy (Randy D.)
  By reason of insanity / Randy Singer.
    p. cm.
  ISBN-13: 978-1-4143-1633-8 (hc)
  ISBN-10: 1-4143-1633-X (hc)
  ISBN-13: 978-1-4143-1547-8 (sc)
  ISBN-10: 1-4143-1547-3 (sc)
  1. Serial murders–Fiction. 2. Trials (Murder)–Fiction. 3. Insanity defense–Fiction.
4. Traumatic neuroses–Fiction. I. Title.
  PS3619.I5725B9 2008
  813'.6—dc22   2008005506

Printed in the United States of America.

15 14 13 12 11 10 09
 7 6 5 4 3 2 1

"I'm starting to see my own handwriting on the wall, and it looks mysteriously like a guilty verdict."

QUINN NEWBERG

PART ONE

LAW

Law: *n.,* That which is laid down, ordained or established....Law is a solemn expression of the will of the supreme power of the state.

BLACK'S LAW DICTIONARY

1

QUINN NEWBERG ROSE to face the jury one last time. The pressure of the case constricted his chest and pounded on his temples. He had to remind himself that he had done this more than eighty times before, with stellar results. "A legal magic act" was how one of the newspapers described him. *Juries love me.*

But he couldn't shake Dr. Rosemarie Mancini's words from the prior night, after his spunky expert witness had listened to a dry run of Quinn's closing. "The whole world hates the insanity plea," she said. "Ninety-five percent of these cases result in convictions." She forced a smile. "Including, believe it or not, even a few where I testified."

"Do you have any advice?" Quinn had asked. "Or just doomsday statistics?"

"Take the jury where the pain is," Rosemarie said softly. "Throw away your notes." She must have sensed Quinn's reluctance, noticed his unwillingness to even look at her as he considered this. Notes he could do without, but he had no desire to put Annie through her nightmare again. "It's our only chance," Rosemarie said.

Those words echoed in Quinn's ears as he approached the jury emptyhanded, took a deep breath, and closed his eyes to gather his thoughts. He opened them again and looked at the jury—*his* jury. He heard the judge say his name—his honor's voice coming from the end of a long tunnel. Another moment passed, and the stillness of the courtroom became the stillness of that dank house on Bridge Street, over two decades earlier.

He started pacing even before he uttered his first word. Rosemarie was right—a good lawyer would start by describing this scene. But a great lawyer would do more. A great lawyer would *take* them there. . . .

By the time Annie turns thirteen, her father has been
visiting her bed for nearly a year. Holidays are always the
worst because they give Annie's father an excuse to drink.

Thanksgiving, Christmas, New Year's Eve, Memorial Day—they all end the same. Like this night undoubtedly would: July 4, 1986. Independence Day.

Annie goes to bed early—a holiday custom of her own—hoping she won't see her father come home. She leaves the light on in her room and prays for a miracle. A car accident. A heart attack. A mugger who goes too far.

She prays that tonight her father might die.

The answer to that prayer, the same answer she has received so many times before, arrives a few minutes after midnight. She hears the sound of car tires on the gravel drive. She listens through the thin walls of the small house as the engine stops and the driver's door thuds shut. Her father enters through the laundry room, his heavy footsteps taking him into the kitchen.

Petrified, Annie lies in bed and stares at the ceiling, the covers pulled tight to her chin. She hears the television. The sound of dishes. Murmured curses.

There is silence for an hour, her father probably sleeping in the recliner, but Annie does not sleep. Eventually he stirs and wakes. He trudges up the stairs, his footsteps and labored breathing magnified by the stillness of the house. She smells him. Though she knows it is impossible because the door to her room is closed and her father is only halfway up the steps, she smells him. Stale beer on her father's breath. The putrid odor of a grown man's sweat. The stench of cigarettes and a wisp of aftershave.

Sometimes he comes directly to Annie's room. If he does, Annie will not cry out for her mother. When Annie cried out in the past, her father would violate her mom first. When he returned to Annie, it would be worse.

Tonight he walks past Annie's door and into his own bedroom. Sometimes he will stay there. But sometimes, like tonight, there is muffled shouting. Her mother begs. Annie hears the sound of fist on bone. Annie wants to run to her mother's aid, but she has tried that before too. It only angers her father more. Once he threw Annie to the floor and made her watch as he beat her mother. He called

it an obedience lesson. Another time, when Annie called
the authorities, her mom defended her father. The bruises
were an accident, her mom said. "I fell down the steps."

Tonight there is angry yelling until it abruptly stops.
Her mother will be unconscious, oblivious to further pain.
The silence hangs like the blade of a guillotine.

Moments later, Annie hears the door to her parents'
room creak open. Stumbling footsteps grow closer in the
hallway. She hopes that tonight her ten-year-old brother
will not try to be the hero. She thinks about the beating
he endured the last time he tried to interfere. After subdu-
ing the boy, her father made him drop his shorts as the
old man took off his belt. He promised to whip Annie's
brother until he cried. Her brother, stubborn as the old
man, refused to cry.

Annie hears the doorknob turn and she closes her
eyes. The smell is real now. She senses her father at the
threshold, lingering there for a perverse moment, breathing heavily. He turns off the light. Even with her eyes
closed, Annie can feel the darkness deepen, and terror
overwhelms her.

2

QUINN STOPPED PACING and turned to the jury, fighting back emotions that threatened to undo him. He swallowed once, twice . . . but he could not dissolve the lump in his throat or calm the slight tremor in his voice. He knew he was close to losing it altogether, right there in the courtroom for everyone to see. In the past he had made jurors cry and had even summoned a few manufactured tears of his own. But this time, the tears were real.

Quinn Newberg, legal magician, in danger of not being able to finish his closing argument. Juror number five, a single mother of two, had tears welling in her eyes too. Every juror stared intently at Quinn. The courtroom was as still as the house that Quinn had just described.

Slowly Quinn returned to his counsel table and placed a gentle hand on his client's shoulder. She had been stoic throughout the trial, but now he felt Annie's silent sobs, the small trembling of the shoulder. She dabbed at the tears with a worn-out tissue.

"Who can begin to understand what such abuse does to a young girl's soul? to her mind? to her psyche? The home is supposed to be a safe place. A father is supposed to be a protector." In control again, Quinn squeezed his client's shoulder and returned to the well of the courtroom, never taking his eyes off the jurors.

"If she had shot her father in self-defense that night—July 4, 1986—who would have blamed her? Who would have been so bold as to charge her with murder?"

Quinn lowered his voice, searching the faces of the jury. "You heard the testimony of Dr. Rosemarie Mancini," he said, motioning toward the witness stand. He knew they could still picture his diminutive but flamboyant psychiatric expert—her sharp wit and confident demeanor had captured the entire courtroom. "Dr. Mancini explained that Annie did what most children would have done—she repressed those horrible acts and partitioned them off in her mind. She created an alternative reality even as her father abused her—a dreamworld where her mind could go and leave the horrors of abuse behind."

Quinn stood in front of the jury now, so close he could reach out and touch the rail. "Some say that most women marry men who are just like their fathers. For Annie, it was true. Blinded by love, she gave herself to Richard Hofstetter Jr.—a man ten years her senior. He could turn on the charm, and she fell for it. And yes, she fell for the lure of his money. He was the heir apparent to his father's Vegas empire. Annie knew he had a temper, but nobody's perfect. And he had never raised his voice at Annie, at least not until Annie and her ten-year-old daughter, Sierra, moved into the Hofstetter estate."

Quinn reached down and grabbed the poster board leaning against the jury rail. He placed it on the easel, displaying large photos of Annie's face after the second domestic disturbance call. "You remember the testimony about this 911 call," he said. His voice stayed composed, but he felt his blood pressure rising. "Richard made some calls of his own before the police arrived. I'll give him this much—the man had connections. He begged Annie to forgive him. He promised to get counseling. The police officers, instead of arresting Richard, agreed to let the couple work it out." Quinn shook his head, disgusted. "We saw how well that worked."

He sensed the jury was tiring. They had been at it for three straight weeks. Rehashing all the evidence now would probably do more harm than good.

"And you know from the testimony that it wasn't just the physical abuse," Quinn continued. "Hofstetter flirted with other women right under Annie's nose—purposefully humiliating her. He threatened to turn her in for a younger model, a smarter model. For her thirty-fifth birthday, he scheduled Annie an appointment with a plastic surgeon.

"It's a wonder she didn't snap earlier—what Dr. Mancini referred to as a psychotic break. The prosecution says she should have worked through the system. She should have called family protective services. She should have filed for divorce.

"But you don't think rationally when your thirteen-year-old daughter says that her stepfather touched her private parts. Maybe you can take your husband's abuse yourself, but you can't let him hurt your daughter the way your father hurt you. Your past comes rushing back in full Technicolor—those nights you begged God to make it stop. You thought you had worked through the painful memories, but you had only caged them in for a while. And now your abusive husband feeds the beast every time he abuses you, every time he humiliates you in public. The beast grows, and the anger feeds on itself. You drive the shame and humiliation into that same cage, and they only make the beast stronger."

Quinn was talking faster now—the words coming in an unscripted torrent that flowed from his own troubled past. "You manage the beast until your husband threatens the one thing you hold dear, the one undefiled thing in your life, the only thing worth living for. The rage and fear consume you and overwhelm your inhibitions until you become the monster your father and husband have created. Your husband becomes your father. Threatening you. Abusing you. Abusing your daughter. To protect yourself and Sierra, you must act. You must do what your own mother could not. For the sake of Sierra, you *must make it stop.*"

He paused, lowering his voice. "And you do."

Instinctively, Quinn did something that violated every rule of advocacy—something that ran counter to every defense strategy he had ever learned. He reached down and grabbed the poster board that contained two large photos of the victim. The first showed a bloody close-up of Richard Hofstetter's face—the entry wound in the forehead, execution-style. According to Annie's confession, she had made him kneel and beg for his life. Only then had she pulled the trigger. The second photo showed Hofstetter lying on the living room floor in a pool of his own blood. He placed the two photographs on the easel, side by side.

"Do you punish a mother for protecting her daughter?" Quinn asked. "Do you punish that abused thirteen-year-old girl for finally, twenty-two years later, pulling the trigger on this new abuser? As you've heard from Dr. Mancini, at that pivotal moment in Annie's life, all of her separate realities merged into an explosive fusion—the little girl and the protective mom, the harsh reality of the past colliding with the present, the real world merging with a dreamworld of make-believe justice. In her mind, her father and husband became one.

"Did my client pull the trigger? Yes. But is she *guilty*? Not under the law. Not when she acted under a delusion so strong that it annihilated her ability to understand the nature and consequences of her actions."

Quinn surveyed the jury, trying to read the looks on their faces. He suddenly felt drained. "My client was legally insane when she pulled the trigger," he said softly. "The only thing more insane would be to make her pay for it. Her father abused her. Her husband abused her. Don't let the system abuse her too."

He waited there for a moment before he turned and started back to his counsel table. He stopped halfway and turned to face the jurors again. This time, he felt the tears resurface, stinging the backs of his eyes.

"Twenty-two years ago, that ten-year-old boy tried to help his sister but couldn't summon the courage to act. Instead, he listened to his dad's menacing footsteps and, alone in the dark, begged God for justice. But justice never came."

Quinn looked down, wishing he could have done more. "Today, he's begging again."

He turned in the quietness of the courtroom and took his seat. He folded his hands on the table and stared straight ahead.

Annie reached over and placed her hand on top of his. "You did everything you could," she whispered. "Nobody could ask for a better brother than you."

3

FOR WHAT SEEMED LIKE AN ETERNITY, Quinn could feel the eyes of the packed gallery—and the ubiquitous television camera—boring into him and Annie. The proceedings, like a modern Shakespearean tragedy, had captivated the nation's fleeting imagination. Before this case, Quinn had been a rising star in the Las Vegas trial lawyer community, but nothing had prepared him for this. The insanity plea and sibling act had turned an already high-profile murder case into a national media obsession.

"Ms. Duncan?" Judge Strackman's calming voice seemed to release the hypnotic trance Quinn had beckoned. "Do you have rebuttal?"

"Yes, Your Honor. Thank you."

Carla Duncan rose to her full height and stepped confidently in front of her counsel table in the small Vegas courtroom. She was the very picture of credibility—a fifty-year-old career prosecutor who didn't try to hide her age. Tall and thin with hair streaked gray, she conveyed the sort of gravitas that age confers on leading actors and actresses. To Quinn's great regret, she had tried a nearly flawless case, an Oscar-worthy performance.

"How dare he?" she asked. "I spent my first twelve years as a prosecutor trying child- and spousal-abuse cases. I *cried* with those moms and daughters. I *hated* those monsters who did this to them. I've been called every name in the book by bombastic defense lawyers. I've been threatened by defendants. I've had midnight calls from victims, and I've cried myself to sleep after visiting them in the hospital. . . ."

Quinn had heard enough. "Objection, Your Honor. This case is not about Ms. Duncan and her career as a prosecutor."

"You're the one who put the system on trial," Carla Duncan shot back. "And I'm part of the system you're so quick to condemn."

Judge Ronnie Strackman stroked his beard, a mannerism Quinn had grown to detest. A few months from retirement, Strackman had been reluctant to rule throughout the trial—like a referee who swallows his whistle, leaving the competitors to slug it out. When he did rule, he often favored the prosecution, which Quinn found unsurprising given the amount of cash Quinn's firm had thrown at Strackman's opponent in the last judicial election.

But even Judge Strackman could stumble onto the right ruling once in a while. "This case is about the defendant's mental state at the time of the crime," Strackman said, surprising Quinn. "I will not allow it to degenerate into a referendum on our criminal justice system."

Carla Duncan thrust out her chin. "With respect, Your Honor, you already have. Mr. Newberg's defense really has very little to do with temporary insanity and much to do with whether his sister was entitled to take the law into her own hands. The system is already standing trial, Your Honor. The only question is whether you'll permit me to defend it."

When Strackman hesitated, Quinn knew another objection was lost. Sure enough, Strackman ignored Quinn's protests and Carla Duncan spent the next ten minutes lecturing the jury about vigilante justice and the rule of law. Anne Newberg could have called protective services or the prosecutor's office, Carla said. The prosecutor promised the jury that, regardless of how much money an abuser's family might have, no matter how much clout, *she* was prepared to prosecute him to the full extent of the law. There was no reason, Carla said, for this defendant to take matters into her own hands.

"Even a victim as despicable as Richard Hofstetter is entitled to his day in court," Carla argued. "Abused women can't just appoint themselves judge, jury, and executioner, shooting a man in cold blood while he begs for his life. Ms. Newberg's attorney and Dr. Mancini claim the defendant was delusional when she pulled the trigger. But the evidence shows a crime carefully planned right down to the smallest details.

"Ms. Newberg says she used her husband's own handgun to shoot him, a gun he supposedly purchased on the black market and kept unsecured in his closet. Does that not sound a little too convenient to you, a little too contrived? And why did the defendant send her daughter to a friend's house on the night in question, ensuring that she would be the only one there when Richard Hofstetter arrived home? Immediately after the shooting, the defendant called 911 and then her brother. Why call her brother? Because she knew she needed a lawyer. She knew she had done something terribly wrong.

"The insanity defense is designed to protect someone so delusional that she cannot appreciate the difference between right and wrong. But it was never intended as a ticket for murder. Or a get-out-of-jail-free card for some-body who has been abused.

"Find Ms. Newberg guilty of first-degree murder. You know in your hearts it's the right thing to do."

For three days Quinn and Anne Newberg waited for a verdict and took turns encouraging each other. During the first two days, Quinn stayed at the court-house, talking off the record to reporters and just being there for his sister. On day three, Judge Strackman allowed the lawyers to go back to their offices while the jury deliberated.

When the third day ended without a verdict, Strackman sent the jury home for the weekend. As usual, the judge admonished the jury not to talk with anyone about the case and to avoid all press coverage. "Try not to even think about the case this weekend. Come in Monday with a fresh and open mind. I'm sure you'll have no problem reaching a verdict."

Monday came and went without a verdict. On Tuesday, the jury reported they were hopelessly deadlocked, and Strackman gave them a conventional Allen charge, also known as a "dynamite charge." He reminded them how much the trial had cost everyone. He told them that no other jury would be better able to render a verdict than they were. He admonished them to keep an open mind and to reevaluate every piece of evidence. He sent them back for further deliberations.

Quinn tried to take his mind off the case by returning phone calls and e-mails that had stacked up during the trial. He divided them into four stacks—media, friends, other cases, and potential new clients. The last stack was the thickest. Over the course of his career, Quinn had developed a reputation as a flashy criminal defense attorney for white-collar crooks. But Annie's case had generated so much national publicity that it seemed Quinn was now the go-to guy for insane defendants of all stripes. Apparently there were a lot of crazy people in the world.

The call he had been waiting for came at ten minutes after three on Wednesday afternoon. "Judge Strackman would like you back in the court-room," the clerk said. "We have a verdict."

4

CATHERINE O'ROURKE FELT HER STOMACH CLENCH when she heard the news, almost as if she were the one standing trial. She knew firsthand the type of pain that Annie Newberg had experienced and found it hard not to project her own feelings onto the defendant in the Newberg case. In some ways, it felt like the Newbergs were speaking for all abuse victims, for all victims of sexual crimes.

She tried to maintain a reporter's objectivity as she settled into her third-row seat next to the other beat reporters. Her paper had been randomly selected under a lottery system for one of the coveted media seats inside the courtroom for this latest "trial of the century," a media phenomenon that veteran observers compared to the Scott Peterson trial.

Courtroom 16D was a small, modern courtroom with only three rows of bucket seats for spectators. Most reporters had to watch via closed-circuit TV.

Catherine typically wrote for just one paper in Norfolk, Virginia—the *Tidewater Times*—but on this case her employers had decided to leverage her presence in the courtroom. Her stories on the trial appeared in all four news-papers owned by the McClaren Corporation, and she did stand-up reports "live from Vegas" for the three McClaren television stations as well. The feedback, especially on the television side, was surprisingly positive. "You've got a face for television," a news producer once told her. He'd tried to talk Catherine into using her nickname on air—"like Katie Couric does"—but *Cat O'Rourke* sounded too informal for a serious reporter.

Stuart Sheldon, seated on Catherine's left, covered the case for the *Las Vegas Review-Journal* and therefore had one of the seats reserved for local media. He also ran the reporters' pool. When the jury first retired, Quinn Newberg had been a three-to-one underdog. "It's the insanity defense," Stuart had said, as if no further explanation were needed.

Most reporters had shared Sheldon's skepticism. Nevada insanity law did not favor defendants. "This state is a little unusual," Catherine had explained during one of her stand-up reports, "in that the jury has the option of returning a verdict of guilty but mentally ill. The defendant gets basically the same punishment, but also gets psychiatric treatment while in jail. Some experts are predicting that type of verdict here."

But that comment was before Quinn's closing argument and this prolonged stalemate by the jury. Now, Sheldon's pool had the odds at fifty-fifty.

Cat jotted down a few words to describe the moment—*tension, fatigue, stress*—they all seemed so inadequate.

The Hofstetter family had settled into their usual seats in the first two rows on the other side of the courtroom, behind the prosecution table. They had been outspoken in their criticism of both Quinn Newberg and Carla Duncan. Newberg because he was trying to spring their son's killer. Duncan because she had painted an unflattering but truthful figure of Hofstetter as a womanizer and abuser, just one step above plankton in the prosecutor's view of the world.

Richard Hofstetter Sr. had taken to the airwaves in an effort to rehabilitate his son's name. Richard Jr. was an exemplary businessman. He gave to charity. He provided for his wife, giving her every material thing she craved— no small feat for a man married to someone as extravagant and greedy as Anne Newberg. Yes, he should have sought help in controlling his anger. But the arguments went both ways. Anne was no saint either.

It was enough to make Catherine O'Rourke sick. Smear the victim. She knew how that game was played.

The air hummed with tension when Quinn and Anne Newberg entered the courtroom looking grim, their eyes straight ahead. *Resolve,* Catherine jotted down as the Newbergs took their seats. *Anne Newberg seems resigned to her fate.*

The young woman had already lost both parents—her estranged father in a single car accident when he was forty; her mom to a heart attack nearly ten years later. Now she faced the potential loss of her freedom and, along with it, the opportunity to raise her only child.

The trial had exacted its toll on Quinn, too. His face looked drawn, and his expensive suit seemed to hang a little looser on his frame. Quinn was just over six feet, angular and lean, with the fluid movements of an athlete, though Cat's research did not reveal any sports background. He had this mysterious look, not unlike a Vegas illusionist, with straight black hair and a trim beard that covered only the tip of his chin. Dark eyebrows shaded the man's best feature—the expressive almond eyes that seemed to dance and spark in ways that made Cat feel like nodding her head when he spoke.

Quinn's sister reflected his dark allure in her own feminine features. In Cat's view, this accounted for much of the nation's fascination with the case. *The Menendez brothers. Scott and Lacie Peterson. The Simpson case.* They all had one thing in common—the leading players were easy on the eyes.

Would anybody have cared, Catherine wondered, *if the Newbergs had been poor, rural, and not quite so dashing?*

Quinn felt his stomach corkscrew while his heart slammed against his chest. On the inside, turmoil. But on the outside, another day at the office. He leaned back in his chair, left leg crossed over right, and kept an eye on the door behind the judge's dais.

"How can you stay so calm?" Annie whispered. "Feel this." She touched Quinn's cheek with the back of an ice-cold hand.

"It's out of our control," Quinn said, though he knew this wasn't entirely true. He still had one more ace to play, something that would keep the legal commentators wagging their tongues for a long time. *If* he had the guts to lay it down.

Quinn placed a blank yellow legal pad on the table and wrote "Verdict:" at the top of the page, drawing a line next to the word. He checked under the last page of the legal pad just to make certain his ace was still there—a single sheet of paper, folded in half and signed under oath.

"All rise! This honorable court is now in session, the Honorable Judge Ronald Strackman presiding."

Strackman took his place on the bench. "Be seated." He paused, took a sip of coffee, and surveyed the courtroom.

"Ladies and gentlemen, it appears we have a verdict in this case. I'm going to say this only once. I will not tolerate *any* outbursts when the verdict is read. I have full contempt powers to control this court, and I will not hesitate to use them."

Under the counsel table, Annie put a trembling hand on Quinn's leg.

He reached down and held it. "Remember," he whispered, "all that stuff about whether or not the jurors look at the defendant as a way to determine their verdict is meaningless. On a case like this, they'll have their poker faces on."

Annie nodded bravely and squeezed Quinn's hand.

"Bailiff," Judge Strackman said, "bring in the jury."

Catherine O'Rourke watched the jury members file in—eyes downcast, a mask of solemn duty on every face. Juror five, the single mother of two, had been crying again.

"Is it too late to put twenty bucks on the prosecution?" Catherine asked.

When Stuart Sheldon shrugged, she slipped a twenty into his greasy hand and made another note on her legal pad. The pain she felt as she did so reflected her own assessment of the case.

Guilty, she wrote.

"Ladies and gentlemen, do you have a verdict?"

"We do," answered the forewoman. She was a schoolteacher with four grown kids. Quinn had found her impossible to read.

She handed the verdict form to the bailiff, who handed it to the judge. Strackman looked over the form, his face expressionless. He took another swig of coffee and handed the form to the court clerk.

"Will the defendant please rise?" the clerk said.

Quinn and Annie stood shoulder to shoulder, like two prisoners facing the firing squad, as the clerk read the verdict aloud.

"On the count of murder in the first degree, we the jury find the defendant, Anne Newberg . . ." The clerk paused for what seemed like an inhumane length of time. ". . . guilty as charged."

Gasps came from the gallery. Somebody in the Hofstetter section said, "Yesss!" Quinn's knees nearly buckled, but he managed to stand tall and keep his chin up. He glanced at his sister and saw a look of uncomprehending shock.

He couldn't believe it had come to this.

Quinn reached down and picked up his legal pad, removing and unfolding the single sheet of paper. The reporters were probably too busy scribbling down their reactions to even notice. If only they knew. Juries delivered verdicts every day. But if Quinn followed through on this next move, it would be unprecedented.

"I have a motion to make, Your Honor."

"Yes, of course," Strackman said, undoubtedly expecting a routine motion for a new trial based on an assortment of evidentiary rulings. "But before you make that motion, would you like me to poll the jury?"

"Sure," Quinn said, gladly taking his seat. He needed another minute to think. Once he launched his grenade, there would be no taking it back.

5

AS STRACKMAN POLLED the jury members, asking them one by one if this represented their verdict, Quinn tried to sort through his jumbled emotions. Anger. Despair. Heartbreak for his sister, sitting next to him in shell-shocked silence. Apprehension about whether to make this next move—a self-destructive bombshell, but one that might gain his sister's freedom.

"Juror number three, is this your verdict?"

"Yes."

"Juror number four, is this your verdict?"

"Yes."

Quinn stared at each juror, trying to shame them into changing their minds. But like every other case he had ever lost, they ignored him and looked straight at the judge, affirming the verdict like good little soldiers.

"Juror number five, is this your verdict?"

The woman swallowed hard and hesitated. Tears rimmed her eyes, and a brief flicker of hope stirred in Quinn. *C'mon. . . . C'mon. . . . I know you didn't want this.*

"Yes."

Another gut punch—the cruelty of hope created and shattered.

"Juror number six, is this your verdict?"

"Yes."

"Juror number seven—" Judge Strackman stopped midsentence, his face twisted with concern. Juror five had her hand in the air. "Yes?" Strackman asked.

"It's not my verdict," the woman blurted out. She stole a glance at Quinn, who quickly nodded his encouragement. "I'm sorry, Your Honor. I only agreed to the verdict so I could get this ordeal over with—to get these people off my back. It's not my verdict. I think she's innocent."

A few of the other jurors shook their heads in disapproval; the Hofstetters let loose with a few muted curses. The entire courtroom buzzed with excitement. This was better than Cirque du Soleil!

Energized, Quinn jumped to his feet, demanding a mistrial. Carla Duncan stood as well, but the look on her face said it all. Juror five had just blown this trial right out of the water.

"Order!" Strackman barked, banging his gavel with uncharacteristic force. "Order in the court!"

He glared at the juror, and Quinn knew what was coming. "Ms. Richards," the judge began, taking the unusual step of calling the juror by name, "you have just nullified this entire trial, causing this court a tremendous amount of frustration, wasted tax dollars, and wasted time. If you had reservations, I wish you would have stayed in the jury room and tried to work them out. As it is, I have no choice but to declare a mistrial."

Julia Richards, juror five, nodded solemnly. But she held her head up, as if she might actually be proud of what she had just accomplished. Though she wasn't really his type, Quinn wanted to walk over to the jury box and kiss the woman.

He thought about that old cliché—*a tie is like kissing your sister.* But after hearing the word *guilty,* this "tie" felt like cause for celebration. He placed his arm around Annie's shoulder and settled for a reserved hug. Then, ever so carefully, he folded the single piece of paper in front of him and slid it back into the legal pad. Still abuzz, the reporters all thought they had a blockbuster story for the evening news.

They should have seen the one that got away.

6

CATHERINE O'ROURKE WATCHED the dueling public statements on the shaded steps of the Las Vegas Regional Justice Center.

Richard Hofstetter Sr. appeared first, a cinder block of a man with dyed black hair, his face red with anger. "Justice failed our family and my son," he stated. "A cold-blooded killer remains free on bond, and her brother continues to defame my son and our family. Who stands up for the victims in this court? Certainly not District Attorney Duncan, who took the allegations of abuse at face value. The victims have no choice but to fend for themselves."

As soon as the man stopped for a breath, the reporters shouted their questions. He ignored them all, holding his wife's hand and pushing his way past the microphones, down the steps, and toward the black sedan waiting at the curb. Cat played the angles right and managed to intercept him just before he arrived at his car.

"What did you mean by your statement that the 'victims have no choice but to fend for themselves'?" she asked, thrusting her microphone at him.

To her surprise, Hofstetter stopped, assessing her with the steely gaze of a man not used to being crossed. Something about the look made her blood curdle.

"I'm not taking questions," he growled. Then he brushed away the mike and helped his wife into the car. After one more disturbing look at Cat, he climbed in the backseat and closed the door.

Catherine and her crew scrambled back up the broad steps to catch the next performance, this time featuring Carla Duncan. The subdued prosecutor expressed her disappointment in the mistrial but vowed to retry the defendant "as soon as humanly possible." The fact that eleven out of twelve jurors were ready to convict was a testament to the strength of the prosecutor's case, she said. *Class act,* Catherine jotted down.

Quinn and Anne Newberg emerged next, and Cat thought they might get crushed by the mob of reporters. Quinn issued a brief statement thanking Julia Richards for her honesty and courage. He called on Carla Duncan to drop the case and spend her time and resources chasing real criminals. He asked the press to give his sister a little private space in the days ahead. "All of the intimate details of her life have just been paraded in front of the entire world," he said. "Is it too much to ask for a little privacy for my sister and niece now that the trial's over?"

From the way the press hordes followed Quinn and Anne down the steps and across the street to the parking garage, shouting questions and capturing their every move on film, Catherine assumed that the answer was *yes, it is too much to ask.* Catherine and her own cameraman stayed back, preparing for a stand-up report from the steps of the Justice Center.

Bubbling with adrenaline, Cat tried to control her emotions and focus on her report. She would do three separate stand-ups for three different television stations, each one cutting live to the courthouse in rapid sequence. And it was almost as if central casting had constructed the Regional Justice Center for these special television pieces. The broad concrete steps angled up to a plaza in front of the eighteen-story glass building. Decorative palm trees provided shade for the afternoon camera shots. Cat found an open spot on the steps a few feet from one of the palms, put in her earpiece, and watched for the small red light on the top of the camera. A few seconds later, the anchor desk kicked it to her.

"Well, Richard, the last few hours have been filled with controversy and chaos here in the eighth judicial circuit in the city of Las Vegas," she began, looking earnestly at the camera. "Some might say that insanity carried the day. . . ."

7

AFTER A CELEBRATION DINNER with his sister and a dozen others who had helped on the case, Quinn hailed a cab and rode in the backseat with Rose-marie Mancini to her hotel. Rosemarie didn't really need an escort—she could handle herself—but this was Quinn's subtle way of thanking her. The dynamic little psychiatrist had served as both expert witness and unofficial counselor to the Newberg family, not to mention the thankless role of trying to serve as Quinn's conscience. As they rode, Quinn felt giddy and exhausted at the same time, the euphoria of avoiding defeat slowly succumbing to the reality that they still had a long road in front of them.

Quinn had watched Rosemarie at work during dinner and afterward, while others joked and swapped stories in the small, private room at the MGM Grand that Quinn's assistant had quickly reserved. Rosemarie had pulled aside Sierra, Quinn's thirteen-year-old niece, and spent most of the time with her. Out of the corner of his eye, Quinn noticed his niece smile for the first time in weeks. Rosemarie had been counseling Sierra for the past few months, and the two had somehow bonded, despite the generational differences between the fifty-five-year-old psychiatrist and her teenage client.

"How long before the retrial?" Rosemarie asked as they approached the Embassy Suites where she liked to stay—away from the strip. "I need to block some dates on my calendar."

"If I'm any kind of lawyer," Quinn said, "it won't be until after August thirty-first. Which, coincidentally, happens to be the day that Strackman retires."

"Why is he out to get you?" Rosemarie asked.

Despite what Quinn considered to be Strackman's obvious bias, Rose-marie had never asked this question before. Maybe she didn't want to know prior to taking the stand and testifying. Maybe she did better if she could just assume the system was fair. "Vegas is a juice town," Quinn said, watching the casinos pass by. "And our firm has no juice with Strackman."

"A juice town?"

"A few years ago, the *L.A. Times* wrote an article about the way we elect our judges in Nevada—the fact that 90 percent of the donations for the judges' campaigns come from lawyers and casinos. The article named names and gave examples of judges who had ruled in favor of lawyers who had been some of their main fund-raisers. The money quote in the article was from a friend of mine who said what all Vegas lawyers know but never state publicly: 'Vegas is a juice town, not a justice town. Financial contributions get you "juice" with a judge—not a guaranteed win, but at least the benefit of the doubt.'"

"And your firm didn't back Strackman?"

"Let's just say we would have had serious juice with his opponent."

"How can you operate like this?" Rosemarie asked, disgust evident in her voice. "What if we had lost and Strackman had been the one to sentence Annie?"

"That was my fear," Quinn said. "But we learned our lesson. Now we have some lawyers in our firm hosting fund-raisers for both candidates in any contested race. Guaranteed juice no matter who wins."

The cab pulled in front of the Embassy Suites, and Rosemarie handed a twenty to the driver. Quinn had lost enough battles trying to pay for Rosemarie's dinners and cab rides that he didn't even reach for his wallet.

Rosemarie opened the door and waited for her change.

"Thanks," Quinn said. "For everything."

Rosemarie looked at her friend and, as she seemed to do so often, must have read his mind. "They're going to be okay, Quinn. Annie and Sierra are going to be okay." She took her change and handed a five back to the cabbie. "It's you I'm worried about."

She climbed out of the cab but leaned back in before closing the door. "If I paid you an extra twenty, would you promise to take this man straight home to the Signature Towers?" she asked the cabdriver. "He's got a round of national television interviews tomorrow morning that start at about 4 a.m."

"Sure thing," said the driver. "Unless he pays me an extra forty after you're gone."

"That's what I was afraid of," said Rosemarie, closing the door.

Quinn smiled. He loved this town! Even the cabbies understood the concept of juice. "To the Venetian," he ordered. No sense wasting a lucky day.

PART TWO
VENGEANCE

Vengeance: *n.*, punishment inflicted in retaliation for an injury or offense.
—*with a vengeance:* 1. with great force and vehemence;
2. to an extreme or excessive degree.

WEBSTER'S UNABRIDGED DICTIONARY

8

TWO MONTHS LATER

THE AVENGER OF BLOOD waited patiently for Marcia Carver, a woman who was perhaps the proudest grandmother in all of Hampton Roads, Virginia, to return from the Princess Anne Country Club, where she had just finished showing off the twins. Her husband, of course, would still be at the office, figuring out some new trick for springing the rapists and murderers and drug dealers who paid for his three-million-dollar mansion at the north end of Virginia Beach.

The Avenger crouched in the shrubs, checking the handheld device that used GPS signals to track the small transponder attached to the frame of Marcia Carver's Lexus. She was less than ten minutes away. Her husband's car, according to a similar device the Avenger had appended there, had yet to move from the office parking lot.

Two weeks ago, Marcia's son Bobby and her daughter-in-law, Sheri Ann, had returned from China with the heirs to the Carver family legacy. Twins! According to the young couple's Web site, they had told the adoption agency they would be open to twins but hadn't found out until they arrived in China that they would indeed be the proud parents of two thirteen-month-old twins—a chubby little round-faced girl named Cail Ying and her brother, Chi. The American names were predictably presumptuous—Callie Ann Carver (a takeoff on her new mother's name) and Robert Carver III.

The Avenger assumed that the Carvers had paid somebody off and bought the twins with a hefty bribe. Adoptions of twins were rare in China, especially when one of the twins was a boy. The Avenger wasn't fooled by the sweet little adoption journal Sheri Ann Carver had put online for the world to read. Or the blow-by-blow description of their tour around China so the Carvers could better appreciate their babies' homeland. Or the hundreds of photos of the twins, showing Callie Ann constantly smiling, toothless, and bright-eyed, her brother wearing a perpetual look of confusion, his little mouth forming an O as he clutched a tattered blanket.

Sheri Ann was a spoiled Southern belle, not the kind of woman who could tolerate mommy duties for long. As a result, the Avenger could have taken the kids when they were in the care of their nanny much of the past ten days, during Sheri Ann's many absences for her tennis matches or gym workouts or pedicures. But that wouldn't drive home the point the way this plan would. Grandma and Grandpa needed to share the pain. Blood money had bought them all this happiness. Justice demanded that it also bring them pain.

Breathless, the Avenger hunkered low behind the shrubs as the Lexus approached. The automatic driveway lights, normally triggered by the headlights from the car, did not illuminate. The Avenger wondered if Marcia would notice.

Marcia parked the car and climbed out the driver's side. She opened the rear door and started cooing over her grandkids. It was almost too easy. Staying low, the Avenger came up behind her, put a gloved hand over her mouth, and twisted her neck, at the same time driving a needle into the small of her back. From behind, the Avenger held Marcia in a chokehold until she went limp, then lowered her to the pavement.

The Avenger glanced in the backseat of the sedan at the twins and worked hard to stay unemotional. The little girl smiled at the Avenger, extending her arms as if the Avenger might free her from the car seat. The little boy looked confused, clutching his blanket and contorting his frightened little face as he began to cry. The Avenger shut the car door, drowning out the noise at least temporarily.

Quickly, efficiently, the Avenger dragged Marcia into the bushes and raked over the footprints. Popping the trunk, the Avenger threw the rake inside. Then the Avenger fired up the Lexus and climbed in, trying to ignore the little boy's loud crying as the car backed down the driveway.

Later that night, the Avenger watched the Carvers' televised pleas for the return of their babies. The Avenger shrugged off the million-dollar reward the Carvers immediately offered for anyone who had information that might lead to a safe rescue of the twins. This wasn't about money. *Justice* demanded this.

A package arrived at Robert Carver Sr.'s office two days after the kidnapping. It contained a note from the kidnapper and a piece of Chi Ying's tattered blanket. DNA tests would confirm that the bloodstains on the blanket belonged to both Cail and Chi.

For strategic reasons, the police insisted, and the Carvers agreed, that information about the blanket and accompanying note should not be released to the public. They continued the manhunt as if the babies might still be alive, though the Carvers had already begun the grieving process.

The note was generated by an HP inkjet printer and contained a quote from the Bible, complete with a reference:

> For I, the Lord thy God, am a jealous God, visiting the
> iniquities of the fathers upon the children unto the third
> and fourth generation of them that hate me. Exodus 20:5.

At the bottom of the note, the kidnapper had typed a signature—a biblical allusion that ripped at the heart of the parents and grandparents. *The Avenger of Blood.*

9

CATHERINE O'ROURKE STARED at her computer screen. The day after the Carver kidnapping, her article had appeared on the front page of the afternoon edition. The next day, in both the morning and afternoon editions, her story about the history of the twins' adoption had again been front page, above the fold. Now Catherine's editor was breathing down her neck for yet another story on day three, something worthy of another front-page placement, and Catherine was drawing blanks.

The investigation had stalled. A press conference held by Virginia Beach Police Chief Arthur Compton just a few hours earlier had been a waste of time. The police were following all leads. There had been no ransom demand. They had not been able to find any footprints, fingerprints, or DNA evidence.

Cat stared at the photos of cute little Chi Ying and Cail Ying, photos she had tacked up on her cubicle wall. The twins had round, pudgy faces and bright little eyes. She couldn't believe that anyone would harm them. Money had to be the motive. But why no ransom note? Would the babies be sold on the black market instead?

Cat put the final touches on her sidebar story about the Carver family. The Carvers' law firm, of course, was prominently featured. Three generations of Carver men had made their mark as criminal defense lawyers. *There was no case too controversial for the Carvers,* Catherine had written. To beef up the story, she had quoted a few respected defense attorneys whom she had called earlier that day. A young lawyer named Marc Boland had given her the best sound bite: *"The Carvers believe in the Constitution. They believe they are doing the dirty work that our founders envisioned when they set up our legal system. Their primary operating principle is that somebody has to represent those who can't speak for themselves."*

The sidebar contained a paragraph of titillating speculation about the Carvers' nefarious clients and numerous enemies. Could the kidnapping be an act of revenge?

But sidebars didn't make the front page. Cat needed a *story*.

Her source at the police department called thirty minutes before deadline. She wanted to rush him, but she knew from experience that she couldn't short-circuit his routine.

"Are you using your earpiece?" he asked.

"Yes."

"Take it out and pick up the handset."

Catherine waited a moment. He was a great source, but his paranoia could be frustrating. "Okay."

"This is off the record, not for attribution, and not for publication unless I specifically say so."

"Right."

"You would go to jail, if necessary, before disclosing my name."

"Absolutely."

"You won't give me up to your editor, your fellow writers, or even the paper's attorney."

"Especially the paper's attorney." Catherine checked her watch. One more set of questions before he would start talking.

"Even in the face of extreme torture, you will protect my confidentiality."

The first time he had said this, Catherine thought he was serious. She had since learned it was just his quirky way of driving the point home. "Do you have anything in particular in mind?" she asked.

"As a matter of fact, I was researching this torture method perfected by the Romans. They would strap a person to a dead body, face-to-face, until the decay from the dead body started rotting the live person."

"Ugh," Cat gasped. "Where do you come up with these things?"

"Would you talk under those circumstances?"

"Of course."

The source paused, another part of the game. "Okay, I'll take my chances."

"I'm listening." Catherine wedged the phone against her ear, freeing her hands to type.

"This is not for publication, but we have a note."

"I thought the chief said there was no ransom note."

"There isn't. That's the problem." The source paused again, and Catherine heard the seriousness in his tone. Fun and games were over. "We believe the kidnapper has killed the children."

Catherine glanced at the photos and felt her chest tighten. "Based on what?"

"I can't say. There are things we have to withhold for strategic reasons."

Cat hated these games, but she kept her tone even. She could not afford to alienate her source. "What *can* you say, then?"

"This kidnapping is not an isolated event. We believe it's related to another kidnapping that took place in northern Virginia about two months ago. The powers that be don't want a widespread panic, but I can't justify withholding this from the public. If I had little kids, I'd want to know."

"Does that mean I can publish the link?"

"As long as you don't identify me."

Cat sucked in a breath as her fingers flew across the keyboard. Serial kidnappings! "How do you know this?" she asked.

"I can't say."

"But you've got to give me *something*. If I can't corroborate this, my editors will never let me run it."

The source paused to give the impression he was thinking this through. Catherine waited him out. She knew he had already anticipated this concern.

"The kidnapped baby in Washington, D.C., was Rayshad Milburn, a three-month-old baby taken in a parking garage from his mother, Sherita Johnson. The father is a twice-convicted felon named Clarence Milburn who beat a rape and murder charge several months ago based on an invalid warrantless search. The cops thought they had exigent circumstances, but the judge disagreed."

Cat typed furiously while processing this new piece of the puzzle. "Was he represented by the Carvers?"

"No. But the MOs for the crimes were very similar. In both cases, a victim was immobilized and then injected with the same type of powerful sedative. There are other connections, but that's all I can say for now."

"What other connections? What else can you give me?"

"We never had this phone call," her source said. "Not unless you get tied to that rotting corpse."

"I understand," Catherine said.

Without another word, her source hung up the phone.

10

THE NEXT DAY, Catherine scored another front-page article, trumpeting the news that the Carver kidnapping was not a stand-alone crime. Predictable panic spread among mothers of infants, matched only by the consternation in the Virginia Beach Commonwealth's Attorneys' office. The Carver investigation had sprung a leak! Determined to plug it, the chief deputy commonwealth's attorney subpoenaed Catherine to a grand jury hearing to ask about her source. When Catherine refused to reveal her source, he scowled and threatened to have a circuit court judge hold her in contempt. When Catherine scowled back, he set up a hearing for late afternoon in the Virginia Beach Circuit Court.

At a few minutes after 4:00, Catherine took her place in the witness box and swore to tell the truth. She crossed one leg over the other and then switched them back, trying to get comfortable.

"Please state your name and place of employment," said Boyd Gates, chief deputy attorney. He was a former Navy SEAL and the top prosecutor at the Beach, doing the heavy lifting in court while his boss, Commonwealth's Attorney Anthony Brower, gave political speeches and media interviews about being tough on crime. Gates was bald, midforties, and a bulldog during trials.

Catherine looked at William Jacobs, the lawyer hired by the newspaper. Jacobs was a bookish man with thin gray hair and a worried look on his face. The reporters hated it when the conservative Jacobs got involved in libelproofing their stories. Scared to death of getting the paper sued, he would always make the reporters water down the good stuff. Jacobs gave Catherine a curt nod.

"Catherine O'Rourke. I'm a reporter for the *Tidewater Times*."

"Is this an article you wrote for this morning's paper?" Gates handed a copy to Catherine and a second copy to the judge.

"Yes," Catherine said. "That's generally what it means when we put our name on it."

Jacobs shot Catherine a disapproving look.

"Do you think this is funny?" Gates demanded. "Do you find something humorous in the kidnapping of the Carver twins?"

"No," Catherine fired back. "I don't think this is funny at all. I'm being threatened with jail time if I don't reveal a confidential source."

"Read the last paragraph to the court."

Catherine wanted to say that she thought the judge could read those big words all by herself, but she thought better of it.

She read in a slow monotone, her voice trembling just a little. "According to a law-enforcement source familiar with the investigation, the Carver kidnapping may be linked to a similar kidnapping two months ago in Washington, D.C., in which the three-month-old child of Clarence Milburn and Sherita Johnson was abducted in a parking garage. Investigators are reviewing a host of other kidnappings nationwide to determine if other occurrences fit a similar pattern."

"Who was that source, Ms. O'Rourke?"

William Jacobs stood and lodged a halfhearted objection. "For the reasons I explained at the start of this hearing, Your Honor, we don't think Ms. O'Rourke should be required to testify at all, much less reveal a confidential source."

"A reporter's privilege is not absolute," Gates countered. He spoke curtly, as if lecturing the judge. "A compelling governmental interest can override the qualified privilege in a case like this. We are dealing with an extremely sensitive investigation in a high-profile case. As with any investigation, the police held back certain details so they could filter out frauds and trip up the real perpetrator." Gates motioned to the front row of the courtroom at an athletic African-American detective named Jamarcus Webb. "As Mr. Webb testified earlier, the link with another kidnapping was one of the facts held back. And for good reason—"

Judge Amelia Rosencrance cut him off with an impatient flip of her wrist. "Yes, yes, I know how the argument goes, Mr. Gates. And, for the reasons stated earlier, I tend to agree with you. I'm going to overrule Mr. Jacobs's objection and instruct the witness to answer. The government's interest in finding a leak on an investigation of this magnitude overrides Ms. O'Rourke's right to protect her sources."

"Note my objection," Jacobs said politely. When he sat down, all eyes turned to Catherine O'Rourke.

She folded her clammy hands in her lap and swallowed hard. She felt alone in the courtroom as the prospect of facing jail became real.

"Ms. O'Rourke," Judge Rosencrance said, "I've overruled the objection. Please state your source."

"I can't say," Catherine testified. "With respect, Your Honor, I'm not willing to reveal my source."

Judge Rosencrance leaned toward the witness box and seemed to hover over Catherine, like an eagle ready to swoop in for a field mouse. "Your counsel has made his argument," the judge said tersely. "I have overruled it. The law does not protect your right to withhold critical information in the midst of a kidnapping investigation."

Gates took a few steps closer to the witness box, hemming Catherine in. She cast a pleading look toward her own lawyer, motionless at counsel table. Her eyes darted toward the judge, then down at her hands.

"I won't," Catherine said softly, barely above a whisper.

"Then I'll have no choice but to hold you in contempt," Rosencrance responded, her voice sharp.

"I'm sorry, Judge."

Looking up, Catherine thought she detected a flash of sympathy in the judge's eyes. Or maybe uncertainty. No judge in her right mind wanted to put a newspaper reporter in prison. Catherine would probably be reporting for a very long time, including future stories about this judge.

But Boyd Gates had no such ambivalence. "Ninety percent of all kidnapping cases are solved within the first forty-eight hours," he snapped. "Most of the children recovered during that time survive. After forty-eight hours, the odds drop precipitously. While we're here playing games, trying to determine which officers we can trust with confidential information and which ones might be leaking information to the press, the lives of two innocent babies are slipping away."

Catherine felt her heart racing. In journalism school, it all seemed so clear. You made a promise to your sources, you kept your word. Jail was a badge of courage.

But now, with jail actually looming and the lives of two babies at stake, things seemed murky. She shook her head slowly and set her jaw. She faced Judge Rosencrance for one final plea. "If I must, Your Honor, I'm prepared to go to jail. But if the court could just give me a short recess—just overnight so I can talk to my source—maybe this entire standoff could be avoided."

Rosencrance turned to Gates and raised her eyebrows. "Mr. Gates?"

"It's out of the question, Your Honor. We have a compromised investigation. Time is of the essence. We need to know what other confidential information was released to the press and who released it."

"Mr. Jacobs?"

Catherine's lawyer stood and gathered his thoughts. "These are substantial issues of law, Your Honor. If there is a chance of avoiding this dilemma, we should seize it. I know the court doesn't want to curtail my client's First Amendment rights if it can be avoided."

"I'll give you one night," Rosencrance said brusquely. "I want all parties back in my courtroom at 9:00 tomorrow morning."

Gates voiced another objection, but the judge proved she had a stubborn streak too. Finally she banged her gavel and adjourned court.

Catherine got off the witness stand as quickly as possible and gathered her things from the counsel table.

"I hope you can get your source to agree to let you divulge his or her name," William Jacobs said, emotionless as ever. "I don't think we can win this on appeal. You could be serving for an indeterminate time."

Catherine stood to her full height and stared at the man who was supposed to be protecting her. She had heard that the paper paid Jacobs more than $300 an hour. She had also heard he was golfing buddies with the publisher.

"You're fired," said Catherine.

Jacobs did a second take, confusion wrinkling his face. "I work for the paper," he said. "You can't fire me."

"I just did," Catherine shot back. "The paper's not going to jail. I am." She turned and stalked out of the courtroom. On the way, she brushed up against Jamarcus Webb, the investigator who had taken the stand to testify about the confidential nature of the information Catherine had printed.

Her message to Jamarcus was unmistakable. *You owe me, Officer Webb. And keep the info coming.*

11

QUINN WAS IN A FOUL MOOD when his plane landed at the Norfolk International Airport. The small terminal could probably have fit inside a Vegas casino lobby with room to spare. He pulled his luggage behind him and looked for the driver with the *Quinn Newberg* sign who would be taking him to Regent Law School in Virginia Beach.

Quinn was here as a favor to Rosemarie Mancini. She had agreed to debate the propriety of the death penalty for mentally impaired defendants but then had found out a few days ago that her testimony would be required at the same time in federal court in California. She had called and begged Quinn to take her place. She reminded him of all the flak she had taken for testifying on behalf of his sister. How could he say no?

His opponent would be a prominent young Virginia defense attorney named Marc Boland. Boland was one of the rarest of breeds—a high-profile defense lawyer who supported capital punishment. In capital cases, Boland handled only the guilt and innocence phase of the trial. For the penalty phase, he entrusted the clients to other lawyers, die-hard opponents of the death penalty. "I'm not against proportionate punishment for capital defendants," his firm's promotional brochure quoted "Bo" as saying. "I'm just against proportionate punishment for *innocent* capital defendants."

It apparently worked in the red state of Virginia. Boland, a former Richmond prosecutor, had a reputation as a top lawyer who knew how to exploit weaknesses in the system on behalf of high-profile criminal defendants.

On the way to the law school, Quinn reviewed his notes and the materials Dr. Mancini had sent him. As a Las Vegas lawyer arguing against capital punishment in a more conservative state like Virginia, he felt out of his element.

"Are there any casinos around here?" Quinn asked the driver. "Riverboat gambling? Horse tracks? Anything?"

The driver, a Pakistani man with a heavy accent, smiled and nodded. "Yes, yes," he said enthusiastically. "Beautiful day."

Catherine O'Rourke was beginning to understand how real criminals felt. Immediately upon leaving court, she called the office of Marc Boland. Catherine had been impressed with Boland when she saw him argue a few cases that she reported on for the paper. She had also called him a few times when she needed a quote from a criminal defense attorney, like the day before on the sidebar piece about the Carver law firm, and he seemed to appreciate the free publicity. *He owes me,* thought Catherine. And if anybody could talk Rosencrance into changing her mind, maybe Marc Boland could.

Unfortunately, the best lawyers were also the busiest. According to Boland's legal assistant, Boland had been in federal court all afternoon, handling some motions in a complicated criminal case.

"It's an emergency," Catherine said, emphasizing that she worked for the paper. "I've got a state court judge threatening to throw me in jail if I don't reveal a confidential source."

"I'm sorry," said the assistant. She sounded unimpressed. After all, most of Boland's clients were probably facing jail time. "They won't let him take a cell phone in court with him. I'll leave a message, and I'm sure he'll call as soon as he gets out."

"Can you give me his cell phone so I can leave a message too?"

"I'm sorry. We're not allowed to do that."

"But I need to meet with him tonight," Catherine insisted. "I have to be back in front of this judge at nine tomorrow morning. I know Marc would want to take my call."

This time the assistant sounded annoyed. "I'm sure he'll get back to you as soon as he gets out of court." She hesitated, perhaps wondering if her boss might chew her out if he missed getting in on this case. "If for some reason you don't hear from him, he's doing a presentation tonight at Regent Law School at 7:00. I'm sure you can track him down there."

Following her conversation with the legal assistant, Catherine drove from the Virginia Beach courthouse to Norfolk federal court. By the time she arrived, fighting traffic the entire thirty-five-minute drive, Marc Boland was long gone. She tried his office again but this time couldn't even reach his legal assistant. She waited for Boland to call, checking her phone at least three different times to make sure it wasn't on silent. At 6:15, she decided to head to the law school.

She arrived at 6:45 and pulled into the parking lot of the ornate, colonial-style redbrick building that housed the law school. She drove through the horseshoe-shaped lot once but couldn't find a spot. After a loop through the adjacent lot for the law school library, she still couldn't find one. She checked her watch and drove to the side of the building, where a few coned-off spots were being jealously guarded by serious-looking students.

Catherine rolled down her window and flashed her newspaper credentials. "Where do press members park?" she asked.

The student looked confused. "There are some open spots across the street," he suggested.

Cat turned in her seat and glanced at the big Amerigroup office building located on the other side of the road. She turned back to the student with a pained expression. "For the press?" she asked.

"I'm sorry, ma'am, that's all we have available."

Now he'd done it—called her "ma'am" as if she were fifty years old with gray hair in a bun. "Can I get your name?" Cat asked. She took out a pen and a little flip notebook—a prop she carried for times like this.

"Hang on a minute," the student said.

A few seconds later, the students moved one set of cones for the school's newly designated press parking spot.

Pleased with herself, Catherine walked toward a small gauntlet of protesters who had gathered outside the side entrance to the building. They held signs blasting gays and lawyers and "the sodomites in Sin City." Catherine recognized the stocky ringleader as the Reverend Harold Pryor, a notorious pastor from Kansas who ran around the country pronouncing God's judgment on everyone who didn't attend his church. Because she had parked in the VIP section, the protesters all turned toward her as she approached the side door.

"What's the matter," Cat asked, "couldn't find any military funerals to disrupt?"

Pryor stared at her with small, dark eyes that he narrowed into condemning slits. His face glistened with sweat, and his red complexion matched nicely with his auburn hair. "Woe to you experts in the law," Pryor said, "because you have taken away the key to knowledge. You yourselves have not entered, and you have hindered those who were entering."

A thought hit Catherine, chilling her even in the midst of the warm, humid air of a spring night. What was Pryor doing clear across the country at an event like this? It wasn't exactly the kind of high-profile gathering that fit his MO. How long had he been in Hampton Roads?

She made a mental note to call Jamarcus Webb once she got inside the building. Then she made a face. "You need to get some new deodorant," she said as she disappeared into the massive brick building that served as the home to Regent Law School.

She found Marc Boland in the front of the lecture hall and pulled him aside, rapidly explaining her dilemma. He apologized for not calling her back. "I haven't even had time to check my messages," he said. "Twenty-two e-mails and six phone messages just from the time I spent in court."

They agreed to meet as soon as the seminar was over.

12

QUINN NEWBERG SAT AT A TABLE in front of the standing-room-only crowd in the expansive moot courtroom that doubled as an auditorium. He listened as Marc Boland gave a stirring defense of capital punishment. Bo, as the moderator referred to him, was tall, maybe six-four or so, and big boned, but with a soft-edged baby face that looked like it only required shaving once or twice a week. He had short blond hair and an engaging way with the audience—the style of a Southern gentleman that belied the killer instinct Quinn had already heard about. Bo had played linebacker at Virginia Tech before a torn ACL short-circuited his senior season.

Bo looked impressive in a tailored blue suit and bright tie with bold crimson and yellow horizontal stripes. Quinn had dressed in Vegas casual—khaki slacks, a blue blazer, an open-necked shirt. The event coordinators weren't paying him enough to sport a tie.

Boland didn't spare any of the gory details when he described the crimes committed by those who claimed mental illness. His word pictures of rape, murder, and mayhem would have made Stephen King proud. "These types of crimes are not committed by ordinary citizens," Boland said. "The grotesque nature of these crimes serves as Exhibit A for the defendants' mental imbalance."

Quinn noticed some heads nodding as Boland continued. He had stepped out from behind the podium and was partway up the middle aisle. "If we adopt the philosophy of people like Mr. Newberg, death penalty jurisprudence would be flipped on its head. The more grotesque the crime, the more likely a defendant can make a case that he was mentally impaired, thus avoiding the death penalty. What kind of system is that? If you're going to shoot them, you might as well slice them up and maybe eat a bite or two of your victim." Boland shook his head at the absurdity of it. "That way you can claim the devil made you do it."

As Boland took his seat, all eyes turned toward Quinn. Though Quinn hadn't wanted to be here in the first place, this smooth-talking Southerner had just thrown down the gauntlet. Sure, this was a law-and-order state. But these folks had hearts, didn't they?

Quinn stood behind the podium, just in case.

"In 1986, the Supreme Court barred execution of the mentally insane. But that ruling only protects those without the capacity to understand they are about to be put to death. Or why."

Quinn surveyed the skeptics in the room, mostly lawyers and law students parsing each word, along with the Reverend Harold Pryor and a few members of his church who had slithered into the auditorium and were lined up along the back wall. Quinn liked juries better, especially Vegas juries—average folks who appreciated a little showmanship and common sense. But he did notice some sympathetic looks from a few of the female law students. Something about his sister's trial had made Quinn a hero for many women who suffered abuse or shuddered at the prospect of it. He had received several unsolicited e-mails from women telling their stories and thanking him for what he had done at trial.

"What about a man like Scott Louis Panetti, who claims he was drowned and electrocuted as a child and recently stabbed in the eye in his death row cell by the devil? He has wounds that he swears were inflicted by demons and healed by JFK. And in case you're worried that he's making this up just to avoid the death penalty, you should know that he was hospitalized fourteen separate times and diagnosed with paranoid schizophrenia on eight different occasions before he shot his in-laws in 1991.

"He defended himself at trial, flipped a coin to determine whether or not to strike jurors during jury selection, and wore a purple cowboy outfit, complete with a cowboy hat dangling around his neck. Even though it was Texas, this probably wasn't a good idea. It would be like a lawyer lecturing at tonight's debate without a tie."

Quinn's quip fell flat, except for a courtesy chuckle from a few of the women.

"He was judged competent to stand trial," Quinn continued, "competent to defend himself, and not insane at the time of the murders. Because he understands what it means to be put to death, he doesn't fit within the narrow category of insane inmates protected from the death penalty."

Quinn paused. He thought about the dozen or so cases he had accepted since his sister's trial. Mental incapacity was not a *choice* these people made.

He couldn't help but get a little passionate defending them. "Is this really the kind of person we want to put to death?"

Quinn could read body language with the best of them, and most of the audience was saying *heck yes.*

"Mr. Boland worries that allowing mentally impaired defendants to escape the needle might gut the death penalty," Quinn continued, more animated now. "Good. A study published in the *Stanford Law Review* documents more than 350 capital convictions in this century in which it was later proven, by DNA evidence or otherwise, that the convict did not commit the crime. In Georgia, a study showed that when African-Americans killed whites, they were four times more likely to be sentenced to death than were convicted killers of nonwhites."

Quinn gave them a chance to digest this information and took a deep breath. The more skeptical the audience, the more Quinn would usually pour on the passion. Weak point, talk louder. He was already out on the limb. Might as well saw away. "Capital punishment is a barbaric remnant of an uncivilized society. Why do you think they use a three-drug cocktail for lethal injection? The sodium thiopental, administered first, is an anesthetic. Then they give the condemned person pancuronium bromide, a paralyzing agent, to put them in a chemical straitjacket. That way they can't squirm around and cry out in pain as the heart is squeezed to a stop from the injection of the potassium chloride. How could any court, much less the Supreme Court, say this is not cruel and unusual punishment?

"As for me, I share the sentiments of former Supreme Court justice Harry Blackmun, a man who grew weary quibbling about the proper guidelines for the death penalty. In a 1994 case, he concluded that the death penalty experiment had failed and stated that he would no longer tinker with the machinery of death. In my view, the death penalty is immoral, unfair, and discriminatory. It ought to be abolished in total or at least prohibited when it comes to the mentally impaired."

A few people clapped and a handful of others joined them in order to be polite. But the real indication of how well his talk was received could be measured by the numerous hands shooting up to ask Quinn a question. Judging by the disapproving looks on their faces, it was going to be a long night.

13

HALFWAY THROUGH THE QUESTION-AND-ANSWER SESSION, Catherine's reporter instincts kicked in. During the first half of the debate, she had been consumed with tomorrow's hearing. Plus, she was only mildly interested in the subject matter—capital punishment had been written to death, so to speak, especially since the Supreme Court had weighed in on the constitutionality of lethal injection. But these two lawyers gave it new life. Quinn, a passionate advocate for the mentally ill, and Bo, the defense attorney with a unique sense of frontier justice. Catherine pulled out her laptop and started typing a few notes.

She stopped midsentence when Quinn responded to a question by describing an execution he had witnessed. And then others he had not. Jesse Tafero in Florida, who, according to eyewitnesses, remained alive for four minutes after the juice was turned on in the electric chair, smoke rising from his bobbing head while ashes fell out from under the iron cap. Or a man in Texas, whose name Catherine didn't catch, who stayed alive for twenty-four minutes after a supposedly lethal dosage of chemicals was injected into his arm. The problem, according to Quinn, was that the tube attached to the needle had leaked, spraying noxious chemicals toward the witnesses.

Quinn explained that doctors couldn't participate in the procedures because helping to kill somebody violated their Hippocratic oath. And the prison officials weren't exactly experts at it. "No sensible person who has actually witnessed an execution can still support the death penalty," Quinn stated.

Marc Boland, seated at the other end of the table, pulled his mike closer. "Not exactly true," he said. "I've witnessed three. One as a prosecutor and two as a defense attorney. In each case, I came to the same conclusion: the murderer died more humanely than his victims did."

And so it went, back and forth, until Catherine had almost forgotten about her appointment with an irate judge the next day. Almost. She checked her watch. It was nearly 9 p.m. That sinking feeling returned to the pit of her stomach.

The moderator called on a student in the second row, and the young man rose to address the attorneys. *Interesting,* thought Catherine. Other audience members had asked their questions sitting down.

"How can you lecture us about morality," the young man asked, "when you represent clients you know are guilty?"

Newberg gave the man a condescending smile, as if he'd heard the question a million times and expected better from a law school student. "You may like to judge people before they're tried by a jury," Quinn said, "but others of us like to follow the law and presume they're innocent. It's not my job to be judge and jury. My job is to stand up for people who can't stand up for themselves, and I'm not ashamed of it."

This brought a smattering of applause as the student took his seat. But the Reverend Pryor apparently had a different take. "You're a hypocrite!" Pryor bellowed from the back wall. "You say everybody's entitled to a defense, but you pick and choose based on whether they can pay and what type of crime they commit. What if I took out a few baby-killin' abortion doctors—you gonna represent me?"

Quinn shook his head in disgust. "That's not even worthy of a response."

Cat turned in her seat and noticed a few men in suits and earpieces moving toward the reverend.

"What about *you*?" Pryor shouted toward Bo. "*You* gonna take my case?"

A security guard grabbed an elbow, and Pryor tried to shake him off.

"I'd refer you to Quinn," Bo shot back. "He's the insanity specialist."

The audience laughed nervously while the men escorted Pryor toward the door.

"Woe unto you, lawyers and hypocrites! You are like whitewashed tombs, which are full of dead men's bones on the inside and everything unclean. When the foundations are being destroyed, what can the righteous do?"

Though the security guards couldn't silence Pryor, they did unceremoniously drag him out the door. Catherine could hear his muffled shouts in the hallway.

There was a moment of stunned silence before the moderator spoke up. He turned first to Marc Boland. "It's a little off the subject," the moderator said, "but maybe we should answer the reverend's question. *Would* you take his case?"

"As a practical matter, probably not. There are some types of cases I don't generally handle, like, for example, sex crimes. The killing of abortion doctors would probably be among them." Bo paused, continuing in a more solemn tone. "But under our system, Reverend Pryor is entitled to a defense. And, if nobody else would do it, or if the court appointed me, I would take the case. I wouldn't *like* it, but, for the sake of the rule of law, I'd give him the best defense I could provide."

Bo's remarks brought spontaneous applause from the appreciative audience. When the clapping died down, he turned to Quinn Newberg. "We've disagreed on a lot of things tonight, but I suspect you would concur on that point."

"Actually," Quinn said, "I wouldn't. Pryor might be entitled to a defense. But he's not entitled to a defense *from me*."

Quinn's bluntness caused a momentary silence as the moderator searched for an appropriate follow-up. Quinn beat him to it. "Not unless he could pay my retainer," he said.

The moderator smiled nervously, apparently unsure whether Quinn was joking.

After the session ended, Quinn Newberg made a relatively quick getaway while Marc Boland lingered for a few moments, shaking hands and chatting people up like a seasoned politician. His eyes eventually landed on Catherine, waiting anxiously at the edge of the crowd. "Excuse me," he said to a few of the folks in front of him.

He pulled Catherine aside. "There's a Shoney's right across Indian River Road. Can you meet me there in five minutes?"

"Gladly," said Catherine, trying hard not to sound too hopeful.

14

CATHERINE TOSSED AND TURNED throughout the night, glancing occasionally at the red glow from the digital readout on her alarm. Each time, she calculated her remaining hours of freedom.

She had not even asked Jamarcus if she could reveal his name. She would rather go to jail than burn a source. Marc Boland had agreed to represent her but had not been encouraging. He saw little chance of getting Rosencrance to change her mind. He did think, however, that they had an excellent chance on appeal. He promised to work all night to have an emergency petition ready to file with the Virginia Supreme Court. But even in the best case, Catherine should be prepared to spend a day or two in jail.

She tried not to be melodramatic—if Paris Hilton could survive jail time, Catherine definitely could—but she still felt like a woman on death row. One more night in a comfortable bed. One more morning with a private shower. One more chance to start her day with a cup of coffee from Starbucks and the morning paper.

Exhausted, she rolled out of bed at 6:30 and started getting ready. She lingered in the shower, letting the steamy water soak into her skin as if she could build up a layer of protection against prison grime. She put on a pair of comfortable khaki pants and a pullover cotton T-shirt. She blow-dried her dark hair and pulled it back with a clip, dreading how greasy it would become after a few nights in the slammer. She went light on the makeup, putting on just enough to hide the dark circles under her eyes. She looked in the mirror and practiced her best *I'm innocent* smile for her mug shot.

Prison. It still didn't seem possible.

Catherine was five-eight with long, athletic legs that had served her well during her high school soccer career. She had added maybe five pounds since then and tried her best to stay in shape despite her desk job. Even so, Catherine knew she would be no match for the career criminals, a thought that caused her stomach to gurgle with apprehension. Solitary confinement she could handle. But she dreaded the thought of sharing a cell with some Amazon who might regard her as a new plaything.

Bo had assured her that the local municipal holding cell wasn't that way. But what did he really know about life behind bars?

Banishing those thoughts, Catherine locked her apartment and climbed into her car for her morning ritual—a strong cup of Arabian Mocha coffee at the oceanfront Starbucks while she reviewed the morning paper. She could have looked at the paper online, but that mentality was killing their circulation. Besides, she liked the feel of something in her hands while she read, the bleeding of ink onto her fingertips.

She bought her coffee and walked a half block to the boardwalk, grabbing a seat on a concrete bench facing the ocean. She basked in the rising sun and the gentle breeze of what promised to be a gorgeous spring day, a great day for a walk, or a sail on the Lynnhaven, or to toss around a Frisbee. It would be a lousy day to spend in jail.

She read with satisfaction the sympathetic article about her case by a fellow reporter. The article was accompanied by an unflattering picture of Gates, who looked like he was in midsnarl, veins bulging from his neck and bald scalp.

Catherine finished her coffee, tossed her paper, and headed home to brush her teeth before going to court. She thought about the last thing Bo had told her the previous night, his lame attempt at gallows humor.

"Don't forget your toothbrush."

Catherine felt her skin tingle with apprehension as Judge Rosencrance entered the courtroom. There was a solemnity about the proceeding, a kind of heaviness that Catherine had witnessed when she'd attended sentencing hearings for real crooks.

At least the paper wasn't going to make it easy on Rosencrance. Catherine's allies had shown up in force. Marc Boland, standing tall and straight next to Catherine, gave her a measure of confidence. Stephen Burnson, the publisher of the paper, and a number of Cat's fellow reporters sat jammed into the front row of the courtroom. Catherine's former attorney, William Jacobs, was there as well, consigned to the second row.

On the other side of the courtroom, Jamarcus Webb stood beside Deputy

Commonwealth's Attorney Boyd Gates and stole a sympathetic glance at Catherine.

The clerk called the court to order, and the participants were seated. "Welcome to the proceedings, Mr. Boland," Judge Rosencrance said. "Has your client obtained permission to divulge her source?"

Bo stood behind his counsel table and buttoned his jacket. "No, Your Honor," he began. He said it with such confidence that it seemed he might actually be proud of his client. "And with respect, I don't see any legal basis for forcing her to do so. It's not as if revealing this source will prevent a crime—"

"That's all I need to know, Mr. Boland." The judge had her hand up. "We argued the merits of the case yesterday. Just because you're new to the proceedings doesn't mean you get a second bite at the apple."

"But, Judge, the cases couldn't be more clear." Bo picked up a stack of papers, presumably duplicates of reported cases he had copied the night before. "The state must have a compelling interest to override the First Amendment, and here—"

"I'm not interested in your arguments, Mr. Boland."

"My client doesn't have any new information that the police don't already know—"

"Mr. Boland!" Rosencrance cracked her gavel. "Do you want to join your client in jail?"

"With respect, Your Honor, neither one of us should be going."

"That's for me to decide," snapped Rosencrance, her face turning dark. "Stand up, Ms. O'Rourke."

Catherine stood, surprised that she felt a little light-headed.

"This court takes no pleasure in what it must do this morning. There is no bigger fan of our First Amendment than me." The judge paused, and Catherine could see the frustration clouding Rosencrance's face. "But I am also aware that the commonwealth's attorney is faced with an extremely urgent kidnapping investigation. Time is of the essence. According to Mr. Webb's testimony yesterday, sensitive information was leaked to the press, information that could jeopardize the investigation. Mr. Gates and Mr. Webb are entitled to know which investigative officers or law enforcement personnel cannot be trusted with such information. Accordingly, I am holding you in contempt of court for refusing to divulge your source, and I am ordering you confined to the Virginia Beach city jail until such time as you choose to reveal the source or until such time as a suspect is apprehended, whichever occurs first."

"We request that the court's ruling be stayed for forty-eight hours while we perfect our appeal," Bo said.

"We object," Boyd Gates responded, jumping to his feet. "We have a compromised investigation at a critical stage in the process. In forty-eight hours, it will be too late."

"I agree," said Judge Rosencrance. "Request denied."

Before the deputies led Catherine away, Bo argued for solitary confinement on the basis that Catherine had written unflattering articles about some of the inmates.

"That makes sense," Rosencrance said.

Catherine held out her wrists as a deputy approached and slapped on the cuffs.

"This way, please."

Catherine shot an accusatory look at Rosencrance as the deputies led her from the courtroom. She kept her head high, but she felt as though she were dying on the inside. Being a hero wasn't all it was cracked up to be.

15

THE DEPUTY SHERIFF GUIDED CATHERINE into a secure hallway and through a connecting cinder block tunnel to the city jail. To Cat, it felt like the walls were already squeezing in on her.

They passed in silence through a series of limited-access steel doors with bulletproof glass windows. Each time, the guard had to wait for the door to be opened by remote control. Cat was mindful of ceiling cameras following their every move.

The male deputy passed her off to a gruff female deputy for processing. The woman—Janet Tompkins according to her name badge—didn't seem to realize that Cat wasn't one of the real criminals. She rolled Cat's fingerprints, cataloged her personal belongings, gave Cat a number to hold just under her chin, and lined her up for a mug shot.

Next, Tompkins escorted Cat into a small cell and told her to strip for a full-body cavity search as if Cat were a notorious drug runner.

"Do you know what I'm in for?" Cat asked indignantly.

"No, and I don't care," Tompkins responded, snapping on rubber gloves. "Now shut up and take off your clothes so we can get this over with."

Cat snorted and did as she was told. After the cavity search came the battle of the undergarments. "These are colored and frilly," Tompkins said, critiquing Cat's underwear.

"And?"

"And you're only allowed white underwear. No markings." Tompkins plopped a pile of clothes on the metal bench attached to the wall. Five sets of white underwear, five T-shirts, five pairs of socks, one towel, and two orange jumpsuits. "Get dressed," she demanded, pointing to the clothes. "Flip-flops are in your cell."

"How do you know my size?"

"We eyeball it. This isn't a fashion show."

As Cat changed into her prison garb, Tompkins filled her in on the protocol. "Prisoners who've earned trustee status wear green. The rest of you wear orange. You get a clean set of clothes once a week. The store is open once a week on Wednesdays."

It was Thursday, apparently the worst possible day to start a jail sentence.

"You wake up at 4:30 a.m., and we'll bring you breakfast. We bring you a razor and soap for your shower, and we collect the razors every morning. You're one of the lucky ones in solitary, so you shower alone—with guards watching, of course. Each morning, you get a mop and bucket. Cell inspection is at 8:00 a.m. Lunch at 10:30. Dinner at 3:30. Lockdown at 11:00."

Cat slid into her oversize jumpsuit, composed of a harsh and worn-down fabric. She rolled up the sleeves.

"Let me see your left wrist."

Cat held out the wrist, and Tompkins snapped on a plastic bracelet containing Cat's picture.

"Don't ever take that off," Tompkins said.

"And if I do?"

Tompkins froze and stared at Cat. "Don't ever take it off."

Tompkins escorted Cat back to a small cinder block cell. It had a bolted-down bed with a thin mattress against one wall and a small metal washbasin and a metal toilet on the other. A metal rod for hanging towels was just over the toilet.

"Do we ever get to go outside?" asked Cat.

"Not when you're in solitary confinement, sweetheart."

Tompkins locked the cell door with a loud clang, increasing Cat's sense of claustrophobia. There were no windows in the small cell. *I might not see the sun for a week.*

"Can I have visitors?" Cat asked.

"Depends," said Tompkins, and she headed down the hall.

16

TIME CRAWLED as Catherine endured her afternoon in Cell G17. She was still jittery from the way she'd been treated at booking and was concerned about how long she might be confined. She knew her editor and attorney were pursuing every political and legal avenue to free her, but she also knew there were no guarantees. She could be here for a week, a month, maybe even a year. The thought of sitting in this same cell for a year was depressing beyond words. She actually wondered if it would drive her insane.

After an hour or so, she used the toilet on the opposite wall of her cell. A deputy walked by and glanced at her. An inmate three cells down was constantly hollering incoherently about one issue or another, causing others to yell at her and tell her to shut up. The language was as filthy as anything Cat had ever heard.

She hoped her editors would figure out a way to get some books to her as well as a notepad and pen. She had already decided to propose an impromptu idea to her editor—a jailhouse journal. If nothing else, it might make her a celebrity with the inmates and keep the deputies a little more vigilant so that they wouldn't look bad in the press—the pen being mightier than the sword and all.

She sat on her bed and stared at the wall. One hour. Two hours. The inmates were herded out for rec time to a small asphalt basketball court surrounded by high cinder block walls topped by barbed wire. But Cat wasn't allowed to join them. An hour later, they returned. For Cat, the seconds clicked by in slow motion until . . .

Her first visitor came wearing a three-piece pin-striped suit with a gold pocket watch. He had a trim, gray beard and a long, gaunt face. His skin seemed to hang on protruding cheekbones that underscored freakish eyes devoid of pupils. He took his place against the far wall, holding an inmate number over his chest.

He smiled, exposing the blackened remains of rotted teeth. A camera flashed, causing Catherine to blink. She blinked a second time, but the apparition remained.

A second man entered, younger and more robust, with dark hair and a short goatee. He also had an inmate number draped around his neck, and Catherine felt like she should know this man, but she couldn't quite place him. He took his spot next to the first man. A second flashbulb exploded, and the background noise started.

Frightened, Catherine moved back a little on the bed, still transfixed by the figures standing before her. She heard the sounds of court proceedings, of gavels banging and the excited murmurs that accompany the announcement of jury verdicts. She shook her head, blinked hard, and tried to force herself awake.

A third figure walked toward the others. He was younger than the first and older than the second, dressed in a suit with yet another inmate number, pushing a double baby stroller. In the stroller were two infants whom Catherine recognized immediately—the cute chubby faces and bright round eyes of the Carver twins. The man pushing the stroller took his place between the other men and turned to face Catherine. A third flash went off and Catherine focused on the twins, her stomach sickened by a sense that something awful was about to happen.

Before she could move to them, the stroller morphed into something less definable, like a chair, and then came into sharper focus. It was an electric chair, with a metal hood replacing the pink cap for Cail Ying, the blue cap for her brother, Chi. Catherine heard the clunk of a lever being thrown, and sparks flew from the hoods.

"No!" She leaped forward and rushed the wall, grasping for the kids.

Cat jerked awake, startled to find her hands clenching the sink. She brought them to her mouth, struggling to catch her breath, paralyzed with fear.

Out of nowhere, the fingers of a man's hand appeared and began writing on the wall just above the sink. The words were red, like blood, the handwriting neat and flowing. Cat felt herself go weak as she watched the words form, the blood rushing from her head.

I will visit the iniquities of the fathers unto the third and fourth generations.

The hand disappeared. The words remained, then seemed to melt, dripping down the wall in streaks of red that trickled into the washbasin and slithered down the drain. Striving to maintain balance, Cat stumbled back to the bed, where she sat nervously on the edge until the red fluid disappeared.

It was a dream, she told herself. A hallucination. A vision caused by the trauma of being imprisoned and the tension of covering the Carver kidnappings. The electric chair, she realized, had been seared into her mind by Quinn Newberg's description the night before.

She tried to stop shaking. But somehow the vision seemed more real than life itself, more solid than the bars of her cell.

It was just a dream. It was just a dream. She repeated it like a mantra until her heartbeat returned to some semblance of normal. She repeated it until the goose bumps started to disappear and the chill crawling up her spine went away.

Just a dream, she told herself.

Just a dream.

Though she had never been asleep.

That evening, Cat was a hot item during visiting hours. The whole experience seemed surreal and, like everything else in jail, impersonal. Cat sat alone in a booth, talking into a telephone, looking at her friends on the monitor in front of her. Her visitors sat in a large room adjacent to the lobby of the jail among a maze of cubicles with telephones and closed-circuit television monitors.

"Did you talk my mom out of coming down?" Cat asked one of her friends. Cat's mom and sister lived in central Pennsylvania, and Cat's friends had already told them about the results of the hearing. Cat loved her mom, but the woman knew how to fret.

"I think I can hold her off for a day or two."

"Thanks," Cat said, and immediately felt guilty.

Like a lot of families, the dynamics between the O'Rourke women were complicated. Cat's dad had deserted the family for another woman when Cat was in junior high. The divorce became final the following year. Cat had seen him only three times since.

Cat's younger sister, Kelsey—the "good sister" in Cat's mind—had stayed close to home to take care of their mom and raise a family. Meanwhile, Cat had chased after her own selfish dreams. Compounding Cat's guilt, her mom seemed to think that Cat could do no wrong and at the same time found ample reason to criticize Kelsey. For her part, Kelsey often returned fire, arguing frequently with her mom while Cat held her tongue, feeling like an awkward visitor even among her own family. Cat couldn't remember exactly when it happened, but the burden of being her mom's "perfect" daughter had somehow stolen her ability to be transparent and authentic, even around her own mom.

She wondered how her mom might react to this latest mess.

Halfway through visiting hours, Marc Boland showed up, and the guards escorted Cat into a booth reserved for attorney conferences. Cat sat on the opposite side of a sheet of bulletproof glass from Bo. The lawyer's tie was undone, and his eyes were bloodshot, as if he had been up three straight nights working on Catherine's case.

"We filed our petition for cert with a justice of the Virginia Supreme Court at 5:00," he said, pulling out a bound document too thick to fit through the slot at the bottom of the glass. "We have a hearing scheduled for 2 p.m. tomorrow. We should have a decision by the end of the day. If not, I'm pretty sure we'll get something on Saturday."

Though this was supposed to be good news, Cat's heart sagged a little. "So the most likely scenario is that I'll be in here for at least one more day and maybe two?"

Bo hesitated. "I'm afraid that's right."

"I can't post a bond and get out like violent felons do?"

Bo looked unsure as to whether Cat was kidding. "You can't get bonded out for contempt of court."

"Can you at least get me a few things to read and something to write with?"

"We can make that happen."

They talked for a few minutes about the procedural challenges. Cat asked

Bo to call her mom and calm her down a little. Bo frowned but took down the phone number. He seemed antsy to get back to work, so Cat tried to keep her questions to a minimum. She wanted to talk to somebody about the vision she had experienced, but she didn't want to sound like a wacko to Bo.

"Are they treating you okay?" Bo asked, his big round eyes expressing real concern.

Cat looked at the tired warrior and decided he had enough to worry about. "Like a queen," she said.

17

QUINN NEWBERG PULLED UP to the black wrought-iron gate that protected the Schlesinger estate and entered the security code. As the gate swung open, Quinn goosed his Mercedes-Benz S350 down the winding driveway, jerking to a halt in front of the four-car garage. He glanced around as he climbed the marble steps to the front entrance of the stone-and-brick mansion. As usual, everything about the place—the waterfall out front, the lush green landscaping in the middle of the Vegas desert, the manicured lawn—was painfully immaculate. At one time or another, various parts of the house had been displayed in Vegas lifestyle magazines.

He rang the doorbell, greeted the Schlesingers' butler, and gave Allison Schlesinger a polite, high-society hug. He wanted to tell her that she looked good in her new face-lift but kept his mouth shut. The lady was thirty-five and, by Quinn's count, already on her third plastic surgery.

"Just in time for dinner," Allison said, as if she'd been cooking all day. "You want to go up and get Sierra?"

"Where's the old man?" Quinn asked.

"In the den, watching *Mad Money*."

Quinn groaned. Wayne Schlesinger was giving Trump a run for his money in Vegas real estate, but still he insisted on directing his own investments.

Control. Wayne Schlesinger was all about control.

About two years ago, Quinn had represented Schlesinger's firstborn son, the black sheep of the family, on charges of racketeering, money laundering, and fraud. The prosecutor had offered Andrew Schlesinger a deal in exchange for testimony against some higher-ups in the Vegas crime circles, but Andrew had refused and gone to trial. Quinn won the case, and Dad Schlesinger told Quinn that if he ever needed anything, he should call. "Anything," Schlesinger had stressed.

When Quinn's sister was arrested and Quinn learned that Judge Strackman had been assigned to the case, he had decided to call in the favor. Rookie lawyers might settle for researching a defendant's background or a judge's prior legal decisions when preparing for a bond hearing. But Quinn researched campaign contributions. His firm might not have any juice with Judge Strackman, but Wayne Schlesinger had juice to spare.

At Quinn's request, Wayne and Allison Schlesinger had agreed to take care of Sierra until Annie's trial was over. All of Wayne's children by his first marriage were grown and out of the household. He and Allison had no other kids.

And Quinn had a quasi-legitimate reason for asking. Possibility of flight was always a factor for the judge to consider at a bond hearing. Quinn had argued that Annie would never think about leaving the jurisdiction without her daughter. The Schlesingers would be sure to keep a good eye on her. Quinn didn't even have to mention how much money Sierra's proposed guardians had provided to Strackman's campaign. The result—Strackman had set Annie's bond at $250,000, imposed a few conditions like electronic monitoring, and ignored Carla Duncan's protests about an accused murderer getting bail.

"I'll go and get Sierra," Quinn told Allison Schlesinger. He took the stairs two at a time and headed straight for Sierra's room. The door was locked. Quinn knocked loudly and waited a moment before the door cracked open.

"Uncle Quinn!" Sierra exclaimed. She swung the door open, and Quinn entered the disheveled room, closing the door behind him.

Sierra gave Quinn a quick hug, and he felt the bones from her shoulder blades. Even before her mom was arrested, Sierra had been thin and gangly, all elbows, knees, braces, and long strawberry blonde hair. But she had been losing weight the last few months and had Quinn worried.

He threw some clothes off the bed and took a seat. "Are they treating you all right?" he asked.

Sierra made a face, then apparently decided to make the best of it. "They're okay."

"That doesn't exactly sound like a ringing endorsement."

Sierra shrugged. She started absentmindedly picking up some clothes, throwing them on the floor of her closet. "I'd rather stay with my mom; that's all."

Annie felt the same way, Quinn knew. But in order to get Annie out on bond, Quinn had agreed that she wouldn't have custody or unsupervised time with Sierra until after the trial. Annie had been second-guessing that decision ever since.

"Can we talk about it after dinner?" Quinn asked.

"Sure. I guess so."

Dinner was a stilted, formal affair where everyone avoided talking about the one subject on everyone's mind—Annie's retrial. The waiters cleared each dish as if Quinn and his hosts were dining at a five-star restaurant. Wayne Schlesinger opened a bottle of his best Chardonnay and tried to impress Quinn with how much he knew about it. Cognizant of Sierra's presence, Quinn stuck with ginger ale.

For the most part, Sierra kept to herself, politely speaking only when somebody asked her a question. She picked at her food, following the example of Allison Schlesinger, who gave herself such miniature portions that Quinn was certain she must sneak down to the refrigerator at midnight to eat a snack under cover of darkness.

After the meal, Quinn and Sierra went for a walk around the gardens in back of the main house.

"I hate it here," Sierra said. "I want to come live with you."

"What's so bad about this place?" Quinn asked. "Other kids your age would give anything to stay one night in a place like this."

"I might as well be in prison," Sierra scoffed. "They won't let me talk on my phone or IM until my grades get up. Plus, they won't let me watch TV because they think I might freak if I see something about Mom." She shuffled a few steps in silence. "It's not like I don't go online at school. Or hear my friends talk about it."

"Sierra, I know it's not ideal, but it's the only way I thought we could keep your mom out on bail. The judge made it a condition that you stay here. I guess the judge figured that if you stayed with me, I might let your mom take you someplace far away."

"That's stupid."

"I know. But we can't change it."

In truth, Quinn thought he probably *could* talk the judge into letting him have custody. But did he want to? He could prepare for trial better without the responsibilities of being a surrogate father. The best thing for Sierra was to have Quinn focused on the case. That way, she could get her mom back for good.

But Quinn couldn't deny that there was another reason he didn't want custody right now—a less admirable one. Having Sierra around would definitely cramp his lifestyle. Quinn thought about his place—an elegant suite on the forty-second floor of the Signature Towers, a high-rise of luxury condos linked to the MGM Grand by a long, covered walkway. His condo featured Italian marble in the foyer and bathroom. A view of the Vegas strip. A flat-screen HD television hanging in the living room. He had decorated his suite with stark and contemporary furniture. Luxurious, yes, but not exactly designed for a thirteen-year-old girl.

Besides, what did he know about raising teenage girls?

Quinn glanced over at Sierra as they walked. He saw Annie's expressive eyes in her daughter, and a hint of Annie's beauty, camouflaged by the freckles and awkwardness of a teen. He also saw big crocodile tears forming in the eyes. His gallant little niece tried to fight them back.

"Can you stick it out here until the retrial? Your mom gets to come and see you just about every night."

"I'll try," Sierra said. "It wouldn't be so bad if the Schlesingers didn't try to act like they were my parents."

"I'll talk to them," Quinn promised.

They walked a few steps in silence. Sierra shuffled along with her head down, displaying the awkwardness of a middle school girl who had hit an early growth spurt. Quinn had seen Sierra with her friends, some of whom came up to the girl's chin. Quinn resisted the urge to tell her to straighten her shoulders and hold her head up.

"What's happening at school?" he asked.

Sierra shrugged. "Nothin'."

"Your mom says your grades are dropping off."

"I don't get math."

"You need some help? Maybe we could get you some tutoring or something."

"I already get tutoring." The statement, said matter-of-factly by Sierra, made Quinn realize how out of touch he was with his niece.

They talked about some of the issues at school, and Quinn inquired gently about what other kids said about Annie's case. "Not much," Sierra responded. "They hope my mom wins next time. Except some of the boys. They call her psycho."

"Boys can be jerks in seventh grade," Quinn said softly.

"They call me Daddy Long Legs," Sierra replied. It was almost a whisper, and Quinn wasn't positive he heard it right.

"Daddy Long Legs?"

"Yeah. Mostly the boys, but some of the girls too."

Quinn stopped walking and Sierra did the same. "Look at me for a second," he said. Sierra looked up, and Quinn saw too much sadness in her big round eyes. "Don't let those boys get to you. Women everywhere would kill to have your long legs. All the models have long legs, all the great actresses. You're a beautiful young woman, and in a few years, every one of those boys is going to be asking you out."

Sierra made a face. "Those boys are lame."

"You just keep a mental list of all their names," Quinn responded. "When you get to high school and they start asking you out, tell them to go find some girls with short, stubby legs."

Sierra didn't smile, but Quinn thought he detected a little glint of pride in her eyes. He realized that he would probably make a lousy dad, teaching a thirteen-year-old girl about the fine art of revenge in order to build her self-esteem. Some men just weren't cut out to be fathers.

There was another long silence as they headed back to the house. "Are we going to win next time?" Sierra eventually asked.

"Oh yeah," Quinn assured her. "We are definitely going to win."

"What happened last time?"

"We just got a bad jury. That's all. It won't happen again."

18

THE MINUTES TICKED BY for Catherine O'Rourke on day two of her involuntary confinement. *How can someone ever serve a ten-year sentence? How does anybody do this for life?*

The blows to her dignity and sanity came from all directions. She had barely slept the previous night. Three times a deputy had come around and shone a flashlight in Cat's eyes as part of the shift counts. At 4:30 a.m., a deputy had come by to rouse the prisoners from sleep, and the screeching voice of another deputy came over the loudspeaker, barking out names and commands for the day. When Cat used the toilet, an inmate from the cell across the hall stood and watched.

Cat shot her a disapproving look that only made the woman sneer. "You'd better get used to it, Barbie," the woman said.

The nickname was a carryover from Cat's first day in the slammer. Most of the inmates were housed in two-story "pods"—groups of fourteen cells that opened into a common area containing bolted-down metal tables and benches as well as a wall-mounted television set. Prisoners like Cat, who were serving time in solitary, stayed in a separate wing composed of single cells on each side of the hall. A few other prisoners, however, occasionally passed through the hallway in front of Cat's cell. One of them, a woman with a buzz cut, had said, "Look, it's the brunette Barbie. Hey, Barbie, you're gonna be my baby doll." The inmates within earshot had laughed, and the name, like everything else in prison, had spread like wildfire.

Cat felt the book she was reading slip from her hand and realized she had been dozing. For most of her second day, she had remained sprawled out on her cot, reading a James Patterson thriller, one of several books Marc Boland had provided. Now she closed the book and placed her head on the pillow, facing the wall. The inmates' shouts from the pods or other cells on her hall became a distant hum as Cat dozed in and out, completely exhausted. In a strange way, she was almost too tired to sleep, her body wired to run or fight or somehow survive this awful experience.

That's when *he* entered her cell.

She saw him reflected on the cinder block wall, which had turned into a mirror. She clutched the pillow tightly, keeping her eyes nearly closed, not daring to breathe. Maybe he would go away if he thought Catherine was sleeping.

Catherine didn't recognize the man, though the sight of him paralyzed her with fear. He was tall, maybe six-two or six-three, and solidly built, as if he spent half his life in the gym. He wore baggy jeans and no shirt. An African-American man with close-cropped hair, a three-day stubble, a broad nose, and molten eyes. Tattoo ink covered the upper half of his body.

He stood on the opposite side of the cell, leering at Catherine as she slept. She wanted to cry out but feared the deputies would be too slow to respond, too late to save her. Instead, she held her breath, deathly still, waiting for her visitor to make the first move.

Instead of attacking, he turned toward a corner of the cell, as if he heard something. The leer disappeared, replaced by a look of sadness, and a single tear trickled from the man's left eye as he slowly faded from view.

Now a woman stood in the corner of the cell. Behind her, a hooded figure in a white robe floated closer, quiet and serene until the woman started shaking spasmodically and then, with a violent rush, the hooded figure jabbed a needle into the woman's neck. Catherine gasped and turned on her cot as the woman slumped to the floor, the needle jutting from her neck.

The hooded figure, face obscured, reached both hands up toward the window. Instantly a baby appeared in the outstretched hands, an African-American child with puffy cheeks and dark, curly locks of hair. The baby cooed and stretched and wiggled a little in the tender hands of the hooded one. The person drew the baby in and cuddled him, rocking the little boy back and forth for a few seconds. Then, as if it were the most natural thing in the world, the hooded figure bent down and extracted the needle from the woman's neck.

"No!" Catherine yelled. She jumped toward the hooded figure but it was too late. With the speed of a striking cobra, the figure inserted the needle into the baby's arm. The child wiggled and the needle wedged out, spraying noxious chemicals all over the room.

Catherine reached for the hooded figure but came up empty, the poison stinging her eyes. Frantically, she turned on the water from the sink and splashed it on her face. "Don't do this!" she shouted. "Stop!"

The sound of her own voice echoed in the cell, startling her awake, as she stood in frozen horror, looking for the visitors who had just moments ago seemed so real. Her face was wet, the water in the rinse basin running. Her breath was short; her heart pummeled her chest.

She turned off the water and sat down on the cot, shaking from the horror of what she had witnessed.

"What's the matter, Barbie?" the inmate across the hall asked.

A deputy came by to check out her cell. "What's with the shouting?"

Shaken, Cat looked at the deputy, barely able to bring the woman into focus. "Just a nightmare," she said.

"Happens a lot," said the deputy. She turned and walked away.

And that's when Cat saw it—with her eyes wide open, in the broad daylight of her cell, unmistakable and as real as the cot Cat sat on.

Handwriting on the wall. Bloodred.

The offspring of evildoers will never be remembered. Prepare a place of slaughter for the sons because of the iniquities of their fathers.

19

CATHERINE WRESTLED ALL AFTERNOON with the implications of her second vision in less than twenty-four hours. As a logical person, she realized that all the classic ingredients for nightmares had converged on her life at once.

She assumed that the content for the dreams had been derived, at least in part, by the capital punishment debate between Quinn Newberg and Marc Boland at the law school. Quinn's graphic depictions of botched executions had played a prominent role in both dream sequences.

On top of that, she had been reading an intense thriller when she fell asleep and had been an emotional wreck these last few days. Jail was a frightening place, and in her case, the fear was compounded by occasional whispers from her own conscience about possibly impeding the investigation into the Carver kidnappings. She had seen the pictures of those beautiful twin babies. Just thinking about the way they might have died made her sick to her stomach.

Even apart from all these stimuli, Catherine was pretty sure she would have experienced nightmares just from being confined to this cell. While she didn't believe in ghosts and hauntings, she did acknowledge that some places tended to cause nightmares. Take the woods, for example. Camping out and listening to night creatures as she fell asleep was a guaranteed ticket to a dreamland horror show.

One more reason to hate camping.

But still, she had to face some hard truths about these visions. They were far more powerful than normal nightmares. The deal with the sink and splashing herself with water was bizarre. Frankly, she wondered if she might be losing it. And, if she was, who could blame her? Who wouldn't go a little psycho in here?

The thing that puzzled her most was the biblical language she recognized in the handwriting on the wall. Perhaps this element came from the bizarre rantings of Harold Pryor. But she doubted it. Though she didn't recall exactly what the reverend had said the night of the debate, the words in the visions seemed somehow different. More disturbing. More sinister.

She sensed that the words themselves might somehow be important, so she pulled out her journal to jot them down. The first vision, twenty-four hours ago—how had that gone exactly? She thought hard, closing her eyes so she could visualize the bloodred writing dripping toward the rinse basin. *The sins of the fathers will be visited on the third and fourth generation.* That was the gist of it, the best she could do for now.

Today's words were still fresh. She jotted them in her journal also, confident that she had remembered them pretty much word for word.

The offspring of evildoers will never be remembered. Prepare a place of slaughter for the sons because of the iniquities of their fathers.

Late that afternoon, a deputy came to Catherine's cell and unlocked the door. "Don't forget your toothbrush, O'Rourke," she said. "You're going home."

Just like that? The whole thing seemed rather anticlimactic, but Catherine wasn't complaining. She gathered her books, journal, toiletries, and pen. All of her possessions reduced to this. She took a last glance around the small cell—she sure wouldn't miss this place—and followed the guard to the processing desk. She endured one last pat down—as if she might be trying to smuggle something dangerous *out* of the jail—changed clothes, signed an inventory for her personal belongings, and felt a rush of gratitude when she saw Marc Boland waiting for her.

She gave her attorney a spontaneous hug.

"Chalk one up for the First Amendment," he said. He handed her a three-page document. "The clerk of the Virginia Supreme Court faxed this to my office about a half hour ago. I wanted to deliver it personally."

"I am so glad I fired Jacobs and hired you," Catherine said, folding the order and placing it inside her journal. "How can I ever thank you?"

Bo didn't try to mask his excitement as a big smile lit up his schoolboy face. "It's all part of Boland Legal Services. Slaying dragons, winning Supreme Court arguments, saving damsels in distress."

"I think I'm going to get sick," said the desk clerk.

"We were just leaving," Bo said.

20

QUINN TOOK A CAB to the front door of the Venetian. Oblivious to the hotel's opulence, he walked straight through the massive rotunda with its rich marble floor and white-pillared walkways and wound his way through the sprawling gaming area and its mile-long "Grand Canal," the casino's attempt to replicate Venice. The gaming tables and slot machines were just background noise. Quinn Newberg was on a mission.

The Venetian had spared no expense in its featured poker room, draping it in rich leathers, dark-grained woods, velvet curtains, and tastefully displayed paintings from the Renaissance era. Quinn checked in at the desk and added his name to the list for the tables in the high-stakes area. He slipped the clerk two fifties and watched her make the appropriate adjustments so he could join his desired table. Thirty-five minutes later, a seat opened up, and Quinn took his place, two chairs away from a local card shark named Bobby Jackson.

Jackson was forty-five but could generally talk his way into a senior citizen discount. He had thin gray hair, a face with the tanned texture of a well-worn baseball glove, and a close-cropped beard that sprouted half gray and half black. He pulled his rounded shoulders in tight, shielding his cards, as if the entire world might be part of a giant conspiracy designed to separate Bobby from his money.

Quinn ordered a soda and settled in next to a brawny man with cowboy boots who had accumulated a sizable pile of chips. He had a thick Southern drawl, and the other players called him Tex.

"Aren't you that boy I saw on TV defending his crazy sister after she knocked off her old man?" Tex asked loudly.

"Oh my gosh!" said a brunette standing behind one of the other players. She frantically fished into her purse and pulled out a hundred-dollar bill. "Would you mind signing this?"

Feeling like an idiot, Quinn scribbled a signature across the top of the bill. He gave her a dismissive smile, but she had already pulled out a disposable camera. She handed it to the older gentleman sitting in front of her at the table. "Will you take our picture, honey?" she asked.

Quinn stood next to the woman, and she placed her arm around Quinn's waist to pull him close. Her scowling husband or boyfriend or whatever he was counted to three and snapped a shot.

"Thanks!" said the woman. "I knew I would meet somebody famous in Las Vegas!"

"We gonna play cards or we gonna play Hollywood celebrity?" Tex drawled.

"Sorry," Quinn muttered. He returned to his seat, and the dealer dealt a new hand. For nearly an hour, Quinn played the game methodically, trusting math rather than intuition or luck. He counted cards, studied the body language of opponents, and kept a mental list of hands worth betting on. Discipline and patience were the hallmarks of his success, along with a programmed set of bluffs that he would sometimes spend half an hour developing.

His first big opportunity came at a few minutes after eleven, when Quinn's two hole cards were the ace of clubs and the four of diamonds. Quinn was sitting on the small blind, meaning he had already put five hundred in the pot before the cards were even dealt. Tex, on Quinn's immediate left, was sitting on the big blind, meaning he had anted up a thousand. During the first round of betting, everyone had folded except Tex, Bobby Jackson, and Quinn, who promptly anted up another five hundred so he could see the flop.

The three cards in the flop were no help to Quinn—the ten and eight of clubs and the queen of hearts. He noticed that Tex had grown extraordinarily quiet as he stared at the three cards faceup in front of the dealer. He probably had two clubs in his hand and was hoping for a flush. Bobby Jackson stole a peek at his two hole cards and blinked three quick times.

Jackson nonchalantly pushed in a pile of chips so the pot grew to four thousand. The bid fell to Quinn, who stacked and restacked a few chips, letting them filter through his fingers as he stared at Tex.

The big man sitting to his left couldn't resist a slight grin. "You Vegas boys sure do fold quickly," Tex said. "I thought this was the high-stakes table."

Quinn shoved some chips to the middle. "I'll see your thousand," he said, then carefully counted out a neat new pile. "And raise it twelve."

"Well, well," said Tex. He quickly counted his own stack of chips. "I'll see your twelve, and bump it up another twelve." He grinned broadly; the only thing missing was a cigar.

"I'll call," Bobby said, pushing his own pile to the middle.

Quinn quickly shoved an additional twelve into the pot, and the table grew quiet with tension. "I'll call as well."

The dealer burned another card before she put the fourth card faceup on the table. The turn—the eight of spades—was another throwaway for Quinn's hand. But he could also see the disappointment register on Tex's beefy face, confirming Quinn's suspicion that the man was working on a flush and needed another club. Quinn bid the pot up another few thousand dollars. Both Tex and Bobby stayed in and the dealer burned another card then placed the fifth community card on the table.

The river was the jack of clubs. Tex immediately went into a lone-star scowl, but he wasn't fooling Quinn. The man now had his flush. Meanwhile, Bobby Jackson's blinking had gone on overdrive—three quick blinks followed by two more. Quinn had nothing—a pair of eights from the community cards and the ace high he had in the hole. He couldn't possibly win—unless he could bluff the others into folding.

"I'm good," said Bobby, tapping the table.

Quinn snuck a peek at his hole cards just for drama and allowed himself a big smile. He went for the blue chips and raised the pot nearly ten thousand.

"My, my," Tex said. "Either you're sittin' on a nine or a couple clubs or you've got more guts than a cat burglar." He pushed his own stack to the middle. "Let's find out."

Quinn noticed that Tex didn't go all in. The big man must have been at least a little worried.

"See your ten and raise it five," Bobby said.

Tex stiffened at the move. If he had a flush, as Quinn suspected, he probably wouldn't fold. His flush would beat a straight, but it wouldn't hold up against a full house. Quinn did some quick math. There was now a hundred and ten thousand in the pot. Tex was in for thirty-five.

Quinn took a deep breath, spread his palms, and decided he would test the man's ego. "All in," he said, shoving the rest of his chips into the middle of the table. Then he looked at Tex. "You might want to remember the Alamo."

The dealer counted the chips. The table grew quiet as the players stared at the huge pile in the center.

"Eighty to stay," the dealer told Tex.

Quinn watched the big man's face redden. Tex looked at his two hole cards again, as if checking to make sure they hadn't changed. He looked at Quinn. "If I recall my history correctly, Santa Anna eventually lost that little war." He shoved his chips to the middle of the table.

"I'll call," said Bobby Jackson. Expressionless, he counted his chips and pushed several piles into the middle. All eyes turned to Quinn.

When Quinn dramatically flipped his cards, Tex beamed. "Ace high!" Tex shouted. "You slimy rascal!" He gave Quinn a punch in the arm, a little too hard to be good-natured but not hard enough to risk starting a fistfight. "You almost bluffed me into folding with an ace high!"

Next, Tex flipped his cards with a show of gusto, standing as he did—the king and queen of clubs. He not only had a flush, it was a king-high flush. He grinned as the attention turned to Bobby Jackson.

"Full house," said Bobby calmly, flipping over a pair of tens. "Tens over eights."

Tex made a grunting noise, as if someone had punched him in the gut, and then cursed his luck as Bobby raked in the chips. "It's always the quiet ones that get ya." Tex reached into his pocket and pulled out a few more markers to replenish his depleted pile of chips. He took his seat, shaking his head.

Out of the corner of his eye, Quinn could have sworn he saw Bobby Jackson drooling.

A few minutes after midnight, sitting at the blackjack tables, Quinn felt some-body brush up against the back of his chair. Quinn mumbled some excuses, cashed in his chips, and followed Bobby Jackson to a corner table in the TAO Lounge.

Bobby and Quinn did some quick math on a napkin before Bobby peeled off forty-five thousand dollars in markers and handed them to Quinn. "I thought you overreached when you went all in," Bobby said. "I thought we should have bet him up in ten thousand increments."

"I knew he had a flush," Quinn said. "And when I saw the three blinks followed by two, I knew you were sitting on a full house. You had to have either pocket tens or queens. I figured there was no way Tex was going to fold with the hand he had."

Bobby ordered a drink but Quinn passed. Unlike the Bobby Jacksons of the world, Quinn had a day job. "Nice of you to buy some more chips so you could let that old guy from Phoenix win back his money," Bobby said as Quinn stood to leave. "Me, I'd have kept his fifteen grand too."

"He looked suicidal," Quinn said. "I don't believe in separating fools from their pensions."

"I've played with him before," Bobby responded. "The guy's almost a billionaire. Made a fortune with those check-cashing places that charge poor people obscene amounts of money to cash payroll checks." He smiled. "For a jury lawyer, you're a lousy judge of character."

"Obviously," said Quinn. "Look who I chose for a card partner."

On his way home, Quinn did some more math. Forty-five thousand would cover the fee for the jury consultant from Annie's trial, part of Rosemarie Mancini's fee, and the cost of the trial transcript. His firm's legal fees could wait, but expert consultants expected to get paid if you wanted them around for a retrial.

After he had raised enough to cover all of the expenses for Annie's retrial, Quinn would go back to old school gambling—no partners, no scams, just solid strategy and a few well-timed bluffs. In the meantime, for Annie's sake, he would park his conscience at the door and work with Bobby Jackson, rationalizing that blowhards like Tex would never miss a few thousand bucks.

21

SATURDAY MORNING STARTED BRIGHT, beautiful, and early for Catherine O'Rourke. She slept comfortably in her own bed Friday night, tucked away in her duplex on the corner of Holly Road and 34th Street, just a few blocks from the ocean. She had intended to sleep in late but woke at 6 a.m. and couldn't force herself back to sleep.

She gave up at 7:00, threw on some workout clothes, brushed her teeth, and grabbed the morning paper. She drove to Starbucks and took her coffee to her favorite boardwalk bench, where she could enjoy the unseasonably warm sun. Scanning the local news first, she read the satisfying story of her own release from prison. Boyd Gates stoically said he disagreed with the Virginia Supreme Court's ruling but was prepared to abide by it, as if he had any choice. Marc Boland declared it a banner day for a free press.

The coverage included an unflattering picture of Cat as she emerged from jail. She would give them an earful about that later today.

She sipped her Arabian Mocha coffee and turned to the front-page story about the Carver and Milburn kidnappings written by one of Cat's colleagues. Though the kidnappings had a similar MO, the victims were very dissimilar. The Carvers were rich, white, Southern lawyers, Virginia gentry with lots of money. Clarence Milburn and Sherita Johnson were the unmarried parents of three-month-old Rayshad Milburn, who lived with his mother. They had very little money, and the police report indicated that cocaine residue was found in Sherita's car when the police searched it immediately after the kidnapping. Clarence was a convicted felon who had recently dodged a bullet on rape and murder charges when the police botched a search warrant.

The article featured a number of quotes from Dr. Rebecca Ernst, a well-known criminal profiler. Though other experts thought the Avenger of Blood was a man, Ernst raised the possibility that the Avenger might be an athletic woman. In both kidnappings, the Avenger had used a needle with a fast-acting anesthetic, methohexital, to help subdue the person taking care of the infants.

In the case of Sherita Johnson, the Avenger had also used a Taser to immobilize Sherita before injecting the drug. In the Carver case, the Avenger had attacked sixty-nine year old Marcia Carver from behind, covering her mouth and putting her in a choke hold until the drug could do its work. Most men, according to Dr. Ernst, probably would have just knocked the victims out using brute force. Dr. Ernst therefore believed the Avenger was quite possibly a woman with some type of medical background.

Ernst refused to comment on whether the police were dealing with a serial criminal who could be expected to strike again. There were too many unknowns, Ernst said, but mothers and fathers everywhere should exercise extreme caution.

None of this was news to Catherine, though she almost dropped her coffee when she looked at the pictures of Clarence Milburn and Sherita Johnson. She recognized Milburn! The broad nose, the flat face, the volcanic eyes. It was the same man Cat had seen in her second vision—she was sure of it.

The woman in her vision had been more in the shadows in the corner of the cell. There were some strong similarities, but she couldn't say for sure if the woman was Sherita Johnson or not. But there could be no mistaking Clarence Milburn.

Cat stared at the picture for a moment, wondering if she might have seen this man sometime before her jailhouse vision. Somehow, her mind must have stored a picture of Milburn and then subconsciously recalled that picture when she had the vision in the prison cell. Or maybe the man in the vision hadn't really looked like Milburn at all. Maybe she was just filling in the vague features from her nightmare by using Milburn's features, the ones filling her mind's eye at this very minute.

Either way it was *creepy*. This case was freaking her out.

She folded the paper and headed back to her duplex. She had to get Milburn's image out of her mind. She would go home, lace on her Rollerblades, and head to the boardwalk for a workout. The misty breeze from the salt water would clear her head. Her editor, Ed Shaftner, had authorized her to write a brief journal about her two days behind bars, and she knew she needed to get that finished right away. It would run in the Sunday paper with another story about the Carver case. "We're gonna make you a star," Shaftner had promised.

But after what she had just been through, Catherine didn't want to be a star. She didn't particularly want to deal with any more confidential sources either. She just wanted to be a regular reporter. And she wanted the Avenger behind bars.

She needed to work out some pent-up emotions and feel the ocean breeze blowing in her face. What better way than to go rollerblading at breakneck speed, dodging the tourists and elderly couples and surfers and stroller moms who hogged the boardwalk?

Her editor could wait. The boardwalk couldn't.

Catherine returned to her duplex after a thirty-minute workout and noticed a small brown package leaning against her door. She opened it and found a cell phone inside with a typed note. "Speed dial 2. I owe you. 'A law-enforcement source familiar with the investigation.'"

Catherine recognized the last phrase. It was the way she had described Jamarcus Webb in the article that had landed her behind bars.

She took off her Rollerblades, stepped inside her duplex, and dialed the number.

"Good morning," Webb said in his deep baritone.

"Good morning, Jamarcus."

"Are you inside your apartment?"

It wasn't technically an apartment, but she knew what he meant. "Yes. Why?"

"Let's not take any chances. As you talk, walk down toward the ocean. Make sure you're not being followed."

"Okay. Hang on a second."

This cloak-and-dagger stuff was making Catherine nervous. Nonetheless, she took a quick glance around as she grabbed a pair of sandals. Satisfied she wasn't being followed, she headed for the boardwalk.

"You do owe me," she said.

"I know. And I'm grateful." Jamarcus exhaled. He sounded nervous. "How was the prison food?"

"Why'd you call, Jamarcus? And why this elaborate deal with the new cell phone?"

"There are a lot of folks trying to discover your source. We can't be too careful."

She waited, knowing he had more.

"Did you know we've interviewed about a half dozen persons of interest?" Jamarcus asked.

"No." And in a way, Catherine no longer wanted to know the details. She had a newfound respect for the price of that information.

"Usual rules apply?" Jamarcus asked.

"Meaning you'll let my carcass rot in jail rather than come forward and confess to being my source?"

Catherine's caustic remark created a brief silence. When Jamarcus spoke, his voice was more somber. "Do you want the information or not?"

She studied the horizon beyond the boardwalk—the sun hanging low in a beautiful light blue sky. Honestly, she didn't know.

"Cat?"

"Let me ask you a question," she said at last. "Why do you want to give it to me?"

Jamarcus paused again. "I want to see how one of the persons of interest might react if his name was in the paper. I think he might slip up. I think it might help the investigation."

Catherine sighed. She felt like she was being manipulated. But still . . . "Let me have it."

"The Reverend Harold Pryor," said Jamarcus. "He was questioned yesterday. He has no solid alibi. He was in the D.C. area when Sherita Johnson was attacked. He was in the Hampton Roads area when the Carver kids were taken."

Catherine stopped walking when she reached the concrete boardwalk. She leaned against the railing. "Interesting. But there must be a thousand men and women who meet those criteria. What else do you have?"

"Dead man's talk?" asked Webb.

"If I haven't proven myself by now—" Cat felt a rant coming on, but Webb cut her off.

"Sorry; you're right." He took a deep breath. "The Avenger is sending messages with biblical quotes. Old Testament. Somebody who claims to be a member of Harold Pryor's church sent us an unsigned note that quoted these same verses. Said the reverend has been referring to them a lot recently."

Cat felt her stomach drop. She pressed her ear against the phone. The morning breeze made it difficult to hear. "Did you say biblical quotes? Old Testament?"

"Yeah. Why?"

Cat leaned hard against the railing. She brought her fist to her mouth—confused, frightened.

"Catherine?" Webb said.

The visions flashed in front of her eyes. Biblical quotes. *The sins of the fathers will be visited unto the third and fourth generation.*

"Catherine?"

She tried to get hold of herself. "What were the exact quotes?"

"I can't say, Catherine."

Her voice became sharp, insistent. "I need to know, Jamarcus. *What were the exact quotes?*"

"Catherine, I'm trying to help. But I'm not willing to jeopardize this investigation."

"He will visit the sins of the fathers unto the third and fourth generation," Catherine said. "The offspring of evildoers will never be remembered. Prepare a place of slaughter for the sons because of the iniquities of their fathers."

There was silence on the line. Catherine had known Jamarcus Webb for a number of years. She had never seen or heard him flustered. She had never known him to be at a loss for words.

"Who told you this?" he asked.

"If I said, you wouldn't believe me."

"Try me."

Catherine stared out over the ocean. Once she told him, there would be no turning back. "I saw it in a vision. Actually, two visions."

Another period of uncomfortable silence followed. "I think we need to meet," Jamarcus said.

22

CATHERINE THOUGHT JAMARCUS was being overly paranoid, but she still followed his instructions to a T. She drove into downtown Norfolk to get beyond the jurisdiction of the Virginia Beach police. At the last possible moment, she jumped aboard the Norfolk-Portsmouth ferry and made sure that nobody got on after she did. Then she called Jamarcus and told him she was not being followed.

He picked her up on the Portsmouth side of the river in his white Ford Taurus. For a fleeting moment she considered the possibility that Jamarcus might be the Avenger. From what she could tell, the killer had some sort of law enforcement experience—who else could commit such crimes without leaving even a trace of DNA or hair or fiber samples? And what did she really know about Jamarcus? A nice guy. A good cop from all reports. A family man. But she didn't really *know* him.

It dawned on her that he could snuff her out today and nobody would even know she had been meeting with him.

"Excuse me a second," Catherine said. She dialed her editor on her cell phone. "I'm meeting with my source," Catherine explained. "And I won't be able to get you those journal entries until later this afternoon."

"That wasn't smart," Jamarcus said sternly after Catherine hung up.

"Sorry," she said. She tried to put her suspicions aside and focus on her story. After all, if Jamarcus really wanted to kill her, wouldn't he have asked her to meet him at night?

They drove around Portsmouth, Jamarcus checking the mirrors, while Catherine started explaining about the visions. She watched for a reaction, but the man was stoic, working his tense jaw muscles but little else. When she finished telling him about the handwriting on the wall in the first vision, Jamarcus pulled into a 7-Eleven convenience store parking lot.

"Who have you told about this?" he asked. He looked shaken, his face a lighter hue than normal.

"Just you."

"Good. Until I figure out what to do, you've got to keep it that way."

No way am I making that promise. "So the kidnapper must have used basically the same words in some kind of ransom note or phone call?" Cat asked.

"Not *basically,*" Jamarcus said. "Almost word for word." He stared straight ahead, deep in thought, watching folks file in and out of the convenience store. "Tell me more about your second vision."

Catherine continued her narration, providing Jamarcus with every detail she could remember about the second vision. The detective immediately started quizzing her about the appearance of the hooded figure. White or black? Male or female? What size? What age?

As he did so, Catherine realized that the person inside the hood was more of a formless ghost than a real person. Her answers alternated between "I don't know" and "I don't have any idea."

"I know this sounds crazy," Catherine interjected, "but you know how some police detectives work with mediums to find killers? Maybe I'm some kind of medium." She shuddered a little at her own suggestion. Mediums were supposed to be whacked-out older women, chunky charlatans who spent too much time with Ouija boards and cats, not serious working women. And certainly not a cynical newspaper reporter who didn't even believe in this kind of stuff.

"Maybe you saw Clarence Milburn at some point in the past, and your brain just registered it away in your subconscious," Jamarcus reasoned. "Maybe you recalled his face for this dream."

Catherine had already considered this possibility but couldn't recall ever having seen Milburn before the vision. She wondered if it had been smart to even say anything to Jamarcus. She hadn't wanted these visions, hadn't asked for this gift or curse or whatever it was. But she knew it couldn't be explained away through simple logic—she had already tried that. "How would I know about the messages?" she asked.

Jamarcus shrugged. "You're a newspaper reporter. You've got sources."

Catherine turned in her seat to face him. "Not for this," she said sharply. "I'm not making this up, Jamarcus. I don't go around quoting Bible verses. And I don't particularly like the fact that when people find out, *if* people find out, they're going to look at me like I'm some kind of nutcase. But there are three babies missing, and maybe more that you guys haven't linked up yet. I can't just pretend this didn't happen if it might help you find them."

As Catherine talked, a volatile mix of emotions stirred in her. Fear of the unknown. Frustration at the conversation she was having right now. Confusion at what this meant. And *power*. Undeniably, there was a certain vague sense of some new and mysterious power. But mostly fear.

Given everything she had just been through, she felt like she was losing control of her life, maybe even her sanity, being dragged into something that shouldn't be her burden.

"Off the record, Catherine, we aren't trying to save those babies." Jamarcus spoke softly, the weariness evident in his deep voice. "The note about the Carver twins was sent with a piece of Chi Ying's blanket, spattered with blood. Considering that, along with the contents of the notes and the fact that there has been no request for a ransom . . ."

He paused and turned to Catherine. "We can't sit on this, you know. I think it might be best if you went to the chief and told him everything you've just told me."

"And leave your name out of it, of course."

Jamarcus nodded. "It won't help either one of us to reveal this relationship. And it sure doesn't bear on whether the visions are true."

Something about this didn't sit right with Catherine. Why should she be out on a limb *alone*? Did it really make sense to meet with the chief of police, and probably a host of others, with the intent of telling them about the visions but at the same time hide her relationship with Jamarcus?

She fidgeted in her seat. "What if I say no?"

Jamarcus ran both hands over his face and watched an older man limp into the store. "Then I'll go to him myself."

"Give me twenty-four hours to decide," Catherine said.

"Twenty-four hours," Jamarcus agreed. He checked his mirrors and put the car in reverse.

Catherine felt a knot form in the pit of her stomach as they left the parking lot. It was like she had walked over the edge of a cliff and started freefalling into a land where dreams and reality merged, where normality flirted with insanity.

One thing she was certain about. There was a serial killer on the loose. And if she wasn't careful, Catherine could end up right in the middle of his or her crosshairs.

Perhaps she was already there.

23

THE AVENGER OF BLOOD drove to the home of Paul Donaldson, found a parking spot on the street in front of Donaldson's house, and slouched down behind the wheel. In the past three weeks, the Avenger had been out here two other times.

The Avenger searched the streets for Donaldson's vehicle, a beat-up silver 2002 Volvo that was probably stolen. It was not around. The lights were on in the two-story white vinyl unit squeezed between nearly identical homes in Donaldson's neighborhood, but Donaldson apparently wasn't home.

At 11 p.m., Donaldson's live-in girlfriend, a Goth-looking woman in her twenties, came strutting out of the house, dressed for a night on the town. Black lace stockings. Straight and shiny black hair hanging over her face. A tight cotton top baring one shoulder. Blue lips. Black eyes. White face. The Avenger decided to follow her.

The girlfriend drove to the Mars Bar in the Shockoe Slip area of Richmond, an eerie place where the Avenger felt like a total misfit. Nevertheless, the Avenger found a booth in the corner and kept an eye on Paul Donaldson's girlfriend, watching intently as she flirted with a guy who made himself at home on the bar stool next to her. When they started making out, the Avenger snapped several pictures with a cell phone.

The Avenger found a spot a few feet away from the couple, discreetly snapped another shot, and even smiled while walking past them. The Goth woman stopped mid-kiss and stared back, as if pronouncing a curse with her eyes, but the Avenger just kept moving. A few minutes later, the Avenger drove out of the parking lot, the sweet taste of revenge pungent on half-smiling lips.

For motivation, the Avenger thought about the wasted life of Sherri McNamara, a woman who had been raped by Paul Donaldson. After his arrest, Donaldson and his lawyer had claimed that the sex had been consensual. They had three other witnesses testify that Sherri liked to play rough. Donaldson and his cohorts apparently lied well enough to create reasonable doubt, and the man even had the audacity to cast an accusatory glance at Sherri as he left the courtroom, according to press reports. Two weeks later, Sherri took her own life.

Now Donaldson would pay. And, since he had no children, he would have to pay himself.

By the time the Avenger finished, Donaldson would be wishing that the court had found him guilty. And Donaldson was just the warm-up act. The Avenger's most despised target was yet to come.

Catherine O'Rourke woke on Sunday morning in a cold sweat. She sat straight up in bed, frantically taking in her familiar surroundings, convincing herself that it was all just a nightmare. She felt like she had been wrestling all night, her sheets in a tangled mess.

Though it disturbed her, Catherine tried to focus on the details of her nightmare so she could write them down.

The nightmare started with a familiar scene, one she first experienced eight years ago and thought she had placed forever in the past. A single man, her attacker, came out of the fog, smiling and sweating, taunting her while she tried to run but could not move. His frat brothers, wearing Greek masks, laughed behind him, like a chorus of grotesque ghosts. The man started to unzip his pants.

But this time there was something new. Another man, lurking further in the background. A hooded figure, quietly watching. The Avenger.

Before the first man could attack Catherine, his face turned from lust to concern. He glanced over his shoulder at the Avenger, then dropped to his knees. The chorus of taunting became a chorus of screams. The Avenger extended a hand, pointed a finger, and the first man jerked in violent convulsions as the Avenger laughed.

And Catherine woke up, terrified.

With the images still burning in her mind, Catherine typed a series of cryptic notes into her computer. *Rapist. Frat brothers. Same nightmare as before. Hooded figure entered from the shadows. No discernable face.* She tried to remember the hand, the pointed finger. Was it the hand of a man or a woman? In truth, she couldn't tell. But the laugh, the one that startled her awake, was still very distinct. It was a sinister sound, haunting. *A man's chilling laugh?* Catherine typed. *The hooded figure crippled the rapist. Electrocuted him?*

Catherine saved the notes under the file "Avenger of Blood" and took a deep breath. She realized how tense she had become just thinking about the nightmare—racing heart, clenched muscles, the whole works. She needed to shake this off and get some perspective.

In four hours she was scheduled to meet with the chief of police, the assistant commonwealth's attorney, and Jamarcus Webb. She had concluded late yesterday afternoon that she really had no choice. If her visions could actually help them catch the kidnapper, how could she withhold that information? Still, she worried that coming forward would be crossing some type of line. After this meeting, her life would never be the same.

She put on her workout clothes, picked up the newspaper outside her door, and started brewing her own coffee, an inexpensive store brand, since Starbucks wasn't open yet. It was mid-May, but a cold front had moved through the area, leaving behind an uncharacteristic bite in the air. An outside thermometer said fifty-eight. She grabbed a sweatshirt, pulled it on, and headed out to the patio with her coffee and paper.

She turned first to her own column, "Journal from Jail," and went through the painful experience of reading her own words. Sometimes, the day after she wrote them, the words still resonated. Other times, she wondered what she had been thinking.

> First, you strip off your clothes for an invasive full-body
> search. Next, they begin to strip away your dignity. Being
> in jail is not so much about confinement as it is about
> humiliation and invasion of privacy. If you're not antisocial
> before you enter, odds are you will be when you leave. . . .

It was harsh, Catherine knew. But it was also true. Fortunately for her, she had no plans of returning anytime soon.

As she finished her first cup of coffee, Catherine thought about calling Marc Boland but talked herself out of it. After she fired William Jacobs, the paper's attorney, Cat had been forced to pay her own legal bills. Bo's rate was normally $350 an hour, but he had cut her a break—"only" $300. She couldn't afford to get him involved in this next matter. He would insist on going to the meeting with her. That alone could cost more than a thousand bucks. And Catherine wasn't even a suspect.

She finished reading the paper, changed from her slip-ons into her Rollerblades, and headed to the boardwalk. She started slowly, her muscles sore and tight. She would push through the first five minutes and loosen up. She could do some of her best thinking gliding down the boardwalk, the wind strong in her face, her quads beginning to burn. But this morning, for some reason, she just couldn't get going.

After ten minutes of laborious blading with skates that seemed to have lost their ability to glide, Catherine coasted to a stop. She leaned against the railing on the edge of the boardwalk and stared out at the ocean.

What's wrong with me? She was exhausted, as if she had run a marathon the night before. Plus, her mind was playing games on her. Summoning visions. Constructing nightmares. She felt like a totally normal person who had been dropped onto the set of *The Twilight Zone.*

She needed to talk with someone. Her mother and sister both lived seven hours away in central Pennsylvania, and her mom didn't need one more thing to worry about. The last time she had seen her dad was fifteen years ago, about six months after he left Cat's mom and filed for divorce. Her friends were wonderful but didn't understand a thing about the criminal justice system except what they picked up from *CSI*. A recent ex-boyfriend? She quickly put that thought out of her mind.

She started skating slowly back toward her house. She would tell the cops what she'd seen in the jail cell, and then maybe life would return to normal. She could go back to writing about crimes instead of envisioning them.

On her way, she tried to remember the last time she had failed to complete a workout—the last time she had felt so sapped of energy, so out of control.

She remembered it well. She was a senior in college. And she was trying to cope with the fact that a man she once loved had raped her.

24

CATHERINE WALKED INTO THE CONFERENCE ROOM of the Virginia Beach Commonwealth's Attorney and reminded herself not to be intimidated. Her sweaty palms apparently failed to get the message. She shook hands with Boyd Gates, whose strong grip seemed to hold a hint of a grudge. Police chief Arthur Compton, a grandfatherly figure with a round face, sunny disposition, and thinning gray comb-over, could not seem to muster a smile either. Jamarcus Webb shook hands coolly, like a perfect stranger, and managed a "thanks for coming in."

Catherine took a seat and noticed that the men all gathered on the other side of the table. She refused their offer of a drink, and Gates laid out the ground rules.

"This conference is at your request. You have indicated that you might have some information relevant to the Carver kidnappings. You have the right to have counsel present but have chosen not to do so."

Catherine nodded and felt like she had eaten lead for breakfast. Why did this seem like an interrogation?

"Do you mind if I record this?" Gates asked. He slid a recorder into the middle of the table and turned it on.

Of course I mind. "No, that's fine."

"The floor is yours," said Gates. He leaned back and studied her, the way you might eye a life insurance agent who had snaked his way to the kitchen table for a presentation.

Catherine shot a quick look at Jamarcus for reassurance, then began describing the background and substance of her first jailhouse vision. When she described the handwriting on the wall, Gates caught Chief Compton's eye and sat up straighter in his chair.

"Tell me again what that handwriting said?" Gates asked.

"I can't remember word for word. But it was something to the effect of 'He will visit the sins of the fathers unto the third and fourth generations.'"

Gates lowered his eyebrows and didn't try to mask the skepticism in his voice. "This just came to you. Sitting in your cell. Like a dream or something."

Catherine felt herself blushing and reminded herself that *she* had done nothing wrong. "Not so much like a dream. More like a vision. I don't think I ever really went to sleep."

"A vision."

"Right. Like a vision."

"Okay," Gates said, with a tone he might have used to pacify a nutcase. "And this confidential source you have—he didn't provide you with any information about messages the Avenger might have sent to the Carvers."

"He, *or she,* did not."

"You said there were two visions," Gates said. "Tell us about the second one."

Catherine walked them through the second vision, step-by-step. She recited from memory the words of the handwriting. "The offspring of evildoers will never be remembered. Prepare a place of slaughter for the sons because of the iniquities of their fathers."

This time, the men's faces betrayed no emotion. She waited. During the few seconds of silence, she heard the air vents kick in.

At last, Gates spoke. "Ms. O'Rourke, I'm going to tell you a few things and ask you a few questions. But first, I need you to pledge that this entire conversation will remain totally off-the-record and out of the paper. Are we clear about that?"

"Okay."

"You've just described, almost to the word, the two messages sent by this person who calls himself—" Gates paused—"or *herself,* the Avenger of Blood." He leaned forward and folded his hands, elbows on the table. "And frankly, I'm not at all sure what to make of this."

Gates held the pose for a moment, frowned, and took a sip of his soda, all for dramatic effect, displaying the showmanship of a trial lawyer even in a conference room. "Either you're some type of psychic, or somebody from inside the investigation leaked this information to you, or somehow you've been in contact with the Avenger of Blood. Can you think of any other options I'm missing?"

"I hadn't really thought about it in those terms," Catherine said.

"Well, I suppose," said Gates, "that you could actually be the Avenger. But let's dismiss that one as somewhat unlikely, at least for now."

"You had me worried for a minute," said Catherine, but nobody smiled. Not even Jamarcus.

"Since I don't really believe much in psychics, let me ask you this—have you discussed with your confidential source, either before or after you had these visions, anything relating to the substance of these messages?"

The question sounded accusatory and Catherine tried hard not to be defensive. "No," she said.

The chief leaned forward. "It seems to me," he said, in a slow and friendly Southern drawl, "that the first thing I might do if I had one of these visionary deals would be to contact my source who had been providing me with all this information and bounce it off him. Or her."

"Maybe my source is a little gun-shy about talking to me right now."

"Will you tell us who your source is?" Gates asked.

"I just spent two days in jail protecting him. Why would I give him up now?"

"Or her," said Gates with a thin smile.

"Whatever," said Catherine. Despite her efforts to remain calm, she felt anger bubbling to the surface. She was trying to help. And her reward? Getting questioned like a criminal. "Are we done?"

"You're free to go at any time," Gates replied. "This meeting is entirely noncustodial. But I think it would be in your best interest to cooperate with us."

"What do you mean by that?"

"Are you willing to take a lie detector test? We need some kind of assurance that your source is not leaking bits and pieces of this investigation to you."

Catherine surveyed all three men, giving her a chance to bore into Jamarcus with a quick and accusatory look before locking her eyes back on Gates. "If my source is feeding me information, you think I'm going to come in here claiming I saw it in a vision? For what purpose?"

"Does that mean you'll take a lie detector test?" Gates asked.

"No. I don't trust their reliability."

"Oh, they're pretty dependable," Chief Compton chimed in. "A polygraph measures your pulse, breathing, and galvanic skin response when you answer a question. Stress is increased if you try to tell a lie. Only the most experienced liars can control all three physiological functions at the same time. I think it might help clear things up if you took one."

"Am I some kind of suspect?" Catherine asked.

"Should you be?" asked Gates.

"Of course not. Am I?"

"No," Gates said. He took another drink, keeping his eyes on Catherine the entire time. "I would have given you a Miranda warning if you were a suspect. I'm just trying to rule out possibilities here."

"Let's assume your source didn't talk to you about the case," Jamarcus said, breaking his silence. "Can you tell us anything about what the man in the robe looked like?"

"No. I didn't really see his face."

"Are you sure it was a man?" Jamarcus asked.

Catherine thought he was trying to keep the focus away from her source. "No. I can't say."

"Have you ever had these types of visions before?" the chief asked.

"Not like this. No."

"Have you had any other visions like this," Jamarcus asked, "either before or since?"

Catherine thought about her dream last night. *I wish you hadn't asked me that question.* Was her dream another vision? It felt entirely different, but it featured the same hooded figure. "No," she said. *Plus, it's none of your business.* A vision about a kidnapping was one thing. A dream involving her own victimization was quite another.

"Are you sure?" said Gates, as if he already had the lie detector hooked up.

Catherine stared him down. "I'm sure."

On the way home, Catherine decided it had been a mistake to agree to meet with the men. In addition to asking her to take a polygraph, Gates had asked her about alibis for the nights of the kidnappings. Unfortunately, she had been alone both nights.

When she was nearly home, Jamarcus called and tried to put her mind at ease. "They had to give you a hard time," he said. "You stung their pride when you beat that contempt citation at the Virginia Supreme Court. Plus, they had to be sure you weren't just rubbing their noses in it."

"Why would I do that?"

"They can't figure that out. It's why they tend to believe you."

"They have a funny way of showing it."

"Don't be surprised if they ask you to come back," Jamarcus said. "They may want you to work with a behavioral psychologist who's in charge of pro-filing our bad guy. If we catch this guy, you could have your own television show."

"Spare me," Catherine said. But she did feel a little better after Jamarcus's call. Later that afternoon, she headed to the beach and played volleyball with some friends. It was the first time in nearly a week that she was able to take her mind off the Avenger of Blood.

25

WHEN QUINN FINALLY STROLLED into the office at 9:30 Monday morning, Melanie pounced. Though Quinn's young assistant could be annoying at times, he still considered her one of the three smartest persons in the sixty-lawyer firm of Robinson, Charles, and Espinoza, behind only Robert Espinoza and Quinn himself, not necessarily in that order. Though Melanie had dropped out of college to get married, she still possessed twice the street smarts of most lawyers in the firm, their diplomas from the big-name California law schools notwithstanding.

"You're up to twenty-six unreturned phone calls," Melanie announced as Quinn tried to slide past her desk. She handed him the telephone slips. "The top four are potential new clients. Eleven media calls are next. On the bottom are calls from other lawyers and bill collectors."

Quinn grabbed the pink slips, his schedule for the day, and a printout that showed the billed and collected numbers for the firm's attorneys. On top of everything else, he knew his unanswered e-mails could easily be in the hundreds.

"And Mr. Espinoza said he wanted to see you as soon as you arrived," Melanie said. "He asked me to call him."

"About what?" Quinn asked, though he already knew. Managing partners cared about two things: billable hours and collections. With Annie's case dominating his year, Quinn had done just fine on billable hours. Collections were another matter. If Quinn lost his sister's case, she would be ineligible as a beneficiary of her husband's estate, including his life insurance proceeds. If Annie had been any other client, Quinn would have resigned by now.

Quinn took his seat and started working through his e-mails. He had fired off at least ten responses by the time Espinoza came in and closed the door. The sixty-year-old attorney with salt-and-pepper hair, an angular face, and a long pointed nose took a seat on the other side of Quinn's desk.

"You know why I'm here?"

Quinn shrugged. "This?" He tossed the firm's latest billing and collections report on his desk. "You know I'll hit my numbers again as soon as Annie's case is over. She's my sister, Robert. I can't just leave her hanging."

"I'm not asking you to drop the case, Quinn. But I am worried about the rest of your files. You used to do a lot of white-collar stuff. I've been watching the new file list lately. It's a lot of insanity plea work." He said it with disdain, as if Quinn had a lineup of clients in straitjackets right outside his office door. "Can these folks even pay?"

Quinn shifted uncomfortably in his seat. He didn't like lying to his managing partner. "I'll make it work somehow. Work a few more hours. Only accept *rich* crazy folks." He tried the famous Newberg grin, but it didn't seem infectious this morning. Maybe he should rely on his track record—six strong years as an associate and two even stronger years as a partner. "Have I *ever* missed my numbers for an entire year, Robert?"

"No. And that's what's got me worried now." Espinoza crossed his legs, obviously trying to keep it casual. "Quinn, I think what you're doing is great work. Somebody's got to take these cases. But the other partners are grousing. Your comp is tied to your white-collar work. Plus, they're worried about the reputation of the firm."

At this, Quinn laughed. "That white-collar work, as you describe it, is about 90 percent mob work. Interesting how nobody cared much about the reputation of the firm as long as the bills got paid."

Espinoza frowned. "You remember Dennis Rodman in the NBA?"

"Sure."

"Well, nobody cared about how many tattoos he had or whether he was into cross-dressing as long as he got his rebounds. But you know what happened when he stopped getting his rebounds, Quinn?"

"They turned him into a point guard?"

"Not quite. He became trade bait." Espinoza stood. "So here's what I need you to do. Beat the heck out of Carla Duncan. Get a unanimous not guilty verdict for your sister. But make your numbers, Quinn. I want you around this firm a long time. But your partners aren't willing to subsidize someone to represent the mentally insane, no matter how famous you become."

Quinn had a thousand retorts but knew how the game was played. Espinoza was managing partner. Espinoza got the last word. To this point, Quinn had only been worried about paying his experts and the consultants in Annie's case. But now his own partners were grousing about the firm's unpaid legal bills, most of which were comprised of Quinn's own work. They would never fire Quinn, not with the name recognition he had brought to the firm. But Espinoza had delivered his message. Getting famous was no substitute for his partners getting rich.

When Espinoza left, Quinn leafed through his reports and found the totals for Annie's case. The legal bills alone, not counting consultants and experts, totaled more than three hundred thousand. Not a single dime of the attorneys' fees had been paid.

26

ON TUESDAY MORNING, Catherine had second thoughts about meeting with the criminal profiler, even though she had called Jamarcus on Monday and told him she would. Officially, this was still a kidnapping investigation, though the entire public now assumed the infants had already been murdered. On Monday, police had released the content of both notes, stunning the public just like the notes had stunned Catherine, who now felt like she had met Hannibal Lecter face-to-face in her prison cell.

At 8:30 on Tuesday, two hours prior to the scheduled meeting, she decided to bite the bullet and call Marc Boland. She hated the thought of forking over an additional three hundred an hour just to get some advice on whether she should call off the meeting, but she was growing increasingly uncomfortable. This was her life. And this meeting could now be part of a serial murder investigation.

Unfortunately, Bo was on his way to a court appearance, but his assistant promised to reach him on his cell phone. He didn't return the call until 10:15, and Catherine was already on her way down General Booth Boulevard, heading to the commonwealth attorney's office.

She told Bo everything about the two visions in the cell and her meeting with the chief of police, Gates, and Jamarcus Webb on Sunday.

"They wanted you to take a lie detector test?" Bo asked incredulously.

"Yes."

She heard Bo grunt his disapproval. "And they asked about alibis?"

"Yes."

"And now they want you to spend an hour or two with their criminal profile expert to allegedly tap into your psychic ability to channel this criminal?"

"Well, they didn't phrase it that way. They wanted me to describe these visions to this profiler and see if it might help him."

"And you bought this?" Bo asked. "You really think they're after your expertise?"

The question made Catherine feel stupid, as well as a little defensive. "Bo, I saw two visions, including handwriting on a wall that tracked almost word for word the notes this Avenger of Blood sent to his victims."

"My point exactly," Bo responded. "Which means they believe one of two things: either your confidential source told you what those notes said or you are somehow involved in the kidnappings."

"That's ridiculous," Catherine said. *And doubly ridiculous that I'm paying you three hundred bucks an hour to suggest it.*

"Why didn't you call me before you met with them the first time, Catherine? If you pull out now, it'll look like you're trying to hide something."

Catherine hesitated but then decided she was tired of lying just so she wouldn't hurt people's feelings. "I couldn't afford to call you, Bo. I'm a reporter. I don't know how I'm going to pay you for what you've already done."

"This one's on me," Bo said, his voice going soft.

"Bo . . ." Catherine appreciated the gesture but hated being a charity case.

"I just want to make sure you don't get caught in the middle of this," Bo said. "There's a ton of pressure on the cops right now to make an arrest. If they can't get their man, they'll be looking for a good scapegoat. Let's not give them a reason to make it you."

This entire conversation frightened Catherine. Until now, she had been assuming the best, hoping this would all go away. Maybe she could even help them find the kidnapper. At worst, she might send them on a wild-goose chase. But now she was a *suspect?*

"Should I call off the meeting?" Catherine asked.

"No," Bo counseled. "You should let *me* call off the meeting. I'll tell them you wanted to help but I wouldn't let you. If they need to know specific facts, they can communicate through me. That's what lawyers are for—we like being the bad guys."

"Thanks." Catherine felt like a weight had been lifted from her shoulders. "But you're not going to do this for free."

"We'll talk about that later," said Bo. And before Catherine could protest, he was off the line.

Ten minutes later he called back. "You're off the hook," he said. "I didn't make any friends, but it's the right call."

Catherine felt like she could breathe again. "Thanks," she managed.

"No problem. But this isn't going away. We need to meet in my office."

The urgency in his voice worried Catherine. "What's up?"

"This is a ploy to get you to rat out your source," Bo said. "They build a flimsy case against you as a suspect, then force you to divulge your source so you can explain how you came across this information."

"But I told you; I didn't get this information from my source."

"All the more reason we need to talk. And not on a cell phone."

27

PAUL DONALDSON FOUND the envelope in his mailbox. It contained no postmark but was addressed to him and marked "personal." When he opened it, he found a cryptic note composed of words cut out from various magazines. "Your lover is having an affair. If you want to know more, meet me in the back corner of the Hooters parking lot on West Broad Street at 11 p.m. Bring five hundred dollars and no weapons. Learn the name of the mystery man! Come alone."

The envelope also contained two pictures. The photos were dark and grainy, but Donaldson could tell that the woman was Rachel and that she was draped all over another man. Both pictures were taken from behind the man, so the back of the skinny runt's head was all Donaldson could see.

He studied the pictures carefully to see if this could possibly be airbrushed or whatever it was they did to doctor pictures these days. He analyzed the details for a few minutes, trying to figure out what bar the pictures had been taken in.

He fumed at the thought of Rachel's unfaithfulness, his rage so full that his hand literally began to shake. After everything he had done for her—how could she betray him? humiliate him in public like this? He had been faithful. He had bought her things. Kept her in clothes. Fed her drug habits. He had sacrificed so much to keep her happy.

Now *this?*

How could he have let himself fall for a woman this deceptive? As he stood there considering the treachery, his humiliation and anger turned into a blinding rage. He conjured up thoughts of spectacular revenge. He would cut off this man's head, then leave it on Rachel's side of the bed, Godfather-style. He would kill them both together so they could burn in hell with each other forever. He wanted to make an example of her, to somehow make her hurt even more than she had hurt him.

But he was just dreaming. None of that was really possible. He had beaten the system once. This time he would have to be careful, more subtle. He would find out the identity of Rachel's lover and kill the man. In an out-of-the-way place, he would show Rachel the man's dead corpse and watch her reaction. And after she begged him to forgive her, Donaldson would kill Rachel too.

He would dispose of the bodies far away from Richmond, Virginia. And he would be careful to leave no evidence.

First he needed the lover's name. Next he would have to kill the person who took these photos. He couldn't risk the possibility that this photographer would have a fit of conscience after finding out that Rachel and her lover had disappeared. The photographer might go to the police.

Donaldson walked from his mailbox to his car and slid the envelope under the driver's seat. Before he left, he would sheath his knife in his favorite pair of boots and tuck a gun in his waistband. He would down a few brews—not enough to slow him down, just enough to lower his inhibitions a notch or two. He would show up at Hooters a few minutes after eleven, nine hours from now.

He hadn't asked for this fight, but he wasn't going to run from it. Nobody made a fool of Paul Donaldson and lived to tell about it.

Marc Boland was all business, his shirtsleeves rolled up to his elbows, when Catherine showed up at his office that afternoon. He offered Catherine a glass of water with ice and poured himself one as well, then sat across from her at a round table in the corner of his office. As they talked, he took notes on a yellow legal pad and gently asked probing questions in his soft Southern drawl.

Catherine told him the story of the visions. He asked the usual questions about whether she could make out any features on the hooded figure, and she gave the usual answers assuring him that she could not. He asked detailed questions about her whereabouts on the days and nights surrounding the abduction of the Carver twins and Rayshad Milburn. He frowned as he realized she had no alibis that would hold water.

After nearly forty-five minutes, Bo studied his legal pad for an inordinate length of time, looked up, and lowered his eyebrows. "I believe every word you've told me, Catherine, but we've got to prepare for the commonwealth's attorney's approach to these same facts. To do that, I'll have to ask a few questions that will make you uncomfortable. Remember, our conversations are absolutely protected by the attorney-client privilege. Okay?"

Bo was already making Catherine uncomfortable, but she nodded anyway. "Sure."

"The morning after these two kidnappings, did you feel unusually tired? Was anything out of place? Like, for example, were your clothes or shoes dirty or soiled? Did you notice any blood anyplace? Were you cut or scratched in any way?"

Catherine should have been accustomed to these types of insinuations, but the questions still bothered her. "I don't remember anything unusual," she said tentatively. She thought about Sunday morning and the level of fatigue she had experienced. She had chalked that up to her hyperemotional prison experience. "I mean, I certainly don't remember any blood on my hands or muddy sneakers or anything like that."

"I'm no expert in psychology," Bo said, "but there are cases of multiple personality disorder where a person is actually taken over by a second or third personality, and the various personalities don't even know that the other personalities exist. Most often, multiple personality disorder is caused by extensive childhood abuse or trauma." Bo took a swig of water and placed his pen on the table. "If there's anything like that in your background, Catherine, I really need to know about it."

Silently, Catherine weighed her options. She stared down at her water, trying to summon the strength to talk about the rape. Why couldn't she put this behind her? It had been eight years ago. Was it really necessary to reopen it all?

"Catherine?" Bo prompted softly. He looked at her expectantly, as if he already knew.

Finally she looked up at him. She had only talked about this with one other man, a boyfriend who hadn't worked out. But she found sympathy in Bo's eyes.

"It was a frat party," she said, starting slowly. "The guy's name was Kenny Towns. I had dated him a few months earlier. . . ."

She told Bo all the details she could remember. The three or four drinks she'd had that night. Flirting with Kenny. How he'd coaxed her into the bedroom only to have her pull away in the middle of some passionate kissing. "I can't do this," she had said to him. "Not now. Not like this."

Kenny was agitated, telling Cat she had no right to get him all worked up and just stop. She left the room angry.

Later that night, Kenny came over and apologized. They went outside for a drink on the patio. Cat would never forget what happened next. After a few minutes and half a drink, she felt like she had chugged a whole bottle of tequila. The wooziness, the slurring of her words. To Cat, it was like watching herself lose control, as if she had stepped outside her own body, observing with detached fascination as an incredibly drunk Catherine lost all of her inhibitions and coordination. She tried to stand, but Kenny had to help stabilize her. She remembered wrapping her arms around Kenny to keep from falling. She remembered staggering back to the bedroom with him.

She regained consciousness the next morning, lying on a couch in the fraternity house lobby, the taste of vomit in her mouth.

Cat stopped and looked at Marc Boland, tears rimming her eyes. "You don't need the details," she said. "I was raped. Maybe more than once. I started asking questions of some of Kenny's fraternity brothers and some of the girls at the party. I got a bunch of vague answers. One girl said that Kenny took me back into the bedroom and that later some of the other guys came in too. The next day, I did some research on date rape drugs and found out a bunch of stuff about GHB. The problem is that it only shows up in a urine test and you generally have to take that test within twelve hours.

"One of Kenny's friends was the son of the prosecuting attorney for that county," Catherine said softly, the emotions of the rape making her voice raw. "Some of the other guys said they would testify against me if I claimed I was raped. Some of them said I was really drunk that night and came on to them, which I didn't. It made me realize that maybe they had raped me too and were worried about whether I had preserved the evidence against them. A few promised to testify I had had sex with them at other times, which wasn't true either."

She stared out the window, her eyes clouding with tears. "I decided to just let it go. A few weeks later, the depression settled in. I went to a few counseling sessions. Got a prescription. But mostly, I just avoided that part of campus and tried to pretend it never happened."

Catherine wiped away a few tears with the back of her hand. Bo stood up, walked over to his desk, and brought a box of tissues to the table.

"I still have nightmares sometimes," Catherine said, pulling out a tissue and drying her eyes. "But it was a one-time event. Eight years ago." She smiled gamely. "I don't think it turned me into a serial killer."

"You're a victim, not a psychopath." Bo said it with real conviction, just the words Catherine needed. "I used to be a prosecutor. Guys like Kenny deserve to be locked up for life."

He paused, and Catherine looked into the boyish eyes. She saw an intensity there she hadn't seen before.

"Everybody deserves a defense under our system of justice. But I personally don't represent sex offenders."

"I heard that about you," Catherine responded. "I guess it's one of the things that drew me to you as a lawyer."

Bo asked a few more questions and then suggested a break. When they reconvened, he went into lawyer mode and gave her the don't-talk-to-anybody-about-anything-related-to-this-case spiel. He straightened his legal pad and put his pen down. "There's something else you ought to consider. I would never advise a client to destroy potential evidence, Catherine, and in your case, there is no evidence to destroy." He paused, as if to make sure Catherine caught his next point. "But if the authorities do try to pin this on you, they will swoop into your home with a search warrant and confiscate everything in sight. Computers, journals, shoes, gloves . . . everything. I've seen even innocent clients burned by random statements in an e-mail or instant message or on an Internet site they accessed. And with you actually covering the various exploits of the Avenger, and possibly doing research to supplement your reporting, there's no telling what's on your hard drive."

Bo shifted and took another sip of water. "Right now, there's no outstanding warrant or subpoena that would keep you from disposing of any personal property, and I'm not saying you should. But I think you might be interested to know about one client who thought he had deleted all kinds of incriminating documents from his hard drive. He even took a hammer to his computer and shattered it into a dozen pieces. Darned if the feds didn't reconstruct every keystroke this genius had made over the prior thirty days." Bo smiled to himself. "We pled him out on that one."

"I understand," Catherine said.

"And one last thing."

"Okay."

"I need to know the name of your confidential source."

"Why?"

"For your own protection," Bo answered. No blinking; no hesitation; all business. "I need to call your source and tell him or her to make this go away. Your source needs to know that we want to protect him or her but that I'll burn the source if I have to. Your source needs to have every motivation to help us out."

"I can't reveal my sources, Bo."

Bo set his jaw and stared back at Catherine. He apparently wasn't used to clients with their own opinions. "You've been noble, Catherine, but don't be stubborn. This isn't contempt of court we're talking about here, a few days in the slammer. This is child abduction and possibly murder."

Catherine sat speechless for a moment, trying to sort out her conflicting duties and emotions.

"I'm trying to help you," Bo said. "Freedom of the press is a nice concept. But *you're* my client, not the press." He leaned toward her. "Let me do my job."

"I'll call you tomorrow," Catherine said, her tone indicating the issue wasn't open for further debate.

Later that afternoon, Catherine began the process of backing up all the documents and e-mails she wanted to keep. It would take her a day or two, and then she would drive over the Chesapeake Bay Bridge-Tunnel, stopping to dump her computer into the vast expanses of the bay.

For the first time in her life, Catherine felt like a common criminal.

THE AVENGER OF BLOOD arrived early at the Hooters parking lot and drove around the building twice, checking for any signs that Paul Donaldson had acted out of character and involved the police. He apparently had not. Human beings, especially no-class felons like Paul Donaldson, were so predictable.

The Avenger parked in the far back corner of the lot and faced the car toward the building so that the Avenger's face was obscured by shadows. The Avenger pulled on a ski mask, hunkered down, and waited—jittery and anxious—blowing warming breaths into fists that had grown cold with antici-pation. At 11:10, the Avenger nearly left but decided to give Donaldson five more minutes. A few minutes later, Donaldson's beat-up Volvo pulled into the spot next to the Avenger.

Donaldson got out of his car, checked in both directions, and approached the Avenger's vehicle. Donaldson had pulled his long, blond hair into a pony-tail, accentuating his receding hairline. He had a thin beard of blond peach fuzz growing on the end of his chin and wore a tight black T-shirt and loose jeans, his impressive biceps bulging as he attempted to swagger.

The Avenger rolled the driver's-side window down a few inches. "Get in."

Without speaking, Donaldson walked to the other side of the vehicle and climbed into the passenger's seat. He stared at the Avenger for a moment, concern darkening his face. "What's the deal with the ski mask?" he asked.

"The pictures are not here," the Avenger said, answering an entirely dif-ferent question. "We've got to drive a few minutes to get them."

"Why don't we start with you taking off the mask?" Donaldson asked.

The Avenger watched Donaldson's right hand slip down toward his boot, probably reaching for a knife. Quickly, smoothly, the Avenger pulled the Taser from the left side of the driver's seat and shot the barbs into Donaldson's stomach. Donaldson cried out and tried to defend himself but succumbed as the current did its work, contorting him with pain.

Five seconds, ten seconds—a full thirty seconds at high voltage until Donaldson nearly stopped moving, his previously convulsing body now limp. The Avenger then stuck a needle into Donaldson's vein and inserted a dose of methohexital. The fast-acting anesthetic was nearly three times as potent as sodium thiopental, the anesthetic administered to inmates during lethal injection. With Donaldson unconscious, the Avenger put the car into gear, checked every mirror, and pulled out of the parking lot.

The trial of Paul Donaldson lasted an hour. During the proceedings, Donaldson was bound to a large wooden chair with handcuffs and leather straps. The chair itself was anchored to the floor with eight large bolts.

Donaldson was cross-examined and confronted with the overwhelming evidence against him. For the first half hour, Donaldson tried to defend himself but eventually became abusive and foul-mouthed, spitting threats back at his accuser. Eventually, having heard enough, Donaldson's accuser donned a black judicial robe and pronounced the verdict: guilty for the rape and murder of Sherri McNamara. The sentence: death by electrocution.

The Avenger gagged Donaldson and pulled out an electric razor to create two bald spots, one on each side of Donaldson's head. At first, Donaldson jerked his head back and forth, determined not to let the Avenger shave the long, golden locks that he loved so much. But when Donaldson's jerking caused the teeth on the end of the razor to create a gash in the skin, he settled down and let the Avenger finish the task. Next, the Avenger bent over and shaved the back of one of Donaldson's calves.

While blood dripped down Donaldson's face from the head gash, the Avenger hooked up three copper electrodes—two to the skull and one to the calf. Not certain whether the amount of current from the makeshift electric chair would actually kill Donaldson, the Avenger pulled out a gun as well. The Avenger had read the botched execution stories about burning flesh and convulsing prisoners. Now the Avenger had a front-row seat. The electricity would flow for ten minutes whether Donaldson died or not—the same amount of time that it took him to rape and murder Sherri McNamara.

"Any final words?"

Donaldson screamed into the gag, his bloodshot eyes wide with fright.

Unsmiling, the Avenger flipped the switch.

Fifteen minutes later, using snap-on plastic gloves, the Avenger picked up a lock of Donaldson's hair and placed it in an envelope along with a message. The envelope was addressed to the editor of the *Richmond Times-Dispatch*, Donaldson's hometown newspaper.

The message was simple and direct, constructed using words clipped from a variety of magazines. It read:

> IN THOSE DAYS THEY SHALL SAY NO MORE, THE
> FATHERS HAVE EATEN A SOUR GRAPE, AND THE
> CHILDREN'S TEETH ARE SET ON EDGE. BUT EVERY
> ONE SHALL DIE FOR HIS OWN INIQUITY: EVERY MAN
> THAT EATETH THE SOUR GRAPE, HIS OWN TEETH
> SHALL BE SET ON EDGE.
>
> PAUL DONALDSON DIED FOR HIS OWN SINS.
>
> SINCERELY,
> THE AVENGER OF BLOOD

29

CATHERINE JERKED AWAKE, startled by her own scream from the nightmare that would not go away. Kenny Towns had haunted her dreams again, coming after her, freezing her limbs with fear. His frat brothers had been there too, wearing their despicable Greek masks. But tonight, as Kenny had taunted her, laughing fiendishly, he had begun to bleed from a gash in his scalp. When he touched the gash and checked the blood on his fingers, his eyes went wide with fear. The blood flowed faster, covering his face and choking his laugh. He started shaking his head, like a dog, blood flying everywhere. It splattered Catherine, and she screamed.

It was one of those nightmares so real that Catherine found herself checking for blood on her face, hands, and clothes. Her heart pounded against her chest as she thought about the gruesome images. She forced herself to focus on other things, eventually chasing the images away with a long, hot shower.

On her way to work that morning, she called Jamarcus.

"Just a minute," he said. A few seconds later, the background noise had disappeared. Jamarcus whispered into the phone. "Why are you using your cell phone to call me?"

"My attorney wants your name," Catherine replied. "He says that Gates might try to pin these kidnappings on me if I don't give up my source."

"That's ridiculous," Jamarcus whispered. There was real urgency in his voice, close to panic. "I told you—they believe you. But you aren't helping matters by hiring an attorney and refusing to work with us."

Catherine sighed. Was she being paranoid? "I'm not going to give you up," she promised.

"I knew you wouldn't," Jamarcus replied. Yet Catherine heard the relief in his voice—the man hadn't been certain. "There's no reason to."

"I agree," said Catherine. "At least not yet."

Jamarcus hesitated, apparently absorbing the implications of Catherine's carefully selected words. "Any more visions?" he asked.

"No," said Catherine decisively. "No more visions."

Though he had been trying cases against Carla Duncan for the last eight years, Quinn had never set foot in her office before. The austere decor did not surprise him. She had hung a diploma and bar certificate on the wall and propped some pictures of children and grandchildren on her credenza. That was it. Carla Duncan was not a showy woman.

She sat behind her desk, looking grave and somewhat sympathetic. "Thanks for coming in," she said. "I thought it would be better to discuss this in person."

Quinn crossed his legs. "No problem."

"I'm ready to deal," Carla said, skipping the preliminaries. The words ignited a small flicker of hope. Driving over, Quinn had speculated this might be the reason Carla wanted to meet. And Carla knew by now the deal would have to be good or Quinn would reject it out of hand.

She placed her forearms on her desk and leaned toward Quinn. "I know you might find this hard to believe, but I do sympathize with your client . . . your sister. It's been no fun prosecuting this case, Quinn. I'm doing my job, but I can't help despising the victim."

It was almost like a confession. What did she want—forgiveness? She wasn't forced to pursue this prosecution; they both knew that. And in Quinn's opinion, she had pursued the case with the zeal of a true believer. He intentionally let the silence grow uncomfortable.

"In my opinion," Carla continued, "it's time to put this case behind us. You know I can't just slap your sister on the wrist and make her promise not to shoot her next husband. But I do realize she's got a daughter to take care of. Justice in this case is a murky concept. Your sister doesn't need to spend most of her adult life behind bars."

"What are you suggesting?"

"Manslaughter. I'll recommend six to ten." Carla waited a beat, her intense green eyes conveying the fact that this offer was nonnegotiable. "If she behaves and gets counseling, you can apply for parole after three years, and I won't oppose it."

The offer was better than Quinn expected, though he didn't let on.

If Carla had suggested a slap on the wrist, Quinn would have argued for a love tap.

"Sierra is thirteen," Quinn said. "That's an age when she really needs her mom. By the time she's sixteen, she'll be a different girl. I can't ask Annie to just walk away from her chance to be a mother during these critical teenage years."

"Perhaps she should have thought about that before she pulled the trigger," Carla countered. "Look, Quinn, I've got my own kids. Grandkids. I'm putting a very generous offer on the table and one for which I'll probably receive a lot of criticism." She sighed and leaned back in her chair. "If you force the issue, I'll try this case again. Next time, I'll get a conviction. What will that do for Sierra?"

"Guilty but mentally ill," Quinn countered. "She gets four years with all but twelve months suspended. Three years of probation and psychiatric counseling."

Carla snorted. "This isn't a DUI, Quinn. In good conscience, I've just given you my best offer. I'm not looking for a counter. Think of it as *Deal or No Deal*."

Quinn nodded. "Had to ask." He stood, thanked Carla, and shook her hand. "I'll get back to you."

"The end of the week," Carla said. "I'll give you until 5 p.m. Friday."

30

MANAGING PARTNER ROBERT ESPINOZA plopped down in the client chair in front of Quinn's desk. Quinn quit typing and turned around, regarding the man with idle curiosity.

Melanie stood in the doorway. "Can I get you anything?" she asked. What she really meant, from the look on her face, was *I couldn't stop him and didn't have time to warn you—he barged right in.*

"We're fine," Quinn said. "Don't worry about it."

Melanie left, and Quinn turned to Espinoza. "Twice in one week," Quinn said. "Pretty soon you won't have to ask for directions."

"You're a funny guy," Espinoza replied, unsmiling. "You might want to save it for someone with a sense of humor."

"Good point." Quinn leaned back in his chair.

"It's a good offer, Quinn. You ought to take it."

Quinn gave his managing partner a sideways look and picked up a pen to keep his hands occupied. Not many people unnerved him like Espinoza. "How'd you find out?"

The question brought a thin smile. "We all have our sources, Quinn. Manslaughter. Six to ten. She's out in three. I would have bumped off a few ex-wives myself if I could have been assured of that deal. Cheaper than divorce."

"She's my sister, Robert. I don't find it funny."

Espinoza's face returned to its normal scowl, wrinkles of concern pulling at the corners of his narrow eyes. "I'm not trying to be funny, Quinn. She might be your sister, but she's also your client. She shot her husband in cold blood. It's a good deal. In fact, it's a great deal." Espinoza paused and seemed to be studying Quinn's very thoughts, trying to decipher whether this was all sinking in. "We need you back on some of these white-collar cases," he said. "Don't play games with your sister's life. Take the deal."

Quinn bristled at the tone, more of a command than a suggestion. "I'll be talking with Annie tonight." His voice had the sharp edge he had perfected for cross-examination. "I'll be sure to let her know you think it's a blue light special."

Espinoza scooted to the edge of his seat. "You're too close to this, Quinn. I'm just trying to give you an unbiased perspective from somebody who really *does* care." He stared at Quinn for a moment and then stood. "It's the deal of the century, buddy. Your sister would be well-served to take it."

Quinn called Bobby Jackson on his way to the Rogue, one of the newest casinos on the south end of the strip. It featured a lush and bustling tropical paradise decor, accentuated by dozens of fountains, sculptures, and flora. Many tourists were drawn by its bad-boy aura, complete with pirate themes and edgy burlesque shows. But Quinn liked it for other reasons. The high-stakes room always had plenty of action involving fresh money from inexperienced gamblers. And Richard Hofstetter Sr. was part owner of the Rogue, bringing Quinn an extra surge of satisfaction at the idea of making a little money at one of Hofstetter's joints.

This wouldn't be the first time Quinn and Bobby had worked together at the Rogue. The last time they'd been here, a few of the floor security guards had paid a little closer attention to their table than Quinn had liked. Bobby was nervous about coming back, but Quinn talked him into it. Quinn's friends sometimes accused him of having a death wish, which might explain why he had chosen this casino out of dozens of others that could have worked just as well.

Maybe he did have a death wish, Quinn supposed. But he was tired of taking heat from his firm's managing partner just because Annie couldn't pay her legal bills. A few more nights of "moonlighting," and he could at least slip her enough to make a decent down payment.

As Quinn meandered past the blackjack tables, a block of a man wearing a blue blazer moved in just behind his left shoulder.

"Hotel security," the man said, keeping his voice low and discreet. "I'll need you to come with me."

Quinn turned to look at the man and, out of his peripheral vision, saw another guard taking up a position about ten feet away.

"Something wrong?" Quinn asked.

"We can talk in Mr. Hofstetter's office," the man said gruffly. He put a hand on Quinn's elbow, directing Quinn toward the nearest wall. "There's a concealed door straight ahead, built into that wall."

Quinn shook his elbow free and walked a step ahead of the guard. "You ought to introduce Mr. Hofstetter to this thing called a cell phone," he said.

"He prefers to meet in person."

They took a hallway to an elevator and were joined by a second guard, equal in girth and attitude to the first. Both guards had gun-size bulges in their blazers.

The elevator traveled up sixty-eight floors to the executive suites, where a third gentleman ushered them down a hall with rich hardwood floors and expensive-looking paintings. Hofstetter's office was located at the end of the hall, taking up acres of prime Vegas real estate, a mammoth tribute to the fact that boatloads of money could not buy taste. Persian rugs and antiques were scattered about haphazardly, combining with floor-to-ceiling windows and the sleek black lines of Hofstetter's furniture to give the room a schizophrenic feel. Or maybe Quinn was just projecting his own jitters on his surroundings.

Hofstetter stood behind his desk. "Have a seat."

"I think I'll stand," Quinn said. He was flanked on each side by one of the bulky security guards.

Hofstetter shrugged. "Suit yourself." He paused and seemed to be searching for his thoughts. "You know why you're here?"

"Because you and your boys want to get sued for harassment?" Quinn sensed the guards stiffening, like assault dogs waiting for a command. Adrenaline pumped through Quinn's entire body, fear staking its claim. But he wouldn't show fear to Hofstetter.

"It's okay," Hofstetter said to the guards, though his nose flared in anger. He walked out from behind his desk, grabbed a remote, and pushed a few buttons. A screen dropped down from the ceiling to Quinn's right. Hofstetter pushed a few more buttons, and Quinn's poker table from the last time he'd gambled at the Rogue appeared on the screen, viewed through an angle behind and above Quinn.

Using an edited series of excerpts and a red laser pointer, Hofstetter pointed out the signals Quinn and Bobby Jackson had used, as well as the hands on which they had bid up other players at the table and scammed their money. He followed it with a video of the meeting between Quinn and

Bobby Jackson at the hotel bar, complete with a stop-action shot of money changing hands.

"You have the audacity to come into *my* casino and cheat *my* customers?" Hofstetter said, his face flushed with anger. "After all you've put my family through?"

Quinn watched warily as Hofstetter flicked off the video and returned to his station behind the desk. The man's anger burned deep, barely under control. Quinn suddenly realized nobody knew he was even here. If Hofstetter gave the order, how far would his henchmen go?

Do not show weakness.

Quinn forced a smile. "That's it? You're going to take your little slide show where? To the gaming authority and try to have me blackballed? To the DA and try to have me arrested? 'Hey, Carla, this guy bid up the pot a couple of times when this other guy at the same table blinked and then afterward, they shared a drink and settled up some bets.'" Quinn shook his head. "Good luck."

"You're a punk," Hofstetter spit back. "A moron. You think I'd take that to the authorities? They'd laugh in my face." Hofstetter sat down in his chair, a smug look on his face that worried Quinn. "I'm not stupid."

Quinn waited. "So what's your point?"

"My point, golden boy, is that you ought to be more careful about the folks you play poker with . . . especially if you're going to steal their money. I've done a little research." Hofstetter opened a manila folder. "Among your victims in the past few months are two gentlemen with local mob connections, one gangster, and another man who has a plain old nasty temper."

Hofstetter looked up at Quinn with a devious smile. He tossed a picture of a battered and bloodied face toward Quinn's side of the desk. "This is another guy who had the bad sense to cheat some of these men. We've got tapes ready to go to every one of the gentlemen you cheated who have any criminal connections whatsoever."

"Unless?"

"We both know your sister is guilty of murder," Hofstetter replied. "You're guilty of worse. Defaming my son and our family." He stopped, his jaw tight, his right hand balled into a fist.

"I'm aware that there's a deal on the table right now that can put this all behind us," he continued, rage riding hard on each syllable. "I don't like it, but at least it ends this ordeal. My family doesn't need to go through another trial, forced to watch you strut around the courtroom with your sanctimonious lies. Take the deal, Mr. Newberg. If you don't, these other card players will be the least of your worries."

Quinn, normally quick on his feet, found himself at a loss for words. At the moment, he just wanted to get out of the man's office unharmed. He could evaluate his options later.

"I've got a job to do," he responded. "We'll take the deal if it's in the best interest of my client."

"Get out of here," Hofstetter fumed. "And if I ever see you in my casino again—ever—your sister will need to get herself a new lawyer."

The guards led Quinn down the hall and into the elevator, pushing the button for the lobby. Halfway down, a guard reached out a stubby finger and pushed the stop button. Another quickly opened the panel and killed the lights.

"What's going on?" Quinn demanded.

He smelled one of them, directly in his face. Then came the answer. A kidney punch from the back. Quinn grunted in pain. One of the guards squeezed the base of Quinn's neck, exploiting a nerve that generated excruciating pain. Quinn tried to grab the guard's thick forearms and pry them off but it was hopeless.

"Next time," the man whispered, inches from Quinn's face, "show a little respect."

Just before Quinn passed out, the guard released his grip, and Quinn slumped to the floor. Somebody flipped a switch, and the elevator started down again, still in the dark. When the door opened at the bottom, the two guards forced Quinn to stand and pushed him down the hall and out an exit door. He stood there for a moment, leaning against the building, trying to catch his breath and regain his lucidity.

The nerve endings in his neck felt like they were on fire, while a knifelike pain jabbed into his kidney. As his mind cleared, he decided against calling the police. He had no cuts or bruises. The cops might write up a report, but the prosecutor would probably argue there was a lack of evidence. Though Quinn could sue Hofstetter and his goons in civil court, he really just wanted to put this whole affair behind him, rather than get in the middle of a two-year legal suit that might result in minimal damages.

In all honesty, he was tired of this case, maybe even losing his nerve. Things would be so much easier if Annie just took the deal. Quinn had already carved out his reputation as an insanity plea expert—he didn't need a second trial for that. And Espinoza would be grateful because Quinn could get back to making some serious money.

On the other hand, there was Sierra. Three years without a mother would be an eternity for a teenager. And regardless of whether he took the deal, Quinn knew that Hofstetter wasn't really going away. The old man wouldn't do anything serious right away—Quinn's greatest protector was the publicity surrounding his sister's lawsuit. If anything happened to him now, people would suspect Hofstetter. But eventually, when Quinn least expected it, Hofstetter would strike. The sad truth was that Quinn was already a marked man. Taking the deal wouldn't change that.

Quinn took a few deep breaths and headed for the parking lot. His stubborn side wanted to head back into the high stakes table at the Rogue and make a killing. But he had been around enough to know that gambling while angry was a bad idea.

He flexed his neck and tried to massage away the pain. Bobby Jackson was on his own tonight. For Quinn, it might be a good time for a rare night off.

31

ON THURSDAY, Catherine found herself increasingly distracted at the office and left work early. She had tossed her laptop into the bay at about 12:30 the night before and then had found it hard to get any sleep. This morning, she had used a calling card to talk with Jamarcus, who reported no real progress on the case. It was as if the Avenger of Blood had just materialized from nowhere, kidnapped three babies, left behind two eerie messages, and vaporized into the atmosphere.

Catherine arrived at her duplex and changed into shorts, flip-flops, and a T-shirt, then sat down to finish loading software onto her new computer. After an hour or so, she took a break and surfed a few of her favorite blogs. A thought hit her, and she googled the words *multiple personality disorder*, resulting in a number of interesting sites. An article from *Psychology Today* was particularly helpful.

The article said the phrase "multiple personality disorder" had been changed to "dissociative identity disorder," also known as DID, sometime in 1994 to reflect the fact that patients actually fragmented their personalities as opposed to "growing" multiple new ones. Most DID patients only had a couple of fragmented personalities, though some had as many as one hundred. Cat thought about that for a moment. *A hundred separate Catherines! How could anyone survive like that?*

The disorder was frequently accompanied by memory loss, especially among the more passive personalities. In other words, a patient would create and live in two or more separate realities, and the passive personality wouldn't even know the more aggressive personality existed. Many times, the more aggressive personality could be very clever in covering up evidence of its existence. According to the article, transitions between personalities were normally triggered by psychosocial stress. One sentence in particular jumped out at Catherine: *"Visual or auditory hallucinations may occur."*

Reading that sentence was like a slap in the face. She stared at the screen for several moments, considering the implications. Could she truly be sick? The part about psychosocial stress sure fit. And the article also said that the disorder was frequently accompanied by depression or anxiety.

She was definitely anxious now.

Cat rose from the computer and got a bottle of water. She started feeling a little light-headed, her skin perspiring as she turned the possibility over in her mind. It was ludicrous. She didn't even know the families whose babies had been kidnapped. She couldn't possibly be involved.

Could she?

She sipped the water and started pacing the duplex, rehearsing all the reasons the DID diagnosis couldn't apply to her. She tried to reason through it, but the whole thing seemed to defy rational analysis. Then she had a thought. One personality might forget events that transpired in the life of another personality, but physical evidence didn't just disappear.

Cat went back online and started researching the kidnappings one more time. What weapons did the Avenger use? What were the precise times and dates of the crimes?

She knew her calendar didn't show anything for the nights in question— the police had already asked her about that. So she focused on the Avenger's MO—a needle and, in one instance, a Taser. Where would she even get such a thing?

Methodically, Cat searched through every room in her small duplex, looking for a Taser or needles or research about the Carver kids or the Milburn baby or rubber gloves or a knife or gun. She looked for bloodstains on clothing or ripped fabric. Catherine ransacked her own place, looking for anything inconsistent with the Catherine she knew.

After two hours, she had found absolutely nothing.

When she finished, she lay down on the couch and closed her eyes. She was exhausted physically and emotionally. If she wasn't crazy yet, at this rate, she would be soon.

When the e-mail first arrived, Rex Archibald could hardly believe his luck. The Reverend Harold Pryor, a "person of interest" in the Carver and Milburn kidnappings, was assembling a dream team of lawyers. He wanted Rex to serve as one of his trial lawyers!

Rex played it cool, resisting the urge to report the good news to his assistant and slap her a high five. His legal career had fallen on hard times recently, dragged down by a long string of losses and lack of high-profile clients. But Rex knew he was only one big case away from the boom times. Seven years ago, after the headline-grabbing verdict Rex had engineered for Paul Donaldson, the phones had lit up for months. Winning a high-profile case was good; winning a high-profile case when everybody knew your client should have been convicted was golden.

Despite his eagerness to be part of the dream team, Rex played it by the book. He sent a reply to the Reverend Pryor and provided wiring instructions to the firm account. *As soon as you wire a twenty-five-thousand retainer, we'll talk.*

Dream team lawyers didn't come cheap.

After some negotiations via e-mail, Rex agreed to a retainer of ten thousand. He didn't tell Pryor, but given all the publicity the case would be sure to generate, Rex would have done it for free. Pryor asked whether money orders would be okay, and Rex assured him that money orders would work just fine. Rex had been well schooled in the number-one rule for criminal defense lawyers—never question the source or the means of payment.

But nothing prevented defense lawyers from dreaming about how they would spend the money. In Rex's case, it was already spoken for. He and Crystal, his wife of thirteen years, had finally been successful in their fertility treatments. Rex was going to be a daddy! He was hoping for a daughter to spoil, though at times he imagined throwing a baseball or football with a rugged little son. In either case, the kid would go to college and then on to law school. It was never too early to put a little something away in a savings account.

Because Rex practiced law in Richmond and the Reverend Pryor was busy raising havoc in Virginia Beach, they agreed on a meeting place halfway between, just outside Williamsburg at a small church where Pryor knew the pastor. Rex's assistant took care of the meeting details and printed out a set of directions from MapQuest. Pryor would be bringing a Virginia Beach lawyer with him, the assistant told Rex.

Now, just fifteen minutes away from the church on Thursday night, Rex received a call on his cell phone. "I'm the custodian for the North Williamsburg Baptist Church," said the caller, "and I wanted you to know I'm unlocking the side door located on the right of the building as you face it from the parking lot. I just talked to Reverend Pryor and his lawyer, and they said they're running a few minutes late. You can just come on in when you get here and wait for them in the fellowship hall."

"No problem," said Rex, though he usually liked to stress his own importance by being the last one to a meeting, not the first. "I'm running a little late myself."

"I'll put on a pot of coffee in the fellowship hall," the caller said. "I may be working in another part of the church, so just make yourself at home."

"Okay. Thanks."

After he hung up, Rex decided to pull over at a convenience store and grab a soda. At this pace, he would arrive a good fifteen minutes late, minimizing the possibility that he would be the first one there.

A half hour later, at twenty minutes after eight, he pulled into the gravel parking lot in front of the small box church with vinyl siding and a cross that served as a steeple. There was a sign out front, the kind with interchangeable black magnetic letters. As his headlights flashed across the sign, Rex noted that it contained a reference to a single verse: *Ezekiel 18:20.* Rex had seen a number of these types of signs before, usually containing pithy sayings that tried too hard to be cute—*God: "Don't make me come down there."*—but never one with just a single verse, especially when there was no indication what the verse actually said.

The sun was low in an overcast sky, throwing long shadows across the church property. Rex parked the car, picked up his file folder, and headed toward the right-hand side of the building. Unfortunately, even with his slow-down tactics, Rex had apparently beaten the others to the meeting.

To his surprise, the side door was locked. He knocked—loud enough to demonstrate his confidence. Hearing nothing, he knocked again.

Without warning, two darts hit him in the back, followed immediately by debilitating pain. He winced and shouted, crumbling to the ground, his muscles contracting. An electrical current snaked through every nerve ending in his body, setting him on fire, causing him to groan in agony. He tried to cry out, tried to beg for mercy, but could no longer control his tongue.

He writhed in pain on the cement, glancing toward his attacker with pleading eyes. His thoughts flashed to Crystal and the baby. They needed him! He had to survive! But when the pain became unbearable, his body ignored his will, and Rex Archibald passed out.

Archibald's unrelenting attacker continued the flow of crippling electricity into Archibald's unconscious body for another sixty seconds, causing the lawyer to spasm and jerk like a fish flopping on the deck of a hot fishing boat.

Later, Archibald would be tried, convicted, and sentenced to die by lethal injection. But rather than use the trio of drugs that most states had employed for the past twenty years—sodium thiopental as an anesthetic, pancuronium bromide as a paralyzing agent, and potassium chloride to stop the heart—the Avenger would use only potassium chloride. The Avenger wanted Archibald to be fully conscious and able to squirm when the potassium chloride triggered its fatal heart attack.

32

THE PHONE WOKE CATHERINE at 6:30 a.m. She was still on the couch, still dressed in her clothes from the evening before. She shook her head clear and tried to remember where she had left the phone. The insistent ringing drew her to the kitchen table.

"Good morning, Cat." It was Ed Shaftner. *Editor* Ed Shaftner.

She grunted. She meant to say, "Hi, Ed," but it came out sounding more like a groan.

"Were you sleeping?"

She double-checked the clock. "No, no, I'm awake."

"Good. Have you checked the papers yet?"

"No, Ed. Not yet." He could only be asking for one reason. Cat had been through this drill before—an early morning call. Another paper had scooped them.

"*Richmond Times.* Front page. The Avenger struck again and sent a note to the editor of the *Richmond Times.*"

The statement hit Cat like a bolt of java, jolting her awake. *The Avenger struck again?* "What did he do? What's the note say?"

"You can read the whole thing online and give me a call back. We'll need something from your source. We can't let this story get away from us."

Cat was standing now, running her free hand through her hair, starting to pace. She felt like the whole world was off and running a race while she was mired at the starting line, tying her sneakers. Then another thought hit—what had *she* been doing last night?

"Was it last night, Ed? Did the Avenger strike last night?"

"No. A few nights ago. The *Times* just got the note yesterday and turned it over to police. They sat on the article until this morning."

A few nights ago. Cat thought about her nightmare a few nights ago, the way she woke up tired. She flashed to the nightmare and asked a question without thinking. "Did the victim die from a head wound?"

117

Ed paused, and Cat realized how random the question must have sounded. "They haven't recovered the body yet, Cat. Are you sure you're awake?"

"Yeah, I'm fine." A few minutes later, Cat was off the phone and on her computer, digesting every detail of the article. She called Jamarcus and left a message. Another hour passed before he returned the call.

He began by confirming the *Times* article. Paul Donaldson had disappeared. In a note to the *Times*, the Avenger claimed credit for Donaldson's apparent death and included a lock of Donaldson's hair. Before telling Cat anything else, Jamarcus extracted a promise of confidentiality and a promise not to run a story without independent verification. Then he dropped the bombshell: "We found a different hair fragment stuck to the seal of the envelope," Jamarcus said. "Donaldson's hair is blond. This piece of hair was dark."

Cat felt a rush of excitement—the killer's first mistake. She knew that the Avenger had been careful, using gloves, leaving no traces of DNA or fingerprints or footprints. But now, a single piece of hair.

"How long before the DNA comes back?" Cat asked.

"Forty-eight hours. We'll check it against our data bank. With any luck, we'll have something by Sunday."

Cat felt like she could take her first full breath in a week. She had never been so swallowed up by a story, had never felt her life being sucked into a nightmare like this as the story progressed. Now she could finally eliminate all shadows of doubt.

"We're trying to figure out how the Carvers play into all this," Jamarcus continued. "Paul Donaldson and Clarence Milburn both beat rape charges, but the Carvers didn't represent either one of them."

"Did the Carvers represent other rapists who beat the rap?"

"They're defense attorneys, Cat. That's what they do."

"Maybe this guy's going after rapists and their attorneys."

"That's our working theory," Jamarcus said, though he didn't sound convinced. "Or at least he's going after the innocent children of defense attorneys." He paused, apparently trying to decide whether he should open a fresh wound. "And our forensic psychiatrists are not at all sure that the Avenger is a man, Cat. The fact that the Avenger is targeting rapists might indicate a female."

The words triggered the usual reaction in Cat—churning stomach, tight chest, self-doubt—the symptoms of serious accusations against her. She remembered that Dr. Rebecca Ernst, the criminal profiler her own paper had featured in earlier articles, had come to the same conclusion about the Avenger's gender based on the methods used in the kidnappings. "What night was Donaldson killed?" Cat asked.

"His girlfriend says he didn't come home on Tuesday night." Jamarcus sounded like he was picking his words carefully. "Just to be sure, I would probably ask potential persons of interest about their alibis all the way through Wednesday."

His message wasn't lost on Cat. For the second time that morning, her mind raced back to Tuesday night. She had been home. By herself. Having nightmares. She distinctly remembered waking up Wednesday morning with the feeling that she needed to wash the blood from her hands and clothes.

Cat took a long breath, trying to calculate how much she could trust her source. In a few days, the police would have the results of the DNA test. Her name would be cleared. The only question was whether they would attach any credibility to her visions. If she wanted to help them later, she would have to establish the groundwork for reliability now.

"They haven't found the body yet—is that right?" Cat asked.

"Yes," said Jamarcus. "Why?"

"Will you do me a favor?" asked Cat. "If they find the body and Donaldson's death involves some kind of head wound, would you call me?"

"More visions?"

She trusted him. But not that much.

"Let's just call it a hunch," Cat said.

Two hours later, shortly after Cat arrived at her office, Jamarcus called back. This time he insisted on meeting in person. They agreed on the Aqua Bar inside the Crowne Plaza Hotel at Town Center in Virginia Beach. Cat nursed a sweet tea for ten minutes waiting for him.

When he came, he ordered a Coke. "Usual rules apply," he said cryptically.

"Right," said Cat.

"Which are?"

She sighed. "These comments are off-record and not for attribution. I'll take your name to the grave. I won't publish the facts unless you tell me I can or unless I get independent corroboration from another source."

"What about waterboarding? If they send you down to Guantánamo for waterboarding, will you tell them?"

Their little game with imagined tortures had become decidedly less fun since Cat had actually gone to jail protecting Jamarcus. "No exceptions," Cat said wearily. "Not even for waterboarding." She took a drink and gave him a look of impatience.

"Paul Donaldson's former attorney is missing," Jamarcus said. "The guy's wife was out of town last night, so the attorney wasn't missed until he didn't show at the office this morning. *If* it's related—and nobody's saying for sure whether it is or not yet—that would be two accused rapists and two defense attorneys." Jamarcus paused, allowing Cat to take it in. "The attorney's name is Rex Archibald."

"Whoa." Cat's mind started spinning as she tried to put the pieces together. "Archibald represented Donaldson. But the Carvers didn't represent Milburn."

"That's right," replied Jamarcus with a thin smile. "But I can guarantee you this: when the information about Rex Archibald goes public, the attorney who did represent Milburn will be sweating bullets."

"You almost sound happy about that," said Catherine.

"Oh yeah," said Jamarcus, trying to strike an appropriate tone of sadness in his voice. "I forgot. Defense lawyers are people too."

Early Friday afternoon, at the Neiman Marcus café, Quinn had a heart-to-heart talk with his sister. She looked exhausted, her dark eyes sunken and lifeless. She had been through so much already—abuse by a father and then a husband, a chaotic night of vengeance, separation from Sierra, a murder trial, and now a decision that no mother should be forced to make.

They talked for more than two hours. After Annie left, Quinn called Carla Duncan.

"She'll take the deal," Quinn said.

"You're doing the right thing," Carla replied. "I'll get back to you with some dates for a hearing."

33

CAT LEFT HER SUNDAY AFTERNOON beach volleyball game early and headed back to her duplex. She was wearing shades, shorts, and a bathing suit top and carrying her sandals so the warm sand could squeeze between her toes. She loved this time of year at the beach—late spring, just before the tourists arrived. Today was unseasonably warm for late May—the high eighties—and it felt good to let the sun's rays bake her exposed skin.

When she got to the boardwalk, she rinsed off the sand at the public spigots and slipped on her sandals. Her duplex was only two blocks south on the other side of Atlantic Avenue. As she walked away from the beach, her mind shifted to the Avenger and the many unanswered questions surrounding the Avenger's death spree. She felt the familiar lead weight in her stomach that came each time she thought about this. Later today, Cat would call Jamarcus and find out about the DNA test results.

From a distance, she noticed a few police vehicles but didn't really comprehend at first that they were centered around *her* duplex. She walked toward the scene, curious. Cat counted at least four marked cruisers and several other sedans that she didn't recognize from the neighborhood.

As she grew closer, she noticed a news van and a couple of cameramen. Her skin bristled with anxiety as somebody turned in her direction and pointed. Cameras swung toward her, and there was nothing left to do but walk straight toward them, chin high, looking beyond the two cameramen to her duplex.

Jamarcus Webb and two uniformed officers met her on the sidewalk. "Catherine O'Rourke?" he asked.

She glanced from Jamarcus to the other officers—all of them staring at her with no-nonsense expressions, as if she might be Jack the Ripper.

"Yes?"

"You're under arrest for the murder of Paul Donaldson," Jamarcus said. The other officers moved in to handcuff her. "You have the right to remain silent. Anything you say can and will be used against you in a court of law. . . ."

Stunned, Cat barely heard the rest of Jamarcus's words. This *couldn't* be happening! Not to her!

As the officers hustled her toward a police cruiser, the reality of events came crashing through. *They think I'm a serial killer.*

She suddenly became cognizant of the cameras recording every step, the details of her shocked facial expression. She lowered her head, thankful for her oversize sunglasses. She felt naked and exposed.

An officer opened the back door of a cruiser and put a hand on top of Cat's head so she would duck as she climbed into the car. Cat stopped just before crawling into the cruiser and took a fleeting glance at Jamarcus.

He stood there like an unfeeling statue. Disgust lined every wrinkle of his face.

PART THREE

GUILT

Guilt: *n.*, 1. the fact of having committed a breach of conduct especially violating law and involving a penalty; 2a. the state of one who has committed an offense especially consciously; b. feelings of culpability especially for imagined offenses or from a sense of inadequacy.

MERRIAM-WEBSTER'S DICTIONARY

34

CAT PROCEEDED LIKE A ZOMBIE through processing and booking for the second time in less than two weeks. This time, she was a murder suspect. She still couldn't wrap her mind around this new reality. She was in shock, too stunned to feel even the tiniest sliver of emotion. She tried to clear her mind and think logically.

They took her into the interview room to meet with Jamarcus and another detective, and Cat just wanted to pour out her heart. *This is a huge mistake— can't you see that? How can you think for a second that I would do something like this? Hook me up to a lie detector right now, right here, and I'll show you how ridiculous this all is.*

Instead, she calmly asked for her lawyer.

"Okay," said Jamarcus, his voice registering disappointment. "But we can't help you if you don't talk to us."

"I want to talk with my lawyer first," Cat insisted.

Two hours later, Cat found herself sitting in a small cubicle on the opposite side of thick, bulletproof glass from Marc Boland. Just the sight of Bo, with his imposing presence and self-assured manner, began to calm Cat's raging nerves.

"It's gonna be all right" were the first words out of his mouth. He opened his briefcase and removed a yellow legal pad and pen. "You okay?" he asked.

Cat shrugged. "Not really. I just can't believe this. . . ." Her lip trembled as she fought to keep the tears at bay.

"Boyd Gates made a huge mistake," Bo said calmly. "He rushed the arrest. Cracked under the media pressure."

The words were like balm to Cat. She knew it had to be a mistake. But to hear her lawyer say almost those precise words . . .

"Assuming nothing changes, we'll demand our right to a speedy trial," Bo continued.

Trial?

"They don't have squat on you. We may waive the preliminary hearing and go straight to trial." Bo labeled the top of his first page. Catherine read his writing upside down. *Client conference. Commonwealth v. O'Rourke.*

"I've already talked to Gates," Bo explained. "He's determined to see this through despite the weaknesses in his case. Here's the way this works. I start by telling you what I know about the commonwealth's evidence. You think it over for a few minutes and then tell me everything, from the beginning."

Cat nodded. She had regained a razor-thin semblance of control. "Okay."

"Including the name of your source, though I'm pretty sure I already know."

Cat wondered how Bo could possibly know. "Okay," she said tentatively.

"Good. Now, I need to warn you," Bo said, "this might sound pretty devastating. But trust me, it's not going to get you convicted."

Cat tensed, her stomach flipping again. What could they possibly have?

"They did a preliminary mitochondrial DNA analysis on a piece of hair found on the flap of the envelope that the Avenger sent to the *Richmond Times.*"

Bo hesitated and Cat knew what was coming. The thought of it squeezed her head and caused the room to spin.

"The DNA results indicate that your hair was on that envelope. They matched it to DNA from saliva on a water glass you drank from earlier last week. Detective Jamarcus Webb is prepared to testify about the chain of custody for the glass."

Cat gasped. *Betrayed by Jamarcus?*

"After the arraignment tomorrow, they're going to ask for another swab sample to confirm those tests," Bo continued. "We'll need to come up with an explanation for that DNA evidence. But apart from that, they've got no body and no motive. Just one piece of hair on an envelope, coupled with your visions about the two kidnappings."

DNA evidence. Psychotic visions. To Cat, it felt like the jury had already pronounced her guilt.

35

THIS TIME, THEY PLACED CAT in a cell with two other women. The cell was part of a pod that housed a total of thirty-four inmates. Cat's older cellmate, a woman probably in her forties, looked like she hadn't bathed or showered in a month. The woman had stringy hair, gingivitis breath, and a spare tire that would put a plumber to shame. She complained loudly when the guards stuck Cat and an extra mattress in the cell, turning her venom toward Cat as soon as the guards disappeared.

"Shut up, woman," said Cat's other cellmate, a young African-American woman with ripped biceps and a hard look that scared Cat. "She didn't ask for this cell."

Cat's defender jumped down from the top bunk and shook Cat's hand, her grip conveying a message that Cat had already deciphered. *This woman's in charge.*

"I'm Tasha," she said.

"Catherine."

"Don't mind Holly," Tasha said. "She gets this way when she doesn't take her medication."

But it wasn't Holly that unnerved Cat. The mouthy ones, in Cat's opinion, were not the dangerous ones. Tasha, on the other hand, had this eerie calmness and unsettling stare.

"What are you in for?" Tasha asked, sizing Cat up.

"They think I murdered someone," Cat responded, though she still couldn't believe it herself. "Maybe more than one person."

"And you're innocent, right?" Tasha said, her sarcasm obvious.

Cat felt almost embarrassed to admit it. "Yes."

"Imagine that," Tasha responded. "Holly's innocent too. They tried to say she's a druggie."

"I *am* innocent," Holly protested, eyeing Cat suspiciously.

"What are the odds?" Tasha asked. "I get the only two truly innocent women at the Virginia Beach city jail as my cellmates."

Cat didn't respond.

"You don't look like a serial killer," Tasha said.

"She does to me," said Holly. "Look at the eyes. She's psycho in the eyes."

Tasha leaned a little closer, staring at Cat and freaking her out. Cat looked down, avoiding Tasha's gaze.

"Maybe she's just scared," Tasha said.

Quinn caught the scene on the late news, bringing his channel surfing to an abrupt halt. An attractive woman in a bathing suit top and cotton shorts, her hands cuffed behind her back, accused of being a serial killer! The sunglasses prevented him from seeing the eyes, the first place Quinn had learned to look for signs of insanity.

From what little he could see, the woman looked scared. Confused. Ashamed. Could a woman this pretty really be a cold-blooded serial killer? Could she be the "Avenger of Blood"?

For some reason, the woman's name rang a bell. Catherine O'Rourke. They identified her as a reporter for the *Tidewater Times*. That was why the name sounded familiar; she had covered Annie's case. Intrigued, Quinn got on the Internet and googled a few of the woman's articles. Catherine had given Quinn the benefit of the doubt during Annie's trial. He decided to do the same for her.

He studied a head shot of Catherine from a few months ago and compared it to her mug shot, already posted online. In the first picture, Catherine's large hazel eyes sparkled with life. They were playful and alluring, a woman comfortable in her own skin. In the disheveled mug shot there was desperation. She looked beyond the camera with a fearful and haunting stare that made Quinn wonder what was going on inside that pretty head.

Annie's case had been huge. But this one, the Avenger of Blood case, would dwarf it. The Avenger of Blood was a serial killer, not just an abused wife who struck back.

He took one more look at the earlier photo and then the mug shot. Interesting. It almost seemed like he was looking at two different women.

36

CATHERINE WAS ALREADY DISTRAUGHT, but her nerves frayed even further that first evening in jail. Friends tried to lift her spirits during visiting hours, but afterward the guards put her back in the same overcrowded pod. In the center of the pod was a two-story common area with a few bolted-down metal tables and picnic bench chairs. A total of fourteen cells lined the walls of the pod on two opposite sides and opened into the common area at all hours except during lockdown. A third wall contained open shower stalls. The fourth wall, the one opposite the shower stalls, was taken up by the thick bulletproof glass protecting the guard station where the deputies could watch every move of the inmates and lock every cell door or even spray the inmates down by remote control.

Inmates had a choice of hanging out in their own cells or going into the common area. But even if they stayed in their cells, the cell doors would be open except during lockdown, and there would be no escaping the taunting of other inmates. For Cat, the barbs during the first day had been nonstop.

Holly and several other inmates who had been in jail during Cat's first stay continued mockingly referring to her as "Barbie." Holly's first nickname for Catherine, which also started with a *B*, got nixed by the short-tempered Tasha.

"Call her that one more time, and I'll drive my foot all the way up to your backbone," Tasha threatened.

From then on, it was Barbie.

Cat hadn't realized how fortunate she had been during her first brief stay in the jail. Isolation had meant having her own private cell and at least a semiprivate toilet. But this time, there was no privacy. The "showers" were nothing more than three nozzles attached to the wall at the end of the pod opposite the guard station. The guards and everyone else in the pod could watch. The toilets weren't much better. Every cell had a stainless steel toilet and a stainless steel rinse basin attached to the wall, open for all to see. When

Holly used the toilet after lockdown at 11:00 p.m. and Cat glanced around the cell, Holly jumped on her.

"What are you starin' at, Barbie?"

"I'm not staring at anything. Certainly not you," Cat responded, tired of her cellmate's nonsense.

"I'll stuff your head in this bowl when I'm done," Holly threatened.

Holly finished and walked slowly toward Cat's mattress. Tasha sat up on her bed and stared, though she didn't say a word. Cat tensed, ready to fight if necessary. Holly towered over her for a minute, laughed, then turned and went back to her own bed.

When Cat used the toilet a few minutes later, Holly stared at her the entire time. "How do you like it, Barbie? How do you like it?"

"Leave her alone," Tasha grunted.

Cat stayed awake the entire first night, wary of even the slightest movement from the bunks. She had already decided she would not submit quietly. If one of the others attacked her, Cat would punch, kick, and claw, screaming the entire time. Jail required a new level of toughness; only the strongest survived.

Cat was a survivor. She would forge alliances and fight to defend herself. Though the guards prohibited gangs, after just one day in the pod Cat sensed the existence of gang loyalty among certain women.

It was probably just a matter of time before Holly found an opportune time to make a move. If and when it happened, Cat would hold nothing back. Her reputation and survival, she knew, would depend on the results of that first fight.

Exhausted, Cat stared at the ceiling, counting the minutes until dawn.

At 8:30 a.m., the deputies placed handcuffs on Cat and walked her through several thick metal doors and down a long tunnel to the circuit court building. Once there, she was jammed in a small cinder block holding cell with about ten other inmates, all clad in orange jumpsuits and shackled at the wrists and ankles. Eventually a deputy led her into a conference room where Marc Boland was waiting. The deputy stood just outside the door.

"Normally attorneys have to stand in that small chamber just outside the holding cell and talk to their clients through the slit in the door," Bo explained. "Because of the confidential nature of what I'm going to tell you, the judge has allowed us to use this conference room just this once."

"Thanks," Cat said. She had a hard time imagining talking to her lawyer in a holding cell, surrounded by ten other inmates.

"Are you doing okay?" Bo asked.

"You've got to get me out of here," Cat said, her resolve from the night before melting away in the face of exhaustion and uncertainty. "Can't you get me bailed out?" She could hear a certain desperation in her voice, but she didn't really care. She *had* to get out of this place.

"This morning's hearing is an arraignment, not a bond hearing. We'll plead not guilty, and I'll make my first appearance as counsel of record. That's all we're doing today."

"How long before a bond hearing?" Cat asked.

"Actually, I'm not even sure we should ask for bail," Bo said.

Cat gave him an incredulous look. *No bail?*

"Number one, I don't think there's any chance the judge would give it to you. And second, I don't think this Avenger of Blood character can control himself. If he strikes again while you're in here, you'll walk free the very next day."

She knew it was an overstatement, but Cat appreciated Bo's attempt to calm her. She shifted in her chair. "We need to at least try," she countered. "If we get it, I'll stay within sight of somebody 24-7. I'll have a total alibi at all times."

Bo didn't look like he was buying it.

"I can't survive in here, Bo."

"Catherine," Bo said calmly, as if attempting to transfer some of his resolve to her, "you can make it. You *will* make it. Every client tells me the same thing the first time we meet. As strong-willed as you are, you'll be running the joint before long. We're going to clear your name, Cat, but it's going to take some time."

We don't have time! she wanted to scream. But she didn't. *Bo's on my side,* she reminded herself. *Looking out for my best interest.* Her part was to be strong.

"Okay," she said, though she heard the uncertainty in her own tone.

Bo nodded. "You need to be aware, Catherine, that the commonwealth claims it has some additional evidence."

"Like what?"

"They obtained an emergency subpoena for your bank records first thing this morning. There's a five-thousand-dollar deposit from American Finance, one of those loan application deals triggered when you deposit the check. It was put into your account last Thursday. In your house, they found the tear-off page for another application for an unsecured credit card loan, this one for ten thousand. They'll be monitoring your mail for the approval on that loan from Bank of America."

"What does that prove?" Cat asked.

"Apparently somebody sent Rex Archibald a ten-thousand-dollar retainer in money orders. They're trying to prove that you had access to that kind of money."

For Cat, it was like they were talking about a different person. She received credit card and loan offers all the time. She never, *ever*, filled any of them out, much less deposited them. "So now they're trying to pin the murder of Rex Archibald on me too? I didn't make that deposit, Bo. I didn't apply for any quick loans."

Bo paused before responding, his facial expression unchanging. "A hand-writing expert says the signature on the back of the check and the handwriting on the deposit stub are yours. There's also something else." Bo watched her, apparently gauging her reaction. "Boyd Gates says they're running DNA tests on some bloody paper towels they found in a white plastic bag in your neighbor's trash container. The same bag contained a small vial of methohexital, the drug used to sedate Marcia Carver and Sherita Johnson. Is there anything you're not telling me?"

"I didn't murder anyone. I didn't kidnap any babies. Why would I do such a thing?"

"I'm not suggesting you did, Cat." Bo kept it low-key, a consummate professional. "But somebody is doing one heck of a job setting you up."

"Why would I dump those things in my neighbor's trash? Who would be that stupid?"

A deputy stuck his head in the door. "Your case is up next," he said to Bo.

"Can you drop it down?" Bo asked.

"No, sir," said the deputy. "Judge Rosencrance wants to make sure this one starts on time. There's a lot of media attention out there."

"Give us a minute," Bo said.

When the deputy left, Bo stood. "We've got to talk about adding another lawyer. On a capital case, you need two lawyers. I only handle the guilt phase. Every capital defendant needs someone who specializes in the penalty phase. We can talk about it after the arraignment."

Penalty phase. Capital defendants. The words were clinical enough, but Cat knew what they meant. She felt nauseous as the reality of it all sunk in, piece by awful piece. In a few minutes, she would be accused of first-degree murder. The commonwealth would be seeking the death penalty.

Bo closed his briefcase. "I've given one of the female deputies the clothes we had your friend pick up, along with a hairbrush and some rubber bands so you can pull your hair into a ponytail. She'll unlock your handcuffs so you can get changed."

"Okay," Cat mumbled, distracted by the challenges looming before her. She felt like she had stumbled into her own worst nightmare—a maze of injustice and false accusations. How could it get any worse?

Cat stepped into court feeling embarrassed and more than a little ugly. The night before, the deputies had released her duplex keys to Bo, who in turn had asked one of Cat's friends to pick out a respectable outfit for court. Cat wore a nice pair of slacks and a modest white cotton blouse. She had pulled her hair into a tight ponytail but wore no makeup. She knew her eyes were as bloodshot as a drug addict's.

She kept her head down and shuffled along, flanked by deputies. She sat next to Bo, mindful that the cameras recorded every movement. She couldn't bring herself to turn and look at the packed gallery. She knew her friends and coworkers would be there, as well as her editors. She had talked to her mother and sister on the phone last night, and they had planned to drive in from central Pennsylvania. Cat wondered how many people in the courtroom had already judged her.

The judge read the charges against Catherine—first-degree murder—and Bo confidently entered a plea of "absolutely not guilty." The lawyers settled on a date for a preliminary hearing, and, almost before it started, the proceeding was over.

Bo talked the guard into giving him a few more minutes with Catherine in the conference room before she headed back to jail.

"This will be the last time," the guard warned.

When they were alone, Catherine didn't wait for Bo to set the agenda. She was still unsure of herself, but she tried to sound decisive. "I want to bring Quinn Newberg on as co-counsel," she said. "He's competent, aggressive, and adamantly opposed to the death penalty."

Bo thought about it for a moment, his face registering concern. "I don't know. . . . He specializes in insanity. People will automatically assume you committed the crime and will be pleading insanity. Plus, he's not local. He doesn't know our courts."

Catherine trusted Bo. But it was *her* life on the line. For some reason, this felt right.

"You know the local courts, Bo. I need someone who hates the death penalty." She placed a hand on Bo's forearm. "Will you call him for me? Please? I think it would have more impact coming from you."

Bo hesitated again; clearly he didn't like this idea. "Quinn Newberg *is* a good attorney. But he's also going to be very expensive."

Cat gave Bo a pained expression. She hadn't really thought about costs. With her family's help, she thought she could scrape enough together for Bo's retainer. But she could never afford two lawyers.

"Vegas attorneys like Quinn charge a minimum of four hundred an hour," Bo said. "He'll charge for travel time back and forth, the time it takes him to get up to speed on Virginia procedure . . . everything. His retainer alone could be twenty-five, thirty thousand."

"It's a high-publicity case," Cat countered. "Won't he do it for a big discount? Maybe even for free?"

Bo gave her a sympathetic smile, the kind he probably reserved for clients with dumb questions. "Lawyers like Newberg don't discount their rates. The man's got enough publicity; he works for cash."

Cat felt desperation welling up in her again. The more she thought about this, the more she *knew* she needed Quinn for the capital phase. "Please? At least call?"

"I'll call him," Bo said, though his tone said it would be a waste of time.

"Thanks," Cat said. She steeled herself to return to jail.

37

"LINE ONE," MELANIE CALLED OUT.

"Take a message," Quinn yelled back from his office.

"You'll want to take this one," Melanie said.

Quinn grunted and picked up the phone. "Quinn Newberg."

"Quinn, it's Marc Boland from Virginia Beach."

Boland explained that he represented Catherine O'Rourke, a reporter accused of being the Avenger of Blood. He said they needed "death counsel" on the case and that Catherine had suggested Quinn.

"I'm flattered," said Quinn. He thought he detected something less than enthusiasm in Boland's voice, and Quinn didn't blame him. The last thing Quinn ever wanted on a big case was another high-powered defense lawyer acting as co-counsel, second-guessing Quinn's every move. "Are you going to plead insanity?"

"We haven't decided yet," Boland responded, "but I doubt it. We'd really just be looking for you to handle the sentencing phase . . . if you're interested."

It didn't take a genius to pick up on that hint. "How do you feel about having me involved?"

When Boland paused, Quinn had his answer.

"I think you're a heckuva lawyer," Boland said eventually. "It's just that when you get involved, the public will automatically assume Catherine killed this guy and that she's lining up an insanity plea. I think she's innocent, Quinn, and I don't want to send conflicting messages."

Is that what it's come to? Anybody who hires me will automatically be assumed either guilty or insane? "I hear what you're saying, Marc, but I don't think my involvement leads to that conclusion. I've actually represented one or two sane people in my day. Why don't you tell me about the evidence?"

It took about twenty minutes for Quinn to conclude that his view of the strength of the commonwealth's case was far different from Boland's.

The commonwealth had DNA evidence. They had a vial of methohexital in the neighbor's trash. They had O'Rourke's "visions." Eventually they would figure out the motive—according to Boland, O'Rourke had been raped in college, and the Avenger's victims were rapists and attorneys who represented rapists. O'Rourke had no alibi.

The visions bothered Quinn most of all. Boland said the jury would just conclude that his client had some kind of sixth sense. "If police rely on mediums to help solve cases, we can certainly argue that supernatural powers really exist. At first, even the criminal profilers thought maybe Catherine could help them solve the case, not be their number one suspect."

Quinn didn't want to argue the point now, but he was definitely part of the skeptic camp on this. In his view, "supernatural" phenomena always had natural causes. Cases were won on evidence and logic, not hunches that came from communications with another world. O'Rourke's visions, to Quinn's way of thinking, were powerful evidence that Catherine O'Rourke was insane. It seemed like a case of dissociative identity disorder, the hardest kind of case for any defense lawyer to win.

Yet something about this case was drawing Quinn. Maybe it was the magnet of national media coverage. Maybe it was seeing Catherine O'Rourke on television, an attractive woman at the mercy of the system. Maybe it was the challenge of a tough case or the fact that Quinn now saw high-profile insanity cases as his birthright. What lawyer knew the complexities of the human mind like Quinn did? Certainly not Marc Boland.

And besides, Annie's case would plead out in a couple of days. Quinn would have the time.

But he didn't really trust Marc Boland to deliver the right message to the client. Quinn didn't want to get involved just to carry Boland's briefcase. If he was going to be an equal partner, Quinn would need his own relationship with the client.

"I'd like to talk to Ms. O'Rourke," Quinn said. "Maybe I *could* help."

"I'll let her know," Boland responded, sounding skeptical. "But I also need to let her know your rates and retainer. She's a reporter. As you can imagine, funds are pretty tight."

Quinn wanted to ask Boland how much *he* was making per hour. But why get off on the wrong foot with a man who might end up being your co-counsel?

"That's okay," Quinn said. "I'll give her a call and see if we can work something out."

"Catherine prefers that you work through me," Boland said.

"She can tell me that when I call her," Quinn said. "And then I'll be glad to abide by her wishes."

38

CAT CRIED WHEN SHE SAW HER MOM and younger sister crammed into the small visitor kiosk. Even though Cat could only "meet" with them via closed-circuit TV from the visitors' station, just knowing they were in the same building gave her comfort.

"I took out a line of credit on the house," her mom said. "I'll give thirty thousand to Mr. Boland as a retainer."

"Mom, I don't want you to do that." But Cat knew there was no other choice. She had about fifteen thousand in savings. Her sister, Kelsey, had even less.

"Don't be ridiculous," said her mom. "What could be more important than proving my daughter's innocence?"

"I'll pay you back," Cat said, wiping away the tears. "Every penny."

"You'd better add interest to mine," Kelsey said, and they all smiled.

Later that night, Cat curled up on her mattress, facing Tasha and Holly on the iron bunk beds, exhausted but too afraid to let herself sleep. Her mind burned with worries and doomsday scenarios, the frayed edges of her nerves catching fire from the pressures of the day and nearly forty-eight hours without sleep. She lay awake for hours, staring straight ahead. Intermittently, one of the psychotic inmates in the pod would scream a string of curse words, which would, in turn, start the other inmates yelling and cursing as well.

At one point a deputy came around, shining her flashlight into the cell. Cat jerked her head up and stared at the blinding light.

"Go to sleep, O'Rourke," the deputy said.

Eventually the rhythmic breathing and congested snoring of her cellmates calmed Cat's nerves. Images blurred in her head; she saw people she knew doing bizarre things, the product of a troubled mind on the verge of sleep. She felt the last vestiges of reality slipping away, and she stopped fighting it.

The nightmares, unbidden, were not far behind.

Kenny and his fraternity brothers invaded her sleep again. They wore their Greek masks and ridiculed Cat, taunting her as they circled around, first one darting toward her, then another. She would turn and fend each off, ready to fight, and then someone else would come running at her from behind. She turned to face her new attacker, setting off a squeal of laughter from the others, while yet another frat boy darted toward her.

Abruptly they stopped, and Kenny, the only one not wearing a mask, stepped forward. He walked slowly toward Cat, and the look on his face said he would not be denied. She tensed, eyeing him warily as he approached, step by agonizing step. He lifted an index finger and curled it toward himself, commanding her to come, but Cat stood her ground. Slowly, almost playfully, Kenny kept coming until he was just inches away, his finger still bidding her come, a sneer curling on his lips.

He stood there, his breath nauseating her, while his frat brothers watched in what seemed like stunned horror, as if even they couldn't believe what Kenny was about to do. He reached out with his index finger and placed it on Cat's lip—

She screamed.

Heart pounding, Cat's eyes popped open, and she focused on the face in front of her, inches away. The insidious smile of Holly.

Cat screamed again, sitting straight up. "Get away from me, you pervert!" she yelled. "What are you doing?"

"Watching you."

Before Cat could respond, Tasha jumped down from the top bunk. She shoved Holly, knocking her over from a kneeling position, pushing her into the wall. "You *are* a perv," Tasha said.

Cat's heart pounded against her chest. She scooted back against the bars at the end of the cell, wide-eyed.

Holly just stared at Cat, smiling. "You talk in your sleep," she said. "You're crazy."

"*You're* crazy. Now get back to bed," Tasha growled.

Holly stood up and retreated to her bed, watching Cat the entire time. "Good night, beautiful," she said. "Pleasant dreams."

"She's harmless," Tasha mumbled, climbing back into the top bunk.

But Cat didn't believe her.

Shuddering, Cat crawled back onto her mattress. This time, she sat up with her back to the wall, her blanket pulled around her shoulders.

She caught only fleeting moments of sleep that night, even after Holly had turned over on her mattress and faced the wall, snoring again. When morning came, Cat was beyond exhaustion.

39

THE NEXT DAY, as Cat finished her lunch at one of the bolted-down picnic tables, she heard an argument break out on the other side of the pod. Apparently a young Hispanic woman named Eva had accused a larger African-American woman of cheating at cards. They stood up and pushed each other a few times while the inmates gathered around, shielding the women from the guard station.

Cat stood to get a better look and watched in horror as the larger woman grabbed Eva and threw her against the bars of a cell, holding her upright while she banged Eva's head against the steel. Eva screamed in pain, her eyes going glassy, but somehow managed to grab a hunk of the other woman's hair and pull with all her might.

She released it when the African-American inmate brought an elbow smashing into Eva's face, causing blood to spurt from the smaller woman's nose. Cat, her sight blocked by the other inmates, couldn't see exactly what happened next, but she heard the fist of the larger woman slamming into bone. The sickening thud was audible even as the inmates cheered and the woman cursed at Eva.

Cat glanced at the guard station—*Do something!* She pushed her way into the inmates who had formed a semicircle around the combatants.

"Stop them!" Cat shouted, repulsed by the bloody face and limp body of the smaller woman. "She's killing her!"

When nobody moved, Cat stepped in to try to stop the beating. But somebody bear-hugged her from behind and pulled her away from the brawlers.

"It's not your fight," Tasha said, speaking into Cat's ear.

Over her shoulder, Cat saw the larger inmate scrape her fingernails across Eva's face, spit on her, and then toss her prey to the floor. By now, six deputies had entered the cell. "Break it up," one of them ordered, shoving a few of the gawking inmates out of the way. "Fun's over."

The deputies helped Eva to her feet and took the woman, barely conscious, to receive medical treatment. They handcuffed the other inmate, presumably to move her into isolation. Then another deputy appeared with a mop and bucket and pointed to Cat, the newest fish. "Mop up the blood, O'Rourke."

While Cat cleaned the blood, the other inmates went back to their card games and lunches, as if they had witnessed nothing more than a verbal spat between friends. Cat trembled at the brutality of what she had just witnessed, amazed at how long the deputies had let the fight proceed before they broke it up. Cat kept her head down and mopped every inch of the concrete floor where the women had been fighting.

When things returned to normal, Tasha pulled Cat aside and gave her some advice. "Trouble will find you soon enough," she said, her jaw barely moving. "Stay out of other people's business."

Cat wanted to protest. She knew Tasha and this other woman were part of a gang that included most of the African-American inmates, though they were closed-lipped about it. But *everyone* couldn't be in that gang. How could the others just stand around and watch a fellow human being get beaten to a pulp?

Cat already knew the answer.

This is jail, she reminded herself. Civilized societies had complex moral codes to restrain behavior. But in here, things were basic. Raw. People were treated like animals. And, like animals, they were governed by one overriding principle.

Survival of the fittest.

40

BEFORE HIS SCHEDULED PHONE CALL with Catherine O'Rourke on Tuesday, Quinn called Dr. Rosemarie Mancini. She was driving her convertible, and the noise from the wind blowing into the phone made it hard to hear.

Quinn explained his potential involvement in Catherine's case and asked Rosemarie about the visions. To Quinn's surprise, his favorite shrink was a lot less skeptical than he was.

"There's a substantial body of research on this type of thing," she said, speaking loudly over the sound of wind and traffic. "Both the University of Arizona and the University of Virginia have psychology professors investigating the paranormal. I hear the guy at Arizona has a government grant from the National Institute for Health for nearly two million."

"Maybe *I* should apply for a grant," Quinn muttered. "Most of my clients certainly qualify as paranormal."

Rosemarie ignored him. "You know that NBC show called *Medium*?"

"I've seen the advertisements."

"That's based on a real person. Allison DuBois. I'll give you her entire story some other time, but she's helped resolve lots of actual cases. She's part of a study at Arizona called the Asking Questions Study—basically an attempt to communicate with dead people through mediums and ask questions that dead people never seem to answer. Stuff like, 'What do you do every day?' and 'What type of body or container for the soul do you have?' and 'Do you eat? Do you engage in sex?' That kind of stuff."

Quinn shook his head. You could apparently get a government grant for anything. "What's the answer to that last question?"

"Seems like all the mediums have their own take on things," Rosemarie said. "They're probably projecting their own biases."

Quinn knew that Rosemarie had both feet firmly anchored in the present dimension, so he decided to get her take. "What about you, doc? Do you think some people actually have this ability to communicate through some other dimension—dreams, premonitions, that type of thing?"

Quinn heard horns honking and, knowing Rosemarie Mancini, assumed she had just cut somebody off. "You asking me as an expert witness or as an individual?"

"As an individual, based on your psychiatric training."

Uncharacteristically, Rosemarie hesitated. "There are some interesting studies on phenomena called 'crisis apparitions,'" she said after a few seconds. "That's when somebody has a strange sense of foreboding or a dark premonition about a relative or someone else just before they die. It's basically what your potential client is saying happened to her."

This surprised Quinn. "You believe that stuff?" For Quinn, if you couldn't touch it, then it wasn't real.

"I'm not saying I buy it. I'm just saying there is some statistical data. Personally, my take focuses more on the spiritual angles."

This didn't surprise Quinn. Rosemarie's diagnoses always seemed to include a spiritual dimension. "Like what?" he asked.

"There's another realm out there, Quinn. A spiritual realm inhabited by real demons and also forces for good. I think God sometimes gives people dreams or visions about things that haven't yet happened or, occasionally, extraordinary insights about things that have already occurred. I'm not sure why, but I'm pretty certain the phenomena exist."

Quinn thought about this for a moment. He wasn't buying this theory that hinged on Catherine O'Rourke's being an innocent conveyor of visions. In Quinn's thinking, Catherine had to be guilty. The "visions," if they were even real, were probably nothing more than manifestations from a repressed personality desperately trying to communicate with the Catherine that everybody knew.

But if this case went to trial, and if Catherine insisted on trying to prove her innocence, it would be heard by a jury in Virginia Beach not Las Vegas. Those folks might be more open to a spiritual explanation than one based on communicating with ghosts of dead people or even "crisis apparitions." Rosemarie might not be Southern, and her northeast accent might grate on the jury, but she could speak their spiritual language. And even if O'Rourke ultimately pled insanity, an expert like Rosemarie Mancini would be priceless.

The doctor seemed to be in a good mood. Quinn decided he might as well push his luck. "If I take this case, will you help me?"

"I'm sure what you really meant to ask," Dr. Mancini said, her tone chiding, "was if you took the case, would I evaluate the potential client and give you my professional opinion about these visions."

"Right. Of course."

"Can your potential client afford me?"

"What?" asked Quinn. "I think you're breaking up."

"I asked if your client can afford me," Rosemarie repeated, raising her voice and speaking more slowly.

"Absolutely," Quinn said. "We both adore you."

Dr. Mancini laughed. "That's what I was afraid of."

But Quinn knew she would do it, especially after the check he had just sent her for Annie's case.

"Does that mean you're in?" he asked.

Even over the cell phone, Quinn could hear her sigh. "Against my better judgment," she said.

41

THE NEWS SHOWS on the wall-mounted television in Catherine's pod carried extensive coverage of her arrest and arraignment for the second straight day. The commentators had dubbed her "the Bikini Killer," a reference, Cat knew, to the repeated footage of her arrest on Sunday afternoon, wearing her swimsuit top and greased down in suntan oil. "Yo, woman," hooted an inmate. "That's what I call a 'killer bod.'"

A few of the women guffawed while others watched Cat to see how she handled it. She tried to force a playful smile.

"She's innocent!" another shouted at the TV. "What's wrong with you people? It was al-Qaeda. Barbie's getting framed!"

Cat tried to react good-naturedly as the inmates rode the subject matter into the ground. Eventually they moved on to something else.

While the inmates played cards or watched TV, Cat grabbed a copy of the *Tidewater Times* and headed into her cell. She had been dreading this moment all day. She knew it would be smart to stay abreast of developments, but the thought of her colleagues writing about her arrest as the Avenger of Blood was almost more than she could handle.

She settled onto her mattress, alone in her cell, and digested the lead story. Front page, above the fold, the headline screamed at her: *ALLEGED KILLER PLEADS NOT GUILTY.* The article had a picture of Cat standing in court as well as a picture on page A7, where the story continued, of Cat being arrested in her bathing suit. Brian Radford, a young reporter who had started at the paper within six months of Cat, had written the main story.

Today's story was much worse than yesterday's initial coverage of her arrest. In this article, Brian had detailed the evidence against her; *DNA* appeared at least a dozen times. An unidentified "law enforcement source" mentioned that they had found methohexital, believed to belong to Cat, in her neighbor's trash. There were comments from the families of the victims, though seeing a rapist like Paul Donaldson called a "victim" made Cat's stomach curl. It seemed to Cat that the crimes of Donaldson and Milburn were downplayed, making them seem more sympathetic.

The more she read, the more her anger flared. To appear balanced, the article contained a few quotes from Marc Boland, who promised that Cat would be vindicated, and a few of Cat's friends, who said they couldn't imagine Cat committing such grievous crimes. But other friends seemed less willing to jump to Cat's defense, saying it seemed out of character for the Catherine they knew, or some other vague comment. Cat's duplex neighbors expressed their shock at the arrests, explaining that Cat seemed so normal they never realized they were living so close to a possible serial killer. "I guess we could have been the next victims," the husband said.

It was trial by press, a phenomenon that Cat had experienced only from the other side. She was enraged by the way the article appeared on the surface to be so evenhanded and professional, because she recognized the cheap tricks of the trade that left every reader with the distinct impression that Cat was guilty. She thought about her mom, her sister, her college friends, and her friends at the beach. The anguish she had unwittingly caused them. If Cat read such an article about someone else, she would automatically assume the person was guilty.

That's when she made her decision. She had always been frustrated by the way accused persons would hide behind "no comment" while the prosecutors would systematically convince the public of their guilt. Cat would call her colleagues and offer an interview. Plus, she would write more journal columns from inside the Virginia Beach jail. She would argue for needed reforms in the incarceration system. Sure, she had made the deputies mad with her last set of columns. But if they realized that Cat was writing some new columns, naming names and detailing specific abuses, maybe they would shape up and protect Cat from the other inmates. Plus, if some quick reforms occurred, Cat could be hailed as a hero in her pod.

Survival of the fittest required the maximization of every available asset. Cat's best asset was her pen. She would fight back in the only way she knew.

42

QUINN TALKED TO CATHERINE O'ROURKE by phone on Tuesday afternoon. The potential client made a strong impression on Quinn, once Quinn convinced her that she didn't need to call him "Mr. Newberg." She sounded poised and articulate, very much in control for a young woman facing a possible death sentence. She answered his questions succinctly and without pretext. Like a lot of his crazy clients, Catherine sounded entirely sane. While he talked, Quinn stared at a downloaded image of her face on his computer screen. *What's going on inside that head of yours, Catherine O'Rourke?*

She became hesitant only when the conversation turned to money. "I can't pay you right now," Catherine admitted. "Honestly, I can barely afford Bo." Her tone turned from embarrassed to determined. "But I'm not a charity case. I'll pay back every penny over time."

Unless you get convicted, thought Quinn.

In a diplomatic way, Catherine made it clear that Marc Boland would be the lead attorney. Though Quinn had expected this, it still came as a blow to his ego. Some lawyers weren't designed to sit in the second chair, and he was one of them.

He had met Marc Boland only once, at the Regent Law School seminar, but Quinn had made a few phone calls today to get a scouting report. Boland came highly recommended—a big Southern boy with down-home charm, a former prosecutor in Richmond, Virginia, a true "courtroom lawyer" who liked to play his cases by instinct.

For the moment, Quinn put aside his misgivings about being second chair. If Catherine pled insanity, he would end up taking the lead.

"I'll get involved under one condition," Quinn said after he had checked off all the questions on his legal pad. "I want you to get evaluated by a forensic psychiatrist I know. She's one of the best in the country."

"Dr. Mancini?" Catherine asked.

At first, Catherine's answer surprised Quinn. Then he remembered that Catherine had covered Annie's case. "Yes, Dr. Mancini."

"Agreed."

"Good. I'll file my appearance tomorrow. I'll try to make it to Virginia to meet with you and Marc Boland early next week."

"Thanks," said Catherine. "And Mr. Newberg?"

"Quinn."

"Sorry. Quinn." Catherine paused, then made one final point. "I'm not crazy. Dr. Mancini will tell you that."

After Quinn ended the call, he asked Melanie to set up a new file. "Our client is Catherine O'Rourke. Criminal defense. Standard rates apply."

"Did you get a retainer?" asked Melanie. She was young and bookish, but she knew how to follow the money.

"Twenty-five thousand. Check's in the mail."

"In other words—no."

"This case is worth a million dollars in free publicity," Quinn argued, but even to him it sounded lame. "We should be paying her."

Melanie sighed and started filling out the new client form. "Are you *trying* to get fired?"

Catherine stayed busy during visiting hours, talking with her mom and sister as well as several friends and coworkers, all via closed-circuit television. Her editor, Ed Shaftner, was too busy to stop by, but Catherine's friends at the paper promised to deliver her message. She would agree to an exclusive interview with her fellow reporter Brian Radford. Also, she would be willing to write an exclusive daily column for the paper about her experience behind bars.

"Didn't you do that last time?" a friend asked.

"That was different. This will be real-time, not after the fact. It will focus on solutions and personalities, almost like a reality show, except printed."

Her friend seemed skeptical.

After a while, the steady stream of visitors wore Cat down. Her mom cried while Kelsey tried hard to stay upbeat, though her eyes were beet red too. With Cat's friends, it was the same questions, the same answers. "How are you doing?" Okay. "What's it like in there?" You don't want to know. "Is there anything I can do for you?" Not really.

When the last visitor departed, a deputy escorted Cat back to her cell.

Tasha was meeting with one of her own visitors, leaving Cat alone with Holly. Without speaking, Cat grabbed her pen and legal pad to make notes for her anticipated column. She looked for the pages she had churned out earlier. She noticed that Holly was watching her.

"Have you seen some notes I made earlier?" Cat asked.

"Yes."

"Do you know where they are?"

"Yes."

Cat raised an eyebrow. "Well?"

"We ran out of toilet paper," Holly said, smiling. "I used them and flushed them."

Cat looked at the nearly full roll of toilet paper sitting on the floor next to the toilet. Anger exploded in her head, ignited by a lack of sleep, the frustrations of the day, and her cellmate's unbridled arrogance. "You jerk," Cat said, seething.

Holly jumped up from her bed and took a few steps toward Cat's mattress. She stood there, towering over a still-seated Cat. "You gonna back that up, Barbie?"

Cat snorted in disgust. She refused to even look up at her cellmate. "Grow up."

"That's what I thought," said Holly. She took another step closer then placed her dirty shoe squarely on Cat's pillow. "Barbie's not so bad when Tasha ain't around."

Cat looked up at her and pointed to the foot. "Do you mind?"

Holly stood there for a moment, chuckled, and pulled her foot away. She walked back to her bed and sat down. Slowly, she removed her shoes. "Don't want to get my sheets dirty," she said.

43

AFTER INSPECTION ON WEDNESDAY MORNING, while the inmates were hanging out in the pod, Tasha pulled Cat into their cell. Cat noticed that a few other African-American inmates stood just outside the cell door, blocking the view from the pod.

"You're in," Tasha said. "A member of the Widows. It's mostly sisters, but we believe in equal opportunity."

Catherine hadn't anticipated this. She didn't want to join a gang, but it didn't seem like Tasha was really asking her opinion. It was more of an announcement, like Cat should be thanking Tasha for the honor.

"Just because you're a Widow doesn't mean you won't get attacked," Tasha warned. "It might even make it more likely. What it does mean, girl, is you got backup."

"How do I know who's in?" Cat asked.

Tasha glanced quickly around at the inmates standing at the door and smiled. "The mark," she said.

She grabbed a plastic cup from the sink and pulled Cat into a far corner of the cell. Tasha took another glance around and reached into a slit in her mattress. She pulled out baby oil and some matches.

"Where'd you get the matches?" Cat asked. She suspected they came from prison "trustees"— inmates specially selected to help with prison chores.

"No questions," Tasha said gruffly.

Tasha filled the plastic cup with baby oil and made a wick out of toilet paper. She lit the toilet paper and held a funneled piece of paper over the makeshift candle for several minutes, collecting black soot on the paper. Next, she mixed toothpaste with the black soot, forming a gooey black ink.

"Amazing," said Cat.

"That part's nothin'." Tasha said. "Wait till you see the tattoo gun. You know Felicia?"

Cat nodded.

"She ripped the motor out of her cassette player and mounted it to an ink pen using dental floss," Tasha explained. "She replaced the ink cartridge with a staple attached to the end of a spring. That staple serves as the needle. This stuff is the ink."

Cat's eyes went wide with disbelief.

"Yep," Tasha said, "Felicia is our resident tattoo artist. Drop your jumpsuit. Left hip, just above the buttocks. Every Widow has a spider tattoo."

Cat thought she might pass out. She hated needles in the first place, but unsanitized prison staples? No telling how many women had been tattooed with this same "needle." Or what diseases they might have.

But how could she say no? Did she want to offend a big portion of the inmate population by refusing to be part of the Widows? How could she survive on her own if she did?

"How big is the tattoo?" Cat asked.

"On your skinny butt? Not much bigger than a real black widow spider."

A few moments later, Cat nearly scraped the cement off the walls as Felicia used her crude tattoo gun on Cat's lower back. When Felicia finally announced she was finished, Cat decided not to even look.

"Two things," Tasha instructed, as Felicia left the cell. "First, you need a weapon. Every night, begin filing down the end of your toothbrush. Also, if you ever see another inmate get careless with their razor in the morning, before the guards collect them, grab it. I'll show you how to hide those things in your mattress. Second, when that tattoo dries, go and take a shower. That way, the other inmates will know you belong to us."

"Is Holly a member of a gang?" Cat asked.

"Uh-uh," Tasha responded. "That woman's psycho. Gangs don't take no psychos."

44

AS USUAL, THE PHONE MESSAGES PILED UP before Quinn even made it to work. He ignored them all, including three messages from Annie. He sent a fax to the Virginia Beach Circuit Court, noting his appearance as counsel of record for Catherine O'Rourke, then closed his office door so he could spend a few hours researching the victims of the Avenger of Blood, searching for common links in their pasts.

There were the obvious links—two criminal defendants who had beaten rape charges and three criminal defense lawyers. One of the lawyers, Rex Archibald, had represented one of the victims, Paul Donaldson. But neither Robert Carver Sr. nor his son, Bobby Carver, had ever represented Clarence Milburn. Quinn would need to research the rape victims. Maybe they would provide the missing connection.

The entire case was bizarre, but a few things in particular really bothered Quinn. The killer was a pro. The way he or she stalked the victims and lured them out. No footprints. No DNA until the single piece of hair on the Donaldson letter.

From what little Quinn knew about her, Catherine O'Rourke did not strike him as a professional killer.

The police had released the e-mails where a person posing as the Reverend Harold Pryor had negotiated with and hired Rex Archibald. Pryor, of course, vehemently denied sending the e-mails. The e-mails had originated from computers in three different public libraries, using a free AOL account set up solely for that purpose. Archibald's $10,000 retainer had been paid by five money orders, each in the amount of $2,000, procured several weeks earlier at five different Hampton Roads convenience stores. No stores kept the videotapes from store security cameras that long.

Quinn assumed that even Harold Pryor was not stupid enough to leave a string of e-mails setting up a meeting where he planned to murder a man. Unless, of course, Pryor had an alter ego, an Avenger of Blood who was not restrained by concerns about evidence trails.

More likely, thought Quinn, the Avenger tried to set Pryor up as a distraction. But this theory had its own problems. The e-mails from Pryor were sent to Rex Archibald *after* the Avenger sent the letter about Paul Donaldson to the *Richmond Times*. In other words, if Catherine was innocent, the Avenger would have been simultaneously setting up both Catherine O'Rourke and Harold Pryor, planting a piece of Catherine's hair on the *Richmond Times* envelope and then sending out e-mails in Pryor's name.

That seemed unlikely, though Quinn didn't like the only alternative— Catherine as the Avenger of Blood, trying to distract the authorities into suspecting Pryor. It demonstrated a level of planning that was inconsistent with an insanity defense.

Other questions also screamed for answers. If Catherine wasn't involved, what was spurring her visions about the Avenger? And why had the Avenger kidnapped babies of the first two victims but attacked Paul Donaldson and Rex Archibald directly? And finally, what was the significance of the biblical verses chosen by the Avenger, including the verse that police had found on the sign in front of the North Williamsburg Baptist Church?

Quinn's head ached as he tried to wrap his mind around these questions. He obsessed over them, turning them this way and that like a jeweler looking at a fine gem under a brilliant white light. The Avenger was crazed but not stupid. In fact, everything pointed to the Avenger having a brilliant tactical mind.

But even brilliant tacticians could make mistakes. Clever criminals could sometimes get away with a single kidnapping or murder, but serial killers eventually tripped up. In Quinn's opinion, it was usually part of their psyches. They *needed* to make mistakes. Somewhere deep in their subconsciences, they *wanted* to get caught. They craved the attention.

Quinn walked over to his window and glanced out at the plaza in front of the high-rise office building. The press trucks were beginning to converge. They had obviously caught wind of Quinn's involvement in Catherine's case. He would wait ten minutes, until the reporters reached critical mass, before he showed his face and proclaimed his client's innocence. Quinn didn't need the attention. But in his opinion, Catherine O'Rourke was getting slaughtered in the press. They needed to turn that tide soon or there would be no point in even having a trial.

His phone rang. An internal call. "Mr. Espinoza is here to see you," said Melanie.

"Tell him I'm busy."

The door opened, and Espinoza burst in. "We're all busy," he said, shutting the door behind him.

Quinn braced himself.

For ten minutes, Espinoza paced around the office and griped about Quinn's taking on Catherine O'Rourke as a client. As usual, he had his facts straight and his arguments in order. Catherine O'Rourke had no ability to pay. Quinn had not sought the approval of the firm's case-acceptance committee. The firm's clients would frown on one of their lawyers representing a serial killer.

"An *alleged* serial killer," Quinn said.

"Don't try that on me," Espinoza countered.

Quinn held out his hands, palms up, the universal sign of surrender. It did no good to argue with Espinoza when he was in one of these moods.

"The problem now is that you pulled the trigger," said Espinoza. "The entire world thinks we're in this case. How do you unscramble the egg?"

"Fire me," said Quinn. And he meant it. "I'm tired of apologizing for being a good-enough criminal defense lawyer that people actually want to hire me."

"That's not the point. Represent all the criminals you want. But they need to have money. And I don't care how good you think you are—you're not above following firm policies."

"Okay, I'm sorry." Quinn starting packing up his briefcase. "What do you want? A pound of flesh? Two?"

"I need you to tell me that you won't pull a stunt like this ever again," Espinoza said, his jaw tight with frustration. "And I don't want you taking any further action on the O'Rourke case until our case-acceptance committee can meet and decide what to do."

Quinn stuffed a few last things in his briefcase and grabbed his suit coat. "I really do have to go," he said. "Walk with me if you want to keep talking."

Espinoza followed Quinn out the door and down the hallway. "There's a whole mob of reporters out there," Espinoza said. "What are you going to tell them?"

"That my client's innocent."

"She's not your client yet."

Quinn stopped. "Look, Robert, I'm not backing out of this case. The firm has every right to refuse to get involved. But I'm in." He stared at his managing partner, a look that others said could melt steel. "I hope you're in with me."

Espinoza didn't respond until Quinn started walking away. Quinn knew the older man must be struggling to contain his anger; young partners didn't treat the managing partner this way. "We don't do well with ultimatums, Quinn."

The press accosted Quinn as soon as he left the building and set foot on the plaza. With the cameras rolling and mikes thrust in his face, Quinn affirmed his representation of Catherine and proclaimed her innocence in no uncertain terms. "The Commonwealth of Virginia has no body, no motive, and no real evidence," he declared. "In Nevada, this case wouldn't even be brought. And even in Virginia, there's this concept called 'innocent until proven guilty.'"

"Is Ms. O'Rourke considering an insanity defense?"

Quinn made a face, as if it were the dumbest question ever. "For something she didn't do?" he asked.

"What about the DNA?" another reporter asked.

"I don't comment on specific evidence," Quinn replied confidently, his chin held high. "But there are a thousand explanations for one piece of Ms. O'Rourke's hair being on that envelope. Nine hundred ninety-nine of them are consistent with innocence, including a scenario where the real Avenger of Blood picks up a piece of Ms. O'Rourke's hair and puts it there in order to frame her."

"What about the other DNA?" a reporter asked. "Have you seen the article just posted on the *Tidewater Times* Web site?"

Quinn quickly processed the possibilities. He knew the prosecutors were running DNA tests on the bloody paper towels. They must have announced a match.

"Have you been to a Vegas magic show?" Quinn asked the reporter. She didn't respond. "Things are not as they appear," he stressed. "Your eyes and your mind play tricks on you, but there's always a rational explanation."

"Care to share that explanation with us?" a skeptical voice chimed in.

"That's why we have trials," said Quinn. He started moving again, pressing his way through the crowd, ignoring the rest of their shouted questions.

More DNA evidence. What had he gotten himself into? And why had he made it a go-to-the-mat issue with his firm?

Maybe I'm the one who's insane.

45

IRONICALLY, TASHA MOOREHOUSE'S alleged crime—lying on a firearms transaction record as the straw purchaser of guns for the black market—was considered a nonviolent offense, making her eligible for the work duty the luckier inmates performed each Wednesday. As a third-time drug offender, Holly could join the crew as well. But not Catherine. Alleged serial killers were not qualified to pick up trash along local highways and endure the scorn of passing motorists. In theory, they posed too big of a flight risk, too much danger to others. Violent offenders were not entitled to see the sun.

When the other inmates returned from work duty late in the afternoon, Tasha was not among them. "One of the male guards tried to take one of the Widows into the woods along North Landing Road," a gang member explained. "When Tasha jumped in and started cursin' him out and makin' a big scene, she ended up in solitary."

While Cat was fretting about spending the night alone with Holly, more trouble showed up, this time in the form of a television newscast. DNA testing on the paper towels found in Cat's neighbor's trash revealed traces of Paul Donaldson's blood and contained a match from Cat's saliva. On hearing the news, Cat stepped from the pod into her cell so she could brood alone.

By now, she was almost immune to the avalanche of incriminating evidence. Though she still believed in her own innocence, it no longer surprised her when seemingly rock-solid scientific evidence pointed straight at her. Somebody was setting her up. And that somebody was doing a very good job.

The noise from the pod and the general chaos that now defined Cat's life made it hard to think rationally. But one question kept haunting her: how had the police even known to look in the neighbor's trash? And a corollary question: how would the person setting her up know that the police would look there?

The more she thought about it, the more she realized there was only one logical conclusion: Cat was being set up by somebody on the police force or in the prosecutor's office. Somebody who could guarantee police would find this evidence. But also—and this was the part that freaked Cat out—somebody who had access to Paul Donaldson's blood even though the body had not yet been found. *Could the Avenger of Blood be a cop?*

Actually, there was one other possibility, and the very thought of it made Cat want to puke. Multiple personality disorder. Or dissociative identify disorder, whatever you wanted to call it. A demon-possessed Catherine exacting revenge on those who raped and got away with it, then attempting to hide evidence next door. She put her face in her hands and closed her eyes, rubbing her forehead.

It couldn't be. For starters, there was just no possible way that Catherine could harm innocent babies like the Carver twins and Rayshad Milburn. Sure, she still felt rage boil up when she thought about that night at the frat house. But it was rage directed at Kenny and his frat brothers, not others who Catherine didn't even know. Especially not attorneys like Rex Archibald and Bobby Carver. They were just doing their jobs, detestable as they might be.

There had to be some other explanation. Because if Catherine truly believed she had done these awful acts, Boyd Gates wouldn't have to worry about prosecuting her. There wouldn't be any need for a trial.

She would take her own life first.

46

THAT EVENING, CATHERINE HIT ROCK BOTTOM. Depression reached out to embrace her as the last vestiges of hope faded away. Her visitors were fewer that night, and she saw the first signs of skepticism even among her closest friends. Her sister, Kelsey, always upbeat, couldn't manage a smile. And Cat couldn't blame her; she had her own doubts.

The new evidence seemed to shake even the confidence of Marc Boland, who stopped by to see how Cat was doing. He asked her point-blank questions about the paper towels, but Cat couldn't help. She could think of no way those paper towels, with their incriminating evidence, could have ended up in her neighbor's trash. She still suspected it was a setup, she told Bo, and he tended to agree with her. But tonight, unlike their prior visits, he warned Cat that this would be a tough trial and that nothing was guaranteed. Cat nodded stoically, too numb for any emotional reaction. She wondered if Quinn Newberg would stay on the case.

Cat promised Bo that she would cancel her interview with the *Tidewater Times*. Cat's editor reacted by sending his own message through a coworker who visited Cat—the paper wouldn't be able to run Cat's journal from jail. They had already done a similar series right after Cat's contempt sentence, the coworker explained. And, to be frank, the public was obsessing over Cat, wondering whether she was a ruthless serial killer. People probably weren't in any mood to read her complaints about jail food or lack of a soft bed.

In other words, thought Cat, *my own paper has already convicted me.* That troubled Cat the most—that her coworkers and some of her friends had turned so quickly against her.

That night in the cell, Cat did her best to ignore Holly's mindless rants. Holly, of course, had heard about the new evidence against Cat and prowled around the cell, complaining about being cellmates with a serial killer. Holly would recite the evidence over and over and tell Cat to face it, she was going to get the needle.

Cat shook her head in disgust. "Take your medication."

"Mind your own business, Barbie."

Minutes dragged by, and eventually Holly settled down. When the lights went out for lockdown, Cat sat in her bed with her back to the wall, staring into the dark void of the cell. Before long, Holly's rhythmic breathing and occasional snorting indicated she had fallen asleep. It gave Cat time to think and process the emotions she had been holding at bay through most of the day.

More than anything, Cat was struck by the realization that she needed help. She had always been strong, savvy, and self-sufficient. But now, she was merely Catherine O'Rourke, inmate number 08-317. She needed help from the Widows to survive prison. She needed Marc Boland and Quinn Newberg to help her survive the trial. She needed family and friends for emotional support.

And for the first time in her life, she realized how much she needed professional psychiatric help. Cat could repress her emotions and avoid issues with the best of them. But actually dealing with her emotions required vulnerability. Until she had nothing left to lose, she just wasn't willing to be quite that vulnerable.

The stigma of seeking psychiatric help no longer mattered. Who cares about such things when most of the world thinks you're a serial killer?

She would check out what types of services were available first thing in the morning. In the meantime, she lay on her side and curled up on the mattress. She wouldn't go to sleep, she promised herself, but she could at least lie down in a more comfortable position.

As she relaxed, her swirling thoughts seemed to calm, like the still waters of a river following a section of harrowing whitewater. She tucked her hands up under her pillow and closed her eyes. She drifted in and out for a few minutes, mindful of the danger lurking in her own cell but exhausted to the bone.

Ten minutes later, Cat fell into a fitful sleep.

47

QUINN SQUIRMED in his seat at the Mirage high-stakes table, realizing that this was the moment. He had played methodically throughout the night, netting nearly fifteen thousand dollars. Not bad, considering he was playing everything straight by the book—no signals, no allies, just Quinn and his carefully calculated risks.

But fifteen thousand was not going to get it done. There were high-stakes tables where Quinn played all the time, and there was *the* high-stakes table, where the ante alone was a thousand dollars. Two hours ago, Quinn had claimed his seat at *this* table, cashing in a marker for fifty thousand. He had two more fifty-thousand markers still in his pocket.

One hundred fifty thousand.

Quinn had a knack for making money, but his real gift was spending it. His Mercedes and his plush address in the Signature Towers did not come cheap. Plus, he had used every dime of his recent gambling winnings to pay the expert witnesses on Annie's case. Which was why, earlier this week when he decided to liquidate his financial assets for tonight's big play, he could scrounge together only a hundred and fifty thousand.

This afternoon, he had checked on a few things and done the math. It would take at least four hundred thousand to start his own firm. He would have preferred to stay at Robinson, Charles, and Espinoza, but he didn't like where things were headed. Quinn was now focused on his insanity trials, not the white-collar cases that had been so lucrative in the past. He was tired of trying to justify every case and having the managing partner breathing down his neck about billable hours and fee collections. Quinn needed space and freedom to take the cases he believed in. He needed his own firm.

But there was a problem. He also needed cash flow for office space, support staff, malpractice insurance, and supplies. The fees wouldn't start coming in for a few months. Four hundred thousand would be bare-bones minimum.

He decided to give himself three nights at the high-stakes table to parlay his hundred fifty thousand into four hundred thousand. He would work the games patiently, waiting until the odds were unmistakably in his favor to strike. He would do it on his own, concerned that Robert Hofstetter had already passed the word to other casino owners about his tag-team approach with Bobby Jackson. If Quinn won this much money, he wanted it to be squeaky clean.

Quinn had never expected his opportunity to come so quickly. He was holding the ace and ten of diamonds and, after the turn card, was sitting on an ace-high flush. The community cards were the four of diamonds, the queen of spades, the nine of diamonds, and the king of diamonds.

Two other players had yet to fold. An Asian gentleman sitting to Quinn's immediate left had been hard to read, but the fifty-five-year-old in the gray ponytail across the table might as well be wearing mirrors for glasses, allowing Quinn to see every card in his hand. His lip curled up a little, and his neck muscles tightened whenever he drew a good hand. When the river had turned up the king of diamonds, the lip curl and neck muscles had gone on overdrive.

The Asian guy bet first and tapped the table. All eyes turned to the man with the ponytail, gold neck chain, and earrings. He had supposedly made his money in the movie business. Hollywood smirked as he counted out the chips. "Fifty thousand," he said, trying hard to suppress his excitement.

Quinn studied the pot for a moment and took another look at his cards, an attempt to convey indecision. Each man already had twelve thousand in. If Quinn called Hollywood's bet, the pot would swell to more than a hundred and forty-three thousand, counting the amount already in by virtue of the blinds and early betting.

"I'll see your fifty," said Quinn, shoving his chips into the middle, "and raise it twenty-five." Quinn resisted the urge to go all in. He didn't want to intimidate Hollywood, causing him to fold early. Quinn cashed in a marker, counted his chips, and slid the piles to the middle of the table.

"I'm out," said the Asian man, tossing down his cards.

Hollywood didn't even hesitate. He must have figured that he had already suckered enough of Quinn's money into the pot. He spread his palms and shoved his chips forward. "All in," he announced. He stood and started pacing in tight little circles behind his chair, just the way they did on TV.

The dealer counted the chips—an additional ninety-five thousand. "It will cost you seventy to stay," he told Quinn.

Cards in his left hand, Quinn picked up a stack of chips with his right, then let them sift through his fingers as he restacked them on the table. He did this once. Twice. He knew the tension was killing Hollywood and thought the man might burst a blood vessel at any moment. Quinn could tell the man wanted to shout, "Put it in, Lawyer Boy!" Instead, he managed to keep his mouth shut while his neck muscles pulled ever tighter.

An ace-high flush. Only a full house, four of a kind, or a straight flush could beat it. With the cards already showing, Quinn knew that he was the only person who could draw a straight flush. Quinn figured that the king of diamonds had completed Hollywood's own flush. Maybe the man had the queen, thinking he would probably win unless Quinn had the ace of diamonds. Or maybe Hollywood was sitting on two pairs, or three of a kind. Unlikely, since then he would have to assume that Quinn had a flush. Only a guy with as much naive swagger as Hollywood would like the odds of trying to draw a full house or four of a kind.

"I'll call," Quinn said. He cashed in his last marker and counted his chips, sliding seventy thousand to the middle of the table.

Hollywood stopped pacing long enough to reach down and flip his cards—the queen of diamonds and the queen of hearts. Three of a kind. Without so much as changing his facial expression, Quinn calmly did the same. Hollywood grimaced, cursing under his breath.

With one card still to be dealt, the odds were strongly in Quinn's favor. The only cards that could bail Hollywood out were another four, another nine, another king, or the queen of clubs. Any of the remaining thirty-two cards would mean victory for Quinn.

The dealer waited for just a moment, the tension building, then burned a card and flipped over the river. The king of clubs!

"Yes!" Hollywood pumped his fist and did a clumsy little dance. "Unbelievable!" He slapped a high five to anyone around him, demonstrating a complete lack of class.

"Nice job," Quinn said.

"Yeah," responded Hollywood. He smiled and shook his head. "What are the odds?"

About four to one, thought Quinn, *you lucky jerk.*

Still beaming, Hollywood sat down and pulled the enormous pile of chips toward him. He started stacking them and glanced over at Quinn's pitiful stack of chips, down to eight thousand dollars. "Stick around afterward and I'll buy you a drink," Hollywood said.

"No thanks."

Three hands later, completely out of chips, Quinn rose from his seat and headed home. The dreams of starting his own firm were now piled in front of the ponytailed player from California, poker chips waiting for the next big pot.

48

CAT SAT STRAIGHT UP on her mattress when the deputy ran a metal flashlight across the outer bars of the cells, setting off a chorus of complaints from the inmates. For a moment Cat felt disoriented. She had slept hard last night, her body finally shutting down after getting so little sleep since her arrest on Sunday.

She waited a second for her head to clear and realized that Holly was sitting on her own bed, staring at her. Cat reached up to brush some loose hair out of her eyes and felt it. Something gooey sticking to her hair. Alarmed, she pulled the strands of hair in front of her face, her fingers sticking to the gooey substance. Gum!

"Ugh!" she moaned.

Holly laughed.

Panicked, Cat stood and felt the rest of her hair. Gum everywhere! Soft, sticky, matting her hair together. Wherever she touched, her hair felt like a rat's nest, tangled together by wads of chewing gum.

"Good morning, Barbie."

Furious, Cat walked toward the bunk beds.

Holly jumped to her feet, grinning, her flabby muscles tightening. She must have bought the gum from the jail store, saved it for a few days, chewed a couple packs, and placed it strategically throughout Cat's hair last night while she slept. Why would Holly do such a thing?

All Cat could think about was the gnarled mess in her hair. She would need to cut it short, ridiculously short, just before her court appearance for her preliminary hearing. She would look like a nutcase! This wasn't just Cat's hair Holly had messed with, it was her life.

Rage boiled within her, clouding her vision. She had been patient. Tolerant. And now this! Cat wanted to smack this woman in front of her, grinning at her, daring her to take action. Holly was a bully. And bullies only responded to force.

"You're an idiot," Cat said, trying to pry some of the gum out of her hair. She felt like exploding, the tears stinging her eyes. "What did I ever do to deserve this? Why do you hate me so much?"

Unexpectedly, Holly popped Cat in the shoulders with the heels of her hands, rocking Cat back. "Don't call me names, Barbie. You're lucky I didn't mess with your face."

Cat retreated a step and Holly moved forward. "You think you're all that. Too good for us jailhouse women . . . for ugly girls like me. Girls you picked on your whole life!" Holly's face was dark red, her eyes popping in their sockets. "Who's picking on who now?" She lifted her chin, sneering at Cat.

Holly's intensity startled Cat, causing her to retreat another step, wrestling with her emotions. Her cellmate had serious issues. Cat didn't want to respond in anger, harsh words for harsh words. But if she didn't do something, where would it stop?

Cat stood there for a long second, staring at Holly.

Holly lifted her eyebrows and tilted her head, daring Cat to make a move. *It was just my hair last night,* Cat thought. *But what's next?*

Cat turned to walk away. She took a half step, still simmering at the humiliation of it all, the abuse of her privacy, the threats of worse to come. She thought about how stark she would look for her court appearance, the whole world laughing at her, the judge and jury thinking she must be a homicidal lunatic. To make it worse, Holly had tried to throw the guilt trip on Cat, holding Cat responsible for a childhood of pain.

Cat hated herself for being the victim again, for letting the bully humiliate her without a fight.

In Catherine's mind, Holly became Kenny—leering, triumphant, arrogant. *You jerk!*

Something snapped inside, and Cat spun with all her fury, backhanding Holly across the face. The blow stunned Holly, sending her reeling to the side.

Finish it! The anger and fear demanded action—violent and adrenaline fueled. Cat couldn't back down now. Quickly, before Holly could recover, Cat grabbed Holly's hair with one hand and the collar of her jumpsuit with the other. Cat twisted hard, using her body weight like a discus thrower to send Holly pummeling toward the opposite wall and floor. Holly screamed as her head cracked against the edge of the metal rinse basin. Cat heard the crunching sound of bone on metal as a gash opened and spurted blood.

Holly lay on the floor unmoving, and Cat thought maybe she had killed her. Horrified, she backed a few steps away and started screaming for the guards, yelling at the top of her lungs for help. She wanted to bend over and check for a pulse, move Holly's neck from the grotesque position it had landed in, do something to stop the bleeding. Instead, Cat backed into a corner, her hands covering her mouth. Emitting a silent scream, she slouched to the floor.

Oh, God, what have I done?

49

QUINN ARRIVED LATE for work on Thursday, and Melanie followed him into his office. "You're fifteen minutes late for a conference call," she said. "I'll dial you in and get some coffee."

Quinn grunted his approval. His head felt like it was ready to explode from the night before. He had lost $150,000 and along with it his dream of starting his own firm, all on one lousy hand of Texas hold 'em when the odds were in his favor. It had taken two hours of hard drinking to erase the pain. This morning, the pain came rocketing back, pulling in its wake a pounding headache and a case of cotton mouth.

"A couple of other things," said Melanie, who seemed terribly perky for first thing in the morning. "The case-acceptance committee has scheduled a meeting at eleven to discuss the O'Rourke case. I've prepared a memo outlining the facts and put together a folder."

"Okay." Quinn plopped down in his chair. *Did she always speak this loud?*

"In the meantime, assuming they give you the green light, I've scheduled your Norfolk trip," Melanie continued, placing a manila travel folder on Quinn's desk. "You meet with O'Rourke Monday afternoon, just before she is evaluated by Rosemarie Mancini. You interview investigators Tuesday and then meet with Mancini and Marc Boland. On Wednesday morning you can spend some time with the investigator you hire and then fly back out Wednesday night for Annie's plea agreement first thing Thursday morning."

Quinn normally appreciated Melanie's compulsive organization, but this morning it only served to make him more tired. He slouched a little lower in his seat. "Anything else?" he asked. Even raising his eyes to look at her seemed to require a monumental effort.

"Excedrin for the headache," Melanie said. "And substitute Gatorade for coffee."

"What?"

"Yeah. When your body breaks down alcohol, it pumps out lactic acid and other byproducts that impede the production of sugar and electrolytes. That's what gives you that woozy feeling in your stomach. Gatorade helps replenish electrolytes and sugar."

Quinn smiled awkwardly—his assistant knew him too well. Why did he do this to himself?

Two hours later, after three Excedrins and a bottle of Gatorade, Quinn was ready for his meeting with the case-acceptance committee. He entered the ornately decorated conference room and greeted Espinoza and the three other committee members—two frowning business lawyers and one of the firm's few female partners, also scowling.

"Thanks for coming, Quinn," Espinoza began, as if Quinn had a choice in the matter. "We've all been watching the news, so we're somewhat familiar with the case." He leaned back and started spitting out facts. "You've got a serial killer running around Virginia terrorizing rapists and their defense attorneys. Two kidnappings and at least two presumed murders. Two of the victims—Paul Donaldson and Rex Archibald—are connected, right?"

Quinn nodded as Espinoza continued. "Archibald represented Donaldson in a rape case. The kidnapping victims include the children of a criminal defense lawyer and an alleged rapist who beat the rap."

"Right," said Quinn, his headache returning with a vengeance. "At this point our client has only been charged with the murder of Paul Donaldson."

"Fair enough," Espinoza said. "So far, the authorities haven't found the babies or the bodies of either Donaldson or Archibald. But our client apparently had some visions about the murders, and these visions contain confidential information known only to police. Right? And then they search her place and find all sorts of DNA evidence and a drug used to subdue the victims."

Quinn glanced around at the committee, his own patience wearing thin. Espinoza had painted the case in the worst possible light. "I must have been out when we passed the rule about only representing innocent clients," Quinn said.

"I didn't say she had to be innocent," Espinoza said quickly. "I'm just trying to figure out what the defense is going to be."

"She got framed," said Alfred Pennington, an old codger who made no secret of his disdain for Quinn's hotshot antics. "Mark Fuhrman placed the bloody paper towels in the neighbor's trash. It was really Kato Kaelin's hair on the envelope flap. Quinn can figure out some Alice-in-Wonderland defense. I'm more concerned with how we get paid. What's the retainer? What's the collateral for our fees as the case moves forward? What hourly rate are you charging?"

"I'm taking the case pro bono," Quinn said. "Our pay will be the millions of dollars in free publicity."

Pennington looked shocked, as if Quinn had just suggested assassinating the president.

For the next thirty minutes, the lawyers vigorously debated the merits of Quinn's proposal. Fortunately for Quinn, Melanie had armed him with a profitability analysis for several national law firms, correlated with the amount of publicity each firm had generated on its high-profile cases the preceding year. The conclusion: It didn't matter if you won or lost. Getting your name in the paper was all that counted. Profits followed publicity.

Just when Quinn thought his head might split open on the spot, Espinoza dismissed him so the committee could deliberate in private. Ten minutes later, Espinoza came to Quinn's office to announce the firm's decision.

"The committee will allow you to stay in the O'Rourke case on two conditions," said Espinoza. "First, you make your billable-hour goal apart from the O'Rourke case. And second, you conclude your sister's plea agreement immediately so you aren't spending all your time on two nonpaying clients."

Quinn didn't know whether to thank the man or tell him off. Quinn was a partner. These conditions sounded like something you would impose on an associate or something a parent might dictate to a rebellious teenager. On the other hand, Quinn was surprised they were letting him take the case at all.

"Okay," Quinn said. Not *thanks*. Not *I'll make this work and you won't be sorry*. Just *okay*.

Espinoza stood gazing out one of Quinn's windows, his arms crossed over his chest. "I had to go to bat for you on this one, Quinn. Your partners were not happy that you circumvented the system. They probably would have rejected the case if we hadn't already been knee-deep in it."

Which is exactly why I filed first and asked for permission later. "I appreciate it," Quinn said. He was already wondering how he could possibly handle this case *and* make his billable-hour requirement. Maybe that requirement was just a setup to run him out of the firm. "Tell my partners I appreciate their dedication to the principle that everyone is entitled to a defense under our system of justice."

Espinoza shook his head and turned to Quinn. "Don't push any harder on this one, Quinn. I can't go to the mat for you again."

As always, Quinn knew that his managing partner would require the last word, and this comment seemed as good a candidate as any. Accordingly, Quinn thanked Espinoza and watched the man head for the door.

Espinoza surprised Quinn by turning around just before he left. "Myself, I prefer Chaser Plus," he said, his lips curling into a half-smile.

"What?"

"For hangovers. You might want to keep some in your medicine cabinet."

50

AFTER HER FIGHT WITH HOLLY, Catherine O'Rourke was placed in an isolation cell pending a psychiatric evaluation. First she was handcuffed so the jail barber could cut the chunks of gum out of her hair. It was such a mess that the barber eventually resorted to a rock-star spike. It looked terrible, giving Cat a hard, street-savvy look, but she knew it was probably the best the barber could do.

After a few hours in solitary, Cat was led into one of the sterile conference rooms with bolted-down furniture so she could be evaluated by the prison psychiatrist. Cat learned from the psychiatrist that Holly would survive with no long-term disabilities. For a few moments Cat couldn't even talk as a wave of relief flooded her body.

"Are you okay?" the psychiatrist asked. She was an older and soft-spoken woman named Dr. Glissen or something like that. Cat couldn't remember; her thoughts had been totally focused on Holly when the lady introduced herself.

"I'm fine," Cat said.

The woman asked Cat all the usual questions, and Cat answered them honestly. She was tired of pretending to be brave and tough. She needed help.

"Have you ever considered suicide?" Dr. Glissen asked. "Or have you tried to hurt yourself in any way?"

"Yes," said Cat. "To the suicide question, I mean." She paused, embarrassed to admit such a thing. "I was thinking about what this person did, this serial killer, and, well, I know it's not me, but I was thinking that if I was wrong and it somehow really *was* me . . ." Cat's voice trailed off and she felt herself trembling a little. It all sounded so bizarre, actually voicing the possibility out loud, like somehow it made the prospects more real.

Dr. Glissen slid forward a little. "What would you do, Catherine, if you found out that you really were this serial killer?"

"I'm not sure," Catherine admitted. "But I think I'd find a way to take my own life."

There. She had said it. Strangely, there was something therapeutic about just saying it out loud.

The two women talked for a long time about Catherine's feelings, the stresses of being in jail, and the pressure of being accused of such horrible crimes. Cat felt safe opening up with this woman. It seemed like the doctor actually cared about what was going on inside Cat's head. At the end of the visit, Dr. Glissen said she would prescribe some antidepressants. She gave Cat a lecture about how important it would be for her to take her meds faithfully.

"A lot of patients quit taking their medication prematurely," Glissen said. "They don't like the way it makes them feel, or they don't like the stigma associated with it, or they just pronounce themselves cured. You've got a lot on your shoulders right now. There's nothing wrong with getting help."

Cat thanked the doctor and returned to solitary confinement, where she spent her time second-guessing herself. She had lost control in a way that scared her. For a brief moment, she had wanted to kill Holly. And she nearly had. A part of Cat that she never even knew existed had virtually taken control of her body. It was like the adrenaline and rage had fueled a different Catherine O'Rourke, one blind to consequences, intent on exacting vengeance and inflicting harm. During the fight, these emotions seemed to disembody Cat, as if she had merely been watching in horror while this other person attacked Holly, using Cat's body as the weapon.

This other Catherine had bought into the prison's moral code—survival of the fittest, kill or be killed—completely. Sure, Holly had done everything within her power to instigate the fight. And Catherine had a right to stand up for herself, especially in prison, where women like Holly picked mercilessly on women like Catherine, hoping to find an inmate they could intimidate and ultimately "own." But what scared Cat was the blind intensity of her rage. For an instant, her entire focus had been on hurting Holly badly enough so that she couldn't fight back. In that single dark moment, Cat knew, she had been capable of murder.

Was this the first time?

Perhaps the answer lurked somewhere deep inside her own head, waiting for her to dig out the hard truth of past wounds and her own festering rage. On the other hand, perhaps this morning was just a courageous response to a relentless bully, Cat's way of screaming that she'd had enough.

Maybe she was overanalyzing this entire incident. Who wouldn't have attacked Holly after what she had done? And besides, Cat remembered every second of the fight. In that respect, this was totally different from having another, unknown personality actually take control of her body.

These questions, and dozens more like them, were driving Cat mad. She had plenty of time to think about them, her paranoia growing by the minute. She needed the medication as soon as possible. And she needed some noise. For the first time since her arrest on Sunday, Cat longed for the chaos created by the other inmates.

Even the little things could drive you nuts in prison. Like never seeing the sun. Cat desperately needed some sunshine.

But there were no windows in her cell, only muted artificial light and an eerie silence. The only sounds were the voices of doubt echoing in her head. Wondering. Questioning. Convicting.

Was this the first time? Or had she done it before?

She folded her hands, put her elbows on her knees, and looked down at her flip-flops. She looked around and noticed there were no sheets on this bed, just the bare mattress, grubby and stained, and an old pillow. She had been given no spare clothes in this cell. Cat immediately understood why. They couldn't trust her with anything that could be ripped apart and fashioned into a rope.

She was not just in isolation.

Catherine O'Rourke was on suicide watch.

51

THREE DAYS LATER

THE SCREENING PROCESS at the Virginia Beach city jail made Quinn think he had stepped back in time and ended up at Alcatraz. Perhaps this was the way they always treated out-of-state lawyers, or perhaps he should have stopped to change out of the jeans, boat shoes, and polo shirt he had been wearing on the plane. Whatever the reason, Quinn endured two pat downs, a metal detector, and a hand search of his briefcase before he found himself waiting in a cinder block–walled cubicle for Catherine O'Rourke.

He was separated from the prisoner's side of the cubicle by a block wall and a window of heavy glass. There was a slit at the bottom of the window for passing notes or pleadings—anything else and a lawyer could lose his visitation rights.

They brought Catherine in ten minutes later, her wrists cuffed together. She slumped forward as she took her place on the opposite side of the glass, watching Quinn with a certain wariness.

"Thanks for coming," she said.

"No problem."

Quinn stared at her for a moment, surprised by the transformation. He had watched the video of her arrest a dozen times, till the image had been burned in his brain. Plus, the networks had been running stories about Catherine all weekend, once they learned about the altercation at the jail. They used stock footage with photos that showed a captivating young woman with a sly half smile and mysterious dark eyes.

But the woman sitting before Quinn had short, unkempt hair, dark circles under those eyes, and the beginnings of a red rash on the side of her neck.

She managed a wan smile. "That bad?"

Quinn felt himself blush. "I've seen worse," he said. "A lot worse." He jotted the date on his legal pad. "Jail's no picnic."

"So I've learned."

Quinn launched into his standard spiel about the need for honesty and full disclosure. He learned Catherine was taking some antidepressants, 20 mg per day of Lexapro, which she said she intended to stop taking once she left solitary confinement. He asked questions about her alibi and the methohexital and the DNA evidence against her. He had her describe in detail the rape by Kenneth Towns and possibly others, as well as the cover-up by Towns's frat brothers. As she did, Quinn put down his pen and studied her carefully, struck by the way she narrated the episode in an even voice, looking mostly at the slit in the glass, as if the entire event had happened to another person.

"How did that make you feel?" he asked.

Catherine looked at him, the almond eyes turning hard as they came into focus. "Violated. Ashamed because I didn't report it. Angry." Her tone underscored the lingering effects. "I've had nightmares for years."

"Tell me about them."

In a subdued voice, Catherine described the recurring scenes of Kenny and his frat brothers. Occasionally she would stop to collect her thoughts or scratch the side of her neck. Quinn probed for specifics, asking follow-up questions that clearly made her uncomfortable.

Next he turned to the matter of Catherine's visions—what she had seen, how she had felt, the differences between her visions and her nightmares. When he felt his client wearing down, he packed up his briefcase and emphasized the importance of Catherine's being absolutely forthcoming with Dr. Mancini. He asked Catherine if she had any questions.

"Aren't you going to ask me if I did it?"

Quinn furrowed his brow and studied his client. "I normally have the psych eval done first."

Catherine returned his gaze. "I'm innocent, Quinn. I need you to know that." She paused, glancing down for just a moment. When she returned her gaze, tears rimmed her eyes. "With God as my witness, I didn't even know those people."

Quinn wanted to reach out and touch her, a hand on her arm, anything to show his support. But three inches of bulletproof glass separated them. "I believe you," he said.

He wondered if she could sense his doubt.

Catherine shuffled back to her solitary-confinement cell, a place that had become hell on earth. Her spirits had sunk lower each day, her isolation interrupted only by an occasional visit from the jail psychiatrist and one brief visit from Marc Boland. The rest of the time, Catherine wrote in her journal and obsessed over the mounting evidence against her, demoralized by her inability to do anything about it.

But Quinn, like Marc Boland, seemed to believe in her case. She liked Quinn's style—thorough, confident, realistic. She could understand why the man did so well with juries. He didn't seem as outgoing as Marc Boland, but Quinn had a quiet intensity that he expressed through his eyes, the smoldering look of a man who knew more than he was saying. You wanted Marc Boland to be your friend. You wanted to make sure Quinn Newberg was not your enemy.

She took a few deep breaths in the quietness of her cell. Day by day, the place seemed to be closing in on her. But for once, it seemed like she could actually fill her lungs, the vicelike pressure on her chest relaxing just a little. She stood and headed for the rinse basin. For the first time since going into solitary confinement, she felt like washing her face and what little hair she had left. It wasn't a nice warm shower at her beach duplex, but the feel of water trickling down her face and dripping from her chin made her feel close to human again.

She had opened up about some painful moments to Quinn, though she had tried to do it on autopilot, keeping her feelings at bay. It felt therapeutic. Yet there were still a lot of things he didn't know. Like her guttural revulsion when a recent boyfriend had tried to get intimate, releasing a flood of horrific memories.

She was smart enough to know that some thoughts are so painful, some memories so intense, you need to hide them even from your own lawyer.

52

QUINN DECIDED TO CONDUCT HIS INTERVIEWS of potential investigators in a corner of the Westin lobby bar, munching on peanuts and drinking iced tea. The first two candidates were unimpressive.

When Quinn saw the third and final candidate meandering toward him, he knew he would have to ask Melanie to go back to the drawing board. Billy Long was a thick bowling ball of a man, about five-ten, with rounded shoulders, a stubble of dark, receding hair, a five-o'clock shadow, and seriously hairy arms and chest. He was dressed in khakis and a Hawaiian shirt.

"Billy Long," he said, squeezing Quinn's hand in a bearlike grip. "I understand you need a private investigator."

"I'm interviewing a number of folks," Quinn said, as Billy took his seat. "I just have a few questions."

Unfortunately, Billy called for a waitress. "I'll take a Bud," he said.

"I'm good," Quinn said. "I need to be leaving soon."

Quinn fired off a list of perfunctory questions and was somewhat impressed with Billy's responses. He struck Quinn as being one of those "dumb like a fox" guys who puts you at ease and then steals you blind. Billy told some fascinating war stories about his prior life as a detective. His wife's job had caused the couple to move around Virginia a little—Hampton, Williamsburg, Richmond—before they got a divorce and Billy moved to Virginia Beach to start work as a private investigator. He had been in Virginia Beach for six years now and seemed to know all the major personalities. Still, Quinn had pretty much decided not to hire the guy; he needed someone more professional.

And then Billy pulled out his ace.

He swallowed the last of his beer and slid a manila folder across the table to Quinn. "This one'll be on the house," he said. "It's gonna be a long day for you boys tomorrow."

Quinn assessed Billy with a sideways look. Billy stood and Quinn did likewise, taking Billy's card before he shook the PI's hand. After Billy left, Quinn opened the manila folder.

It was a summons for Virginia Beach General District Court, Criminal Division, on charges of assault and battery. The named defendant was Catherine O'Rourke, and from the description, the charges were obviously the result of Catherine's attack on her cellmate, a woman named Holly Stephenson.

What surprised Quinn about the document was the date: June 3. Tomorrow. Somehow Billy had gotten his hands on a summons from the commonwealth's attorney's office that wasn't even scheduled to be filed until the next day.

This charge would compound the difficulty of Catherine's defense. If nothing else, it would give the media one more nail as they constructed Catherine's coffin, even before she went to trial. Plus, if Gates could get this assault case to trial first and obtain a conviction, he might be able to use it on cross-examination if Catherine took the stand in her murder trial.

Included with the summons were several oversize photographs showing Holly Stephenson's bloody scalp as she lay unconscious on the floor of her cell. There were photos of the rinse basin, photos of the bloody concrete floor, and close-ups of Holly's stitches. They would undoubtedly be plastered all over the television tomorrow.

At least now Quinn knew it was coming. He called the number on Billy Long's card.

"We didn't talk rates yet," Billy said when he answered.

Quinn smiled to himself. Long was exactly the kind of man he needed.

53

QUINN AND DR. MANCINI met Marc Boland at 3:45 in his eighteenth-floor office suite at the Armada Hoffler Tower in Virginia Beach's Town Center. Quinn couldn't help but notice that the premier conference room for Boland and Associates looked like a janitor's closet compared to the luxuries of his own firm. Sure, Boland's conference room had plush burgundy leather chairs, rich mahogany trim, and ornate wood molding, but those were considered the bare minimum in Vegas, your ante just to get in the game. Boland had no original masterpieces hanging on the wall, no teakwood imported from Thailand for the conference table, no authentic Persian rugs.

It wasn't that Quinn was snobbish about furnishings; he saw it more as symbolic of the sophistication of Vegas criminal defense lawyers versus their Virginia Beach counterparts. It was like a member of the Yankees visiting the clubhouse of the Toledo Mud Hens. It wasn't the clubhouse; it was just a different level of ball.

Boland burst into the conference room a few minutes after Quinn and Rosemarie had settled in. Quinn told Boland about the new charges that would be filed against Catherine, but Boland shrugged it off. "Have you guys made dinner plans?" he asked.

Not even 4:00, and the man is talking dinner?

Quinn and Rosemarie looked at each other. "Not really."

"Good, then pack up your stuff. We've got some major decisions to make and we've got to be at our creative best," Boland declared. "Stuffy conference rooms don't do it for me."

Quinn was skeptical. It was a muggy day in early June, and it seemed to Quinn like Boland was suggesting something outside, like an elementary class sitting in a circle on the schoolhouse lawn. But Boland's enthusiasm carried the day, and a few minutes later Quinn and Rosemarie were following Boland down the interstate in Quinn's rental car. They headed straight for the oceanfront until they took the Birdneck Road exit, wound their way through an established neighborhood, and parked in the lower parking lot of a place called the Cavalier Golf and Yacht Club.

Boland alighted from his car with his tie gone and his sleeves rolled up. Quinn had dressed casual, though Rosemarie Mancini, ever proper, had on a professional blue dress and matching pumps. Boland waved to the boat hands milling about as he led Quinn and Rosemarie down a long pier lined with expensive yachts. They reached the end of the docks and the boat that dwarfed all others—Boland's boat, *Class Action* according to the moniker on the front.

Class Action was a sixty-eight-foot custom-designed yacht, Boland explained, complete with all the gimmicks and toys. The boat looked sleek, Quinn had to admit, with its polished white shell and its dark tinted windows reflecting the sunlight. He and Rosemarie followed Boland aboard, passing through the sliding glass doors on the back of the boat and into a room Boland called the salon.

The room had a soft leather couch and easy chair along one set of windows and a pop-up large-screen television on the other side. A full bar lined the far wall. Apparently this yacht was the Virginia Beach equivalent of the Signature Towers.

They followed Boland up a set of steps into the covered pilothouse and galley area, which gave Quinn's kitchen a run for the money. The bank of controls to the side of the pilot's seat looked like it would be sufficient to pilot a 747.

"Something to drink?" Boland asked, opening the door to a well-stocked refrigerator. Quinn and Boland each grabbed a Corona; Dr. Mancini stuck with bottled water. Boland picked up some hamburgers, hot dogs, buns, and condiments, tossed a bag of tortilla chips and a jar of salsa to Quinn, and assembled his grilling tools. He took his guests up another set of steps to the flybridge area on top of the boat, a semicovered sitting area with plush white leather swivel chairs, another hardwood bar, and an outdoor grill. Boland put on an old baseball hat he pulled out of a compartment and fired up his grill.

"Now can we start arguing about strategy?" Quinn asked. He had to admit he was enjoying the view and the nice little breeze coming from the river. It was a branch of the Lynnhaven, Boland had explained, that eventually led out to the Chesapeake Bay. Quinn opened the bag of chips and the salsa. The smells of the gas grill made him hungry, though it was only 5:00.

"We've got a preliminary hearing next week," Boland began, "and we're getting slaughtered in the press. Quinn and I need to start hitting the airwaves immediately, countering this new charge and getting Catherine's case out there." He plopped some burgers on the grill and pointed toward the river. "Look at that! Egrets!"

Quinn twisted in his chair to watch the beautiful white birds in flight.

"We can't be seen as flip-flopping on this," Boland continued. "If we go out there right now and claim innocence, we'll look like shysters later on if we claim insanity. On the other hand, if we claim insanity now, we're admitting Catherine killed this guy, so we'd better be certain that's where we want to go." He looked at Rosemarie. "Would you even be willing to support such a claim?"

"It's too early to tell. An insanity plea would depend on a diagnosis of dissociative identity disorder, and that's a very tricky diagnosis. I would need several sessions with the patient before I could make a definitive recommendation."

"I thought the whole idea of split personality disorder was pretty much discredited these days," Boland said, poking at the meat on the grill. "I thought most psychiatrists believed it was simply the result of suggested scenarios from therapists."

Rosemarie shot Quinn the briefest sideways glance before she gave Boland a condescending smile. *He'll learn not to challenge the woman,* thought Quinn, kicking back and tilting his face to the sun.

"There is some controversy about the diagnosis, to be sure," Rosemarie said, with just a tinge of snootiness. "But it's still in the *DSM-IV-TR,* and dissociation is recognized by most experts as a symptomatic presentation in response to trauma or extreme emotional distress and in association with emotional dysregulation and borderline personality disorder. Documented cases of full-blown DID, where the patient's ego actually fractures into distinct personalities to deal with different situations, are rare, but they do exist."

Quinn smiled to himself. *This* was why he used her as his big-case expert.

"You said trauma or extreme emotional distress," Boland countered. "Mostly childhood abuse, right?"

"Impressive," Dr. Mancini said. "You've done some homework."

Boland shrugged and flipped the burgers. "Wikipedia. Not exactly admissible in court."

"Clinical studies show that most patients with diagnosed DID report early childhood abuse," Rosemarie said. "However, researchers were only able to document such abuse in about 85 percent of the cases. Still, one of the things that bothers me about Ms. O'Rourke's case is that she denies any such abuse. Rape is a severely traumatizing event that can trigger a lot of psychological issues. But it was not repetitive and it did not happen during her childhood."

"And what's the significance of that?" Boland asked. "And, more importantly, how do you like your burgers?"

"Medium rare," Quinn said.

"Extremely well done," Rosemarie said. She switched back into lecture mode. "It's during childhood that we learn to integrate different types of experiences into a complex and integrated view of ourselves. Our multifaceted personality develops. When certain traumatic experiences or situations of abuse overwhelm us, it's possible to segregate them into a separate personality, one that our default personality does not even know exists."

"So that's one of the problems with claiming DID," Boland responded. "She doesn't fit the pattern. That's why I like going with a straight not-guilty plea." He wiped his brow with a shirtsleeve and turned to Quinn. "You're being awful quiet, Vegas."

Quinn raised his palms, as if he didn't care. He didn't want to make his agenda too obvious. "How do you explain the DNA and methohexital?"

"A setup," Boland said quickly, "by the real Avenger of Blood."

"How did he get her DNA?" Quinn asked.

"It's not that hard," Boland pronounced. "Maybe he broke into her house. Went through her trash. Followed her into a restaurant."

"If it were only the DNA and methohexital, I might agree with you," Quinn said, trying to sound pensive. "But I can't get past these visions. How would an innocent person know so much about the crimes?"

"She's got a gift," Boland responded. "Even the cops use people like Catherine to help them solve crimes."

"A gift," Quinn repeated. He let the sarcasm drip from his lips. "What other crimes has our gifted client solved? What calamity did she predict? Does she also read palms for a small fee?"

Boland climbed onto a white leather bar stool, one eye on the grill. "I don't like it any better than you do, Vegas. But we're stuck with the visions in this case. Some people just know things. Supernaturally. Most jurors will buy that."

"Maybe Virginia Beach juries are more gullible than they are in Vegas," Quinn said, his frustration starting to show. He took a final swallow of beer.

"But it would never fly out there. Magicians and illusionists have 'gifts' too, and so do card sharks. But at the end of the day, it's all smoke and mirrors. If we can't find a logical explanation for these visions, *one grounded in reality*, I think we're better off arguing insanity."

Quinn sat up, his elbows on the arm rests. "If we plead insanity, we can talk at length about the effect of the rape on Catherine's psyche. We turn her visions into a cornerstone of our defense. Would anybody who actually realized they had committed these horrible crimes ever share detailed visions about them with a police officer? It may not get her acquitted, but it ought to be enough to save her life."

"They've got no corpse," Boland protested. "No murder weapon. No real motive. We can't just roll over and admit she did this. What if she's really innocent?"

"Then we'd better have a good explanation for these visions," Quinn responded. "Something that makes sense to the 99 percent of us who don't believe in ghosts."

"Let me give that a shot," said Rosemarie Mancini. "And if you two gentlemen could hold your questions until my little presentation is done, I would very much appreciate it."

Marc Boland shrugged and Quinn stood from his seat. "I'll be right back," he said. "I think this calls for another beer."

54

"BOTH OF YOU are probably familiar with a story from the Old Testament book of Daniel, from which we get our expression 'the handwriting on the wall.'" Rosemarie glanced at Quinn. "Well, at least one of you probably is."

Very funny. Quinn raised his beer toward her.

"A Persian king named Belshazzar was at the height of his glory," Rosemarie continued, "hosting a great feast in his banquet hall and guzzling down the wine. Probably had a few too many."

At this, Quinn thought he detected a reproving glance.

"On a whim, he gives an order for his servants to bring in the gold and silver vessels that his predecessor, Nebuchadnezzar, had taken from the Jewish temple in Jerusalem when he made the Jews his slaves. This guy Belshazzar and his wives and concubines drank wine out of these vessels and praised their Babylonian gods."

Rosemarie spoke with her hands, her face animated.

This is why juries love her so much, Quinn thought.

She turned suddenly toward Quinn, a finger extended. "This hand comes out of nowhere and writes a message on the wall." She lowered her voice into a James Earl Jones impersonation. "'Mene, Mene, Tekel, Parsin.' The king is so scared he turns pale, his hip joints shake like jelly, and his knees knock together. You know what the words mean?"

"Pretty Lady to show in the fourth?" Quinn asked.

"Not quite," Rosemarie said, her face scrunched in disapproval. "The king brought in all his mediums and astrologers, but only Daniel could figure it out."

"And?"

"Honestly, I don't remember, but that's actually beside the point. . . ."

"Are you serious?" Quinn asked. "How can you remember the words and not remember what they mean?"

"You're right—I'm kidding," Rosemarie said. "*Mene* meant the king's days were numbered. *Tekel* meant he had been weighed on the scales and found deficient. *Parsin* meant the kingdom would be divided and given to the Medes and Persians—parceled out, so to speak. And sure enough, that night the king died."

"Sad story," said Quinn. "But what's that got to do with the handwriting on Catherine's cell wall?"

"It means there's precedent for this type of thing, Quinn." Dr. Mancini was serious now. "We're in the South, not Vegas. A lot of folks around here believe in a spiritual dimension that transcends what we can touch and see. In both the Old and New Testaments, there are times when God speaks in a dream or a vision, and it's not always through His prophets or apostles. Belshazzar was a Babylonian. The Egyptian pharaohs had dreams that were interpreted by Joseph. Pilate's wife had a dream warning her that her husband should not sentence Jesus to death. Some of the folks on our jury have probably had dreams or premonitions themselves, and many of them think they've heard from God."

"Maybe so," Marc Boland inserted as he moved some hot dogs onto the top grill to wait for the burgers to finish, "but we can't exactly give them a Bible lesson from the witness stand. I'm actually with Quinn on this one— and I'm a God-fearin', gun-totin' Southern evangelical. Just because that stuff happened in the Old Testament doesn't mean it's still happening. When people start claiming they've heard directly from God, it's usually a one-way ticket to crazy."

"Some jurors will be like me and gravitate to the faith angle," Rosemarie countered. "Others will want science or real-life examples. We can give them a little of everything—juror's choice. Take Allison DuBois, for example. In the year 2000, this nice-looking young lady was on her way to becoming a career prosecutor in the Maricopa County prosecutor's office. One day she went downstairs in her apartment building to get the laundry, and this man walks right through her. When she explains what happened to her husband and actually describes the man—he loves clam chowder; he's had a heart attack—her husband says, 'Hey! That's my grandfather.'

"So Allison DuBois is watching *Dateline* one night and sees a story about a guy named Gary Schwartz, a psychology professor at the University of Arizona who has conducted a bunch of experiments related to the afterlife. Allison goes to this professor so she can prove her 'vision' wasn't real and get on with her life. Instead, Schwartz discovers that this lady really does have a gift for seeing and hearing things the rest of us can't. She walked away from her job as a prosecutor and went on to help police as a medium. The NBC show that's been running for the last few years is loosely based on her life story."

What's with this sudden rush of great-looking mediums? Quinn wondered. "So our defense is that Catherine O'Rourke is some kind of medium or maybe a recipient of a message sent by God or Satan or some other kind of spiritual being?"

He looked from Rosemarie to Boland. They actually seemed to be considering it.

"Personally, I think there's a spiritual dimension to this," Rosemarie said softly. "I asked Catherine a lot of questions about past involvement in the occult or that type of thing and she denied any. Still . . . I think she could be holding something back."

Quinn raised an eyebrow. *Dreams. Visions. Handwriting on the wall. Ghosts.* He'd believe it when he saw it.

"We don't have to prove any of this," Boland said tentatively, starting to sound like a convert. "We just have to raise reasonable doubt."

This whole conversation had a feeling of desperation to Quinn. "I'm starting to see my own handwriting on the wall," Quinn said. "And it looks mysteriously like a guilty verdict."

On the way back to the hotel, Quinn and Rosemarie Mancini rode in relative silence. Rosemarie had insisted on driving, and after putting up a token argument, Quinn had given her the keys. He slouched low in the passenger seat.

"How's Annie?" Rosemarie eventually asked.

"Good," Quinn said. "Actually, more like just okay. She's worried about what's going to happen to Sierra in the next three years. What this will do to their long-term relationship."

"Who's going to take care of Sierra?"

"She's staying with the Schlesingers until she starts boarding school in California this fall," Quinn said, noticing the lack of enthusiasm in his own voice. "After that, she'll spend vacations and some weekends with me."

"Boarding school." Mancini simply repeated the words, but Quinn knew what she meant.

"It's not perfect, Rosemarie. But the Schlesingers can't keep her for three years. And there's no way I could do it, given my schedule at work. Besides, I'd be a lousy parent."

"Boarding school is probably better than the Schlesingers," Mancini confirmed. "But, Quinn, what Sierra needs, more than anything else, is unconditional love. You don't have to be perfect; you just need to be there for her."

55

THE NEXT MORNING, Marc Boland took to the airwaves even before Quinn boarded his flight for Las Vegas. Marc was on the offensive, doing his best to take the sting out of the assault-and-battery charges Boyd Gates apparently planned on filing later in the day. Marc expressed sincere concern for the safety of his client. He said that Catherine had been harassed repeatedly by her cellmate in the past few days. He said the guards had not responded to her requests for protection because they were upset about the articles she had written about conditions in the jail.

He said Catherine finally had to take matters into her own hands and defend herself. Then, to Boland's great surprise, prison officials had punished Catherine by putting her in solitary confinement for several days. Now that Catherine was going back into the general inmate population, Boland said he would be filing a motion for a restraining order to keep Holly Stephenson away from Catherine O'Rourke.

It was, Quinn thought, a nice preemptive strike, but he knew it would get swept away later in the day when Boyd Gates released the pictures of Holly's bloody face.

Catherine O'Rourke stared at the wall during her last day in solitary confinement, pleading for another vision. *What is this—some cruel cosmic joke?* The visions had been vivid enough, and accurate enough, to land her behind bars. She hadn't asked for this power, this curse. But now that she needed the visions to come back with greater force and detail so she could actually help the authorities solve these crimes, now that she did everything within her power to enable them, the visions were nowhere to be found.

She tried to empty her mind. She tried focusing on the wall and then on the psychic power within her. She thought about the victims of the crimes and the night of her own rapes and the biblical verses the Avenger had cited.

But no matter how hard she tried, the visions would not come back. Catherine O'Rourke, infamous medium or hated serial murderer, depending on your perspective, could not conjure up even a hint of the Avenger's ghost. She stared at an empty wall, frustrated.

Where were these vaunted powers when she really needed them?

After Quinn survived the media gauntlet waiting for him at the end of his flight, he headed into his office. Melanie left at five and Quinn barely noticed, consumed by the mound of paperwork his three-day absence had generated. He was still hunched over his computer at 9 p.m. when the phone call came.

Annie's number registered on his cell phone. She was probably nervous about tomorrow's hearing, but he didn't have time right now. He hit Ignore. He would call her back in a few minutes, as soon as he finished with these e-mails.

Two minutes later, she called a second time. It wasn't like Annie to be so persistent. He picked up on the third ring.

"Quinn?"

She sounded stressed, enough so to squeeze his heart. "You okay?" he asked.

"No." Her voice cracked a little. "It's Sierra, Quinn. She . . ." Annie took a breath, obviously struggling to maintain composure, her voice thin and fragile. "She tried to kill herself, Quinn. Sleeping pills. Something like half a bottle . . ." Annie's words trailed off.

Quinn bolted from his chair. "Where is she now, Annie?"

"Desert Springs Hospital. The emergency room. The Schlesingers found Sierra in her bedroom and called me. I met them here."

"Don't move," said Quinn, already heading for the door. "I'll be right over."

56

"THEY THINK SHE'S GOING TO BE ALL RIGHT." Annie had called Quinn back just a few minutes before he hit the hospital parking lot. The emergency room personnel had pumped Sierra's stomach and hooked up some IVs, Annie said. Sierra's vital signs had stabilized.

Quinn breathed an enormous sigh of relief, thanked Annie for the update, and felt his own racing heart slow just a little. He wasn't ready for this—a brush with death by someone so young and innocent. He had been thinking about Sierra the entire drive to the hospital. Her confused and endearing face. Her awkwardness as a girl struggling to become a woman. Her honesty and transparency with Quinn. What could he have done differently? What should he have said the last time he was with her?

He wouldn't have been able to live with himself if Sierra had died. *Suicide.* How could this nightmare be happening?

He parked in a handicapped spot and half walked, half ran into the hospital. Sierra had already been moved to a private room. He bumped into the Schlesingers in the waiting area, and Allison promptly had a meltdown.

She cried as she related the story of finding Sierra unconscious in her room, an empty bottle of Allison's Ambien on the bedside table. "It was awful, Quinn," she sobbed. "We called 911. We thought she was going to die before the ambulance even got there."

Quinn murmured a few sentences of empathy, telling Allison it wasn't her fault, then extricated himself and headed to Sierra's room. He didn't know what he would do once he got there. Quinn hated hospitals, and he wasn't good at providing comfort. Still, he had to see Sierra and be with Annie.

He gently pushed the door open and stopped just inside the threshold. Sierra was lying on the bed, eyes closed, a breathing tube in her nose and IV lines attached to her body. Annie was sitting in a chair on the opposite side of the bed, keeping one eye on the door.

Annie forced a thin smile when she saw Quinn and rose to greet him. She looked shell-shocked, like someone who had just escaped a battlefield littered with land mines and dead bodies. "I can't believe this," she whispered.

She took Quinn's hand and led him into the hall. She crossed her arms and spoke in a subdued tone, as if Sierra might wake up at any moment and overhear them. "The doctors said she's going to be okay. They think it's a cry for help. Girls this age who really want to take their life don't take a bunch of sleeping pills at home in the evening knowing that they'll be discovered right away." Annie stopped, working hard to keep her emotions under control. Quinn reached out to rub her shoulder.

"It's not a coincidence that she did this the night before my plea," Annie said. "Three years without a mother is an eternity when you're thirteen." She paused, measuring her words with care. "Plus, to have a mother who admits being a murderer . . ."

"That's not what this is about," Quinn said softly. "Sierra knows what really happened. A plea bargain doesn't change that."

But Annie was apparently in no mood to discuss it. "I want to call off the plea bargain," she said firmly. "This changes everything."

Quinn wasn't sure his sister was thinking clearly. Her harrowed face showed the strains of a mom's worst nightmare. She was reacting out of emotion.

"I'll call Carla Duncan," Quinn said. "We can postpone the hearing for a week or two, give us a chance to regroup and decide what to do."

Annie had been staring at the floor, but now locked her eyes on Quinn, the big sister coming back. "I don't want a postponement; I want to withdraw the plea. And, Quinn, she can't stay with the Schlesingers. They don't have a clue."

On this point, Quinn knew Annie was right. Sierra felt smothered there; she had said as much to Quinn. "What are you suggesting?"

Annie lowered her voice. "If Sierra can't live with me, it might be better if she could stay with you."

Quinn started to object, pointing out that the court wouldn't allow it, but it seemed his sister could always read his mind.

"Even if it means I have to stay in jail without bail until the retrial," she added.

Part of Quinn wanted this. But the other part, the logical Quinn, could think of a thousand reasons why this was a bad idea, though Annie's desperate look vaporized most of them. "We'll talk about it," he said. "Right now, let's just focus on getting Sierra the help she needs."

"*You* are the help she needs," said Annie.

"I'll call Carla Duncan," said Quinn. "We'll take it from there."

Quinn's misgivings disappeared a few minutes later when he and Annie returned to Sierra's room. The girl looked younger than thirteen, frail and vulnerable, her hair spilling in a tangled web onto the pillow.

Physically, she would recover. But her brittle psyche had been shattered by the overwhelming events of the past few months. Quinn knew the feeling from his own troubled childhood. He had blamed himself for most of the events that spun wildly beyond his control, devastating those he loved most.

They could not lose the next generation. Quinn reached out and touched Sierra gently on the arm, surprised by the coolness of her skin. Instinctively, he wrapped his fingers around her slender forearm, feeling the thin bones. In that moment he had his answer. He would do whatever needed to be done.

Quinn looked at his sister, tears brimming her eyes. "I hope she knows how to cook," Quinn said.

57

QUINN HEADED STRAIGHT for the hospital the next morning, calling Melanie along the way so he could tell her to reschedule the day's appointments. He had called Carla Duncan the night before, and she had agreed to reschedule the plea hearing. "I'll give the judge some vague reason," she assured Quinn. "I'll do my best to keep this out of the press."

When Quinn told her that Annie might change her mind about the deal, Carla was not happy. "If you reject it now, you can't come back on the eve of trial," she warned. "I worked hard to get this deal approved. Don't leave me flailing in the wind."

Quinn thanked her for her efforts but explained that Sierra's suicide attempt had changed things. "We'll let you know one way or the other next week," he said.

Because he had already put the prosecutor in a sour mood, Quinn decided this wasn't the best time to talk about a possible change in Sierra's custody. Given the circumstances, he decided he would employ a vintage Quinn Newberg strategy—act first and seek forgiveness later.

At the hospital, Quinn felt a queasiness develop in his gut. What could he say to a thirteen-year-old girl who'd just attempted suicide?

He rode the elevator to the third floor and shuffled slowly toward Sierra's room. Last night, fueled by adrenaline and remorse, he had practically run into the room. Now, knowing that Sierra would be awake, he took his time, procrastinating the awkward moment as long as possible.

"Hey," Sierra said when she saw Quinn step inside the door. The tubes and IV had been removed, and Sierra had brushed her hair. She looked tired but peaceful.

"Hey," Quinn said. He walked to her bedside. Annie was fast asleep in a reclining chair in the corner, her mouth open. A TV hanging from the wall at the foot of Sierra's bed featured an MTV reality show.

"Mom fell asleep about an hour ago," Sierra said. "I tried to get her to go home."

"She's stubborn," Quinn whispered. He wondered if he should bring up last night. What was the protocol? *So, Sierra, you had any death wishes this morning?*

"You feeling okay?" Quinn asked.

She nodded and looked away. "My stomach hurts. Plus, my throat's raw where they jammed that tube down."

"You scared us," Quinn said.

"I know, Uncle Quinn. I'm sorry."

Her voice was so frail that Quinn decided not to push it. "You hungry?"

"They already made me eat."

This was so awkward. *What do I talk about? Where are the points of connection?*

A long minute passed. "What are you watching?" Quinn asked.

"MTV."

No kidding. "Did they say if you could go home today?"

"You mean to the Schlesingers'?"

"Yeah."

"I think so. Mom talked to the doctor, but she didn't really say if I could or not." Sienna hesitated then turned her pleading eyes on Quinn. "I don't like it there, Uncle Quinn."

"We'll work something out," Quinn said. "I promise."

He stayed for a few more minutes, awkwardly trying to jump-start a conversation while both of them avoided talking about the night before.

Finally he had an idea. "What's your favorite movie?" he asked.

"I don't know. Maybe *Pirates of the Caribbean: At World's End.* I like Johnny Depp."

"You want to watch it?"

Sierra looked skeptical. "How?"

"Give me an hour."

Fifty minutes later, Quinn was back. He brought his laptop and DVDs of all three *Pirates* movies, just to make sure he had the right one. Annie was awake this time, and Quinn made her go home and take a shower. He pulled a stiff wooden chair next to Sierra's bed, put his laptop on her tray table, and popped in the third *Pirates* movie.

It was nearly two-thirds over when Quinn heard his niece sniffle. He looked over to see the tears dripping down her cheeks.

"You all right?" he asked, his heart aching for the girl.

"I'm sorry, Uncle Quinn. Please don't hate me."

He leaned over next to Sierra, and she put her arms around his neck. He held her and let her cry. "Of course I don't hate you," he said. "I love you, Sierra. Your mom loves you." He paused, because he had to convince himself first before he could say this next sentence.

"Everything's going to be okay."

Quinn nearly lost it himself when he received a call later that day from Rosemarie Mancini. He could hardly hear her with all the background noise.

"Where are you?" Quinn asked.

"Sin City."

"What?"

"I heard about Sierra," said Rosemarie. "I came to see if I could help."

58

CATHERINE O'ROURKE RETURNED to the general prison population as a conquering heroine. All the other inmates in the pod knew Holly Stephenson deserved whatever she had coming to her. Forget the fact that it wasn't a fair fight; O'Rourke could draw blood. The pictures of Holly's face, unconscious and red with blood, had been broadcast to televisions across the nation, including those inside the pod at the Virginia Beach jail. Catherine's short, spiked hair only accentuated her new tough-guy image. *Catherine O'Rourke, street fighter.*

The Widows welcomed her back as one of their own. The name "Barbie" was no longer uttered with such disdain. Her thirty-second fight had given her the one thing every inmate craved: respect.

Helping matters along, Marc Boland had apparently pulled the right strings to get Holly moved to another pod. Jail was no picnic, but at least now the inmates were picking on other fish. Catherine was one of the girls.

That morning, Brian Radford, Cat's former coworker at the paper, had called again requesting an interview. This time, Cat said yes without running it by Marc Boland. Cat was being demonized in the press. The visions, the DNA evidence, the vial of methohexital, and now the jailhouse brawl had combined to convict her in the eyes of the public even before a jury could be impaneled.

Radford initially scheduled the interview for 7:00 p.m., the start of visiting hours, but then apparently called the prison officials with a conflict. Incredibly, a prison guard came to Cat at 4:30 and hauled her into a conference room to accommodate Radford's schedule. The guards bending over backward for her? Marc Boland must have rattled somebody's cage big-time.

Brian arrived wearing jeans and an untucked T-shirt, obeying the unwritten rule that cool newspaper reporters had to dress more casually than anybody else with an advanced degree.

Cat knew Radford's chubby young face was deceiving; he could stick the knife in your back and turn it with the best of them. She would be cautious, but she would also be authentic. From their seven years covering stories together, Radford knew Cat was no serial killer.

Brian apologized for the schedule change and placed his tape recorder on the table. He started the tape.

"Is it okay if we tape this session?" he asked, pulling out his reporter's pad.

"Sure," said Catherine, though Brian's businesslike manner bothered her. They were former coworkers. He could have at least asked how she was doing.

Brian recited some background information into the tape and then started with his questions.

"Are you the serial killer who calls herself the Avenger of Blood?" he asked.

"No warm-ups?" asked Catherine. "Just, 'Have you stopped beating your wife?' right out of the blocks?"

"I believe in getting to the point."

"I used to know a guy named Brian Radford," Catherine said. "He was fair and cared about the truth." She sighed. "No, I'm not the serial killer who calls herself the Avenger of Blood. I am not a killer at all. I'm a newspaper reporter just like you."

Brian showed no reaction, and Catherine started to second-guess her decision to grant this interview.

"How do you explain a piece of your hair on the envelope flap of the Donaldson letter?"

Catherine paused before answering. His tone was more hostile than she had anticipated, though she had expected the question. "I can't explain it," she confessed. "I guess the Avenger somehow managed to find a piece of my hair."

"And the DNA evidence on the paper towels?"

For the next twenty minutes, Radford dragged Catherine through all the evidence, piece by piece, without ever really giving her much of a chance to explain. She became frustrated with the adversarial nature of his questions and found herself saying "I don't know" entirely too much. If she had known Radford was going to treat her this way, she would never have agreed to the interview. It felt like a chess match, and she knew that Radford had enough material to write the article with any slant he wanted.

Cat had been on the other side of the table too often. You could massage a quote here, add a fact there, and pretty soon the defendant looked guilty as sin.

"Can we go off the record?" Cat asked.

Radford looked surprised. "Sure." He put down his notepad.

Cat reached over and turned off the recorder.

"What's going on here, Brian?" She tried to read her former colleague, but his eyes had an aloof coldness to them, the type of emotional detachment reporters employed when they were going to skewer the person on the other side of the interview table. "I thought you wanted to hear my side. I thought you'd give me a fair shake."

"I'll tell your side," Brian said, "in your words."

Cat stared him down. "What are you holding back?"

"We're back on the record," Brian said, turning on the tape recorder. "Did you know that earlier this afternoon, the police found Paul Donaldson's body?"

Donaldson's body? The news floored Cat, causing her world to spin off balance. "Where?"

"In the Dismal Swamp Canal. He was strapped into his own car. Somebody had wedged the gas pedal down and popped it into gear. A fisherman discovered the vehicle."

Cat sat in stunned silence, trying to take it in. A new lead—it could only be good news for her; it could only lead closer to the real killer. Yet, for some reason, Brian's tone said otherwise.

"Were you aware of this?" he asked.

"No. But I'm hopeful this will help police find the real killer."

It was then, just before Brian asked his next question, that something dawned on Cat. The prison officials hadn't been helping her. They had allowed Brian Radford to move up the interview by a couple of hours so he could catch Cat off guard before the information hit the airwaves. They knew that the cops couldn't interview Cat, so they were using Radford as a surrogate.

"When Ed Shaftner, the editor of the *Tidewater Times*, first told you about Paul Donaldson's death, did you ask him whether Donaldson had a gash on his head?"

Cat remembered the conversation and felt the blood drain from her face. Her heart pounded fiercely; its deafening noise seemed to drown out all other sound. "I'm not going to answer that," she stammered.

"When you subsequently talked with Jamarcus Webb, did you tell him to call you when they found the body of Paul Donaldson? Did you tell him to check for a gash on the skull?"

Cat's racing mind pieced it together. Webb was still an inside source for the paper. Only now he was working with Radford, against Catherine.

"Did you?" Radford pressed.

"I'm not answering that question either." Cat spit the words out, disgusted with herself. She had walked into a trap set by her own friends. She could see the headlines now.

"You know as well as anybody, Cat—this isn't like a police interrogation or the courtroom. If you don't answer, I'll have to put that in my story. You're better off telling your side and getting it out there."

"Get out of here," Cat said. "This interview's over."

"Are you sure?" Radford asked.

"I don't know how you can live with yourself," Cat snarled.

59

QUINN HEARD ABOUT the recovery of Paul Donaldson's body when Melanie called his cell phone. "I saw it on the news," Quinn's assistant said. "They're saying that Donaldson was electrocuted. They say the Avenger hooked him up to a homemade electric chair and fried him."

"Whoa," Quinn said. He felt the case crashing around him. This kind of graphic testimony could really fire up a jury.

"They said the Avenger shaved some spots on Donaldson's scalp and legs to hook up the electrodes. It gets worse—you ready?"

"How can it get worse?"

"He had a gash on his scalp where the Avenger apparently jammed an electric razor into Donaldson's head trying to shave him. Maybe Donaldson was writhing around trying to get away—who knows? Anyway, both the editor of the *Tidewater Times* and Detective Webb are saying that our client implied Donaldson's head would have a gash."

"What?"

"Yeah. I guess she had another vision of some type."

"We're toast," said Quinn.

Melanie paused for a moment, perhaps uncertain as to whether she should broach this next subject. "You going to drop the case?"

"If Annie withdraws her plea, I'll have to. The firm said I could only handle one of these nonpaying cases."

"In the meantime, you want to do some TV?" Melanie asked, trying to sound upbeat. "Marc Boland called and said he really needs some help with the national cable shows."

Quinn thought about it for a moment. Marc was right—they would have to start on the damage control immediately. But Quinn had scheduled dinner with Rosemarie Mancini. Rosemarie had spent a few hours with Sierra that afternoon, and Quinn was anxious to get her advice.

"Tell Mr. Boland that I want to help but I just can't shake free tonight. I can do a few of the morning shows if he needs me to."

"You sure you don't want to call him yourself?" asked Melanie.

"I'm sure."

Rosemarie Mancini met Quinn in the hospital cafeteria. Quinn bought orange juice; Rosemarie settled for a cup of coffee that looked like it might have been brewed in the last millennium.

"She's going to be okay," Rosemarie said. "She's stronger than you think."

"Except that she just attempted suicide." Quinn kept his voice low, although the tables around them were empty.

"I guess you could say that," Rosemarie answered. "I would consider it more of a statement than a legitimate suicide attempt."

It seemed to Quinn like Rosemarie was splitting hairs, but he held his tongue.

"One out of fourteen girls Sierra's age will self-mutilate or attempt to take their lives. Most aren't enduring anything close to the trauma Sierra has experienced. The main thing we've got to do is eliminate the guilt."

Rosemarie watched Quinn closely, apparently trying to gauge his reaction. "She feels responsible for everything that's happened—her stepfather's death, her mother's imprisonment, the separation from her family. The Schlesingers have little or no rapport with Sierra, and she feels ostracized even among her friends. The thought of being uprooted and sent to a boarding school—on top of her mom going to jail—was just too much."

Quinn took a drink of juice and tried to digest what he was hearing. He knew Sierra was struggling emotionally, but suicide seemed like something that happened to other kids, not his own niece. Why hadn't he seen this coming? "What are you suggesting?" he asked.

"One of the greatest fears of any adolescent girl is to lose one or both parents through death or divorce. Sierra has already lost her stepdad. Now, just a few months later, she's faced with losing her mom."

Dr. Mancini swirled the coffee in her cup and softened her voice to a tone she seldom used. "She views you as a surrogate father, Quinn. This idea of sending her away to boarding school seems to her like more rejection."

A surrogate father? The words rocked Quinn. He admired his niece, loved her, but he had never considered that he might have such an important role in her life. He spent so little time with her and always felt somewhat ill at ease around her. What did Quinn know about the world of a thirteen-year-old girl? But Rosemarie seemed to be confirming Quinn's decision about taking Sierra in.

"You're saying she should live with me?"

"As opposed to the Schlesingers or boarding school, yes. My first preference, of course, would be Annie."

"Except that there's this small matter of her murder trial."

"A good lawyer could make that problem go away."

"Good luck finding one." Though he made the statement facetiously, it felt more like the truth every day. Quinn Newberg, legal magician, was losing his touch. He finished his orange juice, thinking about the impact of another trial on Sierra. "What if Annie gets convicted? Could Sierra handle that?"

Rosemarie shifted in her seat. "Here's my suggestion, Quinn. Let Sierra stay with you until the trial, even if that means you have to allow the court to revoke Annie's bail because the Schlesingers would no longer be custodians. Make it clear to Sierra that if, God forbid, we lose this trial, she'll be living with you until her mom is released. If you're willing to do that, I'll work with Sierra and counsel her through some of these tough issues. In a few months, she'll be strong enough to handle another trial."

Quinn had a ton of questions. How was he supposed to raise a teenage girl? How would Rosemarie counsel Sierra from D.C.? But most important: "And if her mom gets a life sentence—what happens then?"

Rosemarie thought for an uncomfortably long time, her face solemn. "That'd be a tough blow for anybody, Quinn. Sierra's psyche will still be pretty fragile." She gave Quinn a tight smile. "I think you ought to plan on winning."

On the way home from the hospital, Quinn checked his missed calls and voice mails. He had three calls and two messages from Marc Boland. Guilt stabbed at Quinn as he returned his co-counsel's call. Soon he would have to tell Marc that he couldn't be part of Catherine's defense team. Just the thought of bailing out made him sick.

Marc gave Quinn a quick rundown of the television interviews he had conducted that night and his schedule for the next day. "I'm getting hammered,

Quinn. There's just too much to explain now—DNA evidence, the metho-hexital, the visions, Catherine's attack on her cellmate, and now a body turns up with a gash to the scalp, just like Catherine suggested."

Quinn could hear the weariness in Marc's voice, the sound of a crusader on a lost cause.

"I think we've got to consider changing our plea," Marc said.

They discussed it for twenty minutes over the phone. Marc had seen the light, he said. He was willing to talk with Catherine about pleading not guilty by reason of insanity, relying on dissociative identity disorder. He wanted Quinn to take the lead. Marc also suggested they waive the preliminary hearing scheduled for next week, since they no longer had any hope of getting the case thrown out at that stage, and instead just ask for an early trial date.

"Every day, this case gets worse," Marc said. "There's no sense giving the government a chance to parade all these grisly facts in front of the press at a preliminary hearing. If we're pleading insanity, let's line up our experts and get to trial before the press can completely crucify Catherine. And let's start laying the groundwork for an insanity plea during tomorrow's TV appearances. You can take the lead."

Quinn hesitated. He couldn't agree to be lead lawyer for a case he would withdraw from in a week. Still, he had always believed that insanity was the right defense.

"Let's take it one step at a time," Quinn suggested. "I'll start hinting at a possible insanity plea during tomorrow's interviews. You need to set up a meeting with Catherine."

"I just can't believe she's a serial killer," Marc Boland said. "It's just crazy."

Despite his sour mood, Quinn found irony in Marc's statement. "That's what I've been saying all along."

60

ON FRIDAY MORNING, Quinn showed up at all the local Las Vegas network affiliates and played cat and mouse with national hosts interviewing him via live satellite feeds. At 5:45 a.m. Pacific time, Quinn was sitting in the CBS studios, staring down yet another camera for his fourth and last interview of the morning. The national host of *The Early Show* was Thomas Kirkland, young and energetic with a full head of blond anchorman hair and a beaming white smile. He sat on a brown leather couch with his cohost and fired questions at Quinn, zeroing in on the latest evidence in Catherine O'Rourke's case.

"You and Mr. Boland have previously denied that your client committed these crimes," stated Kirkland. "Has this new evidence changed that strategy? Some have speculated that Mr. Boland might have brought you in to quarterback an insanity defense."

Quinn focused on the red light and gave the camera a serious look. "First of all, Mr. Boland is a highly capable defense lawyer and wouldn't need my help to put on an insanity defense. But sometimes a second set of eyes will see things the lead lawyer would have missed. With regard to an insanity defense, let's put it this way: the Catherine O'Rourke that I know would never have committed these heinous crimes."

He paused, reminding himself to tread lightly. The problem with live television, as Quinn knew all too well, was that once you uttered a phrase, you could never take it back.

Looking directly into the camera, Quinn continued, "Does that mean some other manifestation of Catherine O'Rourke—a second independent personality that she doesn't even know exists—couldn't possibly have committed this crime? I'm not willing to say one way or the other at this point, Tom. I do know that Catherine has suffered the kind of trauma in her life that can sometimes give rise to multiple personalities. Until we have a solid diagnosis, I just can't say."

Kirkland slid forward a little. "So you haven't actually ruled out an insanity defense?"

"We haven't ruled it in. We haven't ruled it out."

"What specific incidents in Ms. O'Rourke's past are you referencing?"

"I'm not prepared to say at this point."

Thomas Kirkland frowned. He was a host for a national news show. He obviously considered it his birthright to know everything. "When will you make the call on whether to plead insanity?"

"As soon as the psychiatric evaluation is complete."

"Is that in a few days? a few weeks?"

Quinn saw the cameraman flash a card. *Three minutes left in the segment.* Quinn would wait until the last possible moment to make a strong argument for Catherine's innocence. That way, Kirkland wouldn't have time to follow up before the break.

"A week. Maybe two," Quinn said.

"Let me shift gears for a second," Kirkland said.

Though the anchorman's tone was casual, Quinn's red flags went up.

"I want to ask a couple of questions about your sister's case."

Quinn became more rigid. Annie's case hadn't been mentioned in the interview request. "Okay."

"A few days ago, we reported that you were discussing a potential plea bargain with the state of Nevada, a deal where your client would plead guilty to voluntary manslaughter and serve three years. Care to comment on that?"

"Not at this time," Quinn said. "I will say that I'm always willing to talk with the government. No trial is without risk, especially this one."

"Okay," Kirkland said tentatively, twisting his brow as if Quinn's answer didn't make much sense.

Arrogant jerk.

"Then let me ask you this, and I hesitate to even bring this up, but we have confirmed sources, and we believe this to be an important part of a story that has attracted national interest. . . ."

Quinn saw it coming, like a train wreck he couldn't avoid. His throat constricted, and he felt the blood rushing to his face.

"Is it true that your client's daughter was admitted to the hospital after an attempt to take her own life? And if so, will that enter into your decision about whether to take any proffered plea bargain?"

Unbelievable! Quinn wanted to jump through the camera and strangle the man. Humiliating Sierra on national TV!

"I can't believe you would ask that question," Quinn said in a low voice, staring at the camera. "I just cannot believe you would violate this young girl's privacy like this." He felt his voice rising, veins bulging in his neck. "How is that relevant? How can you live with yourself, humiliating a thirteen-year-old?"

"Mr. Newberg, we know this is an emotional issue for your—"

But Quinn wasn't listening. He pulled the earpiece out and jerked the wire loose from his collar. In one motion, he stood and pulled the battery pack from his waist, dropping it to the floor. Without another word, he walked past the camera, grabbed his briefcase, and stormed out of the room before he said something he might really regret.

He fumed all the way to his car in the parking garage, his rage literally blurring his vision. He couldn't believe they would do this. *Aren't there any boundaries anymore?*

He started his car and dialed Carla Duncan's office number. When voice mail kicked in, he remembered how early it was. "I just finished an interview on CBS's *Early Show*," he said, his voice edged with tension. "They asked about Sierra's suicide attempt. I swear, Carla, if anybody from your office leaked that information, they're going to regret the day they were born." He hesitated; the message seemed so inadequate for how he felt. He pushed the End button.

It didn't have to be Carla's office, he knew. The leak could have come from someone at the hospital or someone at the clerk's office or just someone who knew Annie and wanted to make a quick buck. He might never find out who it was.

In the meantime, he had to think about damage control.

He dialed Annie's number, and she answered on the first ring. "I know," she said. "I was watching."

61

AFTER THE FRIDAY MORNING INCIDENT, Quinn swore off media interviews. He would try his case in court, the old-fashioned way. He refused to watch TV or pick up a newspaper. He gave terse "no comments" when the media hounds stuck microphones in his face.

The hospital released Sierra late Friday morning, and both Sierra and Annie came to stay with Quinn. He gave them the single bedroom and relegated himself to the couch. Technically it was a violation of the court's order concerning Annie's bail, but Quinn didn't care. Things had changed. Sierra needed her mom. The media had embarrassed Sierra in front of the entire world. Quinn was going to protect his family.

He talked to Marc Boland on four separate occasions Friday evening. "CBS overstepped their bounds," Marc told him. "You did the right thing by walking out."

Both lawyers agreed they should waive Catherine's preliminary hearing. Marc said he would petition the court for an early trial date, and Quinn gave Marc his available dates. Quinn still felt like Benedict Arnold for not telling his co-counsel that he planned to withdraw.

The phone number from the Virginia Beach jail showed up on Quinn's cell a couple of times over the weekend, no doubt Catherine O'Rourke calling collect, but Quinn ignored it. He felt guilty enough about withdrawing; there was no sense aggravating those feelings by talking to Catherine.

Being around Sierra and Annie throughout the weekend was a painful experience. They all felt like captives in Quinn's two-million-dollar condo. A small pack of reporters waited just outside the gates of the complex for a glimpse of Las Vegas's current celebrities. Annie and Sierra refused to leave the condo, and to Quinn it felt like everyone was walking on eggshells. Sierra retreated inside herself, slumping her thin shoulders even more than usual and mumbling soft answers when Quinn or Annie asked her questions. The three of them watched a lot of movies.

By late Sunday afternoon, Quinn was tired of being confined. "I'll be back," he announced as he grabbed his car keys. "Don't answer the phone."

He went down to the lobby, gave his ticket to the valet, and explained his plan to the security guard. Quinn climbed in his Mercedes and drove past the media hounds camped outside the gate, ignoring their shouted questions. He drove to a mall just north of the strip and picked out a pair of oversize sunglasses and a stylish, floppy hat. Then he circled back to the Signature Towers and drove up to the maintenance entrance. He waved at the security camera, and the guard opened the gate so Quinn could drive into the underground loading dock that backed up to the elevator.

He returned to the condo and gave the sunglasses and hat to Sierra. "What are these for?" she asked.

"We're going out," Quinn said. "Think like you're a movie star with paparazzi outside."

Sierra looked skeptical.

"Trust me," Quinn said. "I've got a plan."

The look didn't change.

"We're going shopping," Quinn said.

This brought a slight flicker of enthusiasm, followed quickly by another downcast look.

"I've got the car hidden in the basement," Quinn explained. "We'll use the freight elevator. They'll never see us."

"He knows what he's doing," added Annie. "He used to sneak out all the time when we were kids."

Sierra finally assented, and Quinn winked at Annie. "We'll be back," he said, and the adventure was on.

For the first time in weeks, a plan worked just the way Quinn had laid it out. They took the main elevator down to the first floor and then transferred to the freight elevator. They made a clean getaway in Quinn's car and headed to the Boulevard Mall, where Quinn was determined to spend a few hundred dollars on his niece. At first Sierra resisted, but she soon succumbed to the Quinn Newberg makeover plan. A new pair of jeans, several new tops, and a pair of sandals later, Quinn actually talked his niece into the Images Hair Salon for a new haircut. In thirty minutes, Sierra's straight, shoulder-length, strawberry blonde hair had been transformed into a stylishly layered hairdo that made her smile sheepishly when she snuck a glance at the mirror.

"You look great," Quinn said.

"Mom's going to flip out."

They shared dinner at the food court before heading back to the condo. This time, Quinn and Sierra donned their sunglasses and drove right past the surprised reporters.

When they walked into the lobby, Quinn felt Sierra relax.

"Who's that beautiful young woman on your elbow?" the security guard asked Quinn.

"This is my niece, Sierra," Quinn replied.

"I knew she was too good-lookin' to be your date," the man responded.

Sierra smiled. It left her face quickly, but Quinn could tell it hadn't been forced.

"Good looks run in the family," Quinn said.

62

ROSEMARIE MANCINI THOUGHT the College of William and Mary, with its traditional brick buildings snuggled next to the heart of Colonial Williamsburg, seemed like an incongruous place for the painful memories that Catherine O'Rourke had described. On this day in late May, two weeks after graduation, the campus was nearly deserted. A few college students played ultimate Frisbee on the sunken grounds that served as the school's quad while bright sunshine warmed the ivy-covered buildings and huge oak trees that reminded visitors of the school's rich tradition. Rosemarie half expected Thomas Jefferson or John Marshall or one of Virginia's other founding fathers to appear, dressed in colonial garb.

But Rosemarie was chasing other memories today. She found the ancient brick building that served as the home for the philosophy and religion department, eventually winding her way to the small, cramped office where she was scheduled to meet Dr. Frederick Channing.

Rosemarie arrived at 9:50 for the 10:00 meeting. Since the office door was locked, she waited in the hallway, reading bulletin board material and thinking about Catherine's case. Professor Channing came shuffling down the hall a full ten minutes late.

The smell of cigarettes arrived just before the short, round man with the crescent moon of hair circling the lower part of his skull. Rosemarie thanked him for meeting with her but avoided telling him not to worry about being late. Her time was valuable too.

Channing moved some papers and books from a wooden spindle chair in front of his desk and invited Rosemarie to have a seat. He plopped down in his worn leather desk chair and started telling Rosemarie how fascinating he found the entire O'Rourke case. The man remained in constant motion, fidgeting here and there, picking up knickknacks from his desk and placing them back down.

"I don't remember her as a student," he said, picking up where their phone conversation had left off. "I even went back and looked at some yearbook photos to see what she looked like in college, but it didn't trigger anything."

"How big is your comparative religions class?" Rosemarie asked. She had carefully combed through Catherine's schedule from her senior year in college. From the course description in the catalog, this class looked like it had potential.

"Students need three credits in either religion or philosophy as part of their core curriculum. A lot of them take this class. I end up with maybe sixty students per section." Channing squinted and scrunched his forehead. "Most of them are underclassmen, though."

Rosemarie pulled out a Dictaphone and placed it on the desk, turning it on. "Do you mind?" She wanted to watch Channing rather than have her head down taking notes.

"No, that's fine," Channing said. "Will you send me a copy of the tape?"

"Sure."

"So based on our telephone conversation," Channing continued without any prompting, "I actually went back and tried to reconstruct my notes from that year." He started fishing around in a pile of documents behind his desk. "Every year I tweak the course material a little, but the gist of it stays the same."

He pulled out some rumpled pages and started leafing through them. "Here—you can make a copy of these if you want."

Rosemarie took the pages and tried to decipher the professor's sloppy writing, margin notes, and pervasive abbreviations. She noticed for the first time that the computer screen sitting on his credenza was dark and dusty.

"You mind taking me through this?" she asked.

He fidgeted. "Sure." He felt his head for some reading glasses, patted around the piles of paper on his desk a little, and finally found a pair in a briefcase next to his shelves.

At Rosemarie's request, he zeroed in on the issue of justice and retribution. According to Channing, many of his students were surprised to learn that the Bible borrowed many of its principles and stories from other ancient religions and vice versa. Rosemarie had a few opinions about that comment, but she let it pass.

"Take this Avenger of Blood thing," Channing continued. "This whole idea of a blood feud is not unique to Judaism or Christianity."

Channing went to his overcrowded bookshelves and pulled down a Bible with yellow Post-it notes sticking out in dozens of places. With the other hand, he grabbed a well-worn copy of *The Eumenides*, an ancient Greek play. He put the Bible in front of Rosemarie and opened it to the book of Numbers. "Under Old Testament Hebrew law," he explained, "an Israelite had the duty to kill someone who had killed his or her relative." Channing put his stubby finger on Numbers 35:21. "'The blood avenger shall put the murderer to death when he meets him,'" Channing said, quoting the verse. "This was true whether the murder was intentional or accidental."

He gave Rosemarie his copy of *The Eumenides* and returned to his seat behind the desk. "Are you familiar with that book?" he asked.

"I might have read it during undergrad."

"The author is Aeschylus. It's the final play in the *Oresteian* trilogy, the story of Agamemnon following the Trojan War. This last play is basically the battle between two generations of gods—the older generation of deities, represented by the three female furies, and the new generation of Olympian gods represented by Zeus and his progeny." Channing looked at Rosemarie with a hint of paternalism—the college professor lecturing a uninformed plebeian. "Do you know what the furies were called?"

"Blood avengers," answered Rosemarie.

The professor raised an eyebrow, perhaps trying to decide whether it was just a lucky guess. "Quite correct! They were to be feared and never provoked—all black and wingless, with heavy, rasping breath and eyes oozing discharge. They exacted vengeance without remorse. Yet by the end of the play, the ultimate blood feud had been brought to an end with the emergence of the first Athenian court—the goddess Athena presiding at the trial, Apollo serving as an expert witness, and the furies acting as prosecutors. Following the trial, the furies become benevolent goddesses rather than vengeful and spiteful beings."

Rosemarie had forgotten the details of the plot and, despite the professor's condescending attitude, was beginning to think the visit had been worthwhile. She considered the implications of *The Eumenides* for Catherine's case. Honestly, she had been so focused on the biblical notion of a blood avenger that she had missed this secular angle. "Is it okay if I borrow this book for a few weeks?" she asked.

"Have at it," the professor said. "Maybe sometime you could come and lecture to my class. 'The psychology of *The Eumenides.*'"

Also known, Rosemarie thought, *as the professor finding another excuse to take a class off.* She tucked the book in her briefcase. "Is this the kind of thing Catherine would have been exposed to as part of her comparative religion course?"

"This and other examples," said Channing, "my basic point being to demonstrate that these ancient religions all sanctioned some type of blood feud. Makes you wonder who copied whom, doesn't it?"

Rosemarie had heard enough revisionist history. "Seems to me that Greek drama came along in about the fifth century BC, thousands of years after the Mosaic law," she said. "And I'm no expert, but if I remember correctly, the biblical system included a number of 'cities of refuge' set up throughout the country. Any killer could flee to the cities, but a blood avenger could not go there. A person fleeing to the cities would not be put to death unless that person was tried and found guilty of intentional murder, not just an accidental killing."

She opened the Bible on the desk and flipped back to the book of Numbers, locating one of the passages she had run across while analyzing Catherine's case. "'The cities shall be to you as a refuge from the avenger, so that the manslayer will not die until he stands before the congregation for trial.'" She looked at Channing. "Seems to me the biblical system was focused on a fair trial, not just blood vengeance."

"Yes, yes, I see your point," he said. "One could certainly view it that way, though I'm still struck by the overwhelming similarities."

Rosemarie thought about pressing the point but decided against it. Channing could be a valuable witness in Catherine's trial. She thanked the professor for his time, turned off the tape recorder, and left his office. Her suspicions had now been confirmed, dropping the first piece of the puzzle into place.

Under a DID diagnosis, an alter ego would often carry with it many of the thoughts and characteristics that the person had exhibited at the time of the event that caused the personality to fracture, as if that other personality had become frozen in time. Catherine's rape had occurred during her senior year in college. That same year, she had studied the blood-avenging Greek goddesses in *The Eumenides* and the biblical notion of a blood avenger. *It could be a coincidence,* Rosemarie thought. *Or perhaps not.*

On the way to her car, Rosemarie dictated a note to herself, a reminder to check Catherine's newspaper articles for any coverage of the Paul Donaldson or Clarence Milburn rape trials. Then she called Marc Boland.

"Whose idea was it to bring Quinn Newberg into the case?" Rosemarie asked. "Yours or Catherine's?"

"Catherine's," Marc said without hesitation. "Why?"

Rosemary ignored the question. "How insistent was she on getting Quinn involved?"

"Pretty insistent. Confidentially, I tried to talk her out of it. I'm glad he's part of the team now, but at the time I wasn't thinking insanity, and I felt like his involvement might send the wrong signal."

"Thanks," said Rosemarie. "That's what I thought."

"Do you mind telling me why you're asking?"

"I do mind," said Rosemarie. "And thanks for being sensitive to the fact that I can't always share everything I've discovered with you and Quinn."

Rosemarie could tell by the silence that Marc didn't particularly care for that answer. She thanked him for his time and hung up the phone. The second piece of the puzzle was now firmly in place.

63

CATHERINE O'ROURKE FELT HERSELF SLIPPING deeper into depression but couldn't seem to stop it. Everything about jail was designed to depersonalize, humiliate, and desensitize. If it weren't for Tasha, she probably would have gone totally berserk.

Even visiting hours compounded the despondency. The steady stream of visitors had dwindled to a few loyal friends and Cat's mom and sister. In a couple of days, her family would have to return to Pennsylvania. "We'll come down just about every weekend," Kelsey promised. But Cat knew the realities—money was getting tight. Kelsey had to get back to work. Trips to Virginia were long and costly.

Catherine continued taking her antidepressants. Her psychiatrist assured Cat she would work through this. The worst thing was that Cat had not seen Marc Boland in nearly a week, and Quinn Newberg had quit taking her collect calls. Updates on her case came from the news or other inmates.

Through it all, she wondered and worried. Was there really another Catherine, one responsible for the murder of infants, defense lawyers, and criminals? Why had the visions stopped? If she wasn't the Avenger, who was?

Catherine was a woman of action, but here she sat, helpless, watching the minutes slowly tick by as she waited for her trial date. If she lost and faced a lifetime prison sentence, she would seriously consider taking her own life. If she truly was the Avenger, who would care?

I can't think that way. But it wasn't that easy. The more she obsessed about the case, the more she isolated herself. And the more that happened, the more depressed she became. She couldn't remember the last time she had genuinely laughed. Cat felt trapped inside a spiral of misery, her mind eroding by the hour.

Even if she won the trial, there would be a significant percentage of Americans who would always believe she was a serial killer. Her best-case scenario was living like O.J. Simpson, enduring the scorn of good people everywhere.

Maybe she could start over again in some remote Latin American country or someplace in Europe. But first, she had to get through today. And then tonight. And then the day after that and the day after that.

Catherine O'Rourke, suspected serial killer. It seemed at times like she could barely remember what life had been like before this nightmare. The sun. The freedom. Friends who believed in her. A promising career.

All gone. And maybe her sanity along with them.

Late Monday afternoon, Quinn suffered one final blow before his scheduled court appearance with Annie. It came as he entered his office building, pushing through a few persistent TV reporters who had set up shop in the lobby.

"Do you have any comment on Claude Tanner's filing in family court?" one of the reporters asked.

"No comment," Quinn said, wondering what the man was talking about. He and Annie had decided to keep the TV off in the condo. He'd never heard of anyone named Claude Tanner.

"Does your client deny that Mr. Tanner is Sierra's father?"

Quinn stopped dead in his tracks, his world suddenly spinning. *Sierra's father?*

"No comment," Quinn said more tersely than before. He resumed walking toward the elevator, hoping he didn't look as flustered as he felt.

"Will Ms. Newberg contest his right to custody?"

Quinn whirled and shot the reporter a withering look. "Of course," he said. "I don't know if this man is Sierra's biological father or not. I do know that Sierra's biological father wanted nothing to do with his child from day one, at least until the smell of money apparently became irresistible."

"Were you aware he asked for a DNA test?" asked a second reporter.

"No comment," Quinn said, reminding himself that this was a game he could not win. He turned and walked away.

Waiting for the elevator, Quinn mulled over this new complication. Sierra's father could not have picked a worse time to reappear. The thought of the man swooping in and acting concerned about his child's welfare infuriated Quinn. He wondered if Tanner realized that Richard Hofstetter's estate didn't amount to much. Even if Annie was convicted and disqualified from inheriting the money, Sierra, as second in line, wouldn't be getting rich. The proceeds from Hofstetter's life insurance policy would be used to pay his debts first, leaving precious little for either Annie or Sierra.

If Tanner thought he could waltz into this mess and obtain custody of his daughter without a fight, he had another think coming to him. Short of murder, Quinn would do whatever it took to protect Sierra.

64

REPORTERS JAMMED THEMSELVES into the limited seats of Courtroom 16D on Tuesday morning, bringing back memories of Quinn's bitter battle to free Annie, which had ended in a mistrial three months earlier.

Carla Duncan walked down the aisle of the courtroom and came over to shake Quinn's hand. "Please reconsider," she said, referring to the phone call Quinn had made rejecting the proposed plea.

"We haven't changed our minds," Quinn said.

Carla nodded and pursed her lips, looking dreadfully solemn. During the phone call, she had explained to Quinn that she would move to revoke Annie's bail if Annie didn't take the plea.

Carla turned and pointed to a man in the third row. He was probably in his thirties, with shaggy dark hair, a stud in his left ear, and an ill-fitting suit. "That's Officer Northrop," Carla said. "He works vice and narcotics and has a few friends on the seedier side of town. He gave me these." She handed Quinn a couple of fresh-looking visas. Quinn's heart did a nose-dive.

Carla gave Quinn a chance to open the visas and scan the pictures of Annie and Sierra, paired with two unfamiliar names and Social Security numbers. She lowered her voice and continued. "If I'm asked about this, I'll deny I said it. But about half the fake ID operations in the city are part of an underground network that provides leads to the cops from time to time in exchange for being left alone. A few times a year, they might come to us with known felons, folks who might fit a terrorist profile, those types of things. A guy named Keshon, who is under subpoena to testify today, put a couple of fake IDs together for your sister the day after Sierra's suicide attempt." Carla nodded toward the visas in Quinn's hands. "He thought the woman looked familiar so he made some duplicate copies, found her picture on the Internet, and then came to Officer Northrop."

It took all of Quinn's willpower not to react. He felt a stunning sense of betrayal. The bond hearing was going to be hard enough just based on the fact that they wanted Sierra to leave the Schlesingers and move in with him. But this. He opened the visas again and stared at the forlorn look on Annie's face. This was devastating. "I'll talk to my client," Quinn said.

Carla returned to her counsel table, and Quinn sat down next to Annie. He placed the visas on the table. "You've got some explaining to do," he said.

Big tears formed in Annie's eyes as she stared at the visas. "If I were going to use them, I would have been gone by now." Her voice was thick with emotion. "I was scared. I got them the day after Sierra's suicide attempt. I didn't know what to do. I just knew I couldn't lose my daughter."

Quinn wanted to tell his sister how stupid she'd been. He had a sudden urge to let her have it right then and there, to let her know how incredibly difficult she was making this case, to emphasize how much this would cost them. But Annie was already devastated—Quinn could see it in her slumping shoulders and the tears spilling from her eyes.

"We can't win this hearing now," Quinn said softly. "If we even try, Carla will poison the potential jury pool with this evidence that you were trying to flee the country. The issue of Sierra's suicide will come out in all its glory—"

"Quinn." Annie placed a hand on his arm. "I'm ready to go to jail until the trial. Just promise me that you'll take care of Sierra."

"I told you I would," Quinn said. "You should have just trusted me."

A few minutes later, Judge Strackman took the bench.

Carla rose to speak first. "As the court knows," she began, "this hearing was originally scheduled for the court to approve a plea agreement. However, in the interim, the defendant has apparently had a change of mind and—"

"Is that true?" Strackman turned a menacing look toward Quinn.

Quinn stood, once again regretting the dollars his firm had put into the coffers of Strackman's last opponent. "Yes, Your Honor."

Strackman hesitated and frowned, as if he couldn't believe his ears. "I'm sure you and your client have your reasons, Mr. Newberg, but it seems to me that Ms. Duncan was being exceedingly generous. This is, after all, a case you nearly lost the first time around."

"I'm aware of that, Your Honor," Quinn replied, choosing his words carefully. "However, there are other considerations impacting our choice."

Strackman frowned even more deeply but apparently decided not to push further. It would be bad form for a judge to publicly bully a defendant into taking a plea. "If that's your client's decision, Mr. Newberg, then let's set a new trial date."

"Before we do that," Carla Duncan chimed in, still standing, "the state would like the opportunity to address the matter of Ms. Newberg's bail."

"For what reason?"

"The terms of the bail agreement have been violated," Carla Duncan explained. "Sierra has been staying with Quinn and Anne Newberg at a Signature Towers condominium owned by Mr. Newberg. Moreover, we have recently discovered evidence that Ms. Newberg poses a substantial flight risk."

"Mr. Newberg," Strackman said, his face reddening, "the court was very clear about the terms of your client's bond."

Quinn took a deep breath. "May we approach?" he asked.

The judge nodded, and the lawyers trudged to the judge's bench.

Strackman put his hand over the mike, and Quinn launched into his explanation. Sierra Newberg had attempted suicide. When she was released from the hospital, she needed to stay with her mom. Quinn motioned toward Dr. Mancini in the first row and explained that she would be glad to testify about Sierra's need to stay with Annie. "If she testifies," Quinn said, "I'd want to do it in your office with a sealed record. I'm not willing to have my psychiatric expert discuss Sierra's suicide attempt in front of the entire world."

Quinn took a quick breath before addressing the fake visas, but Carla Duncan interrupted.

"I sympathize with Sierra," Carla said, moving even closer to the judge. "But when the court sets bond, it cannot do so on the basis of family members who need time with an accused felon. Half the women in jail have children who desperately need them. Plus, Your Honor, as I mentioned, we have very strong evidence that Ms. Newberg was preparing to flee the jurisdiction."

Strackman leaned forward, all ears, as Carla told him about Annie getting a fake visa for herself and Sierra.

The judge turned his icy stare on Quinn. "Is this true?"

"Like any mother, Annie's first reaction was to protect her daughter. Yes, my client obtained false IDs. But that was last week. She didn't use them. She realized that it was best to work within the system."

"Return to your seats," ordered Strackman. "You've made this easy."

Quinn didn't move. "With respect, Your Honor, if you are prepared to rule against Annie on the basis of violating a bail agreement, then we'll just revoke her request to remain free on bond. I don't want all this incriminating evidence talked about in open court where it will poison the jury pool."

"Return to your seat," said Strackman, his face unyielding. "Your client should have thought about that before she got this fake ID."

For the next several minutes, Quinn simmered while Strackman set up his ruling on the bail issue. He had Carla Duncan recite the evidence she was prepared to produce about Annie's violation of the terms of her bond and her procurement of fake visas. He asked Quinn if he disputed any of the statements, and Quinn told the court he didn't dispute the factual accuracies of the statements. Based on those stipulations, and without even mentioning Sierra's attempted suicide, Strackman ruled that Annie had violated the terms of her parole and would have to remain in jail pending trial.

"It's okay," Annie whispered to Quinn. "I'll be all right."

"I'd like to try this case before I leave the bench," said Strackman. "But the only open dates I've got are during the last few weeks before my retirement. What if we started the trial on August twenty-first?"

"I can make it work," Carla Duncan said.

Unfortunately, Quinn's calendar looked open on the twenty-first as well, unless . . .

Just yesterday, Marc Boland had obtained a trial date in Catherine O'Rourke's case. Boland and Boyd Gates had played a game of legal chicken, both claiming they wanted a speedy trial—Boland because he wanted to prove his client's innocence and get her released from jail as soon as possible; Gates because the case was "open and shut." Gates boasted that the commonwealth could be ready to try the case later that week.

The court had taken the lawyers at their chest-thumping word and set the trial for August eighteenth, just a few months out. Quinn seized on that now.

"We'll have to bump it back into September," Quinn said. Under no circumstances did he want this judge sentencing Annie. "I'm scheduled to start the case of *Commonwealth v. O'Rourke* on August eighteenth. It's expected to last at least two weeks. There's no way I can be ready to try this case until the middle of September."

Judge Strackman locked his eyes on Quinn for a moment, peering over reading glasses, as if questioning Quinn's integrity. But Quinn also knew that deep down, Strackman didn't want the hassle of a retrial either. "I'd hate to leave this as unfinished business for my successor," said Strackman, half-convincingly. "But after I leave the bench on the last day of August, the only judging I plan on doing is a wine-tasting contest here and there."

Quinn just shrugged his shoulders. Eventually they all agreed to set the case for September fifteenth, a date that would necessitate a different judge. Quinn thought he detected Strackman fighting off a smile.

Quinn would have been smiling too if he had not just guaranteed that his sister would be spending at least three months in jail before her case would even be heard.

65

QUINN WALKED INTO HIS CONDO that afternoon and found Sierra sprawled out on his brown leather couch, listening to her iPod and typing on her computer. She looked up at Quinn expectantly, worry creasing her forehead. She'd known there was a good chance her mom would have her bail revoked.

Quinn placed his briefcase by the door and took a place next to Sierra on the couch. She put her computer on the coffee table and took out her earphones. Without saying a word, Quinn could tell she already knew. Maybe she had been watching television or surfing the Internet. Maybe she just surmised it from the fact that Annie had not returned with Quinn.

"We lost," Quinn said. "Your mom had to go to jail pending her trial." He saw the pain register on Sierra's thin face as her fears were confirmed. He wanted to reach out and touch her, maybe even give her a hug, but somehow it didn't seem right. "It's only for a few months, Sierra. She'll be free for good once this trial is over."

Sierra stared down at the carpet, tears pooling in her eyes. She brushed them away with the back of her hand, breaking Quinn's heart in the process.

"Are you okay?" he asked.

She nodded. "Thanks for letting me stay here, Uncle Quinn," she said. Awkwardly, she leaned over to hug him. He held her, concerned at how thin and frail she felt.

"We're going to get through this," he said. "One day soon, you and your mom will be together again."

Sierra didn't respond, and Quinn wondered what was going on inside her young head. Sierra was no longer a preadolescent, a child who took assurances at face value. She knew it was possible her mom could spend the rest of her life in jail. And now Quinn would have to tell her about Annie's attempt to obtain fake visas. He didn't want Sierra hearing about that from someone else.

Quinn took a deep breath and, in the softest voice possible, explained to Sierra that her mom had made a big mistake.

Later that afternoon, Quinn ducked his head into his bedroom, a room he now referred to as "Sierra's room." Sierra was sitting on the bed, watching a movie on her computer.

"I'm going to the office for a few hours," Quinn said. "You gonna be okay?"

"I'm fine," Sierra said. Her voice carried less melancholy than it had earlier in the day.

"I'll be back in time for visiting hours for your mom."

"Okay."

"If you need anything to eat, help yourself."

Sierra looked at him and smiled thinly. "I'll be fine, Uncle Quinn. Don't worry about me."

"Okay."

But he did worry. He worried nonstop until he arrived at the office and Melanie started barking out instructions. She handed him pink phone messages and a stack of prioritized e-mails she had printed out. She followed him into the office and started discussing calendar issues before he could even sit in his chair. She said that she had personally talked to Catherine O'Rourke earlier that day when Catherine had called collect.

"You can't lead her on anymore, Quinn. If you're going to withdraw from the case, you need to let her know."

"Right."

Lastly, Melanie started running through the media requests. Quinn rejected them all, gun-shy after his interview on *The Early Show*. It wasn't about trying the case in the press anymore; it was about protecting Sierra's privacy. The best way to do that was not to comment.

"And," said Melanie, "Mr. Espinoza wants to see you."

Quinn rubbed a hand over his tired face. "Close the door," he said. "Have a seat."

Melanie closed the door and sat down in front of his desk. "Are you going to fire me?" she asked.

"Are you kidding?"

She shrugged. "You never do this. I figured it must be pretty important."

"It is." Quinn shifted in his seat and picked up a paper clip to keep his hands busy while he carefully selected his words. "I need to stay on Catherine O'Rourke's case. I've been thinking this weekend about how much she needs me. Her lead counsel is a good lawyer, but he doesn't know much about the insanity defense." He paused. He had never been one to bare his soul to anyone, much less his assistant.

"This is why I went to law school, Melanie. Not to represent these white-collar criminals but to help people like Catherine. Frankly, until Annie got in trouble, I had pretty much lost sight of that."

Melanie looked a little uncomfortable, and Quinn didn't blame her. This was certainly out of character for him.

"The firm told me that they didn't want me handling both Catherine's case and Annie's case because they didn't think I could carry my weight financially—"

"That's ridiculous," Melanie interjected. "You've been one of the highest—"

"Hang on," Quinn said. "Let me finish. They let me take Catherine O'Rourke's case when we all thought Annie was going to plead out. But now, with what happened to Sierra, Annie can't take that deal. And when the judge tried to set an early trial date for Annie, I used Catherine's case as an excuse to push Annie's trial back. Long story short, I locked myself into both."

"Good," Melanie said. "I never wanted to withdraw from Catherine O'Rourke's case in the first place."

"My question," Quinn continued, "is this: if the firm tries to force me to drop O'Rourke's case and I refuse, will you step out with me if I start my own firm?"

"They'd be idiots to make you do that," Melanie insisted. "But I'd be with you in a heartbeat."

"Even if I couldn't pay you the first few weeks?"

She thought about it, undoubtedly running budget numbers in her head. Quinn knew it was unfair to ask her to do this, but it would take him a few weeks just to get a line of credit established.

"Same salary and benefits as here?" Melanie asked.

"Sure."

"And a big bonus at the end of the year to make up for not getting a salary the first two weeks?"

"We can talk about a bonus."

"I'm in," said Melanie. "When do we start?"

Ten minutes later, Robert Espinoza closed the door and parked himself in the same chair that Melanie had occupied. His freshly pressed slacks nearly crinkled as he crossed his legs.

"I'm sorry to hear about Sierra," he said.

"Thanks. She'll be all right."

"Rumor has it that you told Judge Strackman you were committed to a trial date in Catherine O'Rourke's case."

"I did," Quinn said.

"I thought we had an understanding about that," Espinoza said.

"We did, but I changed my mind. I can't just cut and run on a client who's looking at the death penalty, not when her other lawyer is a novice on insanity pleas."

"And Annie no longer wants to plead out her case in light of what happened to Sierra?" Espinoza asked.

"That's correct. But, Robert, listen—"

"*Quinn,*" Espinoza said sharply, "I didn't come to argue. Is your mind made up about staying on the O'Rourke case?"

"Yes."

Espinoza stood and looked down at Quinn. He pursed his lips and hesitated for a moment, apparently measuring his words.

"Law partnerships, Quinn, are about more than just big bonus checks. Sometimes your partners need you. Sometimes you sacrifice for them knowing that one day, they'll do the same for you."

Espinoza took a deep breath, giving Quinn a chance to catch up. "You'd better win those cases, Quinn. Both of them. The firm's reputation is on the line."

"Does that mean—?"

"I said 'both of them,' Quinn. You're a smart enough lawyer to figure that out."

Espinoza turned and left the office, leaving a flabbergasted Quinn. Quinn's partners had come through for him. They would carry Quinn this year; some other year he would carry them.

Strangely, he felt like crying.

66

TWO NIGHTS LATER, after Quinn and Sierra visited Annie, Quinn felt the urge to hit the town. He loved Sierra, but being a surrogate father was smothering him. He needed a little space, a few hours in the city.

Sierra said she would be fine. "I'm thirteen, Uncle Quinn. A lot of my friends are babysitting."

Quinn left the condo and headed down the interior moving sidewalks of the complex, toward the MGM Grand. In truth, he wanted to go gamble and unwind from a stressful day. As a bonus, he could net a few thousand bucks if the fates were with him, which of course they hadn't been for about six months. But he knew an hour at the high-stakes table would turn into two and then three. If it went well, he could be there until midmorning, and if it went bad, he'd stay even longer trying to get back to where he started.

Instead, he decided to walk down the sidewalk of the Vegas strip, lost in a river of tourists and thrill seekers and young singles on the hunt—cameras flashing and skin showing and huge neon signs pulsating. Some people relaxed at the ocean or a mountain retreat; Quinn relaxed in the midst of a Vegas mob. The teeming electricity of the city would calm his nerves.

When he arrived at the front of the Grand, he shuffled along with the flow of foot traffic, lost in his thoughts and the overwhelming challenges facing him that seemed as relentless as the Vegas heat.

Catherine's case presented the most straightforward problem: how to win. She was, in all likelihood, the Avenger of Blood. At first, Quinn had had his doubts, but the theory recently pieced together by Rosemarie Mancini made sense.

Catherine's personality had probably fractured during her undergrad experience at William and Mary, creating the Avenger and lodging it in her subconscious. When it surfaced several years later, it carried with it the references to the blood avengers from Catherine's comparative religion class. Rosemarie believed that the Avenger personality became active when Catherine started following Annie Newberg's case—a sexually abused female seeking revenge against her husband and almost getting away with it. This was why, in Dr. Mancini's opinion, Catherine had been so intent on having Quinn defend her. In Catherine's subconscious, she viewed Quinn as the defender of the blood avengers—those female *furies* who exacted blood vengeance against abusers and rapists and their legal accomplices.

On the surface, Catherine seemed to be a paragon of sanity, a cynical young reporter who relied on logic, street smarts, and a raw beauty she didn't seem to know she possessed. Yet she must be tormented by a buried hurt so painful that, when it surfaced, it completely took over, thirsty for vengeance on real and imagined perpetrators. Quinn suspected that the rape described by Catherine was only one of many. Perhaps there were numerous incidents of rape or abuse—trauma so painful that Cat had repressed it from her own memory.

Quinn would need to get inside her head and win her trust. Somehow he would have to discover the hidden pain that even Rosemarie couldn't seem to access. In a way, the possibility intrigued him. Something about Catherine O'Rourke drew Quinn. Now that he had a green light to handle her case, he wanted to spend time with her, even if only inside the walls of a sterile prison interview room, trying to break down the barriers that separated her from others and even from herself.

Annie's case was more complex. Annie was his client, but Sierra kept forcing herself to the front of Quinn's mind. Quinn and Annie had been through so much, including childhood scars that could never heal. But for Sierra, there was still hope. The biggest challenge on that front was Claude Tanner, a father who had shirked all responsibilities until he smelled money. Quinn had already assigned Billy Long, his Virginia Beach investigator, to dig up dirt on Claude Tanner. Hopefully Billy would find something good.

As Quinn walked, an unsettled feeling interrupted his thoughts. Something was out of place; he felt as if he was being watched, a deer innocently passing beneath a hunter's tree stand. He glanced left and right, over his shoulder. There. Two men in sunglasses and ball caps, hands in their pockets. *How did I know they were there?*

He picked up his pace on the crowded sidewalk and squeezed past people. He turned to check again, and the men were still there, the same distance behind him as before, pushing their way through the crowds.

Just ahead, the sidewalk was under construction, forcing the foot traffic to squeeze into a long tunnel with a plywood ceiling and wooden rails on each side. The pedestrians slowed to a stop, but Quinn elbowed his way ahead, drawing complaints and return shoves. One more glance over the shoulder and he started running, pushing his way through as fast as possible.

He squeezed out of the crowd at the other end, getting hip-checked by a stocky man who had turned to see Quinn coming. Quinn lost his balance but recovered and broke into a full-out run. He glanced behind him again, and the thugs were still coming, zigzagging around people like two linebackers bearing down on a thin and vulnerable wide receiver.

The sidewalk widened as Quinn entered the heart of downtown Vegas. Bally's was on the right, Bellagio across the street. Directly ahead was an enormous escalator, jammed with people, that rose to an elevated walkway crossing Las Vegas Boulevard. If Quinn had any advantage on his two pursuers, it might be speed and endurance. They would overpower him in a second if they caught him, but . . .

Quinn veered right and headed straight toward the escalator, shouting for people to get out of the way as his legs churned upward two steps at a time, climbing as fast as he could. The two thugs jumped on half a minute later and started climbing as well, surprising Quinn with their stamina.

At the top, Quinn frantically glanced left and right, trying to map out an escape route. He sprinted across the sidewalk overpass toward the New York-New York casino. "Call the police!" he shouted. "Stop those guys behind me!"

Just before he reached the other side of the overpass, he saw some women pushing their baby strollers out of an elevator. A few elderly couples climbed on the elevator, and the doors started to close. Quinn sprinted faster, spurred on by a quick glance over his shoulder.

"Hold that elevator!" he yelled, but the senior citizens pretended not to notice. Just before the doors closed, Quinn lunged and stuck his hand between them. They popped open, and Quinn quickly darted through them.

He started frantically pushing the Door Close button. "C'mon, c'mon . . ."

The thugs were sprinting toward them, and the others on the elevator backed into the corners, their eyes wide.

The doors locked closed a split second before Quinn's pursuers arrived.

Quinn looked around the elevator, now headed down to the street level. "Paparazzi," he gasped, shaking his head. "They never leave me alone."

The door opened, and Quinn bolted out, knowing that his pursuers were probably sprinting furiously down the long and crowded escalator that would bring them to street level as well. He raced through the doors of the New York-New York casino, wound through the casino floor and up an escalator, then ducked into the Coyote Ugly club.

Once inside, he stumbled to a dark corner of the club and bent over, hands on his knees, trying to catch his breath.

Who were those guys? He assumed they'd been sent by Hofstetter. What surprised Quinn was their audacity. They had chased him down a crowded city sidewalk with half of Las Vegas watching them. *For what purpose?* If they really wanted to harm him, why not just accost him in some parking garage?

He thought about going to the police, but then he thought about Sierra. Quinn would have a hard enough time maintaining custody as it was. If he reported these men, Hofstetter would probably counter by reporting Quinn's illegal gambling exploits.

Quinn could probably beat those accusations, but he didn't need more legal complexities right now. He needed to maintain custody of Sierra.

Quinn caught his breath and then, glancing this way and that, worked his way up to the bar and ordered a drink. He took his drink back to a spot in the shadows next to a wall, watching as the undulating bodies crammed together on the dance floor. He finished the drink and checked around one more time.

On his way to the door, he felt somebody jam something that felt like a gun barrel into the small of his back.

"It's got a silencer," a man whispered. "I wouldn't recommend any sudden moves."

Another man approached from the opposite side and threw a meaty arm around Quinn as if he were an old buddy. "Let's go for a little walk," he said.

67

TOO LATE, Quinn connected the dots. Hofstetter's thugs had probably used their connections with the security personnel at The Rogue, Hofstetter's casino, to convince the security guards at New York-New York to quickly review the digital security tapes of Quinn entering the casino. Ubiquitous digital cameras recorded every inch of the casino floor. In a matter of minutes, the security guards would have traced Quinn into the Coyote Ugly club.

Quinn shuffled along, led by his two thick captors, the gun still buried in the small of his back. They walked Quinn outside, shoved him into the backseat of a waiting limo, and blindfolded him.

They rode silently together for about ten minutes. When the engine stopped, the men hauled Quinn out of the car and led him into a musty-smelling building. When they removed the blindfold, Quinn glanced around at what appeared to be an abandoned retail store with empty shelf space and dusty counters.

The bigger of the two men—a white guy with bulging biceps, tattooed arms, and a skintight black T-shirt—had the gun in plain sight now, pointed at Quinn's midsection. He still had on shades and a ball cap, but Quinn tried to cement the contours of the man's blocky face and square jaw into his own memory.

"Our client thinks you're being a little hardheaded, Mr. Newberg," the man said. "He could have sworn your sister was going to take the plea bargain today."

"Tell your client to kiss my—"

Umph! The other man sucker-punched Quinn in the kidney, buckling Quinn's legs as he crumpled to the ground. Quinn grimaced for a second as the pain subsided, then struggled slowly to his feet, more wary now and not quite as cocky.

"Don't make this hard on yourself," said the man with the gun. The

Hispanic man who had punched Quinn just smiled, white teeth lighting up a hard countenance.

They shoved Quinn toward a counter, where they pulled out a laptop computer and turned it on. They took the first few minutes to show the same video evidence of Quinn cheating at poker that Hofstetter had shown a few weeks ago in his office. Next, the men pulled up a document entitled "Quinn Newberg Gambling Winnings," asking Quinn if he recalled reporting those earnings to the IRS.

After that, they showed him a picture of Sierra.

The bigger man turned from the computer and got in Quinn's face. "If our client wanted you dead, Mr. Newberg, that would have happened by now. But he doesn't. All he wants is for two gentlemen to work out a deal. All he wants is for this case to go away without further embarrassment to his family. Is that so hard to understand?"

"I understand," said Quinn, choosing his words carefully. "But it's not that easy. This is Annie's call, not mine."

The man clenched his jaw and turned back to the computer. He clicked the mouse a few more times, and pictures of some scantily clothed women popped on the screen. *Young* women. Women Quinn had never seen before.

"These girls, Mr. Newberg, are prepared to testify that you had sex with them when they were underage. This one—" he stopped on the photo of a particularly young-looking girl—"will say she was fifteen years old at the time. Surely, Mr. Newberg, this might impact your upcoming custody battle. No?"

Like a second kidney punch, the implications become painfully clear. "Tell your boss I don't scare easy," Quinn said, his words sounding braver than he felt. "Tell him I'll do what's best for my client."

"Of course," the thug replied, his words dripping with mock sincerity. "We wouldn't dream of asking you to do anything else."

Without warning, the Hispanic man punched Quinn again, this time in the gut, the wind fleeing Quinn's lungs as he doubled over. Before he could even process the blow, the man had locked on Quinn's right arm, some kind of martial arts hold next to the armpit, wrenching the arm up and back with such violence that Quinn felt like his arm had been yanked from the socket. The rotator cuff in Quinn's shoulder shredded with a nearly audible tearing of the ligament.

Quinn screamed. The pain seared his vision, and the arm went limp. Hot stabs of pain radiated from his shoulder as if he had been impaled by the knives of an errant magician.

"We find," said the first man, "that constant pain can serve as an effective reminder."

Later that night, Quinn put on a brave face for Sierra, explaining that he had torn a muscle when he slipped on the steps and grabbed the railing. His obvious pain brought out the nurse in his niece. She fixed up an ice pack and tried to convince Quinn to go to the hospital. But Quinn was stubborn, and eventually Sierra retreated to her bedroom and went to sleep.

Quinn raided his medicine cabinet for some muscle relaxers and painkillers. But every time he dozed off, the arm would fall into an uncomfortable position, and the pain would jerk him awake. At 6:00 a.m., Quinn left Sierra a note and headed to the emergency room.

68

AFTER AN HOUR in the emergency room and an MRI, Quinn learned that he had indeed torn his rotator cuff. A deep tear, in the words of the pessimistic little orthopedic surgeon, a man who made it clear he didn't particularly care for lawyers.

"Will it require surgery?" Quinn asked.

"With rotator cuffs, I don't tell the patient when it's time for surgery. The patient tells me. When you can't sleep at night or live with the pain during the day, it's time." The doctor latched on to Quinn's elbow and twisted the arm around a little, eliciting a yelp.

"Do you do that for non-lawyers too?" Quinn asked.

"Rotator cuff surgery is one of the most painful surgeries imaginable," the doctor said, not bothering to smile. "The recovery period can be up to two months. If you think *I* like pain, you should meet the rehab specialists."

Quinn left the hospital with his arm in a sling and a new prescription for painkillers in his pocket. Catherine O'Rourke's case was only two months away. Massive amounts of pretrial work awaited. Quinn didn't have time for surgery. He barely had time for the bathroom.

On the way back to the condo, Quinn considered his options. One part of him wanted to just walk into Carla Duncan's office and launch a preemptive strike against his tormentors. He could tell her about last night's assault and file charges. With any luck, Carla could tie the whole thing back to Richard Hofstetter Sr.

But the fallout would damage Quinn as well. There would be allegations of sex with underage girls, illegal gambling, and tax evasion. Plus, members of gangs and organized crime rings would know that Quinn had cheated them at the high-stakes table.

Quinn's legal problems might impact his ability to maintain custody of Sierra against a challenge by Claude Tanner. The last thing Sierra needed right now was to be put in the custody of a person she didn't even know.

But even if Quinn could keep custody, he worried about Sierra's safety. The men last night had shown Quinn her picture as a not-so-subtle hint. They knew Quinn's Achilles' heel—he would do anything to protect his niece.

Quinn would have to handle this one without going to the police. The first step would be to neutralize the threat of Claude Tanner winning custody of Sierra. For that, Quinn had a plan. It was so high risk that the very thought of it made his palms sweat even now.

It would take a few days to put the plan together. Perhaps in forty-eight hours his luck would begin to change.

69

SIERRA SHOCKED QUINN that night by announcing that she wanted to go to the movies with some friends. Quinn saw this as a hopeful sign that Sierra was on the road back to normalcy. Teenagers so often leaned on friends.

Still, it made him nervous. "What do you want to see?"

"Young Love," she said. It sounded suspicious to Quinn, and Sierra must have read the look on his face. "It's kind of like a modern *Romeo and Juliet,"* she added.

"What time does it start?"

"We were thinking about going to the one at 9:05."

"Whom are you going with?" *Man, I sound like a dad.*

"Some friends."

"'Friends' as in girls or 'friends' as in boys?"

Sierra grunted her disapproval, as if all the boys her age were below her standards. It made Quinn smile inside.

"Ashley and Jennifer," she said.

After a thorough cross-examination, Quinn agreed to let Sierra go. He had his reservations about it, especially with Hofstetter's goons prowling about, but he couldn't tell Sierra no. He was starting to understand why dads spoiled their daughters.

In Quinn's opinion, Sierra's cotton stretch top was entirely too tight, hugging her bony torso. He kept that opinion to himself but couldn't shake the feeling that he suddenly felt about ten years older than he had a week ago. *What was it with young girls and the way they dressed today, anyway?* Unfortunately, Quinn knew all too well what went through the minds of junior high boys.

He drove Sierra to the theater where she was supposed to meet her friends. He dropped her off, circled around the parking lot once, and found a spot in a distant corner. He waited at least fifteen minutes, pulled on a baseball cap, and headed inside. He wasn't being paranoid, he told himself.

Hofstetter's thugs were real, and he had a constant source of pain in his right shoulder to prove it.

Quinn bought a ticket to *Young Love*, a bucket of popcorn, and a Coke. He waited until he was sure the previews had finished before he entered the theater. He slumped into an open seat next to the wall in the second-to-last row and started scouring the room for Sierra and her friends. He spotted them on the other side of the theater, two-thirds of the way down, and he was pleased to see that no boys had joined them.

Quinn pulled the cap down and slouched a little lower, trying to make his shoulder comfortable. The movie was full of banal jokes, clichés, and good-looking teens who couldn't act—at least for the first five minutes, which was exactly how long it took Quinn to doze off into a fitful but oblivious sleep.

"Uncle Quinn. Uncle Quinn."

Somebody shook him, and pain sliced through his shoulder like a knife penetrating to the bone. Quinn shrugged himself awake, groaned, and grabbed his arm.

"I'm sorry," the young voice said. "Are you okay?"

Quinn shook off the grogginess and blinked. Sierra and her two friends were standing in the row just in front of Quinn, looking at him. Other patrons were leaving the theater.

"What are you doing here?" asked Sierra. She looked betrayed, and Quinn couldn't blame her.

He leaned his head back, stretched, and closed his eyes. "Seeing if you need a ride home?"

"I told you we would call," Sierra insisted.

"Yeah," said Quinn. "I know."

On the way back to the condo, Quinn and Sierra listened to the radio, neither speaking. At the Towers, Quinn handed the keys to the valet and walked into the building with Sierra, where the two of them silently rode the elevator to the forty-second floor. Once they entered Quinn's condo unit, he started with the apologies.

"I'm sorry, Sierra. I didn't mean to embarrass you."

"It's okay," she said, but Quinn knew it wasn't. Unlike her mom, Sierra never addressed things head-on. She internalized and brooded until it all came frothing to the surface in some emotional meltdown.

"Sit down," Quinn said, motioning to the kitchen table. "I need to tell you some things."

For the next fifteen minutes, he told Sierra about his encounter with Hofstetter's men from the night before. He left out the accusations about underage sex and the fact that they showed him Sierra's picture, but he told her everything else. As he talked, Sierra took it all in, displaying no emotion.

"I don't want to live with my dad," Sierra said after Quinn finished. She was a smart kid, cutting right to the core issue that Quinn had left unspoken. "If he even is my dad."

Seeing the fear in her eyes, Quinn wondered if he had done the right thing in telling her. He had always promised himself that if he ever had kids, he would always tell them the truth. Maybe it wasn't that easy. It didn't take a genius to know what Sierra was thinking. Her stepdad had tried to abuse her. She would be petrified at the thought of living with a different grown man she didn't even know.

"I'm not going to let that happen," Quinn said. He reached out and put his hand on her forearm. "I've got a plan."

Sierra stared down at the table and tried to hold back the tears welling in her eyes.

"You've got to trust me," Quinn said. "Together, we'll get through this. This time, we'll win the case. It's all going to work out."

Later that night, as Quinn slept on the couch, the loud and insistent ringing of the phone jerked him awake. Pain shot through his right shoulder, and he grimaced, trying to collect his thoughts.

He found the phone. "Hello."

"This is Jimmy from the front desk," said a familiar voice.

Quinn's groggy brain pieced it together. Jimmy, the night security guard.

"I've got somebody here who belongs to you," Jimmy said.

Quinn tensed and glanced around the apartment. His niece's bedroom door was closed. "Sierra?" he asked.

"Yes, sir."

Suddenly Quinn was fully awake. "Don't let her go anywhere," he said. "I'll be right down."

Quinn had fallen asleep in a pair of shorts and a T-shirt. He put on his sandals and headed toward the door. The note on the kitchen table stopped him midstride.

> Dear Uncle Quinn,
> Thanks for everything you've done. Don't worry about me cause I'll be fine. I just think I might need to take off for a little while. It will be better for both of us. I'll come back after the trial when all this stuff is over. Pleeeeease, take care of yourself! I love you and miss you!!!
> Sierra

Quinn felt a lump in his throat as he headed down to collect Sierra. *What was she thinking?*

When he arrived in the lobby, Sierra had a worried look on her face, like a kid waiting in the principal's office for her parents to arrive. Quinn thanked Jimmy and led his niece back to the elevator.

Quinn used the elevator ride to tell Sierra that this was no way to handle their problems. "You can't just run away," he scolded. "Where would you even go?"

When she started to cry, Quinn backed off. He told her that he loved her and that they needed to stick together. She walked down the hallway to the condo without looking at him.

"I just didn't want to cause you any trouble," she said, waiting for Quinn to unlock the door.

Sierra kept things under control until she and Quinn sat down together on the couch. Without warning, she came unraveled. She sobbed uncontrollably and apologized over and over.

Quinn didn't know what else to do, so he just held her with his good arm, let her cry, and tried to reassure her. "We can get through this together," he said. "But not if you try running away every time I turn my head."

She cried for a few minutes, then pulled back and seemed to regain her composure. "You were snoring in that movie theater," she said.

"I was not."

"You were, Uncle Quinn; I swear. More like a snort. Kinda like this . . ." Sierra made a sound through her nose that made them both laugh.

"I don't snore," said Quinn.

"That is so untrue. I could barely hear the movie."

They argued good-naturedly for a few minutes, and then Quinn suggested they talk in the morning. He had a plan and would tell her all about it then. Running away was not part of it.

She forced another smile and promised to be there when he woke up. Just to be sure, after Sierra closed the door to the bedroom, Quinn pulled a few couch cushions, blankets, and pillows over to the front door and made his bed at the threshold.

Life with a thirteen-year-old was turning out to be very interesting.

70

ON FRIDAY MORNING, Quinn's investigator called with a missing piece of the puzzle.

"Who put the list of assets together for Richard Hofstetter's estate?" Billy Long asked.

"Annie did. She was appointed as the executrix."

"That's what I thought," growled Billy. "Did you know the list contains a slight oversight?"

"I'm listening," said Quinn.

"Your sister might not have known about this, but Hofstetter Jr. had a 15 percent limited partnership interest in the Oasis, a ratty casino about a mile south of the strip. He held the interest under the name of a Delaware corporation—Oasis Holdings—and Hofstetter Jr. was the only stockholder. Guess who recently made an offer for the Oasis?"

"You're the investigator."

"Yeah," complained Billy, "but you're the big-shot Vegas lawyer. You should know these things." He paused so that Quinn could appreciate Billy's brilliance. "Some of Daddy Hofstetter's business partners, that's who. The word on the street is that this property is the final piece of an assemblage of land that would allow for the next big Vegas casino, the granddaddy of them all."

Quinn was taking notes. So far, it still didn't add up. Hofstetter Jr.'s interest in the Oasis would pass to either Annie, if she was found innocent, or Sierra, if Annie was disqualified from inheriting her husband's estate by virtue of a guilty verdict. How could Hofstetter Sr. benefit from this?

"So here's what makes it interesting," said Billy, anticipating Quinn's next question. "Some of the other partners in the Oasis are tied in with nearby casino owners on the south side of the city who don't want the competition. Hofstetter Jr.'s shares might be the deciding votes."

Quinn put down his pen. No more diagrams were necessary. Sierra was only thirteen. If her stepfather's limited partnership interest fell to her rather than Annie, voting rights would be determined by Sierra's guardian. And if Claude Tanner gained custody of Sierra, he would also obtain those voting rights.

"You think Daddy Hofstetter found Claude Tanner and cut a deal with him?" Quinn asked.

"Nah," Billy said. "I think Claude Tanner just had a sudden and irresistible urge to spend time with a daughter he hadn't bothered to see in thirteen years."

Quinn had finally found his match in the sarcasm department. "Can we prove any of this?" he asked.

"The limited partnership interest and Delaware Corporation are matters of record. The rest is just street talk. When somebody does an assemblage deal like this, they use a lot of shell corporations and offshore holding companies that hide the ownership."

"I'll pay whatever it takes," Quinn said. "Just get me proof."

"Legally?" Billy asked.

"This is my family, Billy. Whatever it takes."

"I'll do my best, Mr. Newberg. But these guys don't like outsiders poking around in their business."

Quinn's own rotator cuff could have told him that.

"One last question," Quinn said. "Is there a time frame when this vote might occur?"

"It's probably not a short-term thing," Billy responded. "My guess is that Tanner wants to get permanent legal custody and then wait a few months before he exercises his right as custodian of the limited partnership interest."

So he doesn't need custody of Sierra right away, thought Quinn. When he hung up with Billy, he started making a few adjustments to his plan.

Five minutes later, Melanie barged into his office, her face reflecting the bad news. "You might want to turn on the TV," she said. Quinn kept one on his credenza but rarely used it. "They're saying the DNA for Sierra's father is a match."

Though Quinn had suspected this would be the case, he still felt the blow. "Set up a meeting with Mr. Tanner and his lawyer," Quinn said. "This afternoon, if possible."

Quinn took a seat in a high-backed swivel chair across the table from Claude Tanner and his famous Vegas divorce attorney, Kyle Richardson. Quinn studied Tanner's narrow face for glimpses of Sierra but could find none. Sierra's father quietly regarded Quinn with narrow and wary eyes, letting his attorney do most of the talking. Kyle Richardson had thinning blond hair, a massive ring, and skin cooked medium well by the local tanning booths. When celebrities needed a Vegas divorce attorney, Richardson was generally their first call.

Quinn let Richardson ramble for a few minutes about the results of the DNA tests and his client's stellar chances for obtaining custody of Sierra. "He's not in this for the money or the publicity," Richardson declared. "He just wants what's best for Sierra."

Quinn wanted to throw up.

"If that's what he really wants," Quinn said, his voice even, "he should have stayed away."

The comment drew little reaction from Tanner, just a slight narrowing of the eyes and another layer of animosity added to the hardened stare. He let his lawyer respond for him.

"If your client could have avoided killing someone, Mr. Tanner would have been pleased to stay away."

Quinn swallowed a comeback; arguing would help no one. "I think we should work this out. One thing is certain: a court battle will not help Sierra."

Richardson shrugged. "I'm listening."

"If Annie is acquitted, the court will probably award her permanent custody. After all, she's Sierra's mother and took care of the girl from birth." He waited for a reaction, but Richardson and Tanner both acted noncommittal. *At least they didn't disagree.* "If she's convicted, I think I'll have a fair shot at getting custody myself."

Richardson started to object, but Quinn cut him off with a raised palm. "Let me finish."

Quinn turned to Tanner. Though he couldn't say it this bluntly, he knew the man wasn't interested in temporary custody for the sake of Sierra. Tanner was only interested in legal custody for the sake of voting rights. Quinn's offer would be a calculated bet that Tanner would trade the possibility of temporary custody now in order to increase his chances of getting permanent legal custody, including voting rights, later.

"As things stand right now, if I lose Annie's case, I'll fight you for custody," Quinn said. "Sierra is thirteen. The court will put a lot of weight behind her wishes. She wants to live with me. Plus, courts don't like fathers who take off when their kids are born and pop back into their lives at times of . . ." Quinn hesitated. "Shall we say . . . 'opportunity'? You might get some kind of visitation rights, but I'm prepared to fight for custody."

"Your analysis has so many holes I don't know where to start," Richardson interjected.

"I'm sure," Quinn said. "But here's the bottom line: I'm prepared to waive all that. I'm prepared to sign a deal today, right now, that says I won't contest custody *if* Annie loses. But there is one condition."

He had their attention. Even Richardson didn't interrupt.

"Sierra can't handle a temporary custody battle right now. She needs stability. She needs a familiar environment. She's too emotionally distraught to be forced into a reconciliation arrangement with a father she doesn't even know." Quinn leaned forward and felt his throat tightening. There was so much at stake. "If Annie and I lose the case, even if the jury enters a compromise verdict of guilty but mentally ill, you get sole custody of Sierra. No court battles. No contest of any sort. Just a reasonable visitation schedule for me. In exchange for that promise, you agree not to file for custody or visitation rights until Annie's court case is resolved. And if Annie wins, *she* gets permanent custody, and *you* get reasonable visitation.

"In the meantime, I'll put Sierra in a stable situation where she can get counseling and recover from some of the psychological blows she's been suffering. If you care about your daughter, you'll give her a chance to get back on her feet."

For a few long seconds, nobody spoke. Quinn's heart rate spiked but he tried to seem calm, as if he held all the cards.

"Give me a minute to talk to my client," Richardson said.

Ninety minutes later, Quinn signed the documents and promised to get Annie's signature later that night. He thanked the two men and hustled out of the building before they could change their minds.

The weight of the case now threatened to crush him. Quinn was a trial lawyer, accustomed to pressure and high-risk litigation decisions. But nothing in his past had prepared him for a case this personal, with stakes this high. If he won, he could save the lives of Annie *and* Sierra, the two women he cared about most.

And if he lost, he might destroy them both.

Only time would tell whether this was a brilliant litigation strategy or legal suicide.

71

THE NEXT DAY, Quinn received Dr. Mancini's written psychiatric evaluation of Catherine O'Rourke. They would, of course, only use it if Catherine could be convinced to plead insanity. The first part of the report was loaded with qualifiers—"This report assumes, without independent investigation, the integrity and credibility of the forensic evidence linking Ms. O'Rourke to the various crimes attributed to the Avenger of Blood." But the main part of the report was vintage Mancini, providing insights that had never occurred to Quinn—or anyone else for that matter.

Later that day, Melanie set up a conference call for Quinn, Rosemarie, and Marc Boland so that the expert could explain her findings.

"There are three factors that allow me to support a diagnosis of dissociative identity disorder," she said confidently. "First is the type of rape that Catherine experienced at William and Mary. It was a former boyfriend, compounding the emotional devastation of rape with the betrayal of trust. Also, it occurred while she was drugged, meaning that she endured this humiliation primarily at a subconscious level, wounding her psyche in a way that her conscious mind never totally comprehended.

"Second, as I detail in the report, the identity for the Avenger of Blood seems to come from an undergrad comparative religions course Catherine was taking at the time of the rape. Alter personalities often exhibit traits consistent with the environment that existed when the personality was first created, even if the alter personality does not manifest itself until years later. It's almost like a snapshot frozen in time. This is one of the ways we distinguish between patients who fake an alter personality and patients who are genuinely psychotic. Catherine, of course, would have no way of knowing this."

Rosemarie paused for a moment. "Are you guys still there?" she asked.

"Just taking notes, professor," Quinn said.

"Good stuff," Marc Boland echoed.

"The third thing," said Rosemarie, "is that I think I've discovered the triggering event. I spent a couple of days digesting reams of newspaper articles written by Catherine. She's an excellent reporter. Her writing is clear, fair, objective, sometimes even detached. But the tone of her writing on Annie's case was very different.

"From the beginning, she seemed more of a cheerleader than a reporter. Plus, it seemed to me that she almost obsessed over it. Her writing was much more emotional than the other articles. Quinn, I think this alter personality saw what Annie did and absorbed your strong defense of your sister, even before that case went to trial. In some ways, I think it gave this personality permission to seek its own revenge, mirroring what Annie did. Perhaps coincidentally, perhaps not, the blood avengers that Catherine learned about in college were the three female furies of Greek mythology, acting as blood-thirsty prosecutors for crimes against innocent victims. In a way, Catherine felt a sense of bonding with Annie—they're both female furies for the twenty-first century."

It made sense, Quinn thought, scribbling furiously. He was already thinking about ways to dramatically illustrate this at trial. The jury would eat it up—Greek mythology, handwriting on the wall, a tortured subconscious. Freud couldn't have written a better script.

"Once I started putting this together, I was curious about how Quinn came to be involved in the case," Rosemarie said. "Marc explained that it was Catherine's idea to hire him and that Catherine had been pretty adamant about it. This fits my theory, Quinn. Subconsciously, Catherine's alter ego wanted Annie's defender to take her case too."

Rosemarie paused again. "There's more, but most of it is in my report. Do you two gentlemen have any questions?"

Quinn loved the report and remained quiet. Not surprisingly, Marc Boland jumped in.

"I do have one question," he said. "How do we convince Catherine that pleading insanity is her best hope?"

"I think that job is best left to her white knight," said Rosemarie.

Quinn didn't argue. In fact, he rather liked the analogy.

72

AIRPLANE FLIGHTS HAD LONG AGO lost any novelty for Quinn, but as he and Sierra left Vegas for Virginia Beach, his niece had her face plastered against the window. She had a perfect view of the Vegas skyline, the El Dorado range, and Lake Mead as the plane climbed to cruising altitude. The flight was not crowded, so Quinn took an aisle seat, leaving the seat between him and Sierra empty.

When the Fasten Seatbelt light went off, Sierra broke out her iPod and moved into the center seat, closer to Quinn. Before long, the gangly teenager had curled into an awkward sleeping position, propping her pillow against Quinn's shoulder. Though it hurt the injured shoulder, he didn't move until Sierra fell asleep. Then he leaned over and kissed her on the forehead. It was amazing how much his niece had already changed him.

Quinn's thoughts turned to Annie and her stoic good-bye with Sierra last night. Though being separated from Sierra tore at Annie's heart, she had put on a brave face and tried valiantly not to show her emotions.

Overall, Annie seemed to be weathering jail pretty well. She was a survivor. Plus, Quinn had called in some favors to get Annie her own cell in a minimum-security wing of the Vegas jail, with work responsibilities as a jail trustee. Doing time was never easy, but Annie's situation was certainly better than Catherine's.

Quinn and Sierra landed at the Norfolk airport, dropped their stuff at the Hilton Garden Inn in the Virginia Beach Town Center, and headed straight for the jail. On the way, they stopped at a Borders so Sierra would have something to read while Quinn met with Catherine.

Quinn's goal for today's meeting was not an easy one—convince Catherine to plead insanity. Marc Boland had broached the subject initially, and Catherine had resisted. If Quinn couldn't convince her, the attorneys had agreed they would petition the court to allow them to plead insanity over the objections of the client. It would be much easier if Catherine just agreed.

Quinn left Sierra reading in the visitors' area near the front desk of the jail and proceeded through the metal detector and two thick, remote-controlled doors that separated the jail proper from the lobby area. Going through the doors always gave Quinn a sinking feeling; the claustrophobic block walls of the narrow hallways had a way of sucking hope out of a person. Jail was no place for someone like Catherine O'Rourke. She needed help, not punishment.

Quinn took his seat in the phone-booth-size cubicle that served as the attorney interview room. Within minutes, Catherine arrived on the other side of the thick glass.

It had been only two weeks since Quinn had seen her, but the change was unmistakable. She still had the haunting beauty that had seared itself into Quinn's memory—the dark eyes and sculpted face—and her spiked hair actually looked stylish, the sort of look a movie star might sport a few weeks after shaving her head for an important role. But Catherine's eyes seemed less full of life than Quinn remembered, and her entire face had the contour of unshakable sadness—a downward sloping of the mouth and eyes that made no secret of her depression. Quinn expected her to look hardened. Instead, he saw melancholy.

She thanked him for coming, and he asked her a few questions about life behind bars. She answered politely and then had a question of her own. "How's Sierra?"

The question reminded Quinn that his family drama had played itself out on the world television stage and that inmates watch a lot of television.

"Doing better," Quinn said. "I actually brought her with me."

"Here?" Catherine asked. "To the jail?"

"Yeah. She's out in the visitors' area."

A small spark flickered briefly in Catherine's eyes. "You think I could talk with her tonight during visiting hours? I know a little about what she's going through. Maybe I could encourage her."

Quinn and Sierra had no specific plans that night. "I don't see why not," Quinn said, though the request took him a little off guard. Before receiving Rosemarie's report, Quinn had worked hard to separate these two cases—Annie's and Catherine's—filing them away in different emotional compartments. For some reason, it seemed a little dangerous to blur the lines.

"Thanks," said Catherine. "Visiting hours start at seven."

Quinn nodded. "For now, I want to talk about a possible insanity plea," he said. "I know that Marc has already broached this with you."

Catherine nodded and Quinn noticed her stiffen a little, reminding him that his client had a mind of her own.

He leaned forward. "I know you don't like the implications of an insanity plea, but my job is not to make you like me." Quinn paused, realizing that he cared very much whether this particular client liked him. He might even care a little too much. "My job is to keep you alive and get you out of here. My job is to keep a needle out of your arm."

"Do you believe I did these things?" Catherine asked. Her voice was flat but still conveyed resolve. "Do you think I kidnapped and killed those babies? Do you think I electrocuted Paul Donaldson—fried him to death and dumped his body into the Dismal Swamp Canal? Do you think that's me?"

"It doesn't matter what I think—"

"It matters to *me*," Catherine said.

Quinn swallowed and stayed fixed on her gaze. "I don't know whether you did or not." It was gut-level honest, and he knew Catherine could sense his sincerity. "I only know that right now, we don't stand a chance of convincing a jury that you're flat-out innocent."

"But I *am* innocent," Catherine said. "I need you to believe that. I know it doesn't seem that way. Sometimes I doubt it myself. But, Quinn, I could never hurt those kids. Not this Catherine. And not some other side of me either."

Quinn nodded. "I believe that," he said softly. In truth, he didn't know what to believe. Emotionally, Catherine made a compelling case. If he could just let her talk to the jury like this, the way she was talking to him right now, as if she wanted to reach out and grab his shoulders and make him look straight into her soul, a jury might believe her. But court didn't work that way. The path to justice was littered with the land mines of cross-examination. Emotion would yield to evidence and logic. And logic would always dictate the same unwanted result.

"That doesn't change my advice," said Quinn. "As a friend, I believe you. But as a lawyer, I've got to give you my best *professional* advice. That advice is to plead not guilty by reason of insanity."

"I didn't do it," Catherine insisted. "How can I say that I did?"

An idea hit Quinn. "State your name for the record," he said.

"What?"

"I'm going to show you. We can't possibly win this case on a straight-up not guilty plea if we don't put you on the stand. So you're on the stand, and I'm Boyd Gates. State your name for the record."

A look of determination hardened Catherine's face. "Catherine O'Rourke," she said, squaring her jaw.

73

"DO YOU CONSIDER YOURSELF A MEDIUM, MS. O'ROURKE?"

"No. Not really."

"And yet you just happened to know information about the crimes committed by the Avenger of Blood—information that the police had not released to anyone?"

"I had visions," Catherine said. "I saw the crimes happen in my visions."

"Visions," Quinn repeated, just like a skeptical prosecutor would.

Catherine frowned, as if she hadn't expected him to play the part so enthusiastically.

"Did you happen to see the face of the Avenger in these visions?"

"No. His face was obscured."

"*His* face. So you could tell the Avenger was a male?"

"Actually, no. I couldn't see the face at all."

"How tall was the Avenger?"

"I don't know—average height?"

"What distinguishing features did the Avenger have?"

"I don't know, Mr. Newberg. These were visions, not police sketches."

"But they provided enough detail for you to know, for example, that Paul Donaldson had a gash on his head?"

"Yes, but that was different."

"You saw him bleeding from that gash on his head; isn't that correct?"

"Yes," Catherine admitted reluctantly, "but I didn't know it was Paul Donaldson. I'd never even met the man."

"Yet somehow," Quinn said, leaning forward, "Donaldson's blood and your saliva ended up on the same paper towel in a trash can at your neighbor's house?"

"I never met the man," Catherine insisted.

BY REASON of INSANITY

"How do you explain the paper towels that the police found in the neighbor's trash containing his blood and your saliva?"

"Somebody set me up," Catherine said, sounding defensive.

"How do you explain the methohexital found in your neighbor's trash—another setup?"

"Yes."

"But if somebody decided to frame you, why would they plant incriminating evidence in a *neighbor's* trash can, where the police might not even find it, as opposed to your own trash can?"

Catherine didn't blink. "Maybe someone on the investigative team did it."

"And planted a strand of your hair on the seal of an envelope sent by the Avenger as well?"

"I don't know."

"Accusing the police of framing you for murder is a very serious thing, Ms. O'Rourke." Quinn sharpened his tone. "Do you have one shred of evidence to suggest that anybody on the Virginia Beach police force holds a grudge against you and would want to cover up the crimes of a serial murderer by framing *you*?"

"No."

"Then what could possibly be the motive for setting you up?"

"I don't know."

"Speaking of motive, Ms. O'Rourke, are you aware that Mr. Donaldson was accused of rape but was found innocent?"

"Yes."

"And the other victims of the Avenger were either accused rapists, attorneys who represented accused rapists, or the children of such persons?"

"I'm sorry," Catherine said, her tone weary. "I don't understand the question."

"Fair enough. I'll withdraw it. But let me ask you this—have you ever been raped?"

The question seemed to shrink Catherine, her self-esteem wilting before Quinn's eyes. "Yes," she said softly.

"What was the man's name?"

"Kenny Towns. I knew him in college."

"Was he a former boyfriend?"

"Yes."

"Were there others involved as well?"

"Possibly."

Quinn lowered his voice to match Catherine's tone. "What exactly did he do to you? How did it happen?"

The examination was staged, but the pain on Catherine's face was real. She looked down, her voice growing even quieter. "I don't want to say, Quinn. I get your point."

Quinn thought for a moment about stopping, but there would be no calling time-out on the witness stand. Catherine had to understand how hard a prosecutor would push. "Is it fair to say the pain is still very real, Ms. O'Rourke?"

Catherine sighed, then apparently decided to keep playing along. "Rape never goes away, Mr. Newberg."

"Was Mr. Towns ever convicted? Was he ever even prosecuted?"

"No. I never reported it to the police."

"Do you hate him, Ms. O'Rourke? Do you hate Kenny Towns?"

Catherine lifted her eyes and drilled them into Quinn. "Yes, I despise him."

"You hate him because he's a rapist. Because he violated you and because nobody ever held him to account—isn't that true, Ms. O'Rourke?"

Catherine answered with a stare. The pretend world of cross-examination had burned away in the smoldering anger of unresolved hurt. "I said I don't want to do this anymore."

"This is not a game, Ms. O'Rourke," Quinn responded. "Answer the question."

"It's not a game for me either, *Quinn*," Catherine said. She stood, nearly knocking her chair over backward. "*Rape* is not a game." Catherine's face was flushed in anger, her eyes piercing Quinn through the glass. "He violated me, Quinn. He drugged me and forced himself on me and then probably went out and rounded up his friends so they could have a turn. He *bragged* about it. He made me the laughingstock of the fraternity."

Her body sagged. "I know you're just trying to make a point, but I'm sick of this whole thing. Sick of sitting behind bars while Kenny Towns is out there living as if nothing happened."

She turned away from Quinn and retreated to the door behind her chair. She knocked on the door and waited for the guard.

"Catherine, sit down," Quinn said. "I'm sorry. I just wanted you to see what you're up against."

"You made your point," Catherine said. "I've got to think about it."

The guard came and ushered Catherine out, leaving Quinn alone in the small booth, staring at the empty chair of his troubled client.

"That went well," Quinn said.

74

QUINN AND SIERRA were less than ten minutes away from the jail when a collect call came on his cell phone. The jail number. Catherine O'Rourke was going to be a high-maintenance client.

"I'm sorry," she said. "I know you're just trying to help."

She sounded better, so Quinn decided to keep it light. "I'm used to it. I represent crazy people, remember?"

"I should fit right in."

Quinn let the comment pass.

"Are you still going to bring Sierra back tonight?" Catherine asked. "I promise not to flip out on her."

At this point, Quinn wasn't so sure that tonight's visit would be a good idea. But he also felt a little guilty for what he had just put Catherine through. Maybe Sierra could help mend that rapport.

"We'll be there," he said.

That evening, Quinn registered Sierra at the front desk of the jail and took her into the visitors' room. The room looked like a dingy call center for an infomercial company—it had dozens of small kiosks in three long rows. Each kiosk had a phone and a computer screen, and tonight most of the spaces were full.

Sierra sat down at the designated kiosk and picked up the phone. Quinn stood behind her. They stared at the image of a small booth in the bowels of the jail for a few minutes until Catherine entered the booth and picked up the phone.

Catherine introduced herself and asked Sierra a few polite questions. Catherine still looked haggard to Quinn with blotchy skin and red eyes, but she was more upbeat than she had been earlier that day. She was trying hard to win Sierra's confidence.

She leaned toward the screen and kept her eyes locked on Quinn's niece. "I was at your mom's trial, Sierra. A lot of us who watched think your mom's a hero. What she did wasn't wrong. She was trying to protect you, and that's a mother's most important job."

Sierra nodded, and Quinn inched a little closer; it was difficult to hear because Sierra had the phone pressed against her ear. Quinn felt a growing queasiness from this conversation. How much of this was Catherine just trying to encourage a confused young teenager, and how much of it was the Avenger? Did Catherine's alter ego envision herself and Annie as fellow blood avengers—the furies of Greek mythology exacting vengeance on modern-day America?

"Some of the jurors voted against your mom because they felt like they had no choice—they had to follow the law. But there's a difference between law and justice. Do you understand that?"

Again, Sierra gave Catherine a small nod of the head. She seemed intensely interested in Catherine's take on the matter.

"Just because something's legal doesn't make it right. And just because something's illegal doesn't always make it wrong."

Catherine lowered her voice, making it even harder for Quinn to hear. He studied her lips as she talked, filling in the words he couldn't hear.

"I was raped in college, Sierra. Did your uncle tell you that?"

"No," Sierra murmured.

"To make it worse, the guy who raped me used to be my boyfriend. A guy I trusted."

Catherine hesitated, and Quinn could see the pain on her face.

"For a while, Sierra, I couldn't trust any men. But I eventually learned that not all men are the same. There are some really good men in this world . . . and your uncle's one of them."

"I know," said Sierra.

"I guess what I'm saying is that your stepdad was an awful man, Sierra. And I know he did some awful things. But don't let him keep hurting you now by making you hate other people. I'm not asking you to forgive him, because honestly, I don't think I'll ever forgive the man who raped me. But you can't let your stepfather control your life by making you hate other people. That was my mistake for too many years." Catherine paused, swallowing hard. "Does that make any sense, Sierra?"

"I think so."

"Good," Catherine said, speaking a little louder and more confidently. "Some people think I'm some kind of medium because I have these visions. Well . . . that's pretty ridiculous if you know me. But I am a good judge of character. I see strength in your eyes and a great deal of love for your mom. She needs you to be strong now; do you know that?"

Sierra nodded, keeping her eyes on the screen.

"Your Uncle Quinn's going to win that case, Sierra, and your mom is doing better in jail than I am. She's a lot stronger. A lot more together. But she's counting on you to do your part and be strong too. Can you do that?"

Sierra shrugged. "I guess so."

The response seemed noncommittal, but Quinn sensed a whole lot more going on. He could almost see willpower flowing from Catherine to Sierra, from one victim to another. While listening to Catherine talk so convincingly about forgiveness and strength of character, it was hard to continue thinking of her as a deranged psychotic. At the start of the conversation, she had seemed to fit the mold. But now, she just looked like a wounded victim. Maybe that was the whole point—two personalities in one body.

"I'm sorry I sound so dramatic," Catherine said. "Next time, we can just talk about *American Idol* or something. I get to watch a lot of TV in here."

"I hope my uncle wins your case," Sierra said.

"I'm sure he will," Catherine said, stealing a quick glance at Quinn. "If he can keep his client under control."

75

IN THE MORNING, Quinn and Sierra checked out of the Hilton and drove around for about ten minutes to make sure they weren't being followed. Eventually they headed into downtown Norfolk, parked the car, and walked over to the Waterside complex, a collection of shops and restaurants bordering the Elizabeth River.

They walked through the Waterside, taking in the odor of french fries and Mongolian barbeque and New York style pizza. They continued out the back door of the complex, found a spot on a concrete bench, and watched the seagulls bother a mom and a few toddlers who were trying to eat ice cream. Sierra laughed, and Quinn thought about how much he would miss her.

A few minutes later, Rosemarie Mancini showed up, looking stylish in jeans, a pullover, sandals, and sunglasses.

Quinn bent over to hug Rosemarie, then watched as Sierra and Rosemarie embraced. Rosemarie had developed quite a rapport with Quinn's niece during their counseling sessions after Sierra's suicide attempt. If nothing else, they enjoyed picking on Quinn together.

Quinn had decided he needed to get Sierra out of Vegas, at least temporarily. He needed her someplace far away, someplace Hofstetter's goons wouldn't suspect. It was actually Rosemarie who first suggested that Sierra stay with her. Sierra would be safe with Rosemarie. Plus, the psychiatrist claimed to know a number of middle school girls from her church who could be counted on to befriend Sierra. The fact that Rosemarie could provide some informal counseling was a bonus.

The Quinn Newberg from a few months ago—or even a few weeks ago—would have jumped at the chance to get his apartment back to himself. But something was different now. He was already starting to miss Sierra, just thinking about flying back to Vegas without her.

Sierra would attend summer school under an assumed name while living in D.C. with Rosemarie. Quinn would return to Virginia Beach a few times each month, meet with Catherine, and drive the four hours to D.C. to spend the day with Sierra. One of the hardest things had been convincing Sierra to go the entire summer without visiting her mom in jail. But Annie had insisted, refusing to even cry until after Sierra had left.

Quinn, Rosemarie, and Sierra talked for a few minutes while they watched the Norfolk-Portsmouth ferry land at the wooden dock. Quinn had his left arm on the back of the bench behind Sierra, psychologically protecting his niece for the last time in a couple of weeks. He'd had no idea it would be this hard to let her go.

"We'd better get going," he eventually said. "This isn't getting any easier."

The three stood and Sierra gave him a long hug, squeezing so tight he thought he might have to pry her hands away.

"I love you, Uncle Quinn," she said.

Quinn felt tears coming but managed to choke them back.

"I love you, too," he said. "But this is the best thing for the next few months." Quinn gave her a kiss on top of her head, and Sierra ended the embrace.

Quinn watched with a knot in his stomach as Sierra and Rosemarie walked away. Just before they disappeared into the Waterside complex, Sierra turned and waved, her sad eyes telling Quinn that this hurt her as much as it did him.

After they left, Quinn sat back down and soaked up the loneliness, his heart aching as if a family member had died. *It is the right thing to do,* he reminded himself. He had to prepare for two major trials. Hofstetter was after him and maybe after Sierra. And Sierra needed a strong female figure in her life.

But none of that chased away the loneliness. Sierra had only been gone a few minutes, and he missed her desperately already. She had only been with him a week, but it was hard to imagine life without her.

The ringing of Quinn's cell phone eventually broke the stupor.

It was Marc Boland.

"The media outlets have found out about Catherine's rape," Marc told Quinn. "Kenny Towns will hit every talk show possible, today and tomorrow, denying that the rape ever occurred. The armchair psychiatrists in the media will say the prosecutors now have a motive for the Avenger's killings."

"Then why didn't she just go after Kenny?" Quinn asked. It was the question that had bothered him about this scenario from the beginning. If

Catherine really was the Avenger, even Catherine in a different personality, did it make any sense that she wouldn't avenge the one violent act that had hurt her the most? "Why go through this elaborate Avenger of Blood scenario?"

"Maybe she was saving Towns for last," Marc replied. "Who knows? I'm not saying they're right; I'm just telling you what they're going to say. Which leads to my next question: did you make any headway getting Catherine to change her plea?"

"She's thinking about it."

"If she pleads insanity, the rape will actually work in our favor as a reason for her fractured personality," Marc said, as if Quinn needed to be reminded. "You ready to take half the interviews?"

"Not really," Quinn said. "I'm leaving first thing tomorrow to head back to Vegas."

"Good," Marc said, ignoring Quinn's actual answer. "Why don't you take the cable stations and radio? I'll take the broadcast TV stations."

Quinn sighed as he took out a legal pad and pen. "Give me the phone numbers."

76

CATHERINE ATE LUNCH quickly and went to her cell to read. The other inmates in her pod congregated at the metal tables, finishing their lunches or playing cards or arguing about anything and everything. Tasha and another woman had pulled a mattress from somebody's cell into the open area and now alternated between sit-ups on the mattress and push-ups with their feet elevated on the benches of the metal tables. All the while, the TV blabbered on as the trustee in charge of the television surfed the channels.

When Catherine heard shouting and catcalls from the pod, she looked out to see most of the inmates glued to the TV. The level of noise had dropped by several decibels.

"Get out here, O'Rourke!" Tasha shouted.

Catherine put down her book and shuffled warily out of the cell. The last thing she needed to see was another "update" about her case. . . .

She stopped in her tracks just outside her cell door. On the screen, big as life, was the face that had haunted her nightmares for years. Kenny Towns was eight years older now but looked exactly the same. Shorter haircut. A more professional bearing. But the same arrogant smirk.

She *hated* this man.

"He's hot," said one of the inmates. Others joined the commentary, making lewd comments about what they'd like to do with Kenny.

"Shut up!" yelled Tasha.

Kenny's lawyer sat next to him as Kenny answered questions from a former prosecutor now making a living as a CNBC host.

"Sure, we had sex," Kenny was saying. "But it was always consensual."

Catherine felt the pressure building inside her head and chest. She wanted to turn away, but somehow she couldn't.

"On more than one occasion?" asked the host.

"Yes, more than one occasion." Kenny smirked in a way that said the conquering hero had been intimate with his conquest too many times to count. "We were college students. We had an ongoing relationship."

The catcalls started again, so loud this time that Catherine couldn't hear the next question. But she heard Kenny say that a few other fraternity brothers had called recently to tell him they had been sexually involved with Catherine as well. One of them said that Catherine had threatened to drag Kenny into her murder case.

Cat felt her face flush as the taunting in the cell merged with the roaring in her head. She looked around at the inmates—smiling, mocking her, making all manner of suggestive noises.

"I've got a family," Kenny was saying. "A wife and kids. The last thing I wanted was to be dragged into something like this—a desperate woman's lawyers accusing me of things I didn't do."

"Shut up!" Cat yelled, more to the television than the inmates. *"Shut. Up."*

"Chill, woman," one of the inmates said.

"I wish he'd accuse me of a few of those things!" said another, and everybody laughed.

"I mean it," Cat said. She turned on the trustee as her anger exploded. "Turn this off!" she demanded.

The woman shrugged. "We already voted. Democracy at work."

Cat stormed toward the woman. "Shut it off!" she yelled. She turned toward a table of inmates right behind her. She grabbed an inmate's plastic tray and flung the half-eaten lunch at the elevated TV screen. She missed, so she grabbed another one and this time hit the mark. She cleared another table with one sweep of her arm, sending trays of food flying to the floor.

The bars of the pod seemed to pulse and billow, keeping time to the anger-laced adrenaline flowing through Cat's body. She was vaguely aware of the inmates staring at her, the doors near the guard post clanging open, Tasha coming toward her to calm her down.

Cat whirled toward the trustee again, stopping just inches away. "Turn it off *now!*" she demanded. She grabbed the remote and spun back toward the television just as the guards reached her. One knocked her to the floor, face-down. A second put a knee in her back. They cuffed her hands and dragged her to her feet, escorting her out of the pod toward solitary confinement.

As Cat left, she could still hear the TV in the background, the grating voice of Kenny Towns protesting his innocence. "I feel sorry for Catherine O'Rourke," he was saying. "I hope she gets the psychological help she needs. I just wish she had left me out of this."

Cat walked without resistance toward the isolation unit. She had never felt so powerless in her life. The man who had raped her, a man who was never brought to justice, who had never even apologized, was now playing the victim! Her insides roiled in rage. She wanted to rip his heart out, the same thing he had done to her.

Three days later, when Catherine O'Rourke left solitary confinement, she made a series of collect calls to Quinn Newberg. The first two times she called, he didn't answer. She reached him on her third try.

"I'm ready to change my plea," Cat said.

PART FOUR

JUSTICE

Justice: *n.*, the impartial adjustment of conflicting claims or the assignment of merited rewards or punishments; conformity to truth, fact, or reason.

WEBSTER'S UNABRIDGED DICTIONARY

THE WHOLE WORLD HATES THE INSANITY PLEA.

Quinn was reminded of this basic truth as he pulled into the courthouse parking lot and prepared to face the protesters and media. Reverend Harold Pryor and his spiteful band of followers stood at their posts in front of the courthouse steps, carrying signs with a blowup of Catherine's face and a simple message: *Baby Killer*. Yesterday they had shouted in Quinn's face and pronounced damnation on him as he climbed the steps. Quinn had lost his cool and asked the reverend if he didn't have some abortion clinics he could go bomb. Today Quinn was determined to keep his mouth shut.

The lawyers had finished jury selection the prior afternoon, and Quinn would give the opening statement for the defense this morning. He didn't feel close to ready. In the last two months, Quinn's normally hectic pace had increased until life seemed a blur of frenzied activity, an adrenaline-laced roller coaster ride under the white-hot glare of media cameras. He couldn't remember the last time he'd had a good night's sleep. He spent every minute preparing witnesses for two major trials, "commuting" from Las Vegas to Virginia Beach, visiting both Annie and Catherine in jail, and sneaking up to Washington, D.C., every few weeks to see Sierra.

He had spent an inordinate amount of time talking with Catherine. It was all a necessary part of trial preparation, he kept telling himself. Yet after hours of talking through the metal vents in the bulletproof glass of the attorney interview booths, Quinn still hadn't solved the mystery of Catherine O'Rourke and her multiple personalities, if indeed she had them.

Since the day of Catherine's outburst during Kenny Towns's television interview, she had been nothing but a class act, answering every one of Quinn's questions with quiet grace and seemingly endless patience. She had endured numerous sessions with Dr. Mancini and two separate sessions with the commonwealth's forensic psychiatrist, a precise Asian-American man named Dr. Edward Chow.

Quinn climbed out of his car and pulled his suit coat from a hanger in the back. He pulled it over his limp right arm first, struggling to slip into the jacket without lifting that arm up and away from his body, a movement that still sent stabbing pain through the unrepaired rotator cuff. After he wriggled into the suit coat, he grabbed his briefcase and headed across the black asphalt parking lot, the heat already radiating from the surface even though it was only 8:30 in the morning.

Quinn picked up the pace as the reverend and a few others jogged over to him and started walking beside him, shouting in his face as he approached the courthouse.

"Not today," Quinn grumbled.

"The blood of the kidnapped babies is on your hands!" shouted the reverend.

"Your client is a baby killer!" echoed a younger woman.

"Baby killer! Baby killer!" The protesters and cameramen formed a moving mob around Quinn as he reached the courthouse steps. Red camera lights blinked while shutters clicked and whirred. Quinn kept his gaze straight ahead, tuning out the protesters as he entered the doors of the courthouse.

The door closed, and the welcome sound of relative silence flooded the hallways. The protesters seemed very far away.

"Good morning, Mr. Newberg," said one of the guards at the metal detector.

"Good morning, Deputy Aaronson."

Quinn plunked his loose change and keys inside a small plastic container to pass through the screener. "Quiet day, huh?" Aaronson asked.

Quinn smiled. "If this is your idea of a quiet day, I'd hate to see a riot."

This brought a big grin from the deputy. "If you win this case, you might just get your chance."

Quinn walked into the courtroom, placed his briefcase at the defense counsel table, said a few words to Marc Boland, and slipped through a side door into a small, gray hallway with no outside windows. Just off the hallway were two even smaller rooms hidden behind heavy metal doors with a single narrow slit about a third of the way up. On a typical court day, male inmates would be herded into one room and females into the other. For the past three days, Catherine had been the only occupant of the female cell. Her friends and sister had brought her a fresh change of clothes each day, and the deputy allowed her to put them on before entering the courtroom.

"Good morning," Cat said after the door to the courtroom closed behind Quinn. "Did you get any sleep last night?"

Quinn stood outside the cell, leaning against the wall. He cherished these few moments before court even though he couldn't see his client's face.

"Sleep is overrated."

"I know what you mean," Cat said.

Today, even more so than the last few days, Quinn could sense the tension in Cat's voice. Today the trial began in earnest.

"Did your friends find some clothes that fit?" Quinn asked, trying to lighten the mood. On Monday, Cat had discovered how much weight she had lost during her months of confinement; her dress had practically swallowed her slender body.

She started to say something, but the words apparently caught in her throat. Whenever she spoke about things that really mattered to her, Cat's voice had a deeper tone and a softness that Quinn had grown to recognize, a softness that he intended to showcase for the jury when Cat took the stand. "My friends went out and bought me three new outfits," Cat said. "It made me cry."

"That's the good thing about murder trials," Quinn said dryly. "You find out who your true friends are."

"And who they aren't."

Quinn checked his watch. In a few minutes, the bailiff would call court into session. Quinn needed to take one last look at his notes.

"Things are going to get a little heated today. Boyd Gates is a first-class jerk, and there's no telling what he'll do to get a reaction from you. If you lose your cool even one time, the trial is over. Our whole case is premised on the theory that the Catherine O'Rourke on display in the courtroom did not and would not commit these crimes. A different personality altogether is responsible. Having that alter ego suddenly appear at trial would look staged and manipulative."

"I know that, Quinn," Cat said. "And I promise not to bull-charge the prosecutor or the judge."

"That would be nice."

"No promises on Jamarcus Webb, though."

"Maybe I can hold you back if you go after him."

"Maybe," said Cat. "But then again, you've never seen me mad."

78

"MY NAME IS BOYD GATES, and I have the privilege of representing the Commonwealth of Virginia."

The prosecutor stood ramrod straight in front of the jury box, holding a legal pad in his right hand, his left hanging at his side. He wore a conservative blue suit and red tie. His bald pate seemed to attract and reflect every ray of artificial light in the courtroom, except for those drawn to the ultra-shiny black wingtip shoes, buffed and polished as if Gates's former navy commander might stop by the courtroom for a quick inspection.

"'This is insane. What kind of warped person would commit a crime like this? She must be crazy to think she could get away with it. She must be sick.'" Gates stopped and surveyed the jury. "These are common expressions we use when we hear about a horrendous crime like the one in question. But these sayings do not reflect the legal definition of insanity. If they did, no criminal audacious enough to commit a truly horrible crime would ever go to jail."

The last statement was hyperbole, but Quinn knew better than to object. He tried to look disinterested, scribbling a few notes on his legal pad, chin in hand. "Don't look so mesmerized," he whispered to Catherine.

"The test of insanity under Virginia law is twofold." Gates consulted his legal pad, though Quinn knew he had the test memorized. "The first part is this: was the defendant, Catherine O'Rourke, at the time of the murder of Paul Donaldson, suffering from a mental disorder that kept her from knowing the nature and quality of the act she committed or, if she did know it, that prevented her from appreciating that the act was wrong? Or second, if she understood the nature of right and wrong, was she unable to control her actions, the so-called 'irresistible impulse' rule?"

Gates stopped reading and looked back at the jurors. "That's a lot of lawyer talk, but it all boils down to this: the insanity plea cannot be used by a defendant to excuse coldblooded and premeditated murder. And one of the ways to determine whether the defendant knew her conduct was wrong is to ask yourself this question: did she try to cover up the crime afterward? In this case, the answer is a resounding yes.

"The defense will rely upon a well-traveled psychiatrist named Dr. Rose-marie Mancini, the same psychiatrist who testified that Mr. Newberg's sister was insane when she killed her husband—"

Quinn jumped to his feet. "Objection, Judge. That's improper argument, not an opening statement."

Gates turned to face the judge, adopting a posture of indignity. "It's a fact I'll prove at trial, Your Honor. It's a preview of the evidence, and it happens to be true."

"Of course it's true," responded Quinn. "But so what?"

Rosencrance gave him a stern look. "You can make your so-what argument during closing statements, Mr. Newberg. I'm going to allow mention of your expert's opinions in other cases to be admitted for whatever relevance the jury chooses to grant them."

"Thank you, Your Honor," Quinn said grudgingly. He took his seat.

"As I was saying," Gates continued, "Dr. Mancini will suggest that this defendant has dissociative identity disorder, something that used to be called multiple personality disorder. Dr. Mancini will claim that, because of an alleged rape that occurred eight years ago, Ms. O'Rourke developed a second personality, one that has the ability to completely take over her body, one that the Catherine O'Rourke sitting here today didn't even know existed.

"But Dr. Mancini's opinion raises a slew of questions and ignores a mountain of evidence. First, the questions."

Quinn noticed that the jury seemed to be paying rapt attention to Gates. The prosecutor had chosen to forgo the normal chronological recitation of events and jump right into the core issues. To Quinn's chagrin, the tactic seemed to be working.

"If Ms. O'Rourke was indeed raped in college, could that rape have caused this entirely different personality, this so-called Avenger of Blood, to spring out of nowhere eight years later? Our expert witnesses will tell you that dissociative identity disorder is extremely rare and is almost always the result of persistent childhood abuse. If Ms. O'Rourke does have this psychosis and it developed from one instance of rape, then we are witnessing a first-of-its-kind occurrence, medical history in the making.

"And a second question: why did it take eight years, with no new trauma in the meantime, for the alleged psychosis to develop? Could it be that there is no psychosis here at all but just a calculating serial killer who believes that all rapists and their lawyers should be punished and that revenge is a dish best served cold?"

Quinn noted the way Gates just stood in front of the jury box, his feet rooted firmly in one place, as if unwilling to surrender even an inch of turf. Quinn was more of a pacer. The more intense Quinn became, the more he moved. He felt himself getting antsy even now. But Boyd Gates was a rock.

"There is also a mountain of evidence that proves this DID diagnosis is nothing but a smokescreen. DNA evidence links the defendant to the murder. *Undisputed evidence,* since the defendant admits she committed the crime. But you will also be shown extensive evidence of planning and cover-up. Ms. O'Rourke stalked the victim, luring him to a meeting by sending him pictures of his girlfriend being hugged by an unidentified man, a man whose identity O'Rourke promised to reveal at the meeting. Those photos, and the accompanying message from O'Rourke, were found under the seat of Paul Donaldson's car.

"And that's not all. The head medical examiner for the Hampton Roads area will testify that Mr. Donaldson died from electrocution. The defendant shaved two spots on Donaldson's scalp and one on his leg and then passed high-voltage electrical current through him for several minutes, frying both his skin and his internal organs. The medical examiner will tell you that Ms. O'Rourke continued to electrocute Mr. Donaldson for nearly five minutes *after* he had passed away, after he had quit moving or showed any other signs of life."

Quinn felt Catherine reach under the table and grab his hand. She squeezed, tension powering her grip. She stared at Boyd Gates's back, as if somehow her stare alone might stop him.

"And that's still not all. After the execution, the Avenger wrote a note taking credit for Donaldson's death. A strand of Ms. O'Rourke's hair was found on the adhesive part of the envelope. She also engaged in an elaborate attempt to conceal evidence, including throwing out her computer just before the police executed a search warrant at her house. She dumped some methohexital, a powerful anesthetic drug Ms. O'Rourke used to sedate her victim, together with bloody paper towels that contained both Donaldson's blood and O'Rourke's saliva, in a neighbor's trash can. Police never did find the clothes that Ms. O'Rourke wore that night, clothes that would presumably be spotted with blood from a gash in Donaldson's scalp. Does an insane person who doesn't know that she's done something wrong dispose of the clothes she was wearing and hide things in her neighbor's trash?"

Gates turned and cast an accusatory glare at Catherine. He motioned to her with a sweep of his hand. "This defendant is clever. She knows that the best place for the fox to hide is in the henhouse and—even better—right in the middle of those who guard the henhouse. So she pretended to have visions about the killings and nurtured a confidential police informant for her newspaper articles about the killings, all in an effort to become part of the inner circle of the investigation."

Gates turned back to the jury. "Catherine O'Rourke wanted to know every step the police were taking so she could stay one step ahead. But she made some fatal mistakes. Fortunately, those mistakes led to her arrest and quite possibly saved the lives of other victims, including the man whom the defendant says raped her in college."

Quinn stifled another objection. He wasn't sure about Virginia, but in Las Vegas lawyers couldn't make these types of boldfaced arguments during opening statements; they were supposed to just preview the evidence. But Marc Boland didn't seem to be bothered by Gates's monologue, and Quinn didn't want to call more attention to the prosecutor's arguments by objecting, so he decided to ride it out.

"This is not some kind of spur-of-the-moment, heat-of-passion crime where a demonic personality took control of the defendant's body. The Catherine O'Rourke sitting in this courtroom is the same Catherine O'Rourke who stalked Paul Donaldson, and took the pictures of Donaldson's girlfriend, and set up a meeting with Donaldson, and electrocuted him, and faked visions to ingratiate herself to the police, and later tried to cover it all up. Do you really think that some other personality magically took over the defendant's body at every stage of this crime, floating in and out of her body to do all these things? Do you really believe the defendant wasn't even aware that the crimes had happened? Do you really think she just happened to throw her computer away a few days before the police arrested her?"

Gates blew out a breath. "She's clever. She fooled a lot of friends and coworkers. She fooled the police for a while. Even now, she is fooling the defense psychiatrist, Dr. Rosemarie Mancini. And starting today, she wants to fool you."

Gates took a half step back and tilted his head. "She's clever all right. But crazy?"

He paused just long enough to gain everyone's attention. "Crazy like a fox."

79

FOR CATHERINE, the first day of the trial was surreal. As a reporter, she had covered major trials for years, wondering what went through a defendant's mind at times like this, trying to imagine what it felt like to have your fate in the hands of twelve fellow human beings in the jury box.

Now she knew.

It felt nauseating.

In the momentary silence that filled the courtroom after Boyd Gates's opening, Catherine sensed the eyes of a packed gallery boring into the back of her neck. She could almost hear the accusatory whispers accompanied by the sad shaking of dozens of heads. The presumption of innocence was a myth. She hadn't reserved her own judgment when she watched defendants squirm during the prosecutor's opening statement. And she knew others weren't reserving theirs now.

She thought about the impact this trial must already be having on her mom and her sister, sitting just a row behind Catherine. What about her remaining friends—the ones who had promised to stick with her no matter what—trying to reconcile this damning evidence with the Catherine they thought they knew?

Quinn introduced himself and reminded the jurors about their obligation to keep an open mind until they heard all the evidence. "The presumption of innocence is more than just a nice-sounding phrase," he said, his voice calm and reasonable. "It actually means something. Right now, my client, Catherine O'Rourke, is clothed in the presumption of innocence." He turned to look at Cat. "She is every bit as innocent at this moment as you and me." Quinn turned back to the jury but Catherine's eyes never left his back; she couldn't bear to look at the jurors.

"And she will remain innocent unless the prosecution removes that cloak by proving her guilt beyond a reasonable doubt. In this case, no such proof exists."

Catherine wished she could feel as confident as Quinn. In her mind, the cloak had already been removed, her naked guilt exposed for the world to see.

Habits die hard. And in this moment of ultra-stress, Cat resorted to her reporter persona, jotting down words that captured her emotions.

Vulnerable. Transparent. Frightened. Listening to Quinn, she still couldn't believe this was happening. *Who am I really?* she wondered. And then she jotted down another word.

Confused.

The jurors definitely had their game faces on; that much was clear to Quinn. But it felt good to finally be in front of them, even though he could have used a few more days of prep time. This might be Virginia, but this was still a courtroom, his stomping grounds, and this was what he did best. Plain talk to folks just like this.

Quinn had always been the legal magician, pulling surprise verdicts out of a hat, because he truly *believed* in juries. He wasn't like some lawyers who gave the jury system lip service but in their hearts feared the unpredictability of ordinary citizens. Quinn knew deep in his bones that the jury would understand his case. The rest of the world might not get it, but that didn't matter. Catherine's fate rested with these twelve and nobody else. Quinn trusted *them*.

It didn't hurt that most of them were women. Despite Quinn's belief that men would naturally jump to Catherine's defense, he also knew that he would develop a better bond with the women on the panel. Even now, he favored them with the majority of his eye contact.

"When Catherine's family and friends and coworkers heard about her arrest, their reaction was almost always the same," Quinn said. "Disbelief. 'The Catherine I know would never do such a thing,' they said. Or, 'I can't believe the cops have the right person—Catherine wouldn't do something like that.'

"Her friends and family were right. The Catherine they knew would never have committed such a heinous crime."

Quinn began pacing now, working his way slowly from side to side in front of the jury. He was onstage, his left hand accentuating his words, his right hand holding a legal pad that he checked occasionally, the subtle inflections of his voice as perfect as those of a trained Broadway singer.

"Even Catherine herself could not believe it. For days, even weeks, she protested her complete innocence. 'Somebody must have framed me,' she said. She pled not guilty at the start of the case, as opposed to not guilty by reason of insanity. This is to be expected because the Catherine O'Rourke you see sitting in this courtroom today was not even aware that this other side of her personality existed. The Avenger of Blood and Catherine O'Rourke share the same body, but they are not the same person. They are entirely different personalities."

Quinn paused for a moment, mindful that he was straying close to the line that divided argument from opening statement. He could sense Boyd Gates on the edge of his seat, trying to decide whether to object. *Good,* thought Quinn. *Turnabout is fair play.*

But the objection came from an unexpected direction.

"Mr. Newberg," snapped Judge Rosencrance, "I don't know how it works in Vegas—" the judge drew out the word as if it were a curse, emphasizing Quinn's outsider status in the courtroom—"but here in Virginia, lawyers use their opening *statements* to provide a roadmap for the evidence and their closing *arguments* to lay out their arguments about the evidence."

She said it condescendingly, as if Quinn were trying his first case. He couldn't let it pass, not with his friends on the jury watching so expectantly.

"Thank you, Your Honor," he said. "In Vegas, it's also traditional for the *prosecutor* to make the objections, freeing the *judge* to rule on those objections."

"*Mr. Newberg.* Your sarcastic comments have no place in this courtroom. Is that understood?"

Quinn waited, silent.

"Is that understood?"

"Yes, Your Honor."

"Thank you. You may proceed."

"The prosecution's expert, Dr. Edward Chow, will testify that the rape of Ms. O'Rourke could not possibly be the trigger for dissociative identity disorder." Quinn raised his voice. "'The alleged rape,' Chow noted in his pretrial report, 'was an isolated, nonrecurring episode,' as if rape is such an ordinary occurrence that every woman should have to suffer at least two or three rapes—"

"Objection!" Gates shouted, springing to his feet.

"—before she can avail herself of a defense based on psychological—"

"Objection! Judge!"

Crack! Crack! Rosencrance silenced the room with her gavel and glared at Quinn. "That's *argument,* Counsel. And this is your last warning."

Red-faced, she turned to the jury. "Please disregard those last remarks by Mr. Newberg. They were improper *arguments*, and they have no place in an opening statement."

"Yes, Your Honor," Quinn said, though it felt to him like a double standard. *Virginia lawyers can argue during opening statements but Vegas lawyers can't?*

"During this case, you will learn about two Catherine O'Rourkes. The one who sits in this courtroom is a dedicated professional, kind to her coworkers and friends, the type of person who would never dream of hurting anyone. She loves her job working at the paper, and she's good at it. She is loyal to a fault—willing to go to jail rather than betray a confidential source.

"She is not some kind of religious fanatic who would use Old Testament Bible verses to justify revenge killings."

He studied the jury panel and lowered his voice. "But there is a second person who sometimes inhabits that body, a person who calls herself the Avenger of Blood, a killer so cold and remorseless that she not only killed an alleged rapist, she allowed the body to *cook* for a full five minutes after the rapist died. A rapist, by the way, whom Catherine O'Rourke had never met before in her life."

Quinn stopped, paused, and filled his lungs. "Your job in this case, simply put, is to determine whether there really are two personalities sharing that body, as we suggest, or only one, as the prosecution suggests. One woman so calculating and devious that she can fool a seasoned professional like Dr. Mancini yet dumb enough to fake visions about related crimes, visions that made her a prime suspect. So clever she can dispose of bloody clothes and her computer in places where the police can never find them but so dumb that she throws methohexital and bloody paper towels in her neighbor's trash where they could be easily found. So consumed with rage from a college rape that she would plot the murders of other accused rapists, but not obsessed enough to go after the man who raped *her*.

"These dichotomies, these inconsistencies, make no sense if there's only one Catherine O'Rourke. The evidence in this case *only* makes sense when we realize that two different women occupy the same body at different points in time."

Quinn searched the jurors' faces for traces of an ally. Seeing none, he realized that his earlier misgivings had been correct. The legal magician wasn't ready today. This was not his normal opening statement. He would usually have them eating out of his hand by now.

"The criminal laws in our country depend on a concept called *mens rea*," Quinn said, plowing forward despite his misgivings. "That's a Latin phrase that basically means evil intent. Do any of you have kids?"

From jury selection, Quinn knew there were six moms on the jury. A few of them gave Quinn subtle nods, and he zeroed in on that group.

"Let's say your daughter is three years old and is playing in the backyard. And let's say, God forbid, that she finds a loaded gun and shoots her playmate. You would be outraged if Mr. Gates decided to charge your child with murder. Why? Because that little girl doesn't have the mental capacity to form an intent to murder. She didn't understand that what she did was wrong, that it would result in the loss of life.

"In some ways, Catherine O'Rourke is like that little girl. She needs treatment and counseling from an expert like Dr. Mancini. Sure, she needs confinement until we can bring that other personality to the surface and deal with the issues that created it. But the defendant doesn't deserve the death penalty. Two wrongs do not make a right. Killing Catherine O'Rourke will not bring back Paul Donaldson."

Quinn surveyed the jury one last time. They were all careful not to telegraph their allegiance but, for the most part, they didn't look hostile either. An open-minded jury. For now, that would have to do.

80

AFTER A BRIEF RECESS, Boyd Gates called Dr. Herbert Saunders, the Hampton Roads medical examiner, to the stand. With the precision of a drill sergeant, Gates rattled off questions about the autopsy and cause of death, establishing in painful detail the sadistic manner by which Paul Donaldson had died. He showed the jury grotesque photos of Donaldson's body after it had been recovered from the Dismal Swamp Canal, including close-ups of the head gash and the burn marks where the electrodes had been connected, then circled back around with some final questions about the method of execution.

"In your duties as chief medical examiner for the Hampton Roads area, have you been called upon to certify the death of capital murder defendants who were sentenced to the electric chair?" asked Gates.

"Yes, on several occasions."

"Tell the jury how that manner of death occurs."

The ME shifted in his seat to face the jury. He had the wrinkled face of a grandfather and a gentle manner that conveyed sadness rather than outrage at this whole inexplicable affair. "When someone is executed by the state through use of the electric chair—a method that can still be chosen by death-row inmates in Virginia—every effort is made to minimize the suffering. Standard protocols are put in place to make certain no malfunctions occur. Two thousand four hundred volts are administered for seven seconds, followed by eight hundred volts for seventeen seconds, then twenty-four hundred volts for five seconds. Most convicts choose the needle, but we've never had a botched electric-chair execution in the history of the Commonwealth of Virginia."

"From your review of Mr. Donaldson's body and your past experience with electrocution as a form of execution, how would Mr. Donaldson have suffered in this case?"

Marc Boland stood to his full height. "Objection, Your Honor. Calls for speculation."

"He's an expert witness," Gates countered. "He's entitled to give his opinion based on the medical facts."

"Overruled," said Rosencrance.

A few jurors leaned forward as Saunders continued. "Unfortunately, the executioner in this case was not very skilled. From the damage to the internal organs, the burn marks on Mr. Donaldson's skin, and the deep contusions on his neck and waist from the straps that apparently held him, as well as marks on his wrists and ankles, which were probably secured with handcuffs, it is apparent that Mr. Donaldson struggled violently for quite some time."

Saunders paused, as if the images he would be forced to describe were too horrible for him to continue. "Although I wasn't there, my opinions are based on the evidence I reviewed. Mr. Donaldson would have been straining against the straps with almost superhuman strength. There would have been the awful stench of burning flesh and probably smoke, maybe even sparks emanating from the spots where the electrodes were attached. Mr. Donaldson would have been convulsing with pain, probably screaming for mercy. He had no stomach contents at the time of the autopsy, meaning that at some point during the execution he probably vomited. His skin would have turned bright red, his eyes bugging out."

Saunders lowered his eyes, signifying that he had subjected the jury to enough gruesome details. "It would have been awful."

"That's all I have," Boyd Gates said. His wingtips clicked on the floor as he returned to his seat.

Before Gates could sit, Marc Boland was up and asking a question.

"It's hard to imagine any sane person inflicting that kind of torture, isn't it, Dr. Saunders?"

"Objection," Gates said, swiveling toward the judge. "Dr. Saunders is not proffered as a psychiatrist."

"Sustained."

"Nothing further," Boland said.

81

"THE COMMONWEALTH CALLS Detective Jamarcus Webb," Gates announced.

Rosencrance checked her watch. "I'm assuming you will be keeping Detective Webb on the stand for quite some time, counsel?"

"That's correct," Gates said.

"Then let's resume after lunch when everybody is fresh." The judge banged her gavel, and the bailiff called the court into recess.

Over lunch, Marc Boland reiterated his strategy for Webb. "We've got to give the jury a *reason* to go with our insanity defense," he told Quinn. "For us to succeed, they have to *want* us to win. The insanity plea just gives them a means to make it happen."

Quinn didn't really disagree, so he just shoved another bite of sandwich in his mouth.

"Paul Donaldson was no Boy Scout," Boland continued. "He raped and killed Sherri McNamara. The jury needs to believe he got what he had coming.

"Plus, we've got to suggest other potential villains. Even though Catherine pled insanity, it doesn't hurt to plant some subtle seeds of doubt about whether she even committed the crimes. Jamarcus Webb will be a good place to start."

An hour later, Webb settled his large frame into the witness chair after affirming his oath with a look of grim determination. He cast a quick glance at Catherine before he shifted to face Boyd Gates and the jury.

For most of the afternoon, Jamarcus Webb presented a painfully detailed overview of the investigation linking Catherine to the death of Paul Donaldson—the hair on the envelope sent to the *Richmond Times*, the DNA evidence on the paper towels, the methohexital, the visions Catherine had shared with

Webb, the gash on Donaldson's scalp found when his body was recovered and Catherine's question about whether Donaldson had been bleeding from the scalp. Jamarcus also discussed various issues related to chain of custody for the evidence and the standard police procedures involved in crime scene investigations.

"Is the death of Paul Donaldson the only crime you have investigated by this so-called Avenger of Blood?" Gates asked.

Marc Boland rose immediately to object. The subject matter of other crimes had been the basis of a lengthy pretrial motion to exclude, which the judge had already ruled against. In a written opinion, Rosencrance had held that the prosecution could refer to the other crimes, even though for strategic reasons O'Rourke had not yet been charged with them, because that evidence was critical on the issue of O'Rourke's state of mind and because the other crimes showed a pattern of conduct. For example, both the Carver and Milburn kidnappings tied the methohexital to the *modus operandi* of the Avenger of Blood.

"We renew our earlier motion to exclude this evidence," Boland said. "It's highly prejudicial and not relevant to the sole crime Ms. O'Rourke is being charged with in *this* proceeding."

"And for the reasons I stated earlier, I'm allowing the testimony," Rosencrance ruled. "It might be relevant to show an alleged pattern or MO, and it goes to the defendant's state of mind at the time of this crime."

Marc Boland gave the obligatory "Thank you, Your Honor" and sat down.

The jury, whose collective interest had been waning a little, now looked riveted to the witness, and Boyd Gates took maximum advantage. He had Jamarcus detail the evidence regarding the Avenger's use of methohexital on Marcia Carver and Sherita Johnson, and he asked Jamarcus to describe the notes sent by the Avenger after those kidnappings. Next, Gates asked the witness to discuss any evidence that suggested a pattern of premeditation for the Avenger's crimes.

In response, Jamarcus calmly took the jury through a litany of devastating facts. The defendant had apparently stalked Paul Donaldson and his girlfriend, taking pictures of Donaldson's girlfriend with another man in order to lure Donaldson into a meeting. The photos, heavily damaged by the brackish water of the Dismal Swamp Canal, had been found under the front seat of Donaldson's vehicle.

The Avenger of Blood had used an even more elaborate scheme to ensnare attorney Rex Archibald. First, the Avenger had sent several different e-mails from a variety of publicly accessible computers, posing as Reverend Harold Pryor and pretending that Pryor wanted to hire Archibald. To pay the retainer, the Avenger had procured five two-thousand-dollar money orders at five different convenience stores over the course of several days and had sent that money to Archibald.

The Avenger had then lured Archibald to a meeting at the North Williamsburg Baptist Church, Jamarcus told the jury. Before Archibald arrived, the Avenger had changed the marquee in front of the church to reflect a Bible verse—Ezekiel 18:20—conveying the Avenger's message about justice and punishment.

Gates asked Webb to read the verse, and the jury hung on every word:

"'The soul who sins is the one who will die. The son will not share the guilt of the father, nor will the father share the guilt of the son. The righteousness of the righteous man will be credited to him, and the wickedness of the wicked will be charged against him.'"

"What happened to Mr. Archibald after he met the Avenger at this church?"

Jamarcus hesitated and swallowed. "He hasn't been seen or heard from again."

Boyd Gates pretended to check some notes so the answer could hang in the air and poison the atmosphere. "This sounds like an impressive level of advanced planning for these crimes, Detective Webb. Would you agree?"

Marc Boland jumped up. "Objection. Leading."

"Sustained."

Gates shook his head, as if reprimanding himself. "Does this level of planning—and this level of cover-up, to the extent that virtually no scientific evidence is left behind at these crime scenes—seem consistent with someone who goes temporarily insane and does things she doesn't even remember?"

Boland stood and just spread his palms. "Judge . . ."

"Sustained," said Rosencrance. But the point had been made.

Boyd Gates collected his notes from the lectern and headed back to his counsel table. Webb's testimony had caused a type of somber hush to settle over the courtroom. This was the trial of a serial killer, after all, someone who had probably kidnapped babies even though she was "only" being charged in this trial with the murder of a single adult.

Before Boyd Gates sat down, he turned back to his witness, who was now taking a sip of water. "When the evidence first started piling up against Ms.

O'Rourke, did you want to believe the evidence or did you want to believe that she was innocent?" Gates asked.

Boland objected again, but Quinn marveled at the brilliance of the question. One of Webb's vulnerable points would be his betrayal of Catherine's confidence. But Boyd Gates had just turned it into a strength.

"It goes to his lack of bias against the defendant," Gates explained to the judge. "Certainly *that's* relevant."

"Objection overruled," said Rosencrance.

Webb put down his water glass and looked directly at Catherine. "The defendant and I were friends," he said. "As a newspaper reporter, I trusted her with confidential information I thought the public needed to know. She guarded that information with her life. One time she went to jail rather than reveal me as her source."

Webb pursed his lips and shook his head a little. To Quinn, the angst did not seem manufactured. "I trusted her and believed in her until the evidence became overwhelming. She lied to me. And she used me to get inside information about the police investigation so she could govern her conduct accordingly."

Webb looked down to deliver his most devastating statement, one that Quinn realized would swing any remaining undecided jurors to Webb's side. "I failed in my duties as a detective," he confessed. "I let a personal friendship get in the way."

As if the testimony hadn't been harmful enough, Judge Rosencrance decided to increase its impact by letting the jurors think about it overnight. "It's nearly 5:00," she said. "Mr. Boland, we'll start with your cross-examination first thing tomorrow morning."

The judge warned the jurors not to discuss the case with anyone and not to listen to, watch, or read any media coverage of the trial. They all nodded solemnly, and the bailiff recessed the court. For a few seconds after the judge left, Catherine and her lawyers just stood there, the enormity of their task sinking in.

"We've got some work to do," Marc finally offered. "But tomorrow will be a new day. And I've got a few questions of my own for Detective Webb."

82

A DEPUTY SHERIFF led Catherine into the small chamber adjacent to the courtroom and locked her in the cramped holding cell where she would change back into her jumpsuit. A few moments later, as he had done on other days, the deputy came back into the courtroom and let Quinn know he could go talk with his client.

Quinn walked into the small enclosed chamber that separated the men's holding cell from the women's and connected both to the courtroom. Catherine was in the women's cell, on the other side of a locked metal door with a six-inch opening about waist high so prisoners could slide their arms through to be cuffed or uncuffed.

Quinn heard Cat rustling around as she changed her clothes and thought he heard her quietly crying as well. "Are you okay?" he asked.

She didn't answer.

"Cat? Are you okay?"

The movement inside the cell stopped, and Quinn imagined Catherine sitting on the metal bench attached to the far wall.

When she spoke, her voice seemed small. Frail. "Whoever did those things deserves to die, Quinn. Whoever did those things is an animal."

"Cat, now's not the time—"

"We're talking about *babies*, Quinn," she said sharply. "Somebody is killing *babies*. If *I* did that . . . *I* deserve to die."

The comment left Quinn struggling for a response. In the past few weeks, Cat had seemed to accept her illness, even embrace it. The testimony of Saunders and Webb had apparently shattered that. "Even if you did those things, Cat, that doesn't mean it's who you are. It's a sickness. A disease. It's not something you could help anymore than you can keep yourself from getting cancer."

"Stop," Catherine said. "I know you're trying to make me feel better about all this, but it's just not working. Those babies are dead. Those men are dead. And Jamarcus is right—whoever killed them planned the whole thing with premeditated malice and a cold heart that would make Hitler proud." Cat paused and sniffled back a tear. "Even if we win, I'm still the one responsible in everybody's mind. The insanity defense doesn't change that."

Quinn leaned against the wall. He ached to be with her. "I told you we would have to be strong," he said softly. "I told you we would have moments like this."

"Do you think I did those things?" Catherine asked. Before he could answer, she added, "And I don't want your usual lines about the Catherine you know couldn't have done it. I need to know: do *you* think I did it—*any* part of me, *any* personality?"

Quinn thought about it for a long time. "I don't know," he said at last. "I honestly don't know." He almost left it at that—probably should have. But Catherine wasn't the only one emotionally drained, and Quinn let his emotions run ahead of him. "I only know that I care about you, Catherine. If you did these crimes, I just want you to get help. If you didn't, I want you to forgive me for doubting you. Either way, my only goal right now is to save your life, and the only way I know to do that is through the insanity defense."

This generated another silence that made Quinn realize again how much he hated the steel door separating them. He couldn't see Catherine's face or place a hand reassuringly on her shoulder. He had no idea what was going through her mind at this critical moment.

"Thanks, Quinn," she said. "Thanks for being honest."

On impulse, Quinn walked a few steps to the door and knelt down, reaching his forearms through the slit as far as he could. "Are you dressed?" he asked.

"If you call an orange jumpsuit dressed."

Quinn looked through the slit just in time to see Catherine kneel on the other side and take his hands. He winced as the pain in his shoulder stabbed at him, but he didn't say a word. She leaned closer so her face was nearly touching his hands. Instinctively, he brushed a strand of hair behind her ear. Her face was raw from crying, her eyes red. He wiped the tears away from her cheeks.

"We'll get through this," Quinn said.

He heard the door start to open behind him, and he jerked his hands back, scrambling to his feet. Pain pierced his shoulder a second time.

"You about done in here?" the deputy asked.

"One more minute," Quinn said.

The deputy obligingly shut the door, and Quinn knelt again. This time, he slid his left hand through the slot, and Catherine grabbed it with both of hers.

"Promise me you won't do anything drastic," Quinn said.

"I appreciate everything you're doing for me," Catherine said haltingly. "Everything." She paused, her voice catching. "But honestly, Quinn, I couldn't live with *myself* if this is who I am."

The door opened again, and the deputy came through without seeking permission.

"You can talk with her in the jail, Counselor," he said.

"I know," Quinn answered. He squeezed Catherine's hand one last time and rose to his feet.

Five minutes later, Quinn had talked his way into an audience with Judge Rosencrance in her chambers. Boyd Gates was there for the commonwealth. Marc Boland was already gone, probably on the courthouse steps answering questions from the press.

"I'm requesting that the court put my client on suicide watch until further notice," Quinn said. "I can't divulge attorney-client confidences, but I'm very concerned about her well-being."

Gates snorted. "That's page three of the defendant's standard playbook, Your Honor. Request suicide watch and then leak it to the press. It helps the defendant seem more insane."

"Everything's a game to Mr. Gates," Quinn countered. "Everything's a strategy. I'm talking about a woman's life, Your Honor. And if we're worried about appearances, think about how it will look if we *don't* put her on suicide watch and something happens."

"Mr. Newburg's right," Rosencrance said to Gates. "I don't think I can take the risk of *not* doing this. The jury will not be told about it, so it won't prejudice your case." She turned to Quinn. "News about this had better not leak out."

"Thank you, Your Honor," said Quinn. He left as quickly as possible before the judge could change her mind.

Catherine waited in the holding tank for the deputy to return and take her back to jail.

He showed up about ten minutes later, put the cuffs on her, and opened the door. "You're going in solitary confinement," he said. "Judge's orders."

He escorted Catherine through the long underground tunnel that connected the courthouse to the jail, through the double solid-metal doors that sealed off the jail facility and through another set of double doors to the isolation cells.

"You missed dinner, but I'll see if I can get something brought in," he said.

The man locked Catherine in her cell and had her slide her wrists through the bars so he could release the handcuffs. She thanked him and collapsed onto her cot, emotionally exhausted.

That night, she slept fitfully, awakened by nightmares of hooded executioners coming to her cell and calling her name.

She woke at 4 a.m. and couldn't go back to sleep.

She had survived three months in jail by telling herself that the trial would set things straight. She had two of the best lawyers in the business helping her. She was being tried by a jury of her Virginia Beach peers. But now, after the first day of testimony, it seemed things could only get worse.

If convicted, she would spend years on death row exhausting one appeal after another. And even if she won, the press and public would demonize her. She should know. How many criminals had she demonized in the past?

She could see the headlines now: *Confessed Killer Found Not Guilty.* She might survive the trial, but the real test of strength would be surviving the public scorn.

All she could do was take it one day at a time. Today, Marc Boland would get a chance to cross-examine Jamarcus Webb. In a few days, Catherine would take the stand and tell her story. She thought about the way Boyd Gates would tear into her on cross-examination. She envisioned the news stories that would follow, even the ones that would be printed by her own paper. She tormented herself with these thoughts for another half hour before the deputies came around clanging their flashlights against the prison bars.

Another cruel day had begun.

83

AFTER A LONG NIGHT of research and trial prep, Quinn slept through his alarm and awoke in a panic thirty minutes later. He fought Virginia Beach traffic, searched in vain for a parking spot within a half mile of the courthouse, elbowed past Reverend Harold Pryor and his brood, and arrived in Virginia Beach Circuit Court 7 just a few minutes before 9:00.

He walked past Jamarcus Webb, seated in the front row, without so much as acknowledging the man. Quinn felt bad that he wouldn't get to spend a few minutes with Catherine before court started. He hoped she wouldn't read anything into it.

Marc Boland had dressed down for the occasion, trading in the suits he had worn the first three days for a sports coat and khaki pants, apparently trying to pull off the common-man look. Quinn had taken the opposite approach today, dressing like the big-shot Vegas lawyer the jury expected him to be—a thousand-dollar suit, cuff links, and a monogrammed shirt. If only he'd found time for a haircut, he might actually look presentable.

Quinn took his seat at counsel table and reviewed some notes while Marc Boland chatted with Jamarcus Webb as if they were fraternity brothers rather than enemy combatants in a court of law. They talked baseball and swapped stories about their kids. Quinn would never talk to a witness before he cross-examined him on the stand. It was hard to intimidate somebody who knew your favorite baseball team.

"All rise," the bailiff called out. Judge Rosencrance took the bench, and a deputy escorted Catherine into the courtroom. "Sorry I got here late," Quinn whispered.

"No problem," Catherine whispered back. "Can you come by after court today?"

"Sure."

A few minutes later, Detective Webb took his place on the witness stand, and Marc Boland changed from the nice guy next door into a legal pit bull.

"You mentioned in your direct testimony that you were a confidential informant for Ms. O'Rourke, who at the time was a reporter for the *Tidewater Times*. True?"

"Yes."

"And in that capacity, you would pass along information about certain investigations, right?"

"Information that I thought the public might need to know. I never compromised the integrity of any investigations."

Marc Boland looked surprised. "Oh, then I take it you must have cleared this information with your superiors to make sure they didn't believe it would compromise the investigations."

"No. I used my own judgment."

"And lied to your superiors about it, correct?"

Jamarcus Webb hesitated, looking indignant. "I didn't lie. I just didn't discuss it with them."

"Is that so?" Boland reached down to his counsel table and grabbed some notes. "Isn't it true that you leaked to the press the fact that the Carver kidnappings and the Milburn kidnapping were related?"

"I thought the public had a right to know."

"And when Catherine O'Rourke's article containing that information ran in the paper, she was subpoenaed before a grand jury and asked who her source was. Is that correct?"

"I wasn't in the grand jury hearing," Webb countered. "But I believe that's true."

"You weren't in the grand jury hearing, but you *were* present in court when Catherine was cited with contempt for refusing to identify her source. And rather than come clean and put yourself in jeopardy, you just let Catherine go to jail."

Webb took a drink of water, his discomfort showing. "We both knew that was the deal from the start. We would even joke about it. I would ask Catherine about various forms of interrogation and whether—"

"Maybe you didn't understand the question," Boland interrupted, taking a step toward Webb. "Rather than voluntarily coming forward and putting yourself at risk, you let Catherine go to jail. *Isn't that correct?*"

Webb cast a glance at Gates, perhaps hoping for an objection. "Yes, that's correct."

Boland let the answer hang for a minute. "And this is the lady you called—" he checked his notes—"a 'personal friend' yesterday. Is this the way you treat all your friends?"

"Objection!"

"I'll withdraw it, Your Honor," Boland said calmly. He turned a condescending tone on Webb. "Are you really asking this jury to believe that, at the same time Mr. Gates was prosecuting Catherine O'Rourke and sending her to jail for not revealing her source, you and others in the department were never even asked if you might be that source?"

"No, that's not what I'm saying. We were all asked."

"Then let me repeat my earlier question," said Marc Boland firmly. "Isn't it true that you lied to your superiors about being a source for the newspaper?"

Jamarcus hesitated. "Yes. I told them I was not the source."

"Now we're making progress," said Boland.

Gates leaped to his feet but the judge spoke first. "That comment will be struck from the record. Mr. Boland, you know better."

"Sorry, Judge."

As Boland launched into another line of questioning, Quinn's thoughts turned to Catherine. She seemed better today. Even her posture was more confident—sitting forward in the chair, erect and attentive, taking notes like the reporter she was.

"You doing okay?" Quinn whispered.

"I hate this for Jamarcus," Catherine replied. "But I'm fine."

"Your *friend*," Quinn reminded her, "is trying to get you the needle."

"He's doing his job," Catherine replied, keeping her eyes on the witness.

Meanwhile, Marc Boland kept hammering away. "Did your extensive investigation reveal any connection between Ms. O'Rourke and Mr. Donaldson?"

"Other than the fact that she stalked him and his girlfriend and murdered him?"

"You know what I mean," insisted Boland. "Was there any prior relationship between Mr. Donaldson and Ms. O'Rourke?"

"We didn't find any."

"Did you find any prior relationship between Ms. O'Rourke and Mr. Milburn?"

"No."

"Between Ms. O'Rourke and any of the Carvers?"

"No."

"Between Ms. O'Rourke and Rex Archibald?"

"No."

"So these victims are just arbitrary victims, as far as you could tell from your investigation?"

"That's not correct," said Webb. "The victims are all either alleged rapists who were found innocent or defense attorneys who represented rapists."

Boland pretended to think about this for a moment. "Then I guess you're suggesting that Ms. O'Rourke's motivation for these crimes was the fact that she was raped eight years ago, during college?"

"Possibly."

"Doesn't that seem a little strange to you, Detective Webb—perhaps even a little *insane*—that Ms. O'Rourke would choose to victimize four people she didn't even know instead of going after the one person who actually raped her eight years ago?"

"Objection," Gates called out. "Calls for speculation. Detective Webb is not proffered as a psychiatrist."

"Sustained."

Marc Boland did not look the least bit disappointed. He had made his point. And Quinn began to relax a little. Marc Boland could handle himself just fine.

84

FOR THE NEXT HOUR, it felt to Quinn like he was sitting in on Paul Donaldson's rape trial. Detective Webb admitted he had studied that case as part of his investigation into Donaldson's death. So Marc Boland, who had been working in the Richmond Commonwealth's Attorney's office at the time on other matters, walked the witness through the troubling details of that case step by painful step.

Sherri McNamara had met Paul Donaldson at a bar. According to her testimony, Donaldson followed her into the parking lot, forced her into his car, and raped her on an isolated stretch of road outside the city of Richmond. Donaldson had admitted to having sex but said it was consensual. Rex Archibald, Donaldson's attorney, had emphasized the absence of any evidence of struggle other than torn clothing. That could have been done by McNamara herself, Archibald had claimed. There was no skin under her fingernails, no scratches on Donaldson or bruises on McNamara.

"As an officer of the law, it must be frustrating to hear about a jury that falls for that kind of argument," Marc Boland suggested.

"It is."

"Does it ever make you want to take the law into your own hands—just once, Detective Webb, just to make sure that a guy like Paul Donaldson gets what's coming to him?"

"No," Jamarcus said firmly. "I believe in the system. It's not perfect, but vigilante justice is not the answer."

"Really. You believe in 'the system.'" Marc Boland took a few steps, thinking. "But the system needed a little help, and therefore you broke department guidelines by conveying confidential information to Ms. O'Rourke."

"That's different," Webb insisted. "Helping Ms. O'Rourke was just passing on important information to the public. That's not taking justice into my own hands."

"Fair enough," Boland said. "Then let me ask you this: did your investigation of the Avenger of Blood initially focus on law-enforcement types and religious fanatics?"

"Yes, of course."

"Can you tell the jury why?"

Grudgingly, Jamarcus looked at the jury. "Because two of the victims were accused rapists who were never convicted and because the messages from the Avenger contained references to Bible verses."

"Law-enforcement officers, men and women like yourself, Detective Webb, are the ones who tested the DNA evidence and searched the neighbor's trash cans for bloody paper towels and drugs and had access to all of the so-called scientific evidence; isn't that right?"

Predictably, this brought Boyd Gates to his feet. "I object, Your Honor. Detective Webb is not on trial here. The defendant has already admitted killing Paul Donaldson."

"I agree," said Judge Rosencrance. "Mr. Boland, am I missing something?"

"I apologize, Your Honor, and I'll withdraw that question. I do, however, have one final question. Detective Webb, can you enlighten us as to the significance of the Bible verses left by the Avenger?"

"Not really. I left that to the psychiatrists."

"Thank you, Detective Webb, that's all I have." With a satisfied look, Marc Boland turned, glanced at Boyd Gates, and took his seat.

85

AFTER A RECESS, Dr. Edward Chow took the stand, and Catherine's emotional roller coaster took another plunge. The small man was precise, professional, and well credentialed. Catherine remembered trying hard to dislike him during her two sessions with the psychiatrist. His disarming manner did not make it easy. As he testified now, she could sense the jury bonding with him while they learned about the intricacies of dissociative identity disorder.

It was, Chow testified, hotly debated whether DID even existed as a psychological disorder. A substantial school of thought held that DID patients either faked their alternate personalities or simply responded to suggestive counseling from their psychiatrists. For the purposes of this case, the psychiatrist said, it didn't really matter. Because even if there was such a thing as DID, Catherine O'Rourke was clearly not suffering from it.

Chow repeated much of the theme of the prosecution's case—that the crime was too well planned and too carefully covered up for it to be the spontaneous work of an alternate personality—but he buttressed the theory by lending his own considerable authority to the argument and cloaking it in official-sounding words.

"Catherine O'Rourke evinced consciousness of guilt," Chow testified, "by throwing out her computer before the authorities could execute their search warrant. In addition, a schizoaffective disorder almost always has a precipitate cause that triggers the psychotic break or, in the case of DID, the manifestation of another personality. After meeting with the defendant for several hours and after reviewing all the known facts of this case, I can point to no precipitate cause that might have occurred just before the killing of Paul Donaldson or any of the other victims."

The only thing that stopped Chow from completely dismantling the defense's case on Thursday afternoon was the clock. When the judge banged her gavel to call it a day, Chow seemed genuinely disappointed. He was the only one in the courtroom still looking fresh, his charcoal gray suit hardly wrinkled. To Catherine it seemed like he had so much more to say, more nails he wanted to drive into the coffin.

The next morning, Chow wasted no time continuing the assault. He shifted gears to what he termed "the underlying cause of the alleged dissociative identities." In Chow's opinion, the "alleged rape" during college was insufficient to create a psychotic break that could lead to multiple personalities, especially personalities that didn't manifest themselves until eight years later. DID was almost always caused by chronic abuse during childhood, a time in life when personality integration was occurring and could be stunted. DID caused by a single rape during someone's early adult years, or even multiple episodes of rape in a single night, would be unprecedented.

Not surprisingly, Chow had a few opinions about Catherine's jailhouse behavior as well. Catherine had shown the aggressive side of her core personality when she bludgeoned her cellmate, an event that Chow accentuated with some show-and-tell pictures of Holly's face. Plus, Catherine had pretty much gone berserk when she saw Kenny Towns on television. "The defendant claims to remember both of those incidents," Chow testified. "So they certainly can't be blamed on this mythical 'Avenger of Blood.'"

Gates paused and made a big show of checking his notes. "One final question: based on your assessment of Ms. O'Rourke, your review of the evidence, and your training and background, do you have an opinion as to why she would kill a man she didn't even know?"

Catherine expected Quinn to object but her defender just nonchalantly scribbled some notes.

"I do. It's my opinion that this whole Avenger of Blood persona and the preying on alleged rapists and their attorneys was an elaborate attempt by Ms. O'Rourke to deflect blame so that she wouldn't be a suspect when she committed her ultimate crime."

"Her *ultimate* crime, doctor?"

"I believe that Ms. O'Rourke fully intended to kill Kenneth Towns."

86

CATHERINE FOUND OUT why Quinn hadn't objected about two seconds into his cross-examination.

"Wow," he said, buttoning his suit coat. "Isn't that straying a little far from your field of expertise—making predictions about crimes that haven't yet occurred? You're not a fortune-teller, are you?"

"Objection."

"Sustained."

Quinn smiled. "To your knowledge, did the police find any evidence that my client even knew where Mr. Towns lived?"

"No."

"Any evidence that she had contacted him since college?"

"Not that I'm aware of."

"So your theory is that Catherine O'Rourke gets raped in college and then, eight years later, decides to kill her rapist but figures, 'Hey, before I even figure out where he lives I might as well kidnap a few babies and kill a few men I've never met first in order to deflect attention from me?'"

Gates stood, his face red. "Objection, Judge. That totally mischaracter-izes the testimony."

"He can answer," Rosencrance ruled.

"When you don't deal with the kind of pain that Ms. O'Rourke suffered eight years ago, Mr. Newberg, it can cause you to do some pretty—" Chow hesitated as if searching for the right word—"*desperate* things."

"Is the word you were actually looking for more like *bizarre* or *crazy?*" Quinn asked.

"Objection."

"Sustained."

"Okay, let's switch gears. Were you aware that Detective Webb, acting as a confidential informant for the newspaper, told my client that Reverend Harold Pryor was a prime suspect and that he had no alibi?"

"I wasn't aware of that, no."

"Assuming that was the case," Quinn said, "does that affect your opinion on whether Ms. O'Rourke was just creating this 'mythical Avenger persona' to divert attention away from what you called her ultimate crime?"

Chow looked pensive, his brow knit. "No. I don't see why that would change anything."

In response, Quinn talked slowly, making sure Dr. Chow understood his point. "If Catherine O'Rourke knew she was the killer and wanted to deflect suspicions by inventing these visions, why didn't she provide a description of Reverend Pryor as the Avenger of Blood when she reported her visions to Detective Webb?"

Chow sat there for a moment, his brain apparently churning through different possibilities. "I'm not sure," he eventually admitted. "Perhaps she believed it would seem too obvious."

"Or perhaps," Quinn countered, "my client is telling the truth."

Quinn chipped away at Chow's opinion for several more hours on Friday, belittling the man's opinion that DID could not possibly have been caused by the rape that occurred during Catherine's college years. Quinn also suggested that the precipitating event Chow was supposedly searching for might have been Catherine's coverage of Anne Newberg's murder trial.

"Did it ever occur to you," Quinn asked, "that Catherine O'Rourke's extensive involvement with and coverage of that murder trial—where another woman took vengeance for years of abuse—might have triggered the manifestation of this alter personality in Catherine's life?"

Chow hesitated, but then answered confidently. "No, I don't believe that's the case."

"But you never even considered that possibility until this very moment, did you?" Quinn pressed.

"That's true," Chow admitted. "But that doesn't change my opinion."

"You've been paid too much to switch at the last minute; is that it?"

"Objection!" barked Gates. Then he mumbled loud enough for the jury to hear, "That's ridiculous."

"Sustained."

As Quinn battled with Chow, Catherine silently battled her own emotions. She still found it hard to believe this was *her* murder trial, *her* Vegas lawyer posturing and mocking and drawing objections left and right from the ever-serious Boyd Gates.

The emotion that surprised Catherine most, and the one she had the hardest time dismissing, was a growing attraction to the man who now commanded the courtroom. Catherine had always prided herself in being logical—a skeptical newspaper reporter who knew how to cut through appearances and smoke screens. And Quinn, she reminded herself, was a Las Vegas performer, a showman, a trial lawyer. He seemed to care deeply for her, but it was probably all just an act. Just a lawyer's way of bonding with a client.

Quinn obviously believed that Catherine had killed two men and kidnapped three babies. Bluntly put, he thought Catherine was certifiably crazy. How could he have feelings for her at the same time?

But there was no denying what had happened after court on Wednesday. Sure, Quinn had been comforting a troubled client. But there was more. Catherine had felt the electricity when they touched. She would never forget the way he brushed the hair behind her ear and grazed his fingers along her cheeks. Looking through the slot of the metal door, she had seen something special in Quinn's eyes, a look of pain because he couldn't hold her. Had she just been imagining that? Was this another way her mind was playing games on her, distorting reality by making her believe Quinn was a handsome prince here to deliver Cat from this nightmare, only to be disappointed when he moved on to another client at the conclusion of the case?

"No further questions," Quinn said, staring at the beleaguered witness for a moment before taking a seat. Gates did a quick redirect as the entire courtroom seemed to breathe a little easier, relaxing from the tension that Quinn had summoned for his cross-examination.

"It's nearly 4:00," said a weary Judge Rosencrance when Gates finished. "This may be a good time to adjourn for the weekend."

But Gates apparently did not want to leave the jurors with the words of Chow's cross-examination ringing in their ears. "The commonwealth has one more witness we would like to present today, if possible. Her direct examination won't take more than ten minutes."

Rosencrance sighed and turned to the defense lawyers. Quinn stood. "Your Honor, we'd like to let the jurors get a jump on the Friday afternoon traffic. And we wouldn't mind one ourselves."

The jurors, Catherine noted, looked grateful.

But Gates wasn't through. "As long as Mr. Newberg doesn't drag out *this* cross-examination, we can do both—hear the witness and get a jump on traffic."

"Okay," said Rosencrance, though her tone said she didn't like it, "call your next witness."

"The commonwealth calls Tasha Moorehouse."

Catherine couldn't believe it. She turned to the door that led to the holding cell. The deputy disappeared through the door and a few seconds later came back, trailed by Tasha. She took the stand, dressed in a nice pair of slacks and a blouse, her face stern and unyielding. She didn't even look in Cat's direction.

Why was Gates calling *Tasha* to the stand?

Maybe he just wanted her to provide corroborating testimony about Cat's fight with Holly or the day Cat went crazy when Kenny Towns appeared on television. Cat quickly scrolled through her memory of the thousands of conversations she'd had with Tasha, the way she had confided in her cellmate.

Cat couldn't recall a single incriminating statement. And even if she could, she couldn't imagine Tasha turning on her. They were both members of the Widows. Tasha had been on Cat's side since day one.

But Cat's stomach was in utter turmoil.

Why won't she look at me?

87

QUINN HAD BEEN TRYING CASES long enough to know that jailhouse snitches came with the territory. He sensed Catherine's discomfort at her former cellmate's betrayal, but there was nothing Quinn could do about that except dismantle this woman on the stand.

Gates took the witness quickly through some background questions, and Tasha responded with a surly I-don't-want-to-be-here attitude.

"Did the defendant ever make a statement to you about this alternate persona that she claims was responsible for the killing of Paul Donaldson?"

"Yes."

"What did she say?"

"Lots of things."

Gates took a step closer to the witness. "Did she ever discuss the specifics of whether she should fake such a personality in order to help her case?"

"Are you kidding me?" Cat whispered. "I never talked about that."

"Yes," said Tasha.

"Tell us about it."

"We was talking about Barbie's shrink—Barbie was what we called the defendant—and she had that shrink named Mancini, or some Italian name like that. So Barbie says to me, 'Do you think it would help if Mancini actually meets the Avenger of Blood?' And I'm like, 'Meets her how?' Barbie gets all secretive and stuff, lookin' around to make sure nobody's listening. Then she whispers to me, 'You know, what if I turn into the Avenger while this shrink's counseling me and I get all wild-eyed.' Something like that."

Cat leaned close to Quinn. "She lying; I swear it. I never said *anything* like that."

Quinn nodded, trying to focus on the testimony.

"What did you tell the defendant?" Gates asked.

Tasha shrugged. "I told her not to try and fake it. Lyin' gets complicated, and people know how to trip you up."

Quinn frowned and turned toward Catherine, in part to get his client to look away from the jury so they wouldn't see the shock registering on her face. "What do you know about her?" Quinn whispered. "What's she serving time for?"

"I don't know much," Catherine said, clearly flustered. "She's awaiting trial on some type of firearms charge—being a 'straw purchaser,' I think she said. It's like her third offense."

"To your knowledge," Gates said, "did the defendant manufacture any dangerous weapons while in jail?"

"She sure did."

"Tell us about it."

"She showed me how to make it," Cat whispered furiously to Quinn. "It was her idea."

"She filed her toothbrush down to a shank. Said she was saving it for just the right occasion. Kept it hid inside her mattress."

"Did you tell the prison guards about it after your cellmate was placed in solitary confinement?" Gates asked.

"Yeah."

Gates moved dramatically back to his counsel table and retrieved a tooth-brush in a plastic evidence bag. The handle of the toothbrush had been filed to a sharp point. He showed it to Quinn, who shrugged it off.

Gates had Tasha identify the weapon and introduced it as an exhibit.

"No objection," said Quinn.

Gates consulted his notes. "Let me direct your attention to an incident that occurred on Monday, June 16, in the pod that you shared with Ms. O'Rourke and a number of other prisoners. Did anything unusual occur on that day?"

"Is that the day that dude Kenny was on the tube?" Tasha asked.

Quinn stood to object, but Gates was faster. "I can't give you informa-tion, Ms. Moorehouse. Why don't you just tell us what happened on the day that you and the defendant saw Mr. Towns on television?"

"Well, this man that Barbie says raped her in college comes on TV and gets all indignant and stuff. 'The sex was consensual. Ask any of my frat brothers.' You know, like that. Well, this dude is hot, and so all the inmates start giving Barbie a hard time—they're gettin' in her face, making all these suggestive motions and stuff, and Barbie just basically freaks."

"What do you mean by that—'just basically freaks'?"

"She gets all red in the face and starts cursing and yelling, her eyes bugging out like she wants to kill someone—"

"Objection!" shouted Marc Boland.

Gates turned. "Which one of you guys is going to be examining her? You can't both make objections."

"I'm sustaining the objection," said Rosencrance. "Ms. Moorehouse, just stick to the facts. Don't characterize things.

"And, Mr. Boland, I suggest you and Mr. Newberg decide which one of you will be examining this witness. This isn't a tag-team match."

"I've got her," Quinn whispered to Marc.

"You sure?"

"I want her."

Gates kept plowing forward. "Just tell us what happened, Ms. Moorehouse."

"So then Barbie starts attacking everybody. She grabs trays of food and throws them at the TV. She goes ballistic on the trustee who has the remote. I mean, she just freaked."

"What did you do?"

"I tried to stop her. I didn't want her to get busted on somethin' this stupid. So I'm sayin', 'That guy on TV is a jerk, don't sweat it,' and Barbie just snapped."

Tasha paused, and Quinn sensed the punch line coming.

"So I jumped in front of her and tried holding her back, just to keep her from getting into more trouble."

"What did the defendant do?"

"She's like tryin' to fight through me to get at the trustee, screaming, 'Let me go,' and 'Stay out of this' and stuff like that. After I calmed her down and she stopped strugglin', she just looks at me. She's still hacked but she's not, like, wild-eyed or anything anymore. And she just says to me, all calm-like, 'I should have done Towns first.'"

Moorehouse paused, her statement sucking the air out of the courtroom. Quinn heard a gasp from Cat's mother and sister, seated behind him.

"She's *lying*," Cat whispered to Quinn, her voice choked with desperation.

Quinn put a calming hand on Cat's knee. "I'll handle it."

"You're sure that's what she said?" Gates asked. "That she should have done Towns first."

"God's truth," Tasha responded. "Every word."

"And what did you understand that to mean?"

"That she wished she had capped this dude Towns first, as opposed to all these other guys."

"Did she appear normal at the time?"

"Objection!" This time it was Quinn.

"Sustained."

"Describe her demeanor when she made the statement."

"She was real calm," said Tasha. "I was like, 'Whoa, girl, you are *cold*.'"

88

"YOU'VE GOT A KNACK for picking friends," Quinn whispered to Catherine before he stood to examine Tasha. "Do you know if she took the stand in her last trial?"

Cat furrowed her brow. "I don't know, but I bet she did. She's pretty arrogant."

"Mr. Newberg?" prompted Judge Rosencrance.

Quinn grabbed a thick legal brief from the table, then stood and buttoned his suit coat, taking his time. He walked closer to the witness box than normal.

"Did you discuss your testimony with Mr. Gates before taking the stand?"

Tasha looked wary, even hostile. "I told him what I was going to say. That's all."

"Did he show you this document?" Quinn asked, waving it around a little with his left hand.

"No. I don't even know what that is."

"The prosecutor's handbook," Quinn said, "where it says, on page 53, 'If your expert witness falls apart on the stand, you can always fall back on a jailhouse snitch.'"

Tasha looked confused.

"Objection!" shouted Gates, his face growing red. "That's ridiculous."

Rosencrance looked like she might be trying to suppress a smirk. "It's cute; I'll give you that much," she said to Quinn. "But this is a murder trial, and we don't do cute in my courtroom during murder trials. This is a warning, Mr. Newberg. Next time it will cost you."

"Yes, Your Honor."

Rosencrance turned to the jury. "Please ignore that last comment by Mr. Newberg. It was just grandstanding, not evidence."

"Let's talk about your record," Quinn said. He placed the legal brief back on his counsel table. "How many felony convictions do you have, and what are they for?"

"Two," said Tasha. "One for possession and one for being an accomplice."

"An accomplice to what?"

"Armed robbery," Tasha said grudgingly, shooting daggers at Quinn with her eyes.

"Given the fact that you're in the city jail, I presume you're facing trial for another offense?"

Quinn waited for an objection—convictions were normally fair game but not accusations on crimes that hadn't yet gone to trial. When no objection came, it told Quinn what he wanted to know.

"Yes," Tasha answered. "Violation of state firearms laws."

"That's a serious offense," Quinn said. "Did the prosecutors promise you any kind of deal in exchange for your testimony in this case?"

"They said they might consider a deal."

"Might consider a deal. What kind of deal?"

"Maybe plead to makin' a false statement to a law-enforcement officer."

Quinn smiled. "What a deal! How could you say no to that? That sounds like it's only a misdemeanor. Am I right?"

"Yes."

"So, instead of facing your third felony and a long jail sentence under Virginia's three-strikes-and-you're-out law, you're looking at a simple misdemeanor?"

"Yeah."

"Maybe you could have asked Mr. Gates to throw in a small car."

"Objection." This time Gates didn't even raise his voice, as if Quinn wasn't worthy of getting a rise out of him.

"Mr. Newberg . . ."

"Sorry, Judge. I keep forgetting I'm not in Las Vegas anymore." Quinn smiled, but Rosencrance did not.

"Proceed," she said.

"As I understand your testimony, you told my client not to pretend to be the Avenger during a session with Dr. Mancini because lying gets complicated and she might get caught."

"Exactly."

"Is that based on your own experience with fabricating testimony?"

"I don't know what you're talking about."

"This last conviction of yours—the accomplice thing?—am I correct that you took the stand in your own defense?"

"Yeah, that's right."

"And a jury of your peers decided not to believe you, right?"

Tasha shrugged. "They got it wrong."

"But you're hoping that maybe this jury *will* believe you. Maybe this will be your lucky day."

"Objection. Argumentative."

"Sustained."

Quinn headed back to his counsel table and stopped. *I don't know what possesses me to do this,* he thought.

"When you get out of jail, Ms. Moorehouse, do you have any plans to visit Las Vegas?"

Tasha furrowed her brow. "No."

"Too bad. Guys like me love to see tourists like you walk into our poker rooms—always sure that *this* is going to be their lucky day."

"Objection!" Gates shouted.

This time, there was no smirk hiding under Rosencrance's glare. "Dismiss the jury!" she ordered.

After a tongue-lashing, she levied a two-thousand-dollar fine against Quinn for grandstanding. She instructed Marc Boland to keep his out-of-state co-counsel under control. She told Quinn he was in danger of having his *pro hac* status removed, making him ineligible to continue on this trial.

Quinn acted contrite, apologizing for pushing it too far. He said all the right things in all the right places, but a single thought kept floating through his head.

It was worth every penny.

89

ONE THING ABOUT SOLITARY CONFINEMENT—it gave a person time to think. And to read. On Friday night, her third consecutive night in solitary, Cat did a lot of both.

She might have been the only one, but she still believed in her own innocence. *Most* of the time. Not just innocence by reason of insanity, a game that lawyers played, but total and complete exoneration. She *wasn't* the Avenger of Blood. She *hadn't* killed Paul Donaldson. And she certainly hadn't killed those babies. Why wouldn't anyone believe her?

Cat was convinced that her visions were the key to solving this case. A few weeks ago, when she had embraced this conclusion, she'd decided to explore every possible explanation for the visions. If she knew what caused them, maybe she could figure out why she stopped having them. And, more importantly, the identity of the real killer.

She'd read the biblical book of Daniel at least three times. In Cat's visions, there was handwriting on the wall. Belshazzar, king of Babylon, had seen handwriting on the wall. Daniel had interpreted what that handwriting meant. All throughout the book of Daniel, kings had dreams or visions, and Daniel interpreted them. All the dreams and visions were messages from God. His finger literally wrote the words on the wall.

Dr. Mancini had seemed to embrace this spiritual explanation, at least in the early days before she had proffered her report about Cat's insanity. "God communicates through His written Word," she had told Cat. "And He showed us what love was like when He sent His Son to live among us. But occasionally, He also communicates through dreams and visions. Treat it as a gift, Catherine. Embrace these visions as God working through you."

But Cat was sitting in prison as a result of the visions. They certainly didn't feel like a gift.

She explored other explanations as well, scientific theories, but few of these seemed very plausible. Cat had read two books about science and the paranormal cover to cover. One book, *Spook*, dealt with scientific explanations of various aspects of the afterlife. It was, according to the author, "spirituality treated like crop science." The other book, *Ghost Hunters*, was about William James and a group of scientists called the Society for Physical Research, detailing their search for scientific proof of life after death.

Cat thought the scientists were every bit as confused as she was. They did, however, provide a few theories that made Cat think. Some members of the Society for Physical Research believed that telepathy could be viewed as a unique way that certain gifted humans communicated. Perhaps, in addition to the audible waves generated by voice patterns, humans also communicated through invisible and inaudible waves much like electromagnetic waves. Maybe some humans, like Catherine, were exceptionally tuned in to such waves, more so than the normal person.

This could mean that Cat's visions were the result of receiving information subliminally from another person who knew about these crimes. The most likely suspect was her confidential source, Jamarcus Webb. Maybe she had received subliminal information from Jamarcus and stored it away until it came out during the visions. Such an explanation would also account for why Cat hadn't received any more visions recently, since she had stopped meeting with Jamarcus.

Other scientists believed that dying persons sometimes gave off strong invisible signals—they called them "crisis apparitions"—which explained why many times people reported having an uneasy feeling at the precise moment of a relative's death, even if the dying relative lived quite a distance away. But Cat wasn't related to any of these folks. And her first two visions had occurred well after the actual kidnappings.

There was a final explanation, one so troubling that Cat rejected it out of hand. Demonic forces were sometimes responsible for dreams and visions, especially if someone had dabbled in the occult. Surely this couldn't be the case in Cat's life. She wasn't exactly a nun, but she hadn't been flirting with the dark side either. Not even in her childhood could she remember being part of a séance or even having her palm read by an amusement park gypsy.

On Friday night, Cat fell asleep still reading her books. She awoke, as usual, at 4:30 a.m. to the annoying sound of a guard scraping a flashlight over the prison bars. It had been another dreamless night. Wherever this power was coming from—whether it was spiritual or telepathic or something else— it had apparently deserted Cat during her hour of greatest need. Frustrated, she picked up her books and started reading again. Maybe she was missing something.

90

ON SATURDAY, ROSEMARIE MANCINI AND SIERRA came into town, and Quinn spent most of the day with his niece. He could tell that Sierra's time with Rosemarie had done her a lot of good. She seemed more self-confident and relaxed, full of chatter about her new D.C. friends. She and Quinn spent the afternoon lying on the beach, though neither of them set foot in the water. They went shopping for Sierra's school clothes at the Lynnhaven Mall and ate dinner on the back deck of a fish house nestled along the Lynnhaven River. They talked a lot about Annie, Quinn virtually guaranteeing an acquittal for Sierra's mom the next time around.

"I like D.C.," Sierra said. "And I like Rosemarie."

The first time Quinn had heard his niece use Rosemarie Mancini's first name, he had winced. "She told me to call her that," Sierra had said. Now, it seemed natural, indicative of a growing level of friendship and trust between them. It was hard to believe that a few months ago this same young girl had been suicidal.

On Sunday, Quinn and Rosemarie got down to work, slugging through her direct examination and practicing the questions Gates might bring up on cross. They still had a lot of ground to cover at 5 p.m. when Quinn received a phone call from Billy Long. "Can I call you back?" asked Quinn. "I'm meeting with Dr. Mancini."

"No," said Billy. "This won't keep."

Billy sounded serious enough that Quinn decided not to argue. "Okay, what's up?"

"You need to be alone when you hear this," insisted Billy.

"It's okay. I'm with Dr. Mancini."

"That's not alone."

Annoyed, Quinn asked Rosemarie if she could give him a minute. After she left the conference room, Quinn said, "This better be good. I trust Rosemarie with my life."

BY REASON OF INSANITY

"I found one of the Carver babies," Billy said.

"What?"

"I found one of the Carver twins. The little boy."

"You found the body?"

"I found the baby, Quinn. Alive. Healthy. Crying and crawling and pooping in his diaper."

It took Quinn a second to catch his breath; he wanted to pump his fist in the air. *Alive!* But before he reacted, a crushing truth hit him. This would complicate things. It was great for the Carvers, but what about the case?

"Where?" Quinn asked. Before Billy could answer, another thought: "How'd *you* find him when half the cops in Virginia are looking for him?"

"He's in L.A.," said Billy. "Asian Central. I put the word out that I had a wealthy client who wanted to adopt a little boy without all the red tape. One thing led to another, and I stumbled across a few black-market baby operations. From there, you probably don't want to know, but let's just say I can squeeze folks in a way the cops can't."

"How do you know for sure it's Chi Ying?"

"I've seen him," Billy responded. "And everything fits. The timing, the age, and he looks just like the pictures. I even sent two digital photos via e-mail to a colleague of mine who does digital facial analysis. He says it's the same kid."

Alarm bells went off for Quinn. "What did you tell this colleague?"

"I'm not a complete idiot," Billy said. "I told him one was a picture of the kid while he was with the Carvers and the other, we think, is a picture of the kid when he was still in China. I told him we were trying to locate Chi's birth parents in China to ask them some questions, and we wanted to make sure we had the right kid."

The cover story sounded like a stretch to Quinn, but he let it pass. "Did you track down how Chi got to this new family?"

"I hit a lot of dead ends on that line. To be honest, I wasn't sure I wanted to know."

"Why?"

"Well . . ." Billy stretched out the word, apparently measuring his thoughts. "If Ms. O'Rourke's innocent, somebody's done a masterful job setting her up. If that's the case, I'm presuming they would have made it look like the money for those babies somehow went to Ms. O'Rourke. If she actually killed Donaldson and Archibald, it's even worse."

Billy paused and coughed, then picked up on his line of thought. "One of the things that always made me think our client might actually be insane is the fact that *somebody* killed those babies. Frankly, I've never heard of a woman killing a little baby unless she was totally nuts. But now we know that somebody went to a lot of trouble to make sure at least one of those babies *didn't* die. It seems to me somebody just wanted people to *think* the babies were dead so everyone would assume that whoever did this was crazy. I was afraid that if I figured out who sold those babies to the black-market folks, we might not like the answers."

Quinn reached the same conclusion even as Billy was talking. This would not be good for their case unless they could tie somebody else to the kidnappings. It would be quite a stretch to make a jury believe that the Avenger of Blood, Catherine's alternate personality, had kidnapped Chi only to sell him on the black market. Killing a baby would indicate insanity. But kidnapping a baby and selling him on the black market showed premeditation and deception over an extended length of time.

"Whom have you talked to about this?" Quinn asked.

"I work for you," Billy said. "Why would I talk to anybody else?"

"Are you still in L.A.?"

"Yeah."

"I need you on the first flight back to Norfolk. We might want you to testify."

91

QUINN NEWBERG AND MARC BOLAND had not requested to meet together with Cat since Quinn entered the case. But on Sunday night, the deputy escorting her to the attorney interview booth told her that her "lawyers" had requested a meeting.

"Which one?" Cat asked.

"Both."

When she arrived, Bo was sitting in the chair on the other side of the bulletproof glass, and Quinn was standing behind him—two men squeezed into a booth designed for one.

Cat sat down, nerves prickling the back of her neck. "What's going on?" she asked, trying to read their faces.

"We've got some important news," Bo said.

They both looked so serious that Cat felt her stomach drop. *Have they discovered another body?*

"Billy Long thinks he has found Chi Ying, the Carvers' little boy, alive and well in Los Angeles."

Cat gasped and put her hand over her mouth. She felt herself trembling, tears welling in her eyes. She tried to say something but couldn't speak.

"Obviously, this is great news," Bo said, though his face indicated otherwise, "assuming we can verify it. Billy had an expert look at some digital photos to confirm the identity, but we don't have any fingerprints or DNA analysis yet."

"I don't know what to say," Cat managed. A wave of gratitude flooded her, washing away emotions that had tormented her since her arrest. It took her a few seconds to regain her composure. She wiped at her eyes, then took a deep breath. "What about his sister?"

"We don't know about her yet," Bo said. "Or about Rayshad Milburn. But we think there's a good chance they're alive too."

Cat couldn't believe this. It was the break she had been hoping for, praying for.

"The thing is," Bo continued, "we haven't been able to track down *how* the little Carver boy ended up out there. Billy tells us that Chi got placed through a black-market baby operation but that he ended up with a good family. We can't get a bead on who delivered him to the operation in the first place."

The seriousness of Cat's attorneys took the edge off her euphoria. What did this mean for the case?

Bo anticipated her question. "Quinn and I have been kicking this around for the past hour or so." Both lawyers stared intently at Cat as Bo talked, apparently searching for some type of reaction. "If this information gets out, it would dramatically impact our case in two ways, both negative. First, it would demonstrate a level of planning and deceit that would make it much harder, maybe impossible, to prove insanity. And second, it would look like you had purposefully misled the investigators when you described your visions, since you described the babies being strapped into an electric chair. Boyd Gates will argue that you created this scenario of dead babies just to make a case for insanity if you got caught when you went after Towns."

"But I didn't go after Towns," Cat protested. "And I didn't kidnap those babies. This is what I've been telling you."

"We understand that," Quinn said, though his tone was unconvincing. "But it's our job to do what's best for you. If we try to change our plea now, the judge and jury will crucify us. We need to keep making our case for insanity but at the same time have Billy continue this investigation. If we can link somebody besides you to the kidnappings, we can change our plea when we have hard evidence. If not, we continue to push insanity. Even if we lose the case, we can always move to reopen based on the results of Billy's investigation."

Cat's head swirled with confusion. *Bury the fact that one of the twins is still alive? How can that be right?* She realized, more from the looks on her lawyers' faces than from the words they were saying, that they didn't *want* to know who had sold the babies. They still believed she was guilty.

"I'm not on trial for the kidnappings. Would we be able to reopen this murder case based on information relating to the Carver twins?"

Both men hesitated, which told Cat everything. "It's not a certain thing," Bo said. "And it depends on the type of evidence. But we think it's likely."

"What happens if this little boy disappears in the meantime? I mean, maybe his parents find out about our case and put two and two together. What then?"

Bo leaned forward and lowered his voice. "This isn't without risk, Catherine. But we've got no legal obligation to reveal this information. Both Quinn and I believe it's not in your best interest to have it come out right now."

Catherine looked from Marc Boland to Quinn Newberg and back to Marc.

"You've got to trust us, Catherine," Marc said. "You're not objective in this. We are."

She put her face in her hands and tried to think. Images of the babies in the electric chairs came rushing back to her, making her shudder. She felt pressure building inside her head, saw the walls of the small interview room start billowing.

"What if I say no?" she asked.

Quinn spoke, his expression showing the strain. "We'd ask the court for leave to withdraw," he said softly. "We're committed to the insanity defense, Catherine. I know it's hard for you to accept, but on these facts, it's the only thing that makes sense."

She looked at Bo, who nodded his head.

"Then I don't know why you came by," Cat said, the frustration overwhelming her. "Just do what you've got to do."

She stared at them, her own lawyers, two men she admired and trusted—but even they couldn't accept the possibility that their client just might be innocent.

"Are we done?" she asked.

"We're done," Bo said softly.

"Good." Cat rose from her seat and turned to the door, knocking loudly. She left with the deputy, not bothering to thank her lawyers or tell them good-bye.

92

BACK IN HER CELL, Catherine wrestled with her emotions. Concealing the information about Chi Ying just seemed so *wrong*. She wanted to call Quinn collect and talk with him alone, but she didn't have phone privileges in solitary confinement.

She knew Quinn and Bo cared about her. But she also knew that in their minds she had killed two people and kidnapped three kids. Technically, they might consider her not guilty by reason of insanity. But on a deeper level, they believed she was guilty as sin.

The incredible thing was that for a while she had even doubted herself. She still did, at times. But something about this newest piece of information seemed to shake her out of a fog. *I didn't do that.* The doubts weren't entirely gone, but they no longer dominated.

Cat couldn't shake the image of little Chi Ying from her mind. Should he have to stay with a family that would buy a baby on the black market just because Cat's lawyers thought it was a good legal strategy? And then a thought hit her that chilled her to the bone. What if the real kidnapper, the real Avenger of Blood, realized that the baby had been discovered? Would he or she contact the people who ran the black-market agency? Would those people find a way to eliminate the evidence if they thought they might get caught? Would the Avenger do it first?

Stirred to action, Cat pulled out a piece of paper and a pen. She *had* to do this. Maybe her lawyers would resign, maybe this would lead to a smoking gun against her, but how could she just sit back and do nothing?

> *Jamarcus,*
> *I have protected your confidences on occasions too numer-*
> *ous to count. I have gone to jail for you rather than breach*
> *that confidence. You have trusted me and, despite some of the*
> *allegedly incriminating information that is coming out in*
> *this trial, you need to know that your trust was not misplaced.*

With this letter, I'm placing my trust in you. I'm begging you to look into a matter but not to talk to anyone else about it.

It has come to my attention that my private investigator, a man named Billy Long, has located a baby in Los Angeles that he believes is Chi Ying. I do not know how Mr. Long located Chi. Perhaps you could privately question Mr. Long and find out the details. My concern is for the baby. If certain persons find out that Chi has been located, what would keep them from "eliminating" that problem?

I am completely innocent of these crimes, and I am trusting you to handle this with discretion so it won't come back to haunt me.
Yours,
Catherine

She read the letter twice, placed it in a sealed envelope, and addressed it to Jamarcus Webb. She would deliver it tomorrow morning in court. Assuming she didn't lose her nerve first.

The courtroom seemed larger, but the players were all the same. Judge Rosencrance scowling from the bench. Jamarcus Webb frowning in the front row. Just in front of him, at the counsel table, sat a sneering Boyd Gates, his bald pate reflecting the harsh courtroom lights. Cat's lawyers were there, of course, as was her family. In the back, standing against the wall, quoting Scripture and damning Cat to hell, was the Reverend Harold Pryor.

"Do you have a verdict?" Rosencrance asked, raising her voice to be heard over the rantings of Pryor.

A woman stood in the middle of the jury box. At first Cat didn't recognize her, but then it sunk in. The refined looks. The sorrow etched into the worried face. Marcia Carver! The jury foreperson was Marcia Carver!

"We've reached a verdict," Marcia said.

Pryor stopped talking, and the courtroom fell silent.

"Will the accused please stand?" Rosencrance asked.

Trembling and weak-kneed, Cat stood, Marc Boland on one side, Quinn on the other. An eternity of silence followed while all eyes turned toward Catherine as if the spectators expected a spontaneous confession. Catherine glanced toward Marcia but couldn't hold the woman's severe stare.

"What is your verdict?" Rosencrance asked.

"Guilty," Marcia Carver said, "of murder in the first degree."

Shaking uncontrollably now, Cat nearly collapsed to the floor. How could this have happened?

"So say you all?" Rosencrance asked.

The other jurors nodded their heads. Cat tried to get her bearings.

"I hereby find the defendant guilty of murder in the first degree," Rosencrance pronounced, her words ripping at Cat's heart. "We will begin the sentencing phase tomorrow morning."

"Amen," said the voice of Pryor.

But Marcia Carver did not sit down. "Not the defendant," she said, her voice trembling as the other jurors nodded along. She extended a long, accusatory finger.

"Him!"

93

EXHAUSTED FROM A LATE NIGHT of trial prep with Rosemarie Mancini, Quinn arrived just a few minutes before the start of court on Monday. He had not told Mancini about the discovery of the Carver baby. He and Marc Boland, as Catherine's attorneys, were protected from having to divulge such information, but an expert witness for the defense, subject to cross-examination on the witness stand, would have no such luxury.

Most mornings, Quinn loved getting to the courthouse early enough to spend a few minutes with Catherine before court started. But after last night's disagreement, he sensed his time and energy might be better spent focusing on the testimony. Tonight he would spend hours in the small attorney-client interview booth with Catherine, preparing for her testimony tomorrow. Talking through some of these issues could wait until then.

Still, he found himself craving his time with her and worrying incessantly about what last night's decision might have meant to their relationship. He had to remember that first and foremost she was a client—one facing death row. The decision by Quinn and Bo not to immediately reveal the whereabouts of the Carver baby had been made for Catherine's benefit. Quinn knew she couldn't understand that yet, and he hoped it didn't tear the fabric of their complex relationship beyond repair, but he had to look out for Catherine's legal interests first.

Quinn mechanically unpacked his briefcase, glancing at the courtroom's side door leading to the holding cell where Cat waited. The truly crazy thing was that recently, Quinn would often catch himself thinking about a possible future with her. After a not-guilty verdict. After treatment by Mancini that successfully brought the Avenger character to the surface and helped Cat deal with the past. Quinn and Catherine, spending time together, giving in to the irresistible impulse to be with each other, exploring the undeniable chemistry that existed between them.

How insane was that? Of all the women in the world, Quinn wanted to spend time with only one: a client who was an admitted serial killer. *Maybe,* he mused, *it's just that old problem of wanting the one thing you know you can't have.*

"All rise," the bailiff said, and Quinn knew his personal problems would have to wait.

"You ready?" Bo whispered.

"I was born ready," Quinn replied.

Rosencrance settled into her seat, greeted the lawyers, and had the bailiff bring in Catherine. She looked even more tense than Quinn had expected, her eyes darting around the courtroom. Her normally graceful gait seemed forced. She took her seat between her two lawyers and leaned toward Quinn, latching on to his right forearm. He felt a stab of pain shoot through his rotator cuff.

"We've got to talk," she said. "The first chance we get."

Boyd Gates ended his case on a whimper, calling a fingerprint expert to the stand to confirm that the toothbrush with the pointed end found in Catherine's mattress did indeed belong to her. When Gates finished his questioning, Quinn and Bo looked at each other, as if both expected the other to conduct the cross. Bo stood. "No questions, Judge."

When Gates announced that the commonwealth rested, Quinn stood quickly, wanting to show the jury how excited he was about his first witness. "The defense calls Dr. Rosemarie Mancini to the stand."

Rosemarie walked into the well of the courtroom, nodded curtly at Quinn, and took her oath. She climbed into the witness chair and lowered the mike.

Quinn quickly marched her through the preliminaries while Rosemarie snapped off succinct answers about her experience, training, and background.

As always, Quinn wanted to get the payment question out of the way early so opposing counsel couldn't make a big deal of it on cross.

"Are we paying you for your time?" Quinn asked.

"Not enough," Rosemarie deadpanned.

"How much is 'not enough'?"

"Two hundred fifty an hour," the psychiatrist shot back. "A total of about nineteen thousand on this case to date."

"That sounds like an awful lot."

"Not compared to what you make."

The jury giggled a little, though Rosemarie kept a straight face. "And I'm glad you brought up the subject," she continued, "because so far I've yet to receive a dime of payment. My *bills* are nineteen thousand. My *collections* are zero."

That subject out of the way, Quinn walked Rosemarie through her diagnosis in the case.

"Assuming that the DNA and hair evidence linking Catherine O'Rourke to the crime are reliable," Rosemarie testified, "my working diagnosis is dissociative identity disorder."

Rosemarie explained the basics of the illness, switching into lecture mode as she cited the DSM-IV diagnostic manual, the "bible" for psychiatric evaluations. She admitted that she had not yet been able to surface this alternate personality, the Avenger of Blood, though the conditions for her treatment of Catherine were clearly not optimal. "After the pressure of the trial has concluded, I believe that Ms. O'Rourke will be in a psychological state that is much more conducive for treatment.

"The idea of DID is that a person's primary personality has fractured into several 'alter personalities' and that two or more of these subpersonalities share a single body, each with its own identity, each taking a turn controlling that individual's personality and behavior. These alter personalities emerge as a result of trauma and, to some extent, serve to protect the person from overwhelmingly painful memories. In Catherine's case, it's the memory and trauma of being raped by a man she once loved and possibly by his friends as well.

"In cases of DID, the core or primary person generally experiences periods of amnesia and may even find herself in a strange place with no idea how she arrived there. Sometimes, she feels like she has been asleep and has woken up tired. This is called an amnesic barrier between identities. One personality may have full access to the memory bank, while others get only partial access, and some may be altogether unaware of the others. Many times, someone who suffers from DID may have vague flashbacks, dreams, or visions, which are actually repressed memories of what happened while the alter personality was in control."

Quinn noted that a few of the jurors were taking notes. "Dr. Chow, the state's expert, insists that DID could not have been the result of one incident of rape," Quinn pointed out. "He says that this psychosis, if it actually exists, is almost always the result of repeated sexual abuse during childhood. Do you have an opinion on that?"

Rosemarie glared at Quinn as if he were the one with the contrary opinion. "Dr. Chow's analysis is patently ridiculous," she replied.

"Would you care to explain why?"

"First, it's demeaning to every woman in this courtroom."

"Objection!" Gates said.

But Rosemarie didn't wait for the judge. "To say that rape is not a sufficient precipitating event is nonsense."

"Dr. Mancini," Rosencrance interrupted.

"Yes, Your Honor?"

"You've served as an expert witness enough times to know that you need to wait on my ruling before continuing your answer."

"Sorry, Judge," said Mancini. "You're right. I just assumed you would overrule it, since this goes to the heart of what I'm saying."

"I am going to overrule it," said the judge.

"May I proceed?"

"Certainly."

"Where was I?" Mancini mused. "That's right, I was explaining how insulting it is for Dr. Chow to try to minimize rape. I've treated hundreds of rape victims. It's a life-shattering event that should never be downplayed. The very act of rape violates the sanctity of a woman's sexuality and shatters her emotional security. This is especially true if a woman is raped by someone she loves. Can it cause that person to have a psychotic break with reality? Absolutely."

"Can it also cause you—?"

"Mr. Newberg," Rosemarie interjected. "I'm accustomed to being interrupted by opposing counsel. Usually my own lawyer shows a little more courtesy."

"Sorry," Quinn said, resisting a smile. "I thought you were finished. Please continue."

"Thank you. Dr. Chow is right in saying that most cases of DID come from childhood abuse—85 percent to be exact. Which means that 15 percent originate from other traumatic experiences. With Catherine, we're dealing with a case in that other 15 percent."

Quinn stole a quick glance at the jury. They were listening. The Mancini magic was beginning to weave its spell. "What about this notion that Ms. O'Rourke is just faking it? Dr. Chow said this alternate personality is just a ruse concocted so that if she got caught on a killing spree, she would have an excuse."

Rosemarie nearly snorted at the idea. "I can detect malingerers, Mr. Newberg. I wasn't born yesterday. This would be a very difficult illness to fabricate. But here's the more important fact: Catherine O'Rourke didn't even try to fake it. Certainly someone of her intellectual prowess would know that her case would be stronger if I could say in court that I had been able to draw out this Avenger character, if I could assure the jury that we had begun treatment and that we would be able to integrate this personality into her core personality without further danger to herself or to society."

Rosemarie paused, but Quinn knew better than to interrupt again.

"Unfortunately, I can say none of those things. You can accuse Ms. O'Rourke of a lot of things. Faking an alter personality is not one of them. How can you say somebody is a terrible actress if she doesn't have a part in the play?"

Quinn nodded. The examination was going well. Maybe *too* well. It worried Quinn when opposing lawyers didn't fuss and fight—no objections, just the kind of fastidious note taking that Boyd Gates was doing.

It usually meant they had something devastating for cross.

94

BEFORE QUINN TURNED ROSEMARIE MANCINI OVER to Boyd Gates, there was one final subject to cover. It was an area that Quinn knew precious little about: religion.

"Dr. Mancini, the Avenger of Blood left four different messages at four different crime scenes. How did those messages factor into your evaluation?"

Out of the corner of his eye, Quinn saw Boyd Gates begin to rise as if he might object but then sit back down. Maybe he didn't want to draw any more attention than necessary to this part of Mancini's testimony.

"The Avenger left four messages, all Bible verses, at four different crime scenes. The first two messages, left after the kidnappings of the Carver babies and the Milburn baby, deal with the consequences of generational sin, saying that God visits the iniquities of the fathers unto the third and fourth generation. The last two verses, conveyed in connection with the death of Paul Donaldson and the apparent death of Rex Archibald, talk about individual accountability and punishment for sin. For example, Ezekiel 18:20 states that 'a son will not be responsible for the sins of his father.'"

"Children being punished for the sins of their parents seems unfair," Quinn noted.

"That's just it," Dr. Mancini said, her voice animated. "The Bible doesn't say the children are being *punished*. It says the iniquities of the fathers are *visited* on the children. It's another way of stating a phenomenon that those of us in mental health care have recognized to be true for a long time—there are some addictions or actions of parents that inevitably affect their children and even grandchildren and great-grandchildren. Drug abuse, for example. Or sexual abuse. These are what we call generational chains. The children aren't being *punished* for what their parents did, but they're certainly being *affected* by those actions. And this is true, Mr. Newberg, until somebody comes along with the courage to break those generational chains."

It occurred to Quinn that Rosemarie's testimony might be aimed more at him than the jury. But right now, he didn't have time to process all the implications.

"I don't quite understand the significance of all this to my client's diagnosis," Quinn said, feigning confusion.

"In my sessions with Ms. O'Rourke, I discovered that she is not particularly religious. Nor was she raised in a home where she might have been exposed to a lot of Scripture verses. So I became curious. If she was in fact the Avenger, where did these verses come from?"

Rosemarie stopped and took a quick sip of water, basking in the attention of everyone in the courtroom. "You know where I found the answer?" she asked, then quickly responded to her own question. "I looked at her college transcript. I discovered that the same year she was raped, Catherine was taking a course called Comparative Religious Thought. I actually called the professor who taught the course, Dr. Frederick Channing, and scheduled a time to meet with him.

"Professor Channing was kind enough to dig up some old notes and try to piece together the topics he might have covered in this course when Catherine took it. It turns out he spent a fair amount of time contrasting the justice systems of ancient cultures. For example, he compared the legal system of the Hittites to the Babylonians' Code of Hammurabi, and the Mosaic law to the ideals of the ancient Greeks and Romans. Among other things, he looked at the issue of vicarious punishment, that is, punishing children for the transgressions of their parents, which was common in many ancient belief systems, though not in Judaism. He also looked at the notion of vengeance, and particularly at the issue of blood feuds or blood avengers—a concept found both in the Old Testament and in Greek mythology."

Quinn waited for a moment, hoping the information was sinking in. "Why is that significant? That class was eight years ago."

"That's precisely the point. The same year that Ms. O'Rourke was so severely traumatized that her personality fractured, she was also wrestling with the concept of justice under these ancient belief systems. She was exposed to the role of the blood avenger under Mosaic law and to the three female avengers in the Greek epic *Eumenides*. So eight years later, when her alter personality began to emerge, referring to itself as the Avenger of Blood, it came complete with the seared-on memories and mind-sets from Catherine's college days, including these concepts from her religion class. She merged these two notions together—the wrath of the female furies from Greek mythology and the verses describing blood avengers from the Old Testament."

"Couldn't Catherine have just made that up?" Quinn probed. "Couldn't she have just consulted some old notes and thrown in those verses to fool people into thinking she's crazy?"

Rosemarie smirked. "C'mon, Mr. Newberg. First, that question assumes Catherine O'Rourke knows enough about DID to realize that an alter personality will exhibit many of the attributes and mind-sets from the time when that personality came into existence, much like a snapshot freezes a moment in time. Second, it assumes she also consciously remembers minute details from a class she took eight years ago. And third, if she made that up, don't you think she might have given me some clues about that old class rather than hoping I would dig it out on my own?"

"I see your point," Quinn said. "But it still seems strange that it would take this alter personality eight years to emerge. What could possibly have triggered it after all that time?"

"Ironically, one of your cases did," Rosemarie said confidently. "As a reporter, Ms. O'Rourke was assigned to cover your sister's murder trial." Rosemarie turned to the jury. "Most of you probably watched news coverage of Anne Newberg's case arising from her admitted killing of her abusive husband. I took the time to read dozens of newspaper articles written by Ms. O'Rourke about various murder trials. The articles about Anne Newberg's case are far more emotional and guttural than her normal reporting."

Rosemarie turned back to Quinn. "I believe that when Catherine first heard about your sister's case, she subconsciously saw Anne as the first of the female blood avengers—the furies—from the *Eumenides*. Shortly thereafter, this alter ego of Catherine's became the second. I think that's the reason she was so adamant about bringing you into the case. She saw you as the common link between her and Anne; you are the defender of the furies."

Quinn snuck a glance at the jury. They looked contemplative, as if weighing the merits of this bizarre theory that Mancini had proposed.

Bizarre, Quinn thought. *Just one step away from crazy.*

"No further questions," he said.

95

GATES WAS ON HIS FEET immediately, apparently trying to show the jury he was unafraid to take on Dr. Mancini.

"Since you're so familiar with the defendant's college record, I presume you know that she had a journalism major and a criminal justice minor?"

"That's correct."

"Meaning she would have studied cases involving the insanity defense."

"Presumably."

"In addition, for a number of years she covered the crime and courts beat for our local paper. Is that your understanding?"

"Yes."

"And in that capacity would have sat through numerous trials, including some dealing with the insanity defense?"

Mancini shrugged. "She would have attended numerous trials, yes. But the insanity plea is actually used far less frequently than most people think—"

"Just answer the question yes or no," Gates insisted.

But he was dealing with an experienced witness, one who knew her rights. "I thought I was allowed to explain where necessary," Mancini said to the judge.

"You are," Rosencrance ruled. "But keep it brief."

"Thank you," Mancini said. "As I was saying, Mr. Gates, the insanity plea is used so rarely that I would doubt Ms. O'Rourke ever covered a case quite like this one."

Gates glared at the witness. "She covered the case of Anne Newberg, who pleaded not guilty by reason of insanity, did she not?"

"Yes. And since I testified in that case, I can assure you that it was a totally different scenario than dissociative identity disorder."

Gates checked his notes, apparently deciding to move on. "Normally you can bring out an alter personality by bringing up memories of the triggering incidence either through hypnosis or other means; isn't that right?"

"That is normally the case, though not always."

"Did you try that here?"

"Yes. I don't use hypnosis, but we did dig deeply into the emotions of the rape and what Catherine remembers about that night."

"Did you ever trigger this alternate personality?"

"No, I didn't."

Gates looked puzzled—an act for the jury, no doubt. "You mentioned on direct examination that you expect to be paid a lot of money in this case for your opinions; is that correct?"

"That's correct, Mr. Gates. With emphasis on the phrase 'expect to be paid.'"

"Let's not be cute, Doctor. Twenty thousand dollars is a lot of money, isn't it?"

"To be precise it was nineteen thousand. But yes, it's a lot."

"And that's not the full extent of your bias, is it?"

Mancini knit her brow. "I'm not sure what you mean. Any professional wants to get paid. That doesn't make me biased."

Gates walked toward the front of the jury box, pulling the gaze of most jurors along. "Then let me make it real clear. Isn't it true that you and Mr. Newberg have formed quite a little team on these insanity cases? Isn't it true that you would do anything to help his cause? Isn't it true—?"

"Objection!" Quinn called out, jumping to his feet. He normally didn't object during Mancini's testimony, confident that she could fend for herself, but this was *way* over the line. "That's highly improper. Plus, it's about three questions in one."

"Judge, the bias of this witness is central to our case. I'm entitled to probe how tightly she is connected with defense counsel."

Standing there, it dawned on Quinn—he had been suckered. Gates wanted that objection. He wanted the jury focused on the question; he wanted the press on the edge of their seats. He wanted Quinn to make a big deal out of this, and Quinn had played right into his hands.

"You may ask about bias," Rosencrance ruled. "But one question at a time. And save your arguments for closing."

Gates paused, thinking. He spoke slowly, thoughtfully, theatrically. "Isn't it true that you and Mr. Newberg are so close, so willing to do anything for each other, that you're even helping him raise his niece?"

Quinn couldn't believe it! How dare Gates drag Sierra into this! Even Rosemarie seemed stunned into silence.

"Dr. Mancini," Gates insisted, "isn't it true that Quinn Newberg's niece is living with you right now?"

"Yes," Mancini answered.

Quinn stared at Gates in disbelief. Poor Sierra had nothing to do with this case. Nothing! She was just starting to get her legs back under her.

And with one insensitive question, Gates had blown it all away.

During the subsequent break, Quinn rose and walked over to Boyd Gates's counsel table. The prosecutor had his back turned and was talking with Jamarcus Webb.

"This case has nothing to do with my family," Quinn said. He placed a hand on Gates's elbow, and the prosecutor turned to face him. "Leave my family out of this."

Quinn's words caused a hush in the courtroom; spectators and press members gawked at the two.

"Your client killed five people, *three babies*, in cold blood," Gates said, thrusting out his jaw. "Everything's fair game in this trial, Newberg. *Everything*."

Quinn inched closer, his fury boiling over. "Not my family. My family stays out of this."

"Or what? Is this some kind of threat?"

A split second before Quinn could respond with a shove or a fist, Marc Boland edged between the two men, taking hold of Quinn's arm. "C'mon, Quinn," he said, nudging his co-counsel back from the brink. "It's a low blow. That's what he's known for. We've still got a case to try."

Quinn shot one last menacing look at Gates as he shook his right arm free from Boland, feeling the pain as he did so, then straightened his suit coat. He walked with Bo back to their counsel table "That guy's an idiot," Quinn said.

Bo looked at the reporters. "Show's over," he announced.

As Quinn sat down to cool off, the deputy who had escorted Catherine into the holding cell reentered the courtroom. Seeing him reminded Quinn.

"My client wants to meet with me," Quinn said to the deputy.

"You know the drill," the man said.

Bo decided to go make nice with the press, and Quinn headed toward the chamber where he could meet with Catherine, separated by about six inches of steel door.

He passed Mancini on the way.

"You need me to make an appointment?" she asked.

"For what?"

"For you. Anger management."

"Sorry, Rosemarie. The guy just knows how to get under my skin."

96

AFTER THE BREAK, the tension level in the courtroom had increased noticeably. There was none of the idle chatter and hustling into seats that usually occurred as Rosencrance took the bench.

Quinn sat numbly as the judge told everyone to be seated. He watched as she jotted a few notes. He knew he should be preparing himself for a tongue-lashing over his altercation with Gates, but he was still trying to process what Catherine had told him just moments ago.

Rosencrance had the bailiff bring Catherine into the courtroom. "Before I bring in the jury," she said, "I would like counsel to approach the bench."

Here it comes. Quinn noticed that Marc Boland stayed on his right, physically separating him from Boyd Gates.

The judge put her hand over her mike and leaned forward, her eyes dissecting Quinn. "I've about had it with your conduct in this courtroom, Counselor. My bailiff told me what happened during the break. I want you to know that I'll be filing a complaint against you with the Nevada state bar after this case. I would revoke your *pro hac* status right now, but then Mr. Boland would just ask for a continuance."

"I understand," Quinn said, thankful that she hadn't tried to make him apologize. A man had to have standards.

"And, Mr. Gates, as many cases as you've tried in my courtroom, you should know better than to pull a stunt like that on cross-examination."

Gates mumbled an apology.

"Now, gentlemen, we have a case to finish. Let's try to act like professionals for a change."

All three attorneys mumbled appropriate "Yes, Your Honors," and Gates started back to his seat.

"Wait a minute," Quinn said. "I have a motion I need to make."

Gates returned to the bench, giving Quinn a sideways look. Quinn leaned in and lowered his voice. "Your Honor, with respect, I move for a one-day recess."

"*What?*" Gates said.

"Let him finish," snapped Rosencrance.

"Thank you, Your Honor." Quinn felt the nerves tingle up his spine. Once he made this motion, there would be no turning back. "We've discovered evidence that may require us to change Ms. O'Rourke's plea."

Rosencrance nearly pulled an eyebrow muscle, and Quinn could understand why.

"And a second development that may require me to withdraw as counsel," he added.

At that claim, Marc Boland joined the others in looking at Quinn as if the Vegas lawyer had just turned into a toad.

"This better not be one of your gimmicks," Rosencrance said.

"It's not, Judge." Quinn swallowed his nerves and hoped he was doing the right thing. "We need a day to confirm this evidence. If it checks out, Judge, it could blow this case wide open. As an officer of the court, I would not be able to proceed with an insanity plea. In fact, I would have to withdraw so I could take the stand and testify."

Quinn could tell that Rosencrance wasn't buying it, but he couldn't provide specifics. Not yet. "I would be glad to submit a written proffer first thing tomorrow morning," Quinn said.

Rosencrance still looked skeptical.

Quinn knew he needed to emphasize the one thing trial judges feared more than anything else: appellate courts. Reversible error. "Judge, I don't want to try this case a second time. If this evidence proves out, requiring us to move forward with an insanity defense would be a guaranteed reversal. At the very least, you need to carefully consider this."

Rosencrance turned to Gates and, to Quinn's surprise, the prosecutor shrugged. "As long as you instruct Dr. Mancini that she can't talk to defense counsel between now and tomorrow morning, I'm okay with it."

Of course, thought Quinn. *Now that Gates has heard the entire direct examination of Mancini, he wants more time to prepare for the remainder of her cross. Plus, he wants the jury thinking about his last question during the overnight recess.*

"I want a written proffer of this alleged evidence first thing in the morning," Rosencrance ordered Quinn. "And it better be good. I'm not inclined to let a defendant change her plea in the middle of the trial absent some overwhelming reason. You don't get to take a trial run at the case and then change your strategy if things don't work out. Is that clear?"

"Absolutely, Your Honor."

"Bring in the jury," Rosencrance told the bailiff. "We're going to give them the rest of the day off."

"What the heck was that?" Marc Boland slammed the door of the conference room adjacent to Courtroom 7. Boland and Quinn were alone in the room, but the way Bo was shouting, Quinn was pretty sure the press contingent in the hallway could hear every word. "I thought we agreed to keep that evidence out of the case."

Boland stormed back and forth on his side of the table, opposite a seated Quinn. "You just destroyed our client's insanity plea," he complained. He bumped into a chair and kicked it for good measure. "You sold her out! What were you thinking?"

"Are you done?" Quinn asked.

Boland stopped and put both palms on the table, leaning toward Quinn. "Heck no, I'm not done. And I won't be done until I get some answers. I worked hard on this case—worked my tail off! And you just flippantly flush the whole thing down the toilet with your Las Vegas showmanship *crap*."

Boland cursed and slammed the side of his fist into the plasterboard wall. "What were you *thinking*?" he repeated.

"If you'd sit down and shut up for a second, I'll try to tell you," said Quinn.

Bo sat, his face tight with rage.

Quinn gave him a few more seconds to calm down. "I need to hire you as my lawyer." He kept his voice low and reasonable. "I need to tell you something in absolute confidence. And I need a lawyer who is thinking rationally as opposed to freaking out on me."

This seemed to blunt Bo's rage a little. Nothing flattered a lawyer like another lawyer seeking advice.

"Okay?" Quinn asked.

"I don't understand you," Bo said. "But okay."

Quinn took another few seconds to collect his thoughts. "Our mutual client had another vision last night," he began. "Actually a dream. I'll spare you all the details, but she basically saw the jury verdict. The forewoman was

Marcia Carver. Reverend Pryor was ranting away from the back of the court-room. The jury delivered a guilty verdict on first degree murder but when Rosencrance started to sentence Catherine, the forewoman protested. She said the verdict wasn't against Catherine after all."

Quinn stopped abruptly, barely able to maintain eye contact. He sighed, it was too late to turn back now.

"Cat said she almost fainted when she saw where Marcia Carver was pointing. Cat said she felt so betrayed, like somebody had slid a knife in her back and cut out her heart."

"Why?" Bo asked, narrowing his eyes.

"Because she was talking about me, Marc. The forewoman in Catherine's dream was pointing at me."

97

"I KILLED MY BROTHER-IN-LAW," QUINN SAID.

He took a deep breath, and the facts came out in a torrent.

"Annie didn't shoot Richard Hofstetter; I did. Afterward, we decided she should confess to the crime because she'd have a better chance of getting acquitted. If the jury found her guilty, I'd admit the truth. The judge would have to grant a retrial, and I'd take the stand and confess. At worst, Annie might get hit with obstruction of justice, and I'd get convicted of murder. But this plan also gave us the best shot at both of us walking away scot-free."

Boland listened, his face unreadable.

"Annie called me a few days before the shooting and said she suspected Hofstetter was sexually abusing Sierra," Quinn continued. "She decided to confront him about it. The night of the shooting, she sent Sierra to a friend's house. She called and told me about her plans while she waited for Hofstetter to come home.

"He got there late, drunk and verbally abusive, but Annie confronted him anyway. He flew into a rage, cursing Annie and telling her how repulsive she had become. He threatened to divorce her and file for visitation with Sierra. The way he said it, the way he sneered, Annie knew her suspicions were correct."

Quinn paused in his narration, stared at the wall, and sucked in a breath. "When Hofstetter stumbled off to the bathroom, Annie called me again. I was actually sitting in my car a block or two away. I figured there might be trouble, and I wanted to be close by in case Annie needed me. I brought a gun I'd bought a few days earlier after talking with Annie. Got it at a gun show, undocumented. After the second call from Annie that night, I drove to the house and entered without knocking. I heard Annie call my name when I opened the door. She sounded panicked. I hustled back to the living room and found Hofstetter kneeling on the floor with Annie in front of him as a shield, his knife at her throat. Later, Annie told me that he was threatening to rape her just before I got there."

Quinn stopped, feeling the heat of the conference room. "I aimed my gun at Hofstetter's forehead and started inching my way toward him. 'Even if I miss on the first shot,' I said, 'I won't miss on the second.' I stopped about ten feet away and told Hofstetter to drop the knife. When he did and Annie scrambled away, I put a bullet through his forehead.

"It was Annie's idea to take the rap. We both knew that a battered wife would have a better chance at acquittal. At first, I wanted to put together a case for self-defense, but I realized the forensic evidence wouldn't justify it. I shot Hofstetter from ten feet away while he was kneeling on the floor. I knew that the angle of entry and lack of stippling around the bullet wound would show that Hofstetter was shot from that distance. Plus, I knew it would be virtually impossible to quickly fabricate evidence of a fight to make it look like Annie had acted in self-defense without her getting tripped up in her story.

"That's why we decided to go with the insanity defense. It could be consistent with a shot from ten feet away. I put on a pair of plastic gloves Annie had in the house and wiped down the handle of the gun. I squeezed Hofstetter's hand around it so his fingerprints would register, then handed the gun to Annie. As soon as I left, she called the police.

"Later, I secretly typed up a confession that I was ready to submit to the court in case we lost. I never intended for Annie to spend any time in jail."

Quinn rubbed his face, exhausted from telling his tale. "When Catherine told me about her latest dream, it was like God had pointed a finger at my chest and pronounced me guilty. Bo, our client clearly has some kind of supernatural gift. Combine that with what we know about the Carver baby, and I think she's innocent." Quinn paused. "The problem is that proving her case means *I* would have to testify."

Quinn swallowed hard as he stared into Marc Boland's contemplative eyes. In the few minutes it took Quinn to tell his story, Boland had totally transformed—from roaring beast to seasoned counselor.

"I need some advice," Quinn said.

Bo squinted past Quinn, as if the wisdom of the ages might be written on the conference room wall. He shook his head slowly and blew out a breath. "I'm not even sure if I can give you advice," he said. "Seems to me that I'd have a terrible conflict if I tried to represent both you and Catherine."

"That may be true," Quinn said. "But I don't know who else to ask.

And I know we really don't have much of a choice. If I don't testify and the prosecution finds out the Carver baby is still alive, we don't stand a chance of winning."

Boland furrowed his brow. "You really think she got set up?"

"I know this much," Quinn said. "Those visions are real. And that Carver baby is still alive. You can take it from there."

"I need some time to process this," Bo said.

The two lawyers agreed to meet at 9 p.m. on Bo's yacht. In the interim, Quinn needed to meet Billy Long at the airport and prepare him to testify. Bo wanted to do a little research.

Bo apologized for losing his cool earlier, and Quinn apologized for not talking to Bo before he made his motion.

Bo even managed a smile before he left the conference room. "You Vegas guys sure know how to mess things up," he said.

98

"NO!"

Catherine bolted upright on her cot, her hair matted with perspiration. Her breath came in short, hard bursts. The other visions had terrified her, but they were nothing compared to *this*.

She grabbed the bars of her cell and shouted for a guard. Other inmates cursed at Catherine or told her to shut up, but she kept right on yelling. Finally a young female deputy appeared.

"I've got to talk with my lawyer," Catherine gasped. "It's an emergency."

"You're in solitary confinement," the guard said. "If your attorney wants to talk with you, he needs to come here." She turned and started walking away.

"Come back!" Cat yelled, pounding the bars in frustration. "Get Jamarcus Webb on the phone! I'm ready to confess!"

The guard stopped. "You've got lawyers," she said. "Talk to them tomorrow."

"Forget about lawyers," Catherine shouted. "I *waive* my right to lawyers! I need to confess! My conscience is killing me! *Killing me!* Get Detective Webb—now!"

The deputy left without another word, leaving Catherine calling out after her.

Three minutes later, the deputy returned with the head of the evening shift. This time, Catherine tried to act a little more sane.

"I understand you're ready to confess," the woman said.

Cat nodded.

"We'll need you to sign some forms waiving your right to counsel."

"I thought you'd never ask."

Quinn walked down the pier of the Cavalier Yacht and Country Club, his steps illuminated by foot lamps mounted on each side of the wooden planks, his mind weighed down with the life-altering decisions in front of him.

The August night was hot and muggy, the quarter moon hidden by a bank of clouds, the sky as dark as Quinn's mood. He had changed into shorts, an oxford shirt, and boat shoes. He'd left his briefcase in the rental car but carried two beers that dangled from a plastic six-pack holder in his left hand. He finished off the beer in his right hand and threw the empty into the Lynnhaven River, stumbled, then climbed aboard the *Class Action*. He circled around to the sliding doors in the back and saw Bo in the lighted salon area, hunched forward on the soft leather couch, reams of trial documents spread around the room and covering the coffee table in front of him.

Bo waved Quinn inside and managed a half smile. "I was going to ask if you wanted a drink," he said.

Quinn held the remainder of his six-pack aloft. "BYOB." He slid into the easy chair on the opposite side of the room from Bo, his legs sprawled out in front of him and crossed at the ankles. He popped another beer.

"I'm not testifying tomorrow," Quinn announced. "I'm not testifying ever. Not about my brother-in-law's death anyway."

Bo regarded Quinn with curiosity, as if trying to figure out whether this was the beer talking or Quinn's actual decision.

"And that stuff I told you in the conference room—" Quinn halfheartedly motioned toward Bo—"that's attorney-client privilege. Take it to your grave."

"Not necessarily," replied Bo, his face stern and indecipherable. "I told you I couldn't represent you and Catherine at the same time. My first obligation is to her. I never agreed to be your attorney."

Quinn sat up a little straighter in the chair. "Meaning what?"

"I've got to do what's best for Catherine." Marc Boland spoke slowly, condescendingly. "My duty to the client comes first." He picked up a black remote and pushed a button. Blinds started descending on the tinted windows all around the salon. "But don't worry, Quinn; I'm not going to put you on the stand. Our client is insane. This bizarre vision that triggered your guilty conscience doesn't change that."

Quinn took another swig. "You're quite the actor, Bo. All that sanctimonious, high-sounding lawyer talk; your self-righteous sneer. You think you're better than me?"

Bo narrowed his eyes but didn't answer.

"I think we're a lot more alike than you'd care to admit," Quinn said. He set his beer down and straightened up in his chair, his feigned intoxication instantly gone. It was time for some *real* cross-examination.

"Did you love her, Bo? Did you love Sherri McNamara?"

99

QUINN SUCKED IN A BREATH, stood up, and put his hands in his pockets. He started pacing as he zeroed in on the man sitting on the couch, his former co-counsel, now prime suspect number one.

Quinn shook his head in scorn. "I must be slipping, Bo. It took me too long to see it. You worked in the Richmond Commonwealth's Attorney's office when Paul Donaldson was prosecuted. You were young and idealistic, assisting victims who testified. You and Sherri McNamara got to know each other, maybe even became lovers." Quinn spoke with the sharp edge that characterized his cross-examinations.

"When your colleagues lost that case and Sherri killed herself, you started plotting your revenge."

Bo leaned back on the couch and chuckled. "You're pathetic, Quinn. Representing insane clients has made you start to think like them."

Quinn ignored the comment. "You waited. Months turned into years, but you could never get her out of your mind. You finally decided the time was right. You picked some random victims first, just to throw police off the trail: the Carvers, defense lawyers who represented rapists—something you'd never do—and Clarence Milburn, a rapist who beat the rap. But all you really cared about was Paul Donaldson and his lawyer, Rex Archibald."

Quinn spoke faster now, watching for a crack in Bo's unnerving veneer. Quinn took his hands out of his pockets and began gesturing. "You didn't have the heart to actually kill the Carvers or Milburn, so you kidnapped their kids and placed them on the black market, making sure the kidnappings coincided with times and places when Reverend Pryor was in town. He was your first scapegoat. And then, a stroke of luck."

Quinn smiled, placing a palm on the back of the easy chair, a pose he might strike in the courtroom. It was classic Quinn Newberg—disguise gut-wrenching nervousness with a show of false bravado. "Catherine O'Rourke had visions. Maybe she picked up some vibes from you; I don't know. But you used it as an opportunity to frame her. You planted DNA evidence on the envelope and the bloody paper towels and methohexital in the trash." Quinn paused, frustrated that Boland showed absolutely no sign of concern. "How am I doing so far?"

"Sit down, Quinn," Bo said. "Have another beer. You're starting to lose it, my friend. Too much pressure. Too much work." He stood and took a step toward the sliding doors that led to the deck, placing himself between those doors and Quinn. Bo seemed larger than he did in court, his neck muscles tightening.

Quinn needed him to crack. Just one incriminating statement. The miniature microphone taped to Quinn's chest was capturing every word, transmitting it to Billy Long, waiting out on the pier.

"I gave you a chance to save Catherine's skin by putting me on the stand," Quinn said, "but you refused to jump at it. Why? Because the last thing you want is for Catherine O'Rourke to change her plea to not guilty and actually get acquitted. If that happens, the cops will reopen the investigation and look for the real killer."

Boland didn't flinch. The face of stone was frozen in a half smirk, as if he knew something Quinn didn't know—a pair of aces for his down cards. Quinn looked Boland over again, searching for any bulges that might signify a gun. Quinn's only hope was to keep talking, to somehow draw Boland out.

"The ironic thing is that the person you set up as the scapegoat is the one who nailed you," Quinn said, forcing his own half smile. "I told you that Catherine saw a vision of Marcia Carver pointing at me, but that's not what she saw. Marcia Carver was actually pointing at *you*. How long do you think it will be until Catherine sees another vision with the location of Rex Archibald's body or the electric chair you used on Donaldson? You can't explain away these visions, Bo. You know it as well as I do. The woman has a gift."

Instead of reacting, a very composed Marc Boland started slowly approaching Quinn, a linebacker just before the blitz. "All that time in the Vegas sun has fried your brain," he said.

"The problem you didn't anticipate," Quinn replied, taking a small step back, "was that Billy Long would figure this out by squeezing some folks who are involved in the seedy business of selling babies. I talked to him less than two hours ago at the airport. We've got you dead to rights."

Even this did nothing to knock the confident look from Marc Boland's face.

"So here's the deal," Quinn said. "You've heard my confession about shooting my brother-in-law. But you've got your own issues."

Boland took one last ominous step, bringing him an arm's length away.

"We swear each other to secrecy," Quinn continued. "Get the women declared insane. They get a little treatment, we get—"

Bo lunged, and Quinn ducked to his left, sliding away from his attacker's grip. Quinn grabbed the first thing he could get his hand on, a glass bottle at the bar, and cracked it against the side of Boland's head.

The blow staggered Boland, but the big man didn't go down. Desperate now, Quinn scrambled up the steps to the pilothouse area. "Get in here, Billy! *Now!*"

He headed for another set of steps that would lead to the upper deck. From there he could leap to the dock, maybe dive into the water. But Boland grabbed Quinn's leg and dragged him back down to the pilothouse. He spun Quinn around and drove a right fist into his ribs, knocking the air out of him, doubling him over. A left uppercut to the jaw sent Quinn crashing into the galley sink.

Quinn crumpled to the floor. Boland stood over him like a raging bull.

But instead of trembling, Quinn managed a painful smile. In the shadows behind Boland, gun drawn like a pro, stood the rounded silhouette of a man who had been recording every sound tonight, every word that had been spoken.

"I thought you'd never get here," Quinn gasped.

Breathing hard, Marc Boland stepped aside. "Neither did I."

Billy Long's gun stayed leveled at Quinn's forehead.

"I'd like you to meet an old friend of mine," Boland said, signaling toward Billy. "From the Richmond police department."

Quinn fought to catch a breath, struggling to understand what was happening. He had been transmitting this conversation to an ally of Marc Boland's?

"Known to some," Boland continued, "as the Avenger of Blood." Boland's face lit up with a demonic grin. "I'm not the Avenger you thought I was, Vegas. I'm the judge and jury."

100

BILLY LONG STEERED Quinn down the narrow steps that led below deck; Boland stayed in the pilothouse area. Billy pushed Quinn into the guest suite, which had been converted into a small study with an ornate desk in the middle of the room and bookshelves along the wall behind it. While holding Quinn at gunpoint, Billy pushed a button on a remote, and a mirrored wall in front of the desk slid aside, exposing a solid wooden chair bolted to the floor. The chair had metal handcuffs built into the ends of both armrests and ankle shackles at the bottom of the chair legs, one thick leather strap for a seat belt, and another for a neck restraint.

"You guys are sick," Quinn said.

"Have a seat," Billy responded, shoving Quinn toward the chair.

Quinn considered his options—all bad—and reluctantly did as he was told.

"Slide your right wrist into the handcuff," Billy said.

Long had the gun trained on Quinn's forehead and stood just out of arm's reach. The man had an unstable look in his eyes that made him seem like a different person from the one Quinn had met at the airport just hours earlier. Quinn knew he couldn't make a play to escape right now, but if he put his wrist into the handcuff and cinched it down, the game would be over.

"Billy, you're in deep on this, but I know you're not the mastermind here. Work with me, and I'll take your case to the authorities—"

Whack!

In a movement too quick for Quinn to avoid, Billy pistol-whipped Quinn across the cheek, opening a gash with a blow that felt like it shattered the cheekbone. Shards of pain engulfed Quinn's face, spreading like the spider-web pattern of a cracked windshield. Dazed, Quinn turned back toward Billy and felt warm blood dripping down his cheek. He touched the spot with his left hand.

"Put your wrist in the handcuff," Billy demanded.

Quinn did so, cinching down the handcuff with his free hand. Then, at Billy's order, Quinn placed his bloody left hand in the other handcuff, and Billy locked it down. After Billy had locked both ankles into the metal shackles, he pulled the leather straps around Quinn's waist and neck and cinched them tight. Quinn felt blood oozing in small rivulets down his neck and soaking into the collar of his shirt.

"Do I get a last cigarette?" Quinn asked.

"Always the comedian," said Billy. "The judge will be back soon. Let's see how good your sense of humor is then."

Quinn heard the engines on the big yacht begin to rumble. They would be leaving the dock soon. This might be Quinn's last chance.

"Hey!" he yelled at the top of his voice. The pain from his cheek intensified. "Down here! Somebody call the police! They're going to kill me!"

Billy shook his head and pulled a gag out of the closet, jamming it into Quinn's mouth as the lawyer yelled. Billy tied a bandanna tight around the back of Quinn's head, holding in the gag and putting more pressure on the cheekbone, while Quinn resisted with all his might.

"Nobody can hear you anyway, Quinn," Billy said after he had tied the gag tight. "This is more for my own peace of mind."

With the gag in his mouth, Quinn stopped trying to make noise. He could tell from the cold look in Billy's eyes that the man was determined to complete his task.

Billy checked Quinn's restraints one last time, surveyed his captive with something that approached disdain, and left the room. Quinn sensed movement beneath him, the maneuvering of the boat as it left the dock, and then the acceleration that signaled the beginning of the trip toward the wide expanse of the Chesapeake Bay, maybe even the Atlantic Ocean. His cheek and shoulder throbbed with pain. Soon, that would be the least of his worries.

101

QUINN REALIZED he was probably sitting in the same chair used to electrocute Paul Donaldson. He flashed back to the court testimony—Donaldson fighting against the restraints, his skin bright red, eyes bulging out, sparks flying from the electrodes on his skull like a scene from a horror movie.

Quinn's mind paraded out other images as well—the most gruesome executions described in the death penalty cases he had studied. The electrical current literally cooked internal organs and heated skin to temperatures that required fifteen minutes of cool-down before guards could touch the executed prisoner. Blood literally boiled. Soon, that could be him.

Quinn used every ounce of willpower to banish those thoughts. Survival would require focus and clear thinking, not panic. There would be time enough to dwell on the pain once Marc Boland started the current. For now, Quinn needed a plan.

A few minutes later, Boland entered the office and sat at the desk, his boyish face stern and judgmental. He raked his hand through his hair and gave Quinn a disapproving shake of the head.

"Don't look at me that way," he told Quinn. "You know the system sucks."

Quinn made a noise, indistinguishable because of the gag. *Don't I even get a chance to defend myself?*

"You were never supposed to get caught up in this, Vegas. This wasn't about you. You're actually a darned good defense lawyer. Too good, maybe."

Boland placed his gun on the desk, and his expression softened, like a father reluctantly scolding a wayward son. "Sherri McNamara *was* a beautiful woman, Quinn. Full of life—the kind of person who makes you feel more alive just hanging around her. And yes, I did love her."

Bo looked straight at Quinn now, but really beyond him, years into the past. "We kept our relationship private—people would have considered it inappropriate for a member of the commonwealth's attorney's staff to be carrying on with someone he met in the victim assistance program.

"I sat through every day of that trial. It was like they raped her a second time, the way Archibald ripped her apart on the stand.

"A week after Sherri's suicide, I was having a drink with a couple of detectives on the Richmond force. Conversation turned to the Donaldson trial, and I found out that Billy Long had a prior run-in with Archibald as well. Archibald had sprung a drug dealer on the basis of an illegal search. He accused Billy of lying on the affidavit to obtain the warrant. The judge agreed and crucified Billy in a written opinion.

"That incident, combined with a prior allegation of police brutality by another defendant, pretty much consigned Billy Long to desk-jockey status. Anyhow, Billy and I got together. We figured if the system was too corrupt to exact justice in these cases, then we probably needed to give it a little help."

Bo stopped, studying Quinn as if seeing him for the first time, fixing his gaze on the blood dripping down Quinn's cheek. "Billy can get a little violent, Quinn. But he's not in charge of the sentencing phase. I am. For that you should be grateful. I save the electric chair for the rapists."

Quinn found scant comfort in the words. He felt like a death-row prisoner, exhausting one appeal after another, sometimes winning a delay but having no chance at acquittal. A gun might be less painful, but it would be equally final.

"I didn't want any collateral damage," Bo continued, his voice calm, almost compassionate, the same tone he used on juries. "I just needed a little misdirection. The babies were unharmed and were placed in homes through the black market—untraceable to us, I can assure you. That's why I had Billy 'discover' one of them—the first step toward getting them back with their original families. Once Catherine's case was over, we would have leaked that info to the cops. The Carvers and Clarence Milburn may have suffered a little emotional trauma in the meantime, but they deserved it.

"As for you, my friend, I'm actually glad you bared your soul about shooting your brother-in-law. That may be the one thing that allows me to live with myself when this dirty little business is finished. Makes me think I might just be doing the Lord's work after all."

Bo stood and walked around his desk until he was standing directly in front of Quinn. "I'll give you a chance to write out your confession exactly as you told it to me. You have my word that I'll deliver it to the Vegas district attorney."

Bo began untying Quinn's gag. "Sorry, Vegas, but that's the best I can do—a relatively painless death, a bullet to the forehead, just like your brother-in-law. We'll bury you at the bottom of the Atlantic and send a note to the authorities from the Avenger along with your confession. Just think—by dying, you might actually save your sister's life."

Quinn spit out the gag. "If there's a God," he said, "I hope you rot in hell."

Bo unhooked Quinn's right arm and wrenched it next to his left wrist, causing pain in Quinn's rotator cuff. "A mouth like that, and I can see why Billy got a little carried away." Bo handcuffed Quinn's wrists together, put leg-irons on his ankles, and undid the leather restraints.

"I'm going to let you go to the head right across the hall," Boland said. "Wash the blood off your face. Get ready for your final meal on deck. A good man like you is entitled to one last meal."

Bizarre, thought Quinn. But he wouldn't refuse this small act of decency. Anything to buy a little more time.

"What about Catherine?" Quinn asked. "A rape *victim.* How do you live with yourself, putting this whole thing on her?"

"Catherine will be fine," Boland said sternly. "Her only mistake was dragging you into this. Go clean up. I'll tell you the plan while you write your confession."

Quinn shuffled across the hall, followed closely by Bo, and appraised himself in the bathroom mirror. He washed some blood from his swollen face, wincing in pain as he dabbed at his cheek with a washcloth. The gash continued to seep new blood, looking like it might require half a dozen stitches to sew it shut. But Quinn's mind was elsewhere. If he could just get to the deck, maybe even dive overboard . . . could he even swim with handcuffs and leg-irons on? Would he stand a chance of getting rescued in the dark waters of the Atlantic?

Probably not, but what were his options?

Still at gunpoint, Quinn returned to the converted guest suite. Bo snapped on some rubber gloves, removed a sheet of paper from a package on the desk, and broke a new pen out of its plastic container.

"Start writing," Bo ordered. "Nothing cute or I won't deliver it."

His mind racing ahead, Quinn slowly printed his confession. If nothing else, at least Sierra might be reunited with her mom.

Bo stood behind Quinn, watching carefully. "You're a showman, Vegas; you would have loved this final piece of the operation. There's still one person who hasn't paid for the life of Sherri McNamara—life for life, as the Scripture says. Know who that is?"

Quinn paused in his writing. Another murder?

"The jury forewoman who freed Paul Donaldson, believing him instead of Sherri," Bo said. "The Avenger will take her out in a very dramatic fashion at the precise moment I'm giving my closing statement. Time of death will be easy to verify. Catherine will no longer be a legitimate suspect, and I'll have an airtight alibi if anybody is ever inclined to look in my direction."

Quinn didn't turn to look, but it almost sounded like Boland was smiling.

"Billy Long has no connection to the McNamara case," Bo continued, "so no one will ever suspect him. These crimes will remain unsolved forever."

Quinn felt the barrel of the gun against the back of his neck.

"Hurry up, Vegas. You're stalling and I'm getting hungry."

102

WITHOUT WARNING, EVERYTHING WENT DARK.

Quinn had no idea what had just happened. A blown fuse? The engine was still powering beneath them, the boat gliding forward. Quinn could barely make out the contour of objects in the study—the darkness broken only by a dim light that seemed to be filtering down the hallway from the main deck.

This might be his last chance.

He flung his handcuffed fists back and to his right, like a double-fisted backhand, connecting with what felt like the face of Boland. Pain shot through Quinn's injured right shoulder.

Crack! Boland squeezed off a shot as he fell backward, and Quinn felt the bullet breeze past his head.

Bo crashed into the wall, and Quinn dove at him, landing on top of Bo and grabbing his right wrist with both hands. Quinn slammed Bo's gun hand against the wall, trying to dislodge the gun, but Bo held on. With surprising speed, Bo locked onto Quinn's arm, lowered his own shoulder, and rolled, his weight carrying him on top of Quinn. He jammed his left elbow into Quinn's gut, a blow that caused Quinn to release his grip on Bo's wrist as the air fled from Quinn's lungs.

Bo exploded to his feet, then whirled and towered over Quinn, the gun pointed at his chest. "Nice try, Vegas," Bo gasped. "I like your spunk."

He took a step or two backward, out of Quinn's reach. Not that it mattered. Quinn was in excruciating pain and had no fight left in him.

"Billy!" Boland yelled. "What happened to the fuse?"

Getting no answer, Bo back-stepped to the door and flipped the light switch a few times to no avail. He raised the gun slightly so it pointed directly at Quinn's forehead. Though Boland's hand was steady, Quinn could tell that the darkness and the lack of response from Billy Long had him worried.

"Billy!" Bo yelled again.

He glanced into the narrow hallway and apparently saw nothing. Breathing heavily, he took a step toward Quinn. "You just forfeited your last meal, Vegas. Any last words?"

Surprisingly, looking down the barrel of the gun, Quinn felt no fear. In that final split second, his life reduced itself to a series of images, past and future, flashing across Quinn's brain in nanoseconds, producing a final collage of intense emotions. Annie and Sierra embracing again. Sierra's wedding. Annie's grandchild. Law partners in solemn mourning one second and at their desks the next. Snapshots of clients and friends. And one final picture freezing on Catherine O'Rourke, her compassionate eyes comforting Quinn, her lips mouthing his name. . . .

A shot rang out. Quinn flinched, anticipating the impact.

103

AT FIRST, JAMARCUS WEBB was skeptical. The last six months had been among the hardest in his life. His friend Catherine O'Rourke had gone to jail to protect him as her source. But when the evidence began mounting against her, Jamarcus did what he had to do.

Even at the time, he knew how much it would cost him.

He told the police chief everything he knew about Catherine, revealing his own status as Catherine's inside source and bringing down the wrath of the entire department on his head. A disciplinary board would ultimately decide his fate. In the meantime, he had been reassigned to administrative duty. He cursed the day he had first met Catherine O'Rourke.

So it didn't make sense when he accepted her collect call from jail. It made even less sense when her supposed confession turned into a plea for help. She had seen another vision. Quinn Newberg was in trouble. This time the handwriting was not a Scripture verse but a location. *Class Action.*

"Marc Boland is the Avenger of Blood," Catherine said, pleading with Jamarcus to believe her. "It all makes sense. Please, Jamarcus, I'm begging you. Go check it out."

Against his better judgment, he did.

He watched from a perch on the deck of a neighboring boat as Quinn Newberg climbed onto *Class Action*, carrying what was left of his six-pack. He saw Quinn's investigator, Billy Long, appear a few minutes later, silently waiting in the shadows on deck. Through the tinted glass of the salon area he could see Quinn and Marc Boland engaged in tense conversation until the shades came down and covered the windows. A minute or two later, he watched Billy Long scramble inside the pilothouse, gun drawn.

Five minutes later, the engines of *Class Action* started, and then Marc Boland began unmooring the boat from the dock.

Questions raced through Jamarcus's head. Why had Billy Long been sneaking around the boat? What had happened to make the man hustle inside the pilothouse, gun drawn? Where were these three going at this time of night?

And a final question, one that haunted him most of all: could Catherine O'Rourke really be innocent, her visions the result of some supernatural gift?

To his astonishment, Jamarcus heard some faint shouting from below deck. Somebody—Quinn?—yelling for help, calling for the police. Somebody was facing imminent harm—a legal justification for boarding the boat. Jamarcus knew he would probably regret it later, but as *Class Action* began pulling away from the dock, he crouched low, jogged to the starboard side away from Marc Boland's line of sight, and jumped on board.

As they cruised out to the Chesapeake Bay, Jamarcus squatted on the outside deck, peering through the windows to the main pilothouse. As he watched Boland pilot the boat, Jamarcus flashed back to the phone call with Catherine. In her vision, she had seen Quinn Newberg sitting in a makeshift electric chair. Could that be what was happening below deck?

Jamarcus had to be careful here. He was an officer of the law. He was piling one assumption on top of another. What did he really have?

He slipped around to the back of the boat and quietly entered the salon area through the sliding door. He pulled out his gun and moved quickly to the steps at the front of the salon leading to the pilothouse, being careful to stay out of sight. Billy Long had just come up from below deck.

"He's all yours," Billy said to Bo, taking Bo's place in the pilot's seat.

"I'm going to be a real gentleman about it," Bo said. "Give him a last meal and everything."

"Your call," Long said gruffly. "He's no different than the others."

The exchange confirmed Jamarcus's worst fears, but it also bought him a little time. They were planning to give Quinn a last meal.

Jamarcus listened for any disturbances below and, hearing none, found the location of the fuse box. He waited until *Class Action* hit the big waters of the Chesapeake Bay. Then, as Billy Long hunched over a chart, Jamarcus crept up behind the captain's chair, said a quick prayer, and knocked Billy out cold with the butt of his gun.

Jamarcus had no idea how to pilot a yacht, so he decided not to touch any of the controls. He checked for Billy's pulse, found one, and scrambled to the fuse box. He cut off the lights below deck and headed for the stairs. He let silence answer Marc Boland's calls to Billy.

Jamarcus slipped into the master suite just as Boland peered out the door of the smaller suite. Jamarcus let his eyes adjust to the darkness for a moment, then heard a scuffle from the adjoining room.

Gun drawn, he rounded the corner.

104

STARING DOWN THE BARREL of Marc Boland's gun, Quinn heard the shot and flinched but never felt the impact. Simultaneous with the shot, he saw Boland's right shoulder lurch forward and heard the man scream in pain, the gun dropping from his hand. It took Quinn a second to register what had just happened; then he scrambled to pick up the weapon as Boland hunched over, holding his shoulder.

In the doorway, Jamarcus Webb stood like a Spartan warrior, silhouetted in the dim remnants of light from the main deck. "Drop the gun!" he yelled at Quinn. "Hands on your head."

"I'm not your man!" Quinn protested.

"Hands on your head!" Jamarcus demanded, taking one step inside the room, then another.

Boland was now leaning against the wall, still holding his right shoulder, his face wracked with pain. They could sort this out later, Quinn reasoned. For now, Jamarcus was just playing it safe. But before he dropped the pistol, Quinn saw a small shift in the faint light from the doorway behind Jamarcus. It could mean only one thing.

"Duck!" Quinn yelled. Jamarcus ducked left and spun, all in one motion, squeezing off a shot as he did so. Quinn fired as well, at the same instant that Billy Long flashed into sight around the corner of the doorframe, his own gun blazing. One of the shots snapped Billy's head backward, and he crumpled lifeless against the hallway wall. Even in the virtual darkness, Quinn could see blood trickling down the man's face from a dark hole on the right side of his forehead.

Quinn dropped his gun and placed his handcuffed hands on his head.

Jamarcus rose to his full height, holding his gun with both hands, keeping it trained on Marc Boland. He kicked the gun that Quinn had dropped into a corner. "You know how to drive this boat?" Jamarcus asked Quinn.

"I know how to put it in neutral and call for help on the radio," Quinn said.

"That'll work."

Before Quinn headed above deck, Jamarcus freed Quinn from the handcuffs and leg irons, then cuffed Marc Boland and checked on Billy Long. He felt for a pulse, then looked at Quinn and shook his head.

"Nice shot," said Quinn.

Jamarcus smiled grimly. "That quarter-sized hole in his temple ain't my caliber. I was just trying to wing him. Nice shot yourself, Counselor."

"I was aiming for his heart," Quinn said.

"Sometimes," said Jamarcus, "it's better to be lucky than good."

105

THE NIGHT BECAME a blur of activity. The arrest of Marc Boland, Quinn's treatment at the hospital for bruised ribs and a gash that required eight stitches, hours of police questioning, and Quinn's negotiations with two prosecuting attorneys—Boyd Gates and Carla Duncan—on opposite sides of the country. Quinn didn't make it back to the Hilton until nearly four in the morning. He took some pain pills and asked for a wake-up call at six so he could stop by the jail on the way to court and explain everything to Catherine.

He woke up hurting all over and noticed the sunlight streaming through a slit in the curtains. He vaguely remembered answering a wake-up call and allowing himself a few more minutes of sleep. He glanced at the clock— 8:05!

He blinked. The digital readout didn't change.

Court started in less than an hour.

Quinn sat straight up in bed and almost passed out. Sharp pain stabbed in his ribs, and a dull aching pain pulsed on his cheek, accentuated by the stitches and swelling that would probably make him look like a boxer in a losing cause. The rotator cuff had its own throbbing rhythm of agony, more intense than it had ever been before.

He climbed gingerly out of bed and flicked on the television. Commentators were speculating about the arrest of Marc Boland, who was to be arraigned later that morning, and a press conference Chief Compton had scheduled for 10 a.m. There was additional speculation about the shooting death of a private investigator named William Long, a former law enforcement officer who might have been assisting the defense team on the Catherine O'Rourke case. Police had confirmed the cause of death as a gunshot wound but were saying little else.

Quinn rubbed on some deodorant, splashed on the aftershave, brushed his teeth, and wet his hair. His ribs ached as he raised his left arm to comb it. He pulled on the same suit he had worn two days ago.

357

Over the past week, his hotel suite had become a combination war room and bachelor pad, clothes and documents strewn everywhere. Housekeeping cleaned every day, but the maids were no match for Quinn's ability to clutter things up.

He threw a few things into his briefcase and headed out the door. On the way to the courthouse, he dialed the airlines and secured a first-class ticket.

Quinn fought his way through the media circus, greeted the security guards, and remained closed-lipped as he entered the courtroom. He made it to his counsel table at two minutes before nine, just in time to iron out a few last-minute details with Boyd Gates.

"All rise," said the bailiff. "This honorable court is now in session."

Rosencrance took her seat, told everyone else to do the same, and spoke the words Quinn had been waiting for. "Bring in the defendant," she said.

Quinn watched Catherine O'Rourke enter through the side door, her posture perfect, her head held high. She was too thin after a few months of jailhouse food, but she still looked great—elegant, triumphant, her face practically radiating grace. She was, Quinn thought, the most beautiful woman he had ever seen.

He couldn't help but feel a surge of triumph as she came and sat next to him. She obviously knew about the events of last night; he could see it in her eyes. Freedom looked good on Catherine O'Rourke.

Quinn put his left arm around the back of her chair and tried to ignore the pain in his ribs. "You heard?"

"Jamarcus told me early this morning," Catherine whispered. Her eyes teared up, and she placed her hand on Quinn's knee. "I don't know what to say, how to thank you. When I had that vision last night—you in the electric chair—it felt like I was dying myself."

Quinn wasn't good at touchy-feely, especially in the middle of a trial. "All in a day's work," he quipped as Rosencrance ordered the bailiff to bring in the jury. If Quinn let himself get emotional right now, there was no telling where it might lead. He would regret it later; he was sure of that. "Though sometimes I charge extra for shooting serial killers."

The jury filed in, staring at Quinn and Catherine. Especially Quinn. "By the way, you look great today," Quinn told Catherine, changing the subject. "Very media friendly."

This brought a quick blush, followed by a most unexpected request. "Can we do dinner tonight, Quinn? There's no other way I'd rather celebrate my first day of freedom than by having dinner with you."

He hesitated. Was she asking him out? It would have been the perfect ending to his greatest triumph as a trial lawyer. Attorney Quinn Newberg, slayer of the Avenger of Blood, rides off into the sunset with his beautiful client. He had dreamed for weeks about what it might feel like to spend time with Catherine when they weren't separated by bulletproof glass and the need to focus on the case. He wanted to get to know the real Catherine. He wanted to hear her dreams and appreciate her wit and know what it felt like to hold her.

"I can't," Quinn said.

She looked hurt, and knowing he had caused that pain ripped at his heart.

"There are some things you don't know about me," he told her. "Reasons it could never work."

"Why don't you let me be the judge of that?" she asked.

With the jury in the box, the courtroom fell into a hushed silence. Boyd Gates was on his feet. Rosencrance asked him if he had a motion to make.

"I do, Your Honor." Gates buttoned his suit coat and squared his shoulders, always the soldier.

Quinn took a deep breath, felt a sharp bite of pain in his ribs, and leaned close to Catherine's ear. These would be the hardest words he could ever remember uttering. "It's best for both of us this way, Catherine. Another time, another place, things might have been different."

"Judge, we would ask you to dismiss with prejudice the charges against the defendant," Gates said. As part of the deal negotiated during the early morning hours, Gates had also agreed to *nol pros* the additional felony assault charge he had filed against Catherine for attacking Holly. Quinn had agreed that Gates could save face by dropping that charge quietly at a later date, as opposed to now in open court.

Gates turned toward Catherine and Quinn, causing Quinn to turn his attention to the prosecutor.

"I'm sorry that you had to endure this ordeal," Gates said softly to Catherine. Without waiting for a response, he turned to face the court again. "As Your Honor knows, we have arrested Marc Boland and will be charging him with three counts of kidnapping, four counts of conspiracy to commit murder, two counts of felony murder, and two counts of attempted murder."

Gasps filled the courtroom, and the jury looked like they had collectively seen a ghost. Excited murmuring threatened to break into full-scale chaos while Rosencrance banged her gavel, attemping to restore order.

"Mr. Newberg," she said, "I take it you have no objection to the commonwealth's motion to dismiss?"

Quinn stood and glanced at Catherine O'Rourke before he spoke. *Another time, another place, it might* definitely *have been different.*

"I think we can live with that, Your Honor."

PART FIVE

GRACE

Grace: *n.*, a favor or indulgence,
as distinguished from a right.

BLACK'S LAW DICTIONARY

106

TWENTY-FOUR HOURS.

After extensive discussions the previous night, Boyd Gates had faxed Quinn's written confession for the murder of Richard Hofstetter Jr. to Carla Duncan in Las Vegas. The fax had gone through a few minutes before 3 a.m. Eastern time. A few minutes later, at exactly midnight Pacific time, Carla Duncan had called and given Quinn twenty-four hours to turn himself in for questioning.

Carla had conceded the possibility that the confession could be entirely bogus, designed solely to entrap Marc Boland. Without more, she was not going to have Quinn arrested and extradited to Nevada. She probably considered him a minimal flight risk given the fact that Annie was in jail awaiting trial and relying on his legal services.

But Carla did insist that Quinn come in for questioning.

Twenty-four hours, not a minute longer. Quinn felt like Kiefer Sutherland in *24*, except that this was real. And Quinn didn't have to save the entire world—just Annie and Sierra.

He landed at McCarren International Airport a few minutes after 2 p.m. on Tuesday, mindful that nearly fourteen hours had already passed. He met a trusted consultant at the airport, who rode with Quinn to the Signature Towers. The man was an electronics and audio geek, an expert who billed at five hundred an hour. Quinn would have paid him double.

"I can have what you need in a few hours," the man said.

Quinn called Richard Hofstetter Sr. and demanded an appointment at 6 p.m.

"Why should I agree to meet with you?" Hofstetter asked.

"Because you want the Oasis sale to go through," Quinn said.

"I don't know what you're talking about," said Hofstetter. "But maybe you'll inform me."

"See you at six," said Quinn.

He hung up with Hofstetter and made a phone call to Annie.

"It'll never work," she said after Quinn explained his plan.

"You got a better idea?" Quinn asked.

The Rogue's security guards escorted Quinn into Hofstetter's enormous office. Quinn was still wearing the suit coat and slacks from his courtroom appearance that morning in Virginia Beach, his white shirt open at the collar.

"I heard about the case," Hofstetter said. "Congratulations."

"Thanks."

"How's the eye?" Hofstetter asked, nodding toward Quinn's swollen cheek.

"Better than the ribs," Quinn said.

One of the security guards pulled out a metal wand to check Quinn for weapons and recording devices.

"Hold your hands straight out to your side," he said.

"I can't," Quinn said, giving the man a fake grimace. "Torn rotator cuff, remember?"

"You really ought to get that fixed," said Hofstetter.

They wanded Quinn and picked up a signal from his suit coat pocket. Quinn pulled out a digital recorder and held it in front of him.

"My, my," said Hofstetter. "I thought that was illegal in the state of Nevada. A man could lose his law license, you know."

Quinn smirked. "Secretly *recording* a conversation is illegal. Playing back a prior one is not."

Hofstetter placed his elbows on the desk and studied Quinn over the top of his fists. The man's square face was tan, contrasting with whiter skin in the shape of sunglasses around his eyes. His hairline was unnaturally even, the precise result of a multitude of hair plugs. The eyes held a death wish for Quinn—a mutual loathing, Quinn realized. "This better be good," Hofstetter said.

"It's for your ears only," Quinn countered. He could feel sweat forming underneath his T-shirt—there was no margin for error here.

Hofstetter nodded at his henchmen. They left the room, and Quinn breathed a little easier. He placed the digital recorder on the desk and turned it on.

For the next several minutes, Hofstetter listened to a telephone conversation between Quinn and Annie, recorded during Quinn's call to his sister a few hours earlier. Quinn told Annie about the existence of the Oasis Limited Partnership interest that had belonged to Richard Hofstetter Jr. and the importance of those voting rights in a battle to sell the Oasis casino. "This is why Claude Tanner suddenly came back into Sierra's life," Quinn explained. "And I think he did so at the urging of Richard Hofstetter Sr., who would benefit handsomely if Tanner voted to sell the casino to Hofstetter's business partners."

Hofstetter stared at the recorder without emotion as the exchange played out. Not even a flicker of surprise.

"You've got no proof of any of this," he said.

Quinn didn't answer. The tape could speak for him.

"I'm going to propose a three-way deal to your father-in-law when I meet with him tonight at six," Quinn said to Annie during the recorded call. "It's the only way I know to protect Sierra. I'll talk to Carla Duncan and get your plea agreement back on the table. You plead guilty and serve three years, then get permanent custody of Sierra afterward. In the meantime, I get temporary custody of Sierra. Tanner gets chaperoned visitation rights and gets appointed as trustee of all Sierra's assets, including the voting rights for the Oasis Limited Partnership. Hofstetter gets his casino; we get Sierra."

Quinn and Hofstetter listened a few more minutes as Annie asked various questions about the deal and its implications. After a long pause, she tearfully agreed that it made sense.

The two men continued to listen as Quinn gave Annie some additional instructions. "Before I started taping this call," Quinn's voice said, "I told you about a location that would contain a microcassette tape of the call. I'm going to make two tapes of this conversation. I'll take one to the meeting with Hofstetter and put the other in the location I mentioned to you. If you don't hear from me by 6:30, or if anything happens to me, tell Carla Duncan about the Oasis Limited Partnership, the location of the tape, and my meeting with Mr. Hofstetter tonight."

Quinn picked up his recorder, turned it off, and took his seat. "We can all win, Mr. Hofstetter, or we can all lose. If I walk out of here without a deal, I'll amend the estate filing to include the Oasis Limited Partnership interest. Annie will go to trial and, if she loses, Tanner gets custody of Sierra and voting rights for the Oasis asset. But I'll raise so much stink about the impropriety of him selling that casino to your business partners, and my suspicions that you put him up to it, that he'll never be able to pull the trigger. You lose. Annie loses. And Sierra loses.

"Or we can all win. You call off Tanner—he doesn't really care about Sierra anyway. You get your casino; Annie and I get custody of Sierra without interference."

Quinn looked at his watch. "It's 6:15, Mr. Hofstetter. You have fifteen minutes."

107

HOFSTETTER CALLED IN his security guards and asked them to escort Quinn outside. He told Quinn to take his digital recorder with him. Five minutes later, Quinn was allowed to return.

"If you propose your deal to Mr. Tanner tonight, I am reasonably confident he will accept," Hofstetter said matter-of-factly. Quinn could tell the man was choosing his words carefully. "It's only idle speculation, of course. And, just to be clear, I didn't even know that my son owned this limited partnership interest in the Oasis until you told me about it tonight. But still, I have to agree with your perspective that Sierra's real father seems to be in this just for the money. Given that perspective, I see no reason he wouldn't take the deal."

Quinn stared across the desk at Hofstetter. He *despised* the man. Hated the doublespeak. But Hofstetter was a pro; Quinn had to give him that much. There was a reason he had never been caught with his hand in the cookie jar. "Does that mean we have a deal?" Quinn asked.

Hofstetter smiled, spreading his palms. "It sounds like a good deal to me," he said. "But of course, I don't have any financial interest in it one way or the other. Only Mr. Tanner can tell you whether the deal makes sense to him."

"It's 6:25," Quinn said.

"So call Mr. Tanner right now," countered Hofstetter. "I'm sure you have his cell phone number."

Instead, Quinn dialed the Las Vegas jail. He explained that he was an attorney and had an emergency need to speak with his client. The deputies could call Carla Duncan if they needed verification.

A few minutes later, Annie came on the phone. "We have a deal," said Quinn, staring at Richard Hofstetter. The old man said nothing in return.

When Quinn got in his car, he called his consultant. "What did you get?" he asked, breathless.

"He called Claude Tanner when you left the office."

"And?" Quinn asked.

Quinn knew that Hofstetter would check for recording devices, but he had guessed that the casino owner would do so just once, at the beginning of the meeting. Accordingly, Quinn had his consultant attach a small magnetic transmitter to the underside of the digital recorder. With his pinky—a move Quinn had practiced for fifteen minutes before leaving for Hofstetter's office—Quinn had flipped on the tiny transmitter when he turned on the digital recorder to play back his phone call with Annie. When Quinn had picked up the recorder from the desk just before leaving the office the first time, he'd flicked the transmitter into a crack in the padding of his chair.

"It picked up every word of Hofstetter's phone call with Tanner," said the consultant. "Every incriminating word."

Quinn called Carla Duncan and agreed to meet at her office at eight.

"Where's your sense of the dramatic?" she asked. "You still have four more hours."

At the meeting, Quinn explained his sting operation on Hofstetter and gave Carla a copy of the recording that his consultant had made of Hofstetter's phone call with Tanner.

"Taping somebody's phone call without their consent is illegal," Carla said. "You know that."

"But as long as the government didn't direct it or participate in it, the tape's admissible in court."

Carla nodded. "I can use it against Hofstetter. But it might cost *you* your law license."

"That's the least of my worries," said Quinn. He trusted Carla Duncan. She was a tough prosecutor, but she was fair. "That confession I signed in Virginia Beach is true, Carla. I came to talk about a deal."

108

CATHERINE O'ROURKE FOUND OUT about Quinn's ploy while watching the news on Wednesday morning, her first full day of freedom. The euphoria of sleeping in her own bed and watching the sun rise over the ocean was swept away by the despair of seeing Quinn torn apart on national television. He didn't deserve this; he was a good man. Watching the coverage literally made her sick, yet she couldn't pull herself away from it.

She had thought about him a lot during the first few months of her incarceration, even before the trial started. Dreamed about him, really. He was part of a fairy-tale ending she knew could never happen: being found innocent by the jury, starting a normal relationship with Quinn outside the pressure cooker of the case, falling in love. She allowed herself to dream this dream even though she had pled insanity, even though a not-guilty verdict would lead to institutional treatment, not a relationship with Quinn Newberg.

During the trial, she had felt a deep bond develop, more than a lawyer-client relationship—way more. They had leaned on each other. Needed one another. Quinn had stood with her when others had run away. Not to mention that her vision Monday evening had saved Quinn's life.

And now she was free, just like in her dreams. But Quinn was gone. And Carla Duncan was holding a press conference, announcing a plea bargain that would send Quinn to jail for three years.

He would essentially serve the same length of time that had been offered to his sister, Duncan said. The prosecutor had taken into account the fact that Quinn was trying to protect his sister and had probably saved her life. But the shooting wasn't technically defense of others, because Hofstetter had already dropped the knife when Quinn shot him. And Quinn was also a lawyer, Duncan argued, an officer of the court. He had committed a massive fraud on the system and could not go unpunished. Moreover, he had committed other crimes that were wrapped up in this plea deal as well, including the unauthorized tape-recording of others without their consent.

In a related matter, Duncan announced the indictment and arrest of

Richard Hofstetter Sr. and several of his associates on racketeering, fraud, and assault charges. Networks showed Hofstetter's "perp walk"—his trademark scowl, hands cuffed behind his back. Duncan said she intended to prosecute Hofstetter and his cohorts, including Claude Tanner, to the fullest extent of the law.

There were some who rallied to Quinn's defense. His law partners, personified by a man named Robert Espinoza, defended Quinn's overall integrity, while admitting some lapses of judgment on this one case that was so personal to him. Abuse groups still hailed Quinn as a hero. Annie staunchly defended him, telling the world through tears that her brother should not have to spend a single day behind bars.

Catherine would join the cause—it was the least she could do. Though she had sworn off media interviews after her acquittal, she decided to make an exception for Quinn. She would write an op-ed piece and send it to all the major newspapers. And she would make herself available to the local news stations. What he had done was not right, but she still cared about the man too much to sit this one out.

Some were comparing Quinn to Marc Boland, noting that both lawyers had taken justice into their own hands and then allowed others to take the blame. Vigilante justice with a scapegoat, they said. But Catherine saw the two situations as totally different. Boland had hunted people down and murdered them in cold blood. Quinn had protected a sister whose life had been threatened. Who among us wouldn't have been tempted to do the same?

Before she wrote her editorial, Cat needed to clear her head. She threw on a pair of workout shorts and a running bra. She grabbed her Rollerblades and took them out to the front steps of her duplex so she could lace them up in the warm sunlight that she no longer took for granted. She knew she would be seriously out of shape from months of wasting away in the city jail, but she would hit the workout hard. It would be great to smell the salt water in the air and feel the muscles burn.

The vision hit her as she sat on the steps, tying a double knot in her left Rollerblade. It began with a familiar pressure building in her head like a migraine, a tropical storm sucking her conscious thoughts into a vortex of otherworldly images. Ghostlike and hazy, the figures seemed to materialize from the scalding concrete of the sidewalk as if the heat waves had taken on human flesh and now stood before Cat, unaware of her existence. There was an argument . . . shouting . . . a fight. Cat watched the entire event unfold, almost as if she could reach out and touch the apparitions before her. She sat there in fascinated horror, unable to turn away.

Unlike her previous visions, this time she saw the detailed outlines of the faces—every wrinkle of the man's leathery skin and angry scowl, the determined look on his wife's familiar face. The other visions seemed like they had taken place in a dark tunnel, with nebulous figures and shrouded identities. But this one unfolded in the light of day. This time, Cat could name names.

The gunshot startled Cat and exploded the vision, leaving her shaken and confused. She didn't want this power, this awful knowledge of facts concealed from others, knowledge too dreadful for one person to bear.

She dialed Rosemarie Mancini immediately. "We've got to talk," Cat said. "I've had another vision."

"I'm at a conference in Colonial Williamsburg," Mancini said. "Can we talk by phone?"

Colonial Williamsburg was less than a two-hour drive. Cat could use the time to collect her thoughts and get hold of herself.

"I'll come to you," Cat said. She knew her voice sounded frantic, but she didn't care. "We need to talk in person."

109

THEY MET at the Barnes & Noble bookstore located on the edge of Colonial Williamsburg, across the street from the College of William and Mary. Rosemarie suggested they go for a walk—a quiet stroll down the tree-lined Duke of Gloucester Street, a cobblestone road that took visitors back more than two hundred years. For Cat, it also had the effect of taking her back just eight years, to her senior year in college, adding another layer of stress to an already confusing day. If the quaint colonial setting was supposed to be relieving Cat's anxiety, it was not working.

After walking a few minutes and telling Rosemarie how great it felt to be out of jail, Cat got down to the point of her visit. "I saw the murder of Richard Hofstetter Jr.," Cat said. "It felt like I was sitting right in the Hofstetters' living room." She was still wound tight as she remembered the ghostly figures, images burned into her mind. "I saw Hofstetter and Annie argue."

Cat looked off into the distance. The trees cast shadows across the street while late-summer tourists traveled in small packs, their noses glued to their guidebooks, figuring out what attraction to see next. Cat couldn't even remember when life had seemed so simple.

"Annie pulled out a gun and started threatening Hofstetter with it," Cat continued. "She backed him down, made him kneel and beg. He was on his knees when she pulled the trigger. That's when the vision faded—exploded, really. The last thing I saw was Annie dropping the gun, putting her hands over her mouth, and screaming."

Cat paused. Just recounting the vision had drained her energy and constricted her chest. She glanced at Rosemarie as they walked and couldn't quite read the psychiatrist's expression. "Quinn wasn't even in the room," Cat said. "He didn't shoot his brother-in-law."

She had been wrestling with the implications the entire drive to Williamsburg. Quinn was innocent! How could she keep that information to herself? She had to do *something*.

But if freeing Quinn meant that Annie went to jail, how *could* Cat possibly tell anyone other than Rosemarie? Quinn would hate her for exposing his sister to serious jail time, for separating his niece from her mother. Cat needed Rosemarie Mancini's advice, and as usual, the psychiatrist was one step ahead.

"I know all that," Rosemarie said. "But this was undoubtedly part of Quinn's plan all along. I don't think he ever intended to let his sister stay in jail. He wanted to give the second jury a chance to do the right thing at trial, but if they didn't, he was ready to take the blame. When it became obvious that putting his confession on the table would also help him nail Marc Boland, he played his ace early."

Cat was stunned that Rosemarie seemed to take this all in stride. "He told you this?" Cat asked.

"He didn't have to. I was Annie's psychiatrist, remember?" Rosemarie looked up at Cat as they walked. "You, I could never completely figure out. But Annie was an open book. She killed her husband, Catherine. It happened exactly the way Annie described it in court.

"But Quinn always covers his bets. I knew he had something radical planned. I saw it in his eyes when I talked to him about Sierra, about the need to break the chains of abuse that get passed from one generation to the next. I knew he had a plan he wasn't telling me about, an ace in the hole.

"Did you notice how carefully he crafted his own confession?" Rosemarie continued. "If he had made it appear too much like self-defense or defense of others, Carla Duncan would have been suspicious. She would have seen it as a contrived attempt to make sure nobody went to jail for the murder. But by saying he shot Hofstetter *after* the man dropped his knife, Quinn guaranteed he would end up taking Annie's place in jail."

Rosemarie motioned toward an ancient brick building on their left, rimmed by a graveyard on the side and back. "St. Bruton's Parish," Rosemarie said. "It was on the tour I took yesterday. Want to peek inside?"

Cat shrugged. *Not really.* She had seen the church a few times during her college years. But Rosemarie had already veered off to see if it was open. Finding it locked, she banged loudly on the thick wooden door.

"A shame," she said. "It's really peaceful in there."

"So you're thinking I shouldn't say anything?" Cat asked, trying to get the conversation back on topic.

"Have a seat," Rosemarie said, plopping down on the front steps of the church. She dusted off a place next to her, and Cat reluctantly sat down. Filled with tension, Cat wanted to keep moving. Besides, she needed answers, not a counseling session.

"The answer to your question requires you to understand the purpose of these visions—does it not?" Rosemarie paused, but only for a moment, not really expecting Cat to answer. "I don't think we'll ever know for sure why God chose you as His messenger, but He did. I know the visions sometimes felt like a curse, but look at the results: they exposed a serial killer, restored the Carver family, helped recover the Milburn baby, and saved Quinn Newberg's life. That's hardly a curse."

Cat had been thinking some of these same thoughts recently. Somehow, the visions that had landed her in jail had also helped bring two killers to justice. The visions were still a mystery, unlike anything Cat had ever experienced, but the timing of the visions and the uncanny results were strangely comforting. And the visions seemed purposeful to Cat, not like the random paranormal activity or the "scientific" telepathy theories she had studied. Cat's visions were something different. Something good.

"You've read the book of Daniel," Rosemarie continued. "Did you notice that Nebuchadnezzar called God the 'revealer of mysteries'? God hasn't changed." Rosemarie turned and looked at Catherine. "We can't always understand God's reasons or methods, but we can learn to trust what He reveals to us. Your first three visions were to help others. This last vision, Catherine, might be God's gift only to you. Maybe you're not supposed to use it to set Quinn free. Maybe God is just showing you something about Quinn's character, telling you it's okay to follow your heart.

"Don't get me wrong; I don't condone the way Quinn misled the court about Hofstetter's murder. But Quinn made a choice. He decided to use a false confession to trap both Marc Boland and Richard Hofstetter Sr. He decided to trade his own freedom for the freedom of two women he loves. And he helped a third reclaim her mother. The thing is, if he had to do it again, I'm sure he'd make the same decision."

Cat didn't respond. She had never been very comfortable talking about matters of faith. Now Rosemarie was digging up Cat's feelings toward Quinn and tossing them into the stew as well. She sat there next to Rosemarie in silence as the tourists paraded past: old men with shorts and black socks, children in strollers, couples holding hands.

It was a strange place to have a spiritual moment, but Cat couldn't deny that something significant was happening. It certainly wasn't a leap of faith—more like an insight or realization, the way Cat felt when the pieces of a news story fell together. God had been pursuing *her*. Trusting *her* with these visions. Loving *her* enough to show her these things. Maybe it was time to listen.

Maybe it was time to start returning that trust.

Rosemarie looked down the street and smiled at a kid who had buried his face in a chocolate ice cream cone. She stood and brushed off the back of her pants.

"You ready to head back?" she asked.

"Sure."

Since the street was closed to motor traffic, the two of them shuffled along in the middle of the road, dodging horse manure, feeling the gravel crunch against the cobblestone under their feet. It was Rosemarie who spoke first.

"You know I don't like to preach to my patients," she said.

Catherine turned and raised an eyebrow.

"Okay," said Rosemarie. "Maybe a little. But there's this Scripture verse about Jesus that says, 'No one has greater love than this, that he should lay down his life for his friends.' Think about that—it's the most noble thing a person can do, putting his own life on the line for someone else. And in Quinn's case, it was something more—a ten-year-old boy finally discovering the courage to act.

"Love him for it, Catherine, but don't try to take that away."

110

FOR CAT, IT FELT STRANGE being on the outside going in. She registered as a visitor and passed through a metal detector, palms sweaty just from being surrounded by prison walls again. The guards in Vegas had the same I'm-just-doing-my-job approach as the deputies in Virginia Beach. *Depersonalizing*. Their attitude reminded Cat of how depressing jail had been—how much it had toyed with her sense of dignity and worth.

Ironically, Vegas was not as technologically advanced as Virginia Beach. For that, Cat was grateful. Instead of closed-circuit TV, where Cat wouldn't even be in the same room as Quinn, she would instead be sitting on the opposite side of three-inch glass, face-to-face, a mirror image of the way they had conducted their attorney-client conferences in Virginia Beach.

Cat arrived in the interview booth first and mentally steeled herself for the fact that the Quinn Newberg she was about to meet would not seem like the same person as the dapper attorney who had stood up for her in court. Even though he had been in jail only a few days, the place had a way of changing you—reducing you to the ugly core of who you were.

A few minutes later, the door opened on the other side of the glass and Quinn slid into the booth. He wore an orange jumpsuit, his hair was disheveled, and his face was still swollen from the nasty cut to his cheekbone. He smiled immediately. "What's a gorgeous woman like you doing in a place like this?"

Surprisingly, he sounded upbeat. His smile brought back the old Quinn, except for the swollen eye and the gash on his cheekbone, and for a moment it was Catherine who was incarcerated and this handsome Vegas lawyer who had ridden into town to save the day.

She was glad that she came.

"They said you needed some coaching," Catherine said. "How to survive in jail."

"Yeah. That would be good. Things like how to stay out of fights and how not to confess to my cellmate. Maybe you could teach me how to file my toothbrush into a shank."

"Shut up," Cat said, and they both laughed.

"Actually," Cat went on, "the best thing I did in jail was to convince the world's best lawyer to handle my case." As she said it, she stayed locked on his eyes, sensing that the chemistry was still there, that things hadn't changed between them. "I never got a chance to properly thank you, Quinn Newberg. You saved my life."

"You made it easy," Quinn said. "You happened to be innocent." His halfhearted attempt to shrug it off couldn't mask how much her words meant to him—especially now, alone in prison, where the full weight of abandonment and loneliness hit.

There was an awkward silence, and Cat remembered how hard it was to communicate—not just talk but really get down to heart issues—when separated by glass, wondering if every word was being monitored. "Are you doing okay?" Cat asked. "Is there anything I can do to help?"

"Are you kidding? I love this place. Plenty of crazy folks for clients. Card games galore. You should see the pile of cigarettes I've already won."

Cat decided not to let him off the hook so easy—always the sarcastic charmer, deflecting the tough questions. "Seriously, Quinn. How are you doing?"

He shrugged again. "It helps being a lawyer, even one about to have his license pulled. I'm representing three of the toughest thugs already, preparing paperwork for their outside lawyers—the inmates love it. You don't have to worry about me being attacked. I'm trading legal brains for protection and pretty much have my own Secret Service escort."

Cat couldn't resist a small smile. Quinn had been in jail less than a week, and it already sounded like he was running the place.

Quinn's eyes softened, and his voice became quieter. "The hardest thing is that you only see the sun for about an hour each day—and then you're on a scalding concrete pad with a basketball goal on each end, and it's about a hundred and ten degrees. Three years is going to be a long stretch."

Quinn seemed to catch himself, throw a switch in his demeanor, and turned from melancholy to superlawyer again. "Enough about me, though that *is* my favorite subject. How's my number one client doing?"

"She's fine. She's also free, thanks to you."

"Does she still have nightmares? Did she get her old job back?"

Catherine shifted in her seat. This was the opening she had been waiting for. It was time to get serious and push the point. "I had another vision, Quinn. This time, I saw Hofstetter's murder." She watched closely for a reaction. "You weren't even there when it happened."

Quinn didn't flinch—not a single facial muscle changed. The man had practiced bluffing for years at the poker table and in the courtroom.

"As for my job," Cat continued, "I've got a friend at the *Las Vegas Review-Journal* who thinks he can get me in. I'm moving out here, Quinn. I'm going to come by every day."

Catherine waited when Quinn didn't respond immediately. He glanced down, seemingly trying to figure out what to say. When he spoke, his voice was steady and sad. "You aren't going to mention this last vision to anyone, are you?"

"Nobody else needs to know."

This seemed to relax him a little, though his face was still troubled. "You can't move out here, Catherine. You're twenty-eight years old—smart, beautiful, full of life. There are a million guys who would swallow broken glass just for a chance to take you out. You can't waste your life waiting for me." He hesitated, looking as though he had to convince himself to continue. "Three years is forever. We'll both be different people by the time I get out."

She leaned forward and felt her throat tighten as emotions too complex for words welled up in her. She knew he didn't mean this. He had brushed her off once before, right after her case was dismissed, supposedly for her own good. Not this time. Catherine O'Rourke could be very determined when she knew what she wanted. And she also knew what Quinn needed, despite his protests to the contrary. "I would have been in jail the rest of my life if it wasn't for you—"

"That can't be the reason—"

Catherine held up a palm. "Please let me finish," she said. Quinn nodded.

"That's not the only reason I'm here. I want this, Quinn. I want us. We're made for each other. I know it, and you know it." Her words came out thick with emotion. And they were having an impact. Quinn's poker face turned soft. "Jail taught me that life is too short to play games," Catherine continued. "You can't stop me from coming by, Quinn. You can't stop me from caring."

"You know I've got a pretty strict curfew."

Cat grinned. "At least you won't be running around with other women."

"It's not the women I'm worried about."

There was another awkward silence, and Cat waited him out again. She needed a serious response. "You really want to try this?" he asked.

Cat nodded. "If you do."

"More than anything in the world," Quinn said, looking down. When he raised his eyes to look at her again, Cat could have sworn she felt the warmth spread through her entire body.

"We're going to make this work," Cat said. It was barely a whisper, not loud enough for Quinn to hear but surely he could read her lips. "You're worth waiting for, Quinn. I can be very persistent."

They sat there for a long moment, Quinn staring at her, the same way he had the first time they met, when he was trying to figure out what was happening inside her head. This time, it felt like he was looking straight into her soul. Maybe he could tell she was heading down a different spiritual path, the Revealer of Mysteries at work in her life. Whatever he saw made him smile— that million-dollar smile of Quinn Newberg, legal magician and Vegas heart- throb. Prison couldn't take it away, not even the orange jumpsuit and bruised face could lessen the irresistible pull of Quinn's impish charm.

"I always thought you were a little crazy," he said.

ACKNOWLEDGMENTS
AND AUTHOR'S NOTE

Writing is a team sport, and I'm surrounded by a great team. If you like the book, there's a good chance these folks are the reason why. The mistakes, as always, are on me.

During the research phase, I was helped immensely by Judge Patricia West and her bailiff, Deputy Brian Capps, who answered all my questions about the Virginia Beach jail and allowed me to spend time there without having to commit the kinds of acts that entitle others to an inside view. I also want to thank the Rigell family and the McWaters family for teaching me a thing or two about boats and the Virginia Beach culture—just enough so the locals might think I know what I'm talking about. As for the person who instructed me on the Las Vegas gambling tricks, he (or she) wishes to remain anonymous for what should be obvious reasons.

More help arrived during the editing process. Thanks to Michael Garnier, Robin Pawling, and Mary Hartman for reviewing the manuscript and making great suggestions even before I sent it to my publisher. Thanks also to Karen Watson, Stephanie Broene, Jeremy Taylor, Ron Beers, and a host of other talented folks at Tyndale House who believed in this book and made it better at every turn. Not only are they extremely good at what they do but they have fun doing it. I love being a Tyndale author. I'm also thankful for Lee Hough, who is equal parts agent and friend, for his steady help at every stage of the process.

Now for the disclaimers. (I'm a lawyer; it's in my blood.) The Virginia Beach jail is a well-run institution with deputies who care a lot about their jobs and the inmates. The deputies in this book bear no resemblance to the real-life deputies. On another front, I took the liberty of having one of my nefarious characters belong to the Cavalier Golf and Yacht Club. In the real world, the Club is a distinguished and enjoyable group that would undoubtedly have the good sense to keep most of my characters from joining. Meanwhile, up the road at the United States Supreme Court, a case will likely be decided about the time my book comes out that might change the way most states execute death row inmates. My characters assumed the court overruled the challenge to the constitutionality of the three-drug cocktail used in lethal injections. If it goes the other way, don't blame my characters; they're just following orders. And speaking of drugs, the Avenger's anesthetic drug of choice, methohexital, works faster in the book than it ever would in real life. These things are called literary license, a fiction author's best friend.

This past year has been a year of change for the Singer clan, and my writing wouldn't be possible without the help and forbearance of a lot of people involved in those changes. We have moved to Virginia Beach, and I have rejoined my old law firm. My partners and friends at Willcox & Savage have been incredibly supportive of my writing endeavors while allowing me the flexibility to handle real cases as I write about fictional ones. In addition, I've had the invaluable support and prayers of two families—my church family at Trinity and my long-suffering immediate family and relatives. Thanks especially to Rhonda, Rosalyn, and Joshua for putting up with the idiosyncratic lifestyle of a husband/dad who loves to write stories, and for their help on so many aspects of the book.

I'll end with a word about the inspiration for this story. Some have accused me of writing what I know best—a story about multiple personality disorder from a guy who is part lawyer and part pastor. In truth, the idea comes from a trial that occurred nearly two thousand years ago and is recorded in the pages of the New Testament. When the apostle Paul was on trial for his life, he told King Agrippa about a heavenly vision that the apostle experienced on the road to Damascus. Paul's defense was interrupted by Festus, a governor who had already tried Paul. "You are out of your mind, Paul!" Festus shouted. "Your great learning is driving you insane." Paul's measured response: "I am not insane, most excellent Festus. What I am saying is true and reasonable." Acts 26:24-25.

This book also deals with life-changing visions and accusations of insanity. My hope is that readers might find a few words of reason and a few kernels of truth in these pages as well.

DON'T MISS RANDY SINGER'S NEXT RELEASE:

FOR SOME, JUSTICE
IS A GAME, AND THE
HOUSE IS PLAYING
WITH A STACKED DECK.

FOR OTHERS, IT'S
A MATTER OF LIFE
AND DEATH.

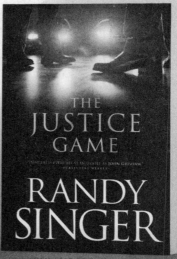

THE
JUSTICE
GAME

RANDY
SINGER

AVAILABLE SUMMER 2009

TAKE A SEAT ON THE JURY...

VISIT WWW.RANDYSINGER.NET

- Listen to closings for the gun-control trial featured in *The Justice Game*.

- Render your verdict.

- Impact the outcome of the case in the actual story.

ALSO BY RANDY SINGER

Fiction

Directed Verdict

Irreparable Harm

Dying Declaration

Self Incrimination

The Judge Who Stole Christmas

The Cross Examination of Oliver Finney

False Witness

Nonfiction

Live Your Passion, Tell Your Story, Change Your World

Made to Count

The Cross Examination of Jesus Christ

www.randysinger.net

CP0232